More praise for *The Gangster of Love*
by Jessica Hagedorn

"One of the most auspicious literary novels about the rock
scene since Don DeLillo's *Great Jones Street*."
—*The Boston Sunday Globe*

"If you've ever had underground-rock-star fantasies, pick
up a copy of *The Gangster of Love* by Jessica Hagedorn and
check out the story of hard-living singer Rocky Rivera and
her struggle to span two different cultures. Hagedorn
writes this book in a jazzy sort of poetry: She switches
voices and viewpoints, weaves in words of Tagalog, harks
back to the stories of her native land and slings obscenities
with abandon . . . an undeniably entertaining glimpse of
life on the edge." —*Mademoiselle*

"Manila-born Jessica Hagedorn explores a Filipino family's
struggle for its slice of the American dream. *The Gangster
of Love* is rich in its share of off-beat characters. The novel
has it all: sex, drugs, and rock 'n' roll. The writing has an
edgy, melancholic beauty. We are reminded that Hagedorn
remains a fresh, irreverent, and richly textured voice."
—*Asiaweek*

"Hagedorn paints a lively portrait that in many ways is im-
pressionistic . . . engrossing, unsentimental, and quite
funny." —*The Washington Post*

"Dramatic, poetically specific, and darkly humorous, this
poignant tale features some truly unforgettable characters."

PENGUIN BOOKS

THE GANGSTER OF LOVE

Jessica Hagedorn's first novel, *Dogeaters*, was nominated for a National Book Award in 1990 and was voted the best book of the year by the Before Columbus Foundation. A performance artist, poet, playwright, and screenwriter, she is also the author of *Danger and Beauty: Poetry and Prose*, as well as the editor of *Charlie Chan Is Dead: An Anthology of Contemporary Asian American Fiction*. She lives in New York City.

The Gangster of Love

Jessica Hagedorn

PENGUIN BOOKS

PENGUIN COMPASS
Published by the Penguin Group
Penguin Group (USA) Inc., 375 Hudson Street, New York, New York 10014, U.S.A.
Penguin Group (Canada), 10 Alcorn Avenue, Toronto,
Ontario, Canada M4V 3B2 (a division of Pearson Penguin Canada Inc.)
Penguin Books Ltd, 80 Strand, London WC2R 0RL, England
Penguin Ireland, 25 St Stephen's Green, Dublin 2, Ireland (a division of Penguin Books Ltd)
Penguin Group (Australia), 250 Camberwell Road, Camberwell,
Victoria 3124, Australia (a division of Pearson Australia Group Pty Ltd)
Penguin Books India Pvt Ltd, 11 Community Centre,
Panchsheel Park, New Delhi – 110 017, India
Penguin Group (NZ), cnr Airborne and Rosedale Roads,
Albany, Auckland, New Zealand (a division of Pearson New Zealand Ltd)
Penguin Books (South Africa) (Pty) Ltd, 24 Sturdee Avenue,
Rosebank, Johannesburg 2196, South Africa

Penguin Books Ltd, Registered Offices: 80 Strand, London WC2R 0RL, England

First published in the United States of America
by Houghton Mifflin Company, 1996
Reprinted by arrangement with Houghton Mifflin Company
Published in Penguin Books 1997

20 19 18 17 16 15 14

The yo-yo definition is reprinted with permission
of Macmillan General Reference USA,
a division of Simon & Schuster Inc., from *Webster's New World Dictionary*,
Second College Edition. Copyright © 1986 by Simon & Schuster Inc.

Portions of this work were originally published in slightly different form in
Ploughshares, BOMB, Conjunctions, and *Charlie Chan Is Dead: An Anthology
of Contemporary Asian American Fiction.*

PUBLISHER'S NOTE
This is a work of fiction. Names, characters, places, and incidents either are the
product of the author's imagination or are used fictitiously, and any resemblance to
actual persons, living or dead, events, or locales is entirely coincidental.

THE LIBRARY OF CONGRESS HAS CATALOGUED THE HARDCOVER AS FOLLOWS:
Hagedorn, Jessica Tarahata, date.
The gangster of love/Jessica Hagedorn.
p.   cm.
ISBN 0-395-75412-7 (hc.)
ISBN 0 14 01.5970 3 (pbk.)
I. Title.
PS3558.A3228G36   1996
813'.54—dc20   96–10281

Printed in the United States of America
Set in Transitional
Designed by Melodie Wertelet

For John, Paloma, and Esther, always.

For the band.

Y *siempre*, for Luis Burgos, in loving memory.

Acknowledgments

Many thanks are due my agent, Harold Schmidt, and my editor, Dawn Seferian at Houghton Mifflin. Thank you, Jayne Yaffe, for your perceptive manuscript editing.

Thank you, Han Ong, for the joke.

I also wish to acknowledge the National Endowment for the Arts Literature Program and the Lila Wallace-Reader's Digest Fund for their support while I wrote this book.

And to the yo-yo artist and Philippine American cultural archivist Orvy Jundis — *maraming salamat*.

Prologue

There are rumors. Surrealities. Malacañang Palace slowly sinking into the fetid Pasig River, haunted by unhappy ghosts. Female ghosts. Infant ghosts. What is love? A young girl asks.

Rumors. Malicious gossip, treacherous tsismis. Blah blah blah. Dire predictions, arbitrary lust. The city hums with sinister music. Scandal, innuendo, half-truths, bald-faced lies. Adulterous love affairs hatched, coups d'état plotted. A man shoots another man for no apparent reason. A jealous husband beats his wife for the umpteenth time. The Black Nazarene collapses in a rice paddy, weeping.

I love you, someone sings on the omnipresent radio. Soldiers in disguise patrol the countryside.

Love, love, love. Love is in the air.

Background, foreground, all around.

But what is love? A young girl asks.

A fatal mosquito bite, the nuns warn her.

Rumors. Eternal summers, impending typhoons. The stink of fear unmistakable in the relentless, sweltering heat.

Yo-Yo

yo-yo n., pl. yo-yos (Tagalog name: the toy came to the U.S. from the Philippines) 1. a spool-like toy with a string attached to the pin holding its two halves together: it may be reeled up and then let down by manipulating the string 2. (Slang) a person regarded as stupid, ineffectual, inept, eccentric, etc. — *adj.* (Colloq.) up and down; fluctuating; variable — *vi.* (Colloq.) to move up and down; fluctuate; vary

Purple Haze

Jimi Hendrix died the year the ship that brought us from Manila docked in San Francisco. My brother, Voltaire, and I wept when we read about it in the papers, but it was Voltaire who was truly devastated. Hendrix had been his idol. In homage to Jimi, Voltaire had learned how to play electric guitar, although he'd be the first to admit he wasn't musically gifted. "It's okay for me to dream, isn't it?" He'd laugh. Voltaire grew his bushy hair out and teased it into what he called a "Filipino Afro." Voltaire caused a sensation whenever he appeared in his royal purple bell-bottoms and gauzy shirts from India. My parents were appalled, especially when Voltaire took the next logical step and adopted an "indigenous Filipino" hippie look. The crushed velvet was replaced by batik fabric; the corny peace medallions replaced by carabao horn, scapulars, and amulets he purchased from bemused market vendors in front of Baclaran Church.

My father once threatened to have Voltaire arrested by the Marcos secret police for looking like an effeminate *bakla*. Then there was the incident of Voltaire's guitar, which he set fire to in a very public ritual in Luneta Park. According to my father, Voltaire was on the military's growing shitlist of subversives and hippie dissidents. Nothing much came of my father's threats, except after one of their more physical confrontations when Voltaire disappeared for weeks. My mother was sure he was dead. "He's probably holed up in some Ermita drug den," my father scoffed, though he was plainly worried. Voltaire eventually showed up without explaining himself, but by then no one cared: my mother's announcement that she was finally leaving my father overshadowed everything.

Voltaire and I convinced ourselves that our parents' breakup was temporary, that the journey we were taking with our mother was some sort of weird vacation. Our lives as the children of

Milagros Rivera had often consisted of startling events and irreversible showdowns. We were relieved to be away from the Philippines after the bang-bang, shoot-'em-up elections. Who gave a damn about voting anyway? Even my father was forced to admit that the elections were a joke. Everyone knew Crocodile had fixed it to win. That's what Voltaire called Marcos now — Crocodile. Imelda was Mrs. Croc, or Croc of Shit, as Voltaire sometimes said when he was in a truly bitchy mood. Voltaire blamed Marcos, the CIA, and the Catholic Church for everything that was wrong with our country. He once said the CIA had contaminated the Pasig River with LSD as part of their ongoing chemical warfare experiments against the Vietcong. He also claimed that we were the original gooks. He and our sister, Luz, the eldest, used to argue about politics all the time. "Didn't you know the term *gook* originated in the Philippine-American war?" he once yelled at her. "Enough!" Luz yelled back at Voltaire.

Excited and distracted by our sudden trip to America, we didn't dare ask too many questions — even when Luz stubbornly refused to leave Manila and my father.

Voltaire croons softly to himself as he leans over the deck railing and studies the faces of the motley crowd waiting on the pier. "'Purple Haze was in my brain, lately things don't seem the same . . .' There she is!" He waves to a tiny woman bundled up like an Eskimo in a hooded down parka and pants. Voltaire must've recognized Auntie Fely from those Kodak cards she sends every Christmas with photos of her with her stepchildren and husband stiffly posed under a lavishly decorated artificial tree and "Merry Xmas & a Happy New Year to You & Yours from the Cruz Family" embossed in gold.

According to my brother, I was three when Auntie Fely left to find work in America. A few years older than my mother, Auntie Fely was unmarried then, and she doted on all of us. She stopped by our house on her way to the airport for one last teary goodbye, though family and friends had already bid their farewells at numerous ceremonial breakfasts, lunches, *meriendas*, and dinners held a month before my aunt's scheduled departure. Luz was the first to receive kisses and hugs, then Voltaire. My aunt gave each of them envelopes stuffed with peso bills. "Don't spend it all on sweets." Because I'm the baby of the family, Auntie Fely saved me for last. She scooped me up with her strong arms and peered into my face as if to memorize it. The intensity of her gaze, magnified through Coke-bottle eyeglasses, frightened me.

Auntie Fely was a nurse, and since I'd been diagnosed as borderline anemic by our family physician, Dr. Katigbak, she had the dubious honor of administering my dreaded vitamin B shot every Tuesday. I would run and hide whenever I saw my aunt approaching in her starched cap and uniform — Auntie Fely took her profession very seriously — carrying that ominous black medical kit packed with glass vials and a sinister array of gleaming silver needles. She'd huff and puff up the winding, graveled pathway, drenched in sweat by the time she reached the front door. "Where's my little patient?" I'd hear her call out in a sweet, singsong voice, as she and my *yaya* Emy hunted for me in every shadowy nook of our rambling ruin of a house.

"Your Auntie Fely's going to miss her little patient so much." She kissed me noisily several times on both cheeks and wept. "Don't ever forget your Auntie Fely."

My right arm still throbbing from yesterday's injection, I howled in terror for my mother, my *yaya* Emy — anyone who could rescue me from my aunt's smothering embrace.

Shortly after she found a job in a public hospital in San Francisco, Auntie Fely was set up by her supervisor, another Filipino nurse named Mrs. Garcia, with a flashy widower from Stockton named Basilio Cruz. Basilio's wife, Dolly, had recently died in the ICU after a mysterious ailment. There were rumors of foul play — worrisome *tsismis* my mother heard all the way back in Manila — but only rumors. Dolly Cruz had worked as a managing housekeeper at the Hilton Hotel, leaving behind a bubblegum pink, two-bedroom tract home in Daly City, quite a bit of insurance money, and no debts. There were three grown children. The eldest was a postal worker named Boni — short for Bonifacio — who moved back to Stockton after his father remarried and never spoke to him again. The twins, Peachy and Nene, seemed more adaptable and took to calling our aunt Mama Fely. They were unbelievable academic achievers, graduating from high school with honors, then majoring in medicine at the University of San Francisco on scholarships. "USF is the best," Auntie Fely had written my mother proudly in her last Christmas card. "A strict Catholic school."

"Look! We're approaching the Golden Gate." My mother points at the shadowy outline of the bridge through the thick morning fog.

"But it's not gold," I say, disappointed.

On the windy pier, a burnished man in a dapper felt hat and fur-trimmed overcoat makes face talk, eyebrows going up and down in furious Filipino sign language: *Welcome! Hurry up! What are you waiting for? Everything okay*, ba?

My mother can't help scowling. "That must be the famous Bas." Then she forgets herself, blowing kisses and making twisted crazy faces of her own. Another passenger hands her confetti and streamers, which she flings at the people huddled and waiting below. "Fely! Fely!" Her eyes are moist and I could swear she is sniffling. Is it possible? I nudge Voltaire with my elbow. My mother has always been too tough to let anyone see her cry. "Fely!" She is jumping up and down in her four-inch heels. Voltaire and I exchange amused glances as the other passengers on deck turn to gawk at her.

Our passports are stamped, our suitcases inspected. "My sister is a citizen," my mother informs the warehouse crowded with immigration officials and customs agents. Voltaire's long hair, beads, and fringed buckskin jacket (bought off an enterprising Australian hippie in Manila) inspire hostile stares as we exit the customs area into the biting wind. "Thinks he's Tonto," I hear one of the officials saying. Someone laughs.

Auntie Fely is weeping and smiling. Her exclamations and questions overlap, uttered with that same lilting, singsong cadence. "Raquel! *Dios ko!* Remember me? My little patient! *Naku!* How old are you now! Not even a teenager yet! Ay! *Talaga!* So big!" She means mature when she says big. Even after all her years in America, Auntie Fely still says "Open the light . . . close the light" when she orders someone to turn a light switch on or off and "for a while" when she has to put a phone call on hold.

My mother is holding back tears. "Fely, we finally made it."

In my childhood, my mother was a volatile presence, vampy, haughty, impulsive. "Who the fuck do you think you are?" my father used to yell at her. He was a mystery to me, aloof and distracted, anxious about money. I was never sure what he did for a living, except that he employed eleven people. The sign at the entrance to his cramped office read RIVERA TRADING CO.

Whenever she fought with my father, my mother would hop on the next plane bound for Hong Kong or Tokyo. Glamorous cities, distant and exotic enough to provide a distraction, yet only a few hours away from Manila. We were her reluctant, loyal, sullen companions, tagging along on our mother's spur-of-the-moment adventures. That time in Hong Kong, for example. Luz, Voltaire, and I were the only children present in Patsy Lozano's presidential suite at the Peninsula Hotel, brought along by my mother for who knows what reason. Patsy and my mother were both pretty drunk, having a grand time with a rather decadent crew. The men all vaguely resembled my father, with feline Chinese Portuguese nymphets clinging to their sharkskin suits.

The radio was on loud, blaring Perez Prado's heated music. My mother danced with a fat, graceful man, and they showed off some breathtaking mambo moves. Suddenly she pulled away from her sweaty partner and climbed up on the coffee table. Lost in her own world, lithe and exuberant in her green mermaid dress, she shook her bare perfumed shoulders and tossed her head back with abandon. I was enthralled and ashamed of my mother's torrid performance. The music ended, and the fat man helped my mother down as Patsy Lozano applauded. More drinks were consumed, and everyone forgot about us. The fat man whispered in my mother's ear.

Luz locked herself in the bathroom to sulk. Voltaire snuck out and was later found by hotel security, aimlessly going up and down the elevators. No one even noticed he was missing. I stayed, sure I was going to die from having to sit there and watch my mother make a spectacle of herself. An eternity later, back in the safety of our much humbler hotel, Luz, Voltaire, and I got in my mother's king-size bed and watched unfunny British comedies on the king-size television. Our mother went nightclubbing with Patsy and the fat man. To spite them all, we ran up a huge bill ordering junk food from room service — making ourselves sick on soda pop, banana splits with chocolate syrup, hot dogs and club sandwiches doused in ketchup and mayonnaise. I threw up all night long, alternating between chills, diarrhea, and a burning fever.

"There, there," Voltaire murmured, helping me wash up for the hundredth time. We ran out of clean towels.

"Are you playacting?" Luz asked me snidely, suspicious as always.

Then there was Tokyo. Voltaire wasn't with us, so there was no one to mediate between my mother and Luz. Now a tall, sour adolescent, Luz shadowed my mother relentlessly like a stern, disapproving chaperone. "Why don't you go sightseeing and let me breathe?" My mother wailed in desperation.

The day we arrived, we ran into a smooth businessman from Manila named Alfonso Something-or-Other. Alfonso's last name was too baroque, too Spanish, and too long to take seriously. We were in the midst of checking in, exhausted and surrounded by luggage, most of it my mother's. "You remember Mr. Something-or-Other, don't you?" My mother gave us one of her warning glances. "He plays golf with your father."

"Ah," Luz said.

"I don't," I chimed in.

We were in no mood for being nice to yet another one of my mother's insincere and fawning admirers. Plus, I never forgot what Sister Immaculada at Our Lady of Perpetual Sorrow had drummed into us in daily catechism class: sex in any form was a mortal sin, and the sin of adultery the absolute worst. Sister Immaculada was the oldest living nun at my school, with bushy gray eyebrows that curled over her eyes. "Not only will you end up in hell forever," Sister Immaculada droned in a raspy voice, "but Lucifer himself will make a special point of torturing you personally. He'll carve out your private parts, barbecue while you watch, then make you eat yourself slowly, morsel by morsel."

"Call me Tito Alfonso," the man said in Spanish to Luz and me. He smelled of leather and expensive soap.

I spoke to him in English. "You're not my uncle."

Luz pinched me, but said nothing.

Alfonso invited us to eat with him in the hotel dining room that evening, and we were annoyed with our mother for accepting his invitation. Luz and I were determined not to leave her alone with him, however, so we tagged along. We made Alfonso suffer by pretending not to hear every time he spoke to us, or else by responding with a terse yes or no. Luz made things worse by speaking to me only in Tagalog.

I drank iced Coca-Cola in a very tall glass, aware of the flirtation going on between my mother and Alfonso. She kept laughing at every other thing he said and leaning closer and closer to him. They had both simply decided to ignore Luz and me. I felt impotent and wished Voltaire was with us, sure that Alfonso wouldn't take as many liberties in his presence. Suddenly I bit down hard on the rim of my glass. The sliver felt cold and dangerous on my tongue. Luz squealed like a pig. "She's going to die! Mama, Raquel ate glass and she's going to die!"

Alfonso and my mother stared at the cracked glass I held in my hand. It took a moment for what I'd done to register in their minds. "Open your mouth," my mother commanded, a strange look on her face. I froze, afraid of what she might do. "Open your mouth," she repeated, glaring at me. The diners from nearby tables looked in our direction.

"Are you all right, *hija?*" Alfonso asked solicitously. He put a hand on my mother's braceleted arm, as if to restrain her from attacking me. The sliver of sharp glass prevented me from speaking.

"She's *insane*," Luz said, to no one in particular. I had gone too far and upset them all, including my sister. The waiter hurried over just as the band onstage began playing "Begin the Beguine." "Filipino," I managed to croak to Luz, pointing at the band. I attempted a smile.

"You're *insane*," Luz repeated.

"*Eb-ri-ting* okay?" our Japanese waiter asked.

"Spit," my mother growled, holding out her napkin. I did as I was told. She wrapped the shard of glass in the napkin, handed it to the startled waiter, then casually ordered another Coke for me.

Our deluded, beautiful mother thought that by running away and spending money my father didn't really have, she could force him to mend his ways. She was a romantic, defiant, and proud woman who sometimes got what she wanted. My father would actually show up and surprise her with presents and flowers, making promises he couldn't or wouldn't keep. He'd take us children on fatherly outings, making a supreme effort not to look bored. We all fell for his charm. When my father didn't feel up to the chase, he would simply wait for my mother to run out of money and return to Manila. He punished her by flaunting his mistress in public. We all knew about his *querida*, a long-legged beauty queen named Evelyn "Baby" Guzman. Another Baby in a long line of Babys. To this day, my mother can't bring herself to speak Baby's name. "That woman" is about all she can manage.

I have made it a point to try and remember everything. I remember that Baby wasn't much older than my sister, Luz — and therefore more threatening to my youth-obsessed mother than any of my father's other women. I always thought it quite fitting and funny that my mother refused to grant my father, Francisco Rivera, a proper divorce. Two years after we moved to America, he chose to bribe Judge Ramos and marry Baby Guzman in an illegal civil ceremony on September 21, 1972, the day Ferdinand Marcos declared martial law in the Philippines.

(Love Is) Like a Heat Wave

Shit. A step down the ladder, *talaga*. Dismal light, peeling paint, tin ceilings. The second-floor Victorian flat we rented near Golden Gate Park somehow evoked a shabbier, smaller version of our haunted house back in Manila. We barely managed the rent, scraping by with the help of skimpy support payments that my guilt-ridden father sent monthly, marked "For the children." My mother was determined not to live with Auntie Fely and her family in Daly City. "I don't need charity," she sniffed. She couldn't stand Uncle Bas, with his stupid jokes and oily manners. Plus, his sweet, studious daughters were a painful reminder of what sullen underachievers Voltaire and I had turned out to be.

In the flat above us lived the Greens, the first black American family we ever knew. The Greens were a total surprise to my mother. They weren't in show business, they weren't athletes, they weren't criminals. We ran into the Greens on their way to work one morning. Our mother embarrassed Voltaire and me by launching into her love for Diana Ross. "She's so thin and pretty," Milagros gushed. "Such nice clothes. Her voice like honey velvet." Mr. Green seemed uneasy; Mrs. Green, amused. "Ma," I murmured, "they're in a hurry."

My mother ignored me. "Velvet," she repeated. "We worship her in Manila."

"How nice," Mrs. Green said.

Mr. Green and his wife were always rushing to and from work, looking exhausted. They owned a depressing little combination liquor-convenience store down the street. Mrs. Green sat behind the cash register, protected by bulletproof glass. The Greens gave my mother credit. Sometimes Mrs. Green asked me to baby-sit their children, Nicky and Rhonda, who were actually old enough to take care of themselves. Mrs. Green probably felt sorry for me and figured I could use the money.

Zeke Akamine, a tall, melancholy Hawaiian, was our landlord. He lived below us in what he called his "bachelor pad," but thought of every excuse to come upstairs and hang around my mother.

"How de toilet doin'? Flush okay?"

My mother humored him. "Fine, Zeke. Fine."

"Sink backed up? How about de kitchen?"

He was smitten. They'd sit in the kitchen and reminisce about Honolulu or Manila, nostalgic, rambling conversations that went on late into the night. I'd come home from school and do my homework at the kitchen table just so I could listen. My mother often seemed bored or distracted, but she never sent Zeke away. "Looks like you got a nice fat letter from home," he'd say, handing her the day's mail.

"You're such a snoop," my mother teased, snatching the envelopes greedily from him. News from Manila — that's what she lived for. But if the letter was from Luz, she'd pass it to me without bothering to open it. My mother could never forgive Luz for staying in Manila and "siding with your father and that woman of his."

"But the letter's addressed to you," I'd say.

My mother's face would grow dark and scornful. "So?"

If Zeke wasn't sighing with regret about the good ol' plantation days that never were, he'd just sit there worshiping my mother as she cooked, a cigarette dangling precariously from her painted lips. She spent a lot of time planning meals and cooking way too much food. "Zeke, I need another carton of Marlboros — and more garlic." She'd make a gesture toward her handbag, but Zeke would wave her away.

"Zeke don't need your money." Off he'd run to the Greens', or to Harry Fong's overpriced supermarket. "What else you need? A fifth of Dewar's? How 'bout snacks for de kids?"

"Zeke, open your eyes. They're too old to be called kids."

Zeke's mopey hangdog presence got on Voltaire's nerves. Voltaire especially hated "cocktail hour," when my mother interrupted her incessant cooking to drink potent Scotch and sodas and gossip with Zeke. She'd grimace theatrically at the first sip. "Where's the soda?" she'd pretend to complain. She could get evil when she was drunk, which wasn't often, but often enough. Looking oddly calm and in control, she'd belittle Voltaire — his succession of failed jobs, his lack of ambition, his yearning for Manila. Zeke tried to stop her. "Tha's your son," he'd protest feebly, shaking his head. "Why you pick on him so?" But Zeke was no match for Milagros Rivera.

Voltaire started not coming home at all. He blamed all the ugly, maudlin evenings on Zeke, though it was clearly our mother who was possessed of a cruel streak. I didn't mind Zeke at all. He was kindhearted and kept our mother entertained, which was useful when I wanted to be left alone — pretty much all the time these days. I stayed in my bedroom listening to Aretha Franklin and Sly Stone on KSOL, while tapping out minimalist poems on the secondhand Underwood my mother had bought me for my birthday. The poems imitated my male favorites of the moment: Antonin Artaud, Mallarmé, Gil Scott-Heron, and LeRoi Jones.

Poor Zeke. It sickened me to catch him gazing at my mother with such desperate, awful longing. As the years went by, Zeke's obsession with my mother seemed to grow worse. I swear, I never want to be in love like that.

"You're like a stupid dog, chasing its tail around," I said to him. Zeke was too far gone to respond. My mother took advantage of his weakness by being late with the rent. Or not paying at all. Zeke never called her on it.

I graduated from Ralph Waldo Emerson High School with no close friends and technically still a virgin, although I'd once permitted Reggie Bambang to French-kiss and maul me at the movies. I never went out with him again. Except for poetry, my grades were average. "You're not living up to your potential, Raquel," my English teacher, Mrs. Cavello, said and sighed.

"Call me Rocky," I mumbled from behind a curtain of unruly Medusa hair, which I cut off impulsively the day after graduation. From Manila, my father sent a curt congratulatory telegram and a money order for two hundred dollars. My mother tried not to look impressed. "As usual, he's trying to buy your love."

I kept just enough cash to run down to City Lights Books for *The Selected Poems of Federico García Lorca*, then over to Tower Records for The Original Last Poets and Nikki Giovanni's "Ego Tripping," then to Flax's for another blank journal bound in black. The rest of the money I gave to my mother to go toward the rent.

I hid my black journals (three so far) under the mattress. I showed no one what I wrote, not even Voltaire, who wasn't home much anyway. He'd gotten himself a temporary stock-boy job at Macy's. According to Voltaire, most of the stock boys were Filipino or Chicano "fly boys." Very young, pretty, and vain. They blew their paychecks on haircuts, clothes, and discos. "They take the bus, but they dress like millionaires." Voltaire chuckled. He was determined to save up enough for airfare back to the Philippines, whereas I was content to hole up in my room, writing and dreaming to the funky music on the radio. High school was finally over, and I drifted happily. Late afternoons I spent with my mother and Zeke, learning how to drink.

At first, my mother was amused. "You can certainly put it away."

Then a note of alarm: "What about college?" She even called Auntie Fely to come over and give me some inspirational advice. I overheard her saying, "I want Raquel to be motivated, like Peachy and Nene."

"Leave me alone," I pleaded.

"Leave her alone," Zeke suggested.

"Stay out of this," my mother warned him.

"I'm really okay," I said, meaning it.

"Your daughter got a good head. She learnin' how to live," Zeke said.

"My husband's going to blame me for everything," my mother said.

"Forget that stupid husband of yours and marry me," Zeke pleaded with my mother.

"Shut up." My mother laughed.

Zeke had a family somewhere, and a wife. But where they all lived, we never knew. He used to disappear on weekends. My mother wheedled some information out of Zeke once. His wife's name was Celine and she was a natural blonde. ("Did you check her pubic hair?" My mother chortled.) He refused to say anything else about his wife, but he described his children with pride. He seemed to have quite a few. His eldest son had been drafted to Vietnam. Another was in a motorcycle gang. The youngest had just turned five. "Zeke, you too old. You're just like all the rest. Keep your wife too busy and too fat," my mother sneered.

"I love my babies," Zeke said. "I love you."

"Ha!" My mother tossed her head in contempt. She enjoyed pushing men like Zeke around. It was another way of getting back at my father, who was thousands of miles away and couldn't care less.

"You never should've left him," Auntie Fely chided her gently. "What about the children? Marriage vows are sacred in the eyes of Our Lord —"

"Putang ina talaga," my mother cursed with gusto. "Are you defending that sleazy, bigamist, gangster husband of mine?"

Auntie Fely looked pained. "Ay, Milagros. Your daughter is sitting right there. How can you talk like that about her father in front of her? How you've changed —"

"I've been the same smart bitch all my life," my mother snapped.

Zeke the landlord, Sal the butcher, Jean-Claude the baker, Harry Fong at the supermarket, Jerry the lawyer, RickFoss (that's how she said his name: as if it were one word) the senior credit officer at Bank of America: Milagros Rivera had them all wrapped around her manicured fingers. I like to think she never fucked any of them. My mother teased, flirted, and hypnotized the men with her cooking. "RickFoss is coming over for lunch," she announced, triumphant. She'd cajoled Rick to approve a small loan so she could launch her one-woman catering service, Lumpia X-Press. Rick offended her by constantly referring to it as her "egg roll business." "Excuse me, RickFoss. Egg rolls are Chinese. Lumpias are Filipino. There's a difference," she corrected him.

It's a known fact: Filipinos are the original party animals. They love to dance, love to sing, love to fuck, but most of all, they love to eat. Lumpia X-Press was a hit. Milagros had no problem finding people to cook for. Filipinos showed up from Berkeley and Oakland, from Richmond, Daly City, and San Francisco. They ordered by the dozen: lumpia Shanghai, fresh *sariwang* lumpia, even innovations my mother concocted like Mexi-Lumpia (stuffed with avocado and jalapeño chili, salsa on the side) and New Wave Lumpia (bite-size, vegetarian). My mother's steadiest customer was the nosy, obese widow Bambang, mother of Reggie the mauler. Mrs. Bambang sold watermelon, okra, and eggplant at the Farmers' Market on Alemany, and made extra money by reading cards and telling fortunes. She loved gambling and went on weekend expeditions to Reno on a charter bus packed with other Filipinos and Chinese. No one slept; they just gambled, rushed through dinner, gambled some more, then got back on the bus. She invited my mother to join her several times, but my mother refused. Politely, of course. Mrs. Bambang never stopped trying to fix me up with her son, so I'd run and hide whenever she came over. My mother gladly put up with her. "Tessie Bambang," my mother said, "keeps us one step away from the poorhouse."

Voltaire and I were paid to help our mother dice, chop, roll, and fry. Rolling lumpia was the hard part, intricate, tedious work that began the night before, as we prepared and cooked the fillings ahead of time. You had to know just how much to put in

— not so much that the wrappers would fall apart as soon as you threw the lumpias in hot oil, but not so skimpy that your clients would accuse you of ripping them off. I was slow and clumsy with my hands, so my mother sent me on errands to Chinatown to shop for ingredients. I also delivered lumpia by taxi. Clients had to order a minimum of three dozen, and pay for my travel expenses. If I was lucky, they also tipped.

Voltaire was usually stuck back in my mother's overheated kitchen, rolling lumpias as fast as he could. My mother's big American dream was to have Voltaire become a partner and handle the financial end of the business. She envisioned Lumpia X-Press franchises sprouting up all over the Bay Area. "I won't need your father's handouts anymore!" she declared. Voltaire wasn't interested, which hurt and angered my mother. "What are you planning to do, sit around in your pajamas until I die?"

"You'll never die," my brother said with such solemn conviction that Milagros Rivera shut up for a little while.

Voltaire lost his job at Macy's after the month-long trial period. "I don't care. Whatever it takes, I'm going back. One day soon I'm going back to Manila."

We were in my room with the door locked, smoking a big fat joint.

"And do what?"

"I dunno. Something. Work for Papa. Marry Cherry Pie de los Santos. Or maybe that other one. You know, the general's daughter."

The weed was so strong I started to cough. "I thought you liked boys. Besides, Cherry Pie probably has six kids by now."

Voltaire giggled. "Che-Che-Cherry Pie. Imagine calling your kid Cherry Pie!"

"Yeah, right, *Voltaire*." I took another deep hit off the Panama red. "How come you stopped playing music?"

Voltaire pretended not to hear my question. "Papa'll make me his number-two man. When he retires —"

"Voltaire."

"I'll take over, fire the entire sales department —"

"Voltaire, please."

He breaks out of his reverie and gives me a hostile look. It was Voltaire who revealed to my mother, "Papa's in love with another woman." My brother even pointed out the bungalow that Papa had rented for her near his office.

No one in the family likes to talk about it, not even Auntie Fely. But something's been eating away at Voltaire since the day he was born. My mother once said that Voltaire was cursed by malevolent spirits who coveted his beauty while he was still in her womb. That's how she explains Voltaire's frequent bouts of *sumpung*, black mood swings that transform him from someone sweet and gentle into someone raging and lost.

Aswangs who prey on pregnant women, *tianaks*, malevolent *duendes* — it all makes perfect sense to me.

Voltaire putters aimlessly around the flat in his faded green pajamas, pulling dead leaves off dying, wilted plants and brewing pots of exquisite Brazilian coffee (courtesy of Jean-Claude the baker) for our adored mother, who has told Voltaire repeatedly, "No thank you, I prefer instant." He chain-smokes, just like she does. Smokes and stares out the greasy bay windows, starting in anticipation every time he hears a car door slam shut. Who is he waiting for? Agitated and giddy with ideas one day, then suddenly withdrawn and somber the next. Once he went to a pawnshop and spent his Macy's paycheck on a gaudy diamond pendant for our mother, which she'd never be caught dead wearing. My brother makes us all sad. He blames himself for wrecking our family.

"Troublemaker," Luz called him with great bitterness, back in Manila. She blames him, too.

Voltaire's madness is a contradiction. He shuts himself away in his room with the blinds drawn, memorizing the Old Testament. But just as abruptly, he can lose interest and head for the

Tenderloin, his unholy *barrio*, teeming with sinners and saints. He roams the streets in a restless, somnambulant daze until he meets "somebody." My brother's always meeting somebody. Men and women ask for him on the telephone. *Is this Voltaire Rivera's house? I need to talk to Voltaire.* They call at all hours, their voices shaky and uncertain. My mother bangs the receiver down in their ears or curses at them in Taglish. "*Hoy, mga* goddam perverts *kayong lahat!*"

Sometimes Voltaire brings them home for dinner, unannounced. A man with a rat's face, obsequious and badly dressed. The man introduces himself as Dr. Amor Amor.

My mother gives him an imperious once-over, hands on hips. "How do you know my son, Dr. Love Love?"

"We met in church. I'm from Manila too," Dr. Love Love says, cautiously. "He borrowed money."

"Bullshit," my mother said.

"No, no, it's true," Voltaire moans. "I owe him money."

Our next visitor is a burned-out ballerina from hell with a straggly ponytail and brown, decaying teeth, wearing a moth-eaten crinoline, leather jacket, and Converse sneakers. "Susan Levine," I gasp in recognition, "don't you remember me? Rocky Rivera, Mrs. Cavello's English class."

"Susan Levine has been erased from the cosmos," Susan replies cheerfully.

"Her name's Eurydice," Voltaire says, embarrassed.

Susan/Eurydice squats on our living room floor and rummages busily through the Hefty plastic bag she's been toting. The stench of aftersex, sweat, and onions fills the room. My mother is about to faint.

Susan/Eurydice unrolls her drawings and displays them for us. Lizards in a geometric maze. Paisley patterns. Flower petals erupting into flames. Naked women with swirling hair and legs wide open. God's eyes and swastikas. "I'm doing posters for the Fillmore," Susan/Eurydice says, then turns to my brother. "Did you tell them? What's your name, honey?" she asks Voltaire, as if noticing him for the first time.

"Pathetic American," my mother grumbles, pinching her nose in distaste.

"The Fillmore's closed," Voltaire informs Susan/Eurydice quietly, but she's focused on me.

"You been to the Fillmore?" Susan/Eurydice asks. Her features still show traces of an odd, crooked beauty. Susan Levine: class artist, class clown. Voted Miss Personality, Most Likely to Succeed. She runs a grimy hand tenderly over the drawings spread out before her, mesmerized by her own images. "Sun Ra," she murmurs, "Quicksilver, Blue Cheer . . ."

"Where'd you find her?" I whisper to my brother.

"Talking to herself in front of this peep show on Turk," Voltaire says.

"Pathetic." My mother sweeps out of the room and starts banging around in the kitchen.

The only uninvited guest who wins my mother over is a statuesque Filipino Mexican drag queen who calls himself Fátima de las Mananitas. "But how come you don't speak Tagalog?" my mother asks, intrigued.

Fátima shrugs. "I grew up in the barrio."

"Well, so did I," my mother says.

Fátima's laugh is raucous. "Dah-ling, I mean the barrio of East LA."

In the middle of our improvised banquet Fátima says to my mother, "Your son is so sensitive." Then he declares, patting Voltaire fondly on the arm, "Well, you are! Sensitive . . . and artistic."

My mother heaps more rice on Fátima's plate. "We're an artistic family."

"I can tell," Fátima says.

My mother beams at the glamorous man before her. It is a rare, happy occasion.

If Voltaire's somebody happens to be female and outdoes my mother in the looks and breeding department, then our mother makes sure it is a tense, brief experience. "My son can't afford you," she once said to a bewildered teen beauty queen named Vicky Villamor, Miss Phil-Am Daly City of 1976. Vicky called for a taxi and left our flat in a hurry.

It often goes like this after Voltaire's guests are gone: I retreat to my room. Voltaire and my mother start sniping, then hurl accusations at each other. "Am I running a goddam soup kitchen?" My mother howls. "Am I made out of money?" The conflict inevitably boils down into the same old argument: life in Manila versus life in America. "I'm never going back," my mother vows. "Never."

Voltaire's sob is wrenching. He scares the shit out of my mother and me. "I'm sorry, I'm sorry for everything," he says.

"You wanted to come," my mother reminds him cruelly. She can't handle her son's tears and ends up yelling in frustration for him to stop. It gets so bad and so loud that Zeke knocks on our door, demanding to know if my mother is all right. "Of course she's all right!" I shout through the door, refusing to open it. It is Voltaire who is suffering, but how can I say that to blind, lovelorn Zeke?

Voltaire recovers long enough to bring Elvis Chang home one night. He's heard Elvis play at Mabuhay Gardens in North Beach, this new wave club run by Pinoys. "*Ano ba iyan? Intsik?*" Our mother scrutinizes Elvis and his guitar case carefully. He stares right back at her, unafraid and polite, while she interrogates him. *Are you a professional musician? What kind of name is that for a Chinese? We have plenty Chinese in the Philippines. Were you born here?*

"Do you mind if I smoke?" Elvis asks.

God, he's cool. Cool enough to wake me from a self-induced trance. Right then, right there, I decided, as Martha & the Vandellas might sing it, to feel the burning flame. *Like a heat wave, burnin' in my heart.* Can he save me? From what, I'm not even sure, but of course he can. There's his guitar, his lanky body, his tight ass, and that mysterious tattoo my brother keeps talking about. Cool.

"Were you in the navy?" my mother asks. "Or jail? Back in the Philippines, only convicts get tattoos."

"Ask him to show it to you," Voltaire dares us.

Elvis's tone is firm. "Let's change the subject, Voltaire."

Elvis almost wins my mother over, but the fact that I am hot for him keeps her on guard. He's more American than we could ever be. How is that possible? My mother is one of those people who means "white" when she refers to Americans. It doesn't matter who was here first, or how many generations they'd been in America: the Greens are Negroes, Mexicans are Mexicans, Jews are Jews, and the Chinese are most definitely always Chinese. And forget calling anybody Black with a capital *B*, an Indian a Native American, or whatever. She'd just laugh in your face. Who could keep up with the latest political trend and correct terminology? Filipino spelled with an *F* or a *P*, Pinoy, Flip, brother, sister . . . My mother has no patience with any of it. She has her very own personal brand of politics.

When the Symbionese Liberation Army kidnapped Patty Hearst and demanded free food distributed to the "people," Voltaire and I stood in line to get our bag of groceries. Part of what had driven us to Potrero Hill Community Center that day was mundane and practical. Our father was behind with his support payments and our mother complained of constantly having to borrow money from Auntie Fely. Our other reasons had to do with genuine curiosity and a guilty sense of adventure. How long was the SLA going to keep Patty locked up in that closet? Visionary thugs and pampered debutantes danced in our heads. Susan Levine wasn't the only one to change her name. Patty became Tania: kidnap-rape victim, revolutionary bank robber, and traitor to her class.

"Where the hell did you get this?" My mother held up a tin of Spam and an unlabeled package of welfare cheese.

"The SLA," Voltaire mumbled.

"William Randolph Hearst," I said.

My mother threw the bag and all its contents into the aluminum trash can she kept in the kitchen.

"What are you doing? Feed the people! Feed the people!" Voltaire kept shrieking. He reached into the trash to retrieve what he could, but every time he pulled something out, my mother would toss it back in.

My mother takes Voltaire aside to ask him if Elvis is queer. "*Bakla ba iyan?*"

"Rocky doesn't think so," Voltaire says.

Elvis is the only non-Filipino we've met who knows the difference between lumpia and egg roll. "I had a Pinay girlfriend once," he explains to my mother, deadpan. When she turns away, he winks at me.

"Who invented the lumpia?" I ask.

"Who invented the yo-yo?" Voltaire asks.

Elvis scarfs down my mother's food, then offers to treat us to the movies. My mother dismisses his invitation with a yawn. "It's much too late for me. Besides, I can't bear to sit still that long."

I try to convince her. "Come on, Ma. It'll be fun. When was the last time you saw a movie?"

She starts making a big production of clearing the dishes. Elvis and Voltaire jump up to help, but she waves them off. "Not necessary."

Of course, I accept. I can't wait to get out of my mother's flat, with its lingering cooking smells and glum atmosphere of genteel poverty. I can't wait to sit next to Elvis Chang in a pitch-black movie theater, feel the heat of his hard sinewy body burning next to mine.

Voltaire is delighted. "What shall we see? What shall we see?" He keeps asking, like a child. I have never seen him so animated.

"*Superfly*'s playing on a midnight double bill with *Blacula*," I say.

Elvis finally looks at me. "The sound track's great. Have you heard it?"

"Of course. Curtis Mayfield." I'm trying to act cool and restrain myself. What if he's a shitty lover? I probably am.

My mother's scrutinizing us closely. "My husband took me to the last movie I saw. *Love Is a Many-Splendored Thing*. That was quite a while ago . . . Do you know it, Elvis? Jennifer Jones was supposed to be half-Chinese." My mother pauses for dramatic emphasis. "My husband was a big fan of Jennifer Jones. I wasn't."

Elvis breaks the uneasy silence. "That was a great dinner, Mrs. Rivera."

My mother looks at me as she speaks. "Don't stay out all night."

Elvis Chang. My virgin crotch tingles with love and anticipation, but like any good rebel Catholic, I know how to wait. The nuns and priests of my childhood had all been liars. How could they know? Divine love, divine lust. What's the difference? Maybe one's more polite and romantic, more songlike. *I love you, baby. I lust you, ooh bay-beh, bay-beh, ooh, ooh, ooh.*

I move in with him exactly one week later.

Love is eternal, love is bloody, love is fleshy, love is meat. Like a heat wave. Yeah, yeah, yeah, yeah.

"Dahil Sa Iyo" (Because of You)

Elvis seemed vaguely disappointed and surprised when I told him that I was a virgin. How I must've confused and angered him. I was hot and passionate in the darkness of a movie theater, and then, when we were finally naked and alone in his bed, I burst into nervous giggles at the sight of his erect penis. I did try, taking guilty pleasure in his sleepy eyes and the hard beauty of his young, tattooed body. He didn't maul me like Reggie Bambang. Elvis was too skilled and confident a lover. Even I could tell the difference. I didn't bleed much, but I didn't enjoy it much, either. Maybe what made it worthwhile for him were those times when I forgot I was Rocky Rivera. "Tell me what you want," Elvis would whisper. How could I? My mother once confessed how much sex revolted her. "Romance is what I crave," she said. "Sex is for men and animals." I guess the vigilant Sister Immaculadas of the world had done their job well. I dreamed about sex, wrote about it, sang about it; I got down and dirty when I talked about it. But actual sex for me was . . . well, too *penetrating*. I was always a mess afterward. Call it what you will. An intrusion, an invasion, a mortal sin — sex was simply too much trouble. Poor Elvis. I was a withered nun trapped in a young girl's nubile body, and the less I was touched, the better.

After I moved out, my mother was cool toward me. She never actually said so, but I think she was a bit stunned by my running off with a man. Especially an arrogant, unapologetic type like Elvis Chang. It was one thing for my worldly mother to act open when it came to sexual liberation, but for her own daughter to take her up on it . . . "Like a slap in the face," Auntie Fely said, telephoning on my mother's behalf. "I'm sorry to say this, Raquel. But have pity on your *nanay*, your *nanay* is so embarrassed."

"Embarrassed by what?" I was furious with my mother's manipulation of Auntie Fely, with Auntie Fely's groveling manner, and with myself for answering the phone.

"Reggie Bambang told his mother that boyfriend of yours sells drugs," Auntie Fely said.

"Reggie Bambang tried to get in my pants," I said. "Reggie's a loser."

"Ay, Rocky. Please," Auntie Fely pleaded. "Your mother is worried about you." She sighed unhappily, just like my mother would.

"And Mrs. Bambang's a sow," I added, enjoying myself.

It was Voltaire who finally insisted that my mother invite me over for dinner one night. My mother caved in, on the condition that I come alone. After that, I showed up at least once a week. She knew it was about her food, and though she resented being used in this way, my mother laid out a banquet at a moment's notice. "I had a feeling you'd show up," she'd say, giving me a reproachful look. "I made *leche flan* with grated lemon peel for dessert. Your favorite."

It's Auntie Fely's birthday, a good excuse for a party. Everyone's crammed around the small dining room table: Auntie Fely, my sort-of cousins Peachy and Nene, Voltaire, and even mopey, red-eyed Zeke Akamine. I'm trapped in my seat next to Uncle Bas, who's bathed in Jovan musk cologne and decked out in a maroon double knit suit, platform ankle boots, and a paisley polyester shirt, partially unbuttoned to show off his hairless chest. Ropes of gold with Virgin Mary and Saint Jude medals dangle from his scrawny neck. "When are you and that boyfriend of yours getting married?" he asks, with a sadistic grin. My mother and Auntie Fely exchange glances. I can feel Voltaire watching me and shake my head vigorously. "Never."

"Never say never," Uncle Bas chides me, then announces brightly, "Good news, everyone. Peachy's engaged to a urologist. And Nene's dating . . . a . . . pediatric . . . oncologist!"

"Papa, please." Peachy and Nene murmur, blushing.

"Peachy's fiancé is from Cavite," Uncle Bas continues.

"He must be good with a knife," I mutter darkly. Peachy giggles.

Uncle Bas ignores me. "And Nene's beau is from Boston!"

My mother turns to him, her smile deadly. "My goodness, Bas. With all these *physicians* in your family, you may as well open up a clinic." Voltaire and Zeke crack up. "Well, maybe I will," Bas responds, unfazed. I am grateful for the feast before me — garlic-fried rice, oxtails braised in peanut sauce, and my mother's supreme lumpias. After dinner, Auntie Fely unearths a contraption that looks like a boom box from one of her ubiquitous plastic shopping bags. "Bas and the girls brought it back from Manila for my birthday," she says. "Isn't it amazing? It's called a Minus One."

"Like karaoke?" Zeke asks, intrigued.

Peachy nods. "Every house in Manila has one."

"You mean every house in the Philippines," Nene corrects her.

"Fely, what are you going to do with that thing?" My mother glares at Uncle Bas. "Fely can't *sing*." Auntie Fely acts as if she doesn't hear, but I know better. I rummage hastily through the bags for a cassette. "Who knows this song?" I ask, catching Voltaire's eye. The instrumental track for "Lady Marmalade" by Labelle comes on. Voltaire and I leap up from the table. Auntie Fely excitedly hands us the microphone, giggling like a schoolgirl. Voltaire and I sing what we can remember of the lyrics. Suddenly, Auntie Fely's head slumps into her chest. She nods off into a dreamless sleep that will last only a few minutes. Voltaire and I gyrate our hips and roll our eyes back in exaggerated ecstasy. Everyone laughs and applauds, including my mother. Auntie Fely wakes up with a start, clapping along and never missing a beat. "What a great party," she says.

I would be lying if I said my life with Elvis Chang was romantic or easy. It wasn't. I had chosen a man as remote and complicated as my father, whose proof of love when you demanded it consisted of staring at you in mock astonishment and saying, "I'm here, ain't I?" From a noisy and tumultuous household, I, Rocky Rivera, daughter of La Reyna Milagros, Queen of the Not-So-Mellow-Drama, had to learn how to find solace in those long silences, had to learn how to read between the jagged lines when Elvis did speak.

The two-room apartment on Noe Street was as spartan and uninviting as Elvis himself could sometimes be. We had a futon on a cheap wooden frame, two cinder blocks and a plank for a table, the back seat of a Chevy covered with a blanket for a sofa. There were amps, an eclectic tape and record collection, and his guitar, of course, a white Stratocaster that Elvis's father had found in a pawnshop in Oakland. Voltaire pointed out that the guitar looked just like Jimi's. "Wouldn't it be cosmic if it were really his?" Voltaire mused one day when he was visiting. One of his pet theories, which he would expound upon quite rationally and eloquently to anyone who cared to listen, involved the CIA assassinating Jimi with a fatal overdose of drugs. "Hendrix was considered dangerous," Voltaire explained, "because of his growing allegiance to the black liberation movement, and his tremendous power and influence over young people." Elvis nodded in grave agreement. "Makes sense to me." I loved him for the respect and indulgence he showed my brother. Hendrix's spectacular, elegiac version of "The Star-Spangled Banner" sizzled over the airwaves of the Nakamichi sound system, our only luxury. Elvis fretted over the Nakamichi every time we left the apartment. He was sure some junkie was going to break in and take it (which some junkie eventually did).

I had brought my notebooks and stuffed my clothes next to his in the tiny closet, leaving everything else behind at my mother's. I wasn't sure how long I was going to stay, and there was an unspoken, temporary feeling to our living arrangement. Out of the blue one day Elvis said, "I'm moving to New York."

"No shit," I said, reacting as casually as possible. On the inside, I was freaking out — *I just got here, you bastard!* — but on the outside, I was the inscrutable, unsentimental one, determined to behave as coolly as he did. *Bahala na*, baby. Whatever will be, will be. Didn't I write that song, after all, "Love Ain't Nothin' but an F-Word"? *Fleeting, fickle, fucked. It ain't life, but love that's cheap.*

Out of the blue a few days later, Elvis mumbled an invitation. "Wanna come along?"

"Sure," I answered, my heart racing. "When?"

"Soon," he said, which I knew could mean either tomorrow or a year from now.

I never quite relaxed around him, and so I stayed in love longer than I expected. He fulfilled my notion of love, which meant no one would ever get what they wanted. Love for me had never been a source of comfort, but of anxiety and longing, desire and regret. It was a terrible emotion, really. I learned that from observing the way my parents cruelly danced around each other.

Make no mistake, though. Elvis and I were lovers, possessive and protective with each other. We quickly settled into our own version of domesticity: sleeping together, eating together, hanging out, waiting up for each other. He even took me to meet his family. They were surprised to see us and insisted we stay for dinner. I had the feeling that Elvis hadn't been home in a long time.

I knew Elvis fucked other women — so what? Women made themselves available at all his gigs. Even if I was in the vicinity, it didn't matter. They were so brazen, it was downright funny. "Just don't bring anything home," I warned him. He'd already given me the clap once. I barely showed any symptoms, except the glands around my crotch were swollen, and I didn't know why. After a couple of days of listening to me gripe about being uncomfortable, Elvis admitted rather casually that he had "the drips." We rushed downtown to the infamous haven on Howard Street known fondly as the Clap Clinic. I didn't even bother getting angry at Elvis. I was mad at myself, actually, for being so naive. I sat apart from him in the waiting area crowded with worn-out streetwalkers, humiliated business executives, and ashen young men who reminded me of my brother.

The doctor who examined me turned out to be a butch-looking, friendly woman named Dr. Maguyan. She inquired in Tagalog, "Are you Pilipina?" After administering my penicillin shot, Dr. Maguyan ushered Elvis into her office and lectured us on the use of condoms. "In this day and age, it would be wise to take all necessary precautions." She caught Elvis yawning and her voice hardened. "Are you listening, young man?" Then she caught me off guard by asking, "What kind of birth control are you using, young lady?" When I managed to squeak, "Rhythm method," the doctor shook her head in dismay. Tsk, tsk, went Dr. Maguyan's clicking tongue. *Ay naku.* "You kids are playing with fire." I was tempted to ask if she knew Auntie Fely, but I didn't. Elvis and I left the clinic that afternoon with a prescription for penicillin tablets and a bagful of condoms.

Dr. Maguyan and my brush with gonorrhea made me start worrying about worse shit — shit that could kill you. There were stories going around. A guy down the hall from us named Hector, who used to cut Elvis's hair, now looked like a wispy ghost. Hector never left his apartment; Elvis and I used to knock and ask if he needed anything from the store. There'd be long periods of silence, a lot of coughing and rustling around. Then you'd hear Hector make wheezing sounds through the door, like he was leaning up against it. He'd finally muster up enough energy to say, "No thanks, really." Friends came and went, carrying bags of groceries. Then one day Hector's parents and sisters showed up, all the way from Mayagüez, Puerto Rico. They left and took Hector with them. Next thing you know, the apartment's being repainted, the floors are being sanded, and the rent's gone up.

My thing about sex got positively morbid. I remained faithful to Elvis, though there were times my thoughts strayed to other remote, rebel types with the faces of fallen angels. There were lots of them prowling the streets. *What if?* I never did anything about it, of course. Or I mused about the boys I grew up with back in Manila — Teofilo, my *yaya* Emy's mute son (mute only because he was too shy to speak), and Jose Mari, with his German last name, hazel eyes, and thick, incongruous Tagalog Spanish accent. Jose Maria Kunstler. "Will you wait for me forever, *naman?*"

He was a very rich mestizo, two years older than Voltaire. They went to the same prestigious Jesuit school, the difference being that Voltaire was on full scholarship. Voltaire found him just as fascinating as I did, and made the mistake of bringing him home one day. "What a creep," Luz said. I had never met anyone who moved so languidly and assuredly through our steamy, chaotic world, as if everything and everyone belonged to him. Jose Mari flirted with me when he thought no one else was looking. He stroked my arm. "My sister still plays with dolls," my brother reminded him politely. Jose Mari was the son of a powerful man, and Voltaire knew he had to be careful. Jose Mari ignored him and concentrated on getting in my mother's good graces. He dubbed her the Ava Gardner of Manila. "But really, Tita Milagros, you are more beautiful *talaga* than Ava could ever be." My mother was flattered but uneasy. Only Luz saw right through him, and Jose Mari avoided her whenever he could. Jose Mari called me "little sweetheart" and sent gushy secret notes through my miserable, intimidated brother. I was confused by all this furtive attention.

Tossing aside the latest obscene love letter, I start to cry. "He's so nasty, Voltaire. Plump and white like a slug. *Nakakadiri.*"

"So tell him to go away," Voltaire grumbles. "I'm sick of being his messenger boy. Who does he think he is?"

It is one of Voltaire's dark days. Without warning, he starts screaming and won't calm down. Luz bursts into the room. She grabs Voltaire by the shoulders and shakes him. "Voltaire," she says, "it's Luz. We're all here, and you're safe." He yelps like a wounded animal. "Stop it," Luz begs him, "or we'll have to call the doctor." Slender fingers flutter around his glistening face like tiny, excited moths. His eyes are uncomprehending. He pushes Luz away. She flees from the room, calling for my mother to help her. I am rooted to my spot, unafraid, eyes fixed on my brother. He hiccups and barks like a dog. He makes an attempt to say something. *Cabron*, he gasps. I strain to listen, enchanted by the curses flying out of his mouth. *Hijo de puta. Puki mo.* Beautiful words, graphic and violent, curses in three languages. *Putang ina.* Goddammit. Shitfucker. Mother. Whore. *Coño.*

Was my brother possessed by the devil, or an *aswang*? I was enthralled, in spite of myself, just as I was enthralled by Jose Mari with the brusque German last name. If I had been more like Luz and stayed behind in Manila, would I be married to Jose Mari and half crazy by now?

Whereas little, hungry Teofilo was not demonic but meek. The servant's son. So gaunt and ingratiating, so much smaller than I though we were the same age, I was compelled to mistreat him. I stuck out my tongue. I slammed doors in his face. I pinched him when we were alone. Unperturbed, he kept following me around the house, staring at me with his big, sad, watery black eyes. "Stop spying on me, you stupid boy," I growled at him one day in exasperation. *Yaya* Emy overheard me and suddenly appeared. Flushed with angry shame, she slapped her son in front of me before yanking him by his bony arm back to the kitchen. He whimpered in pain. The thin, mewling sound of his voice startled me, and I too was ashamed. Days went by. I fantasized about apologizing profusely to Emy and Teofilo, but of course, I didn't. I never saw Teofilo again.

On my twelfth birthday, Jose Mari's chauffeur delivers a twenty-four-karat-gold ID bracelet to our house, wrapped inside a fancy gift box, which my mother rips open. She is shocked. The bracelet is inscribed with our names, "Jose Mari & Raquel," and the word "Always." My enraged father sends the bracelet back with a note addressed to Jose Mari's father. I am punished for encouraging Jose Mari's obsessions. When I am not in school, I am ordered to stay in my room with only Emy for company. I have no allies. Voltaire is in a sanatorium up in Baguio, "resting." My mother and Luz are away visiting him. In the yellow stifling heat of the interminable afternoons, Emy patiently teaches me the lyrics to "Dahil Sa Iyo," the popular Tagalog love song: "*Nais kong mabuhay / dahil sa iyo / hanggang mamatay*." (Because of you / I want to live / because of you / until I die.)

When my mother takes us on the ship bound for America, Jose Mari is absent from the crowd seeing us off. My father and sister are absent, too. "How can she take you away like this? What does your mother think she's doing?" Jose Mari weeps on the phone the night before my departure. He hints at suicide. Even I know he is lying.

"It's none of your business," I retort. "And besides, you're not supposed to call me anymore." I want to cry, but I don't. Two years have gone by, and I am a lot tougher now. Fat slug, I want to hiss, I'm the one who's being dragged away. *Against my will.*

"You'll be back," Jose Mari says, the smug nonchalance returning to his voice. "All grown up, and beautiful *talaga*, just like that crazy mother of yours. I'll never give up. *Hanggang mamatay*, sweetheart, daar-ling. I'll be waiting for you."

No Experience Necessary

Voltaire told me Macy's always hired extra help for Christmas, "no experience necessary," and I knew the time had come for me to quit relying on Elvis and my sorry tips from Lumpia X-Press. Elvis and I usually had just enough to buy a few groceries and the occasional cheap bag of smoke. I was considering applying for food stamps, so when Voltaire suggested Macy's as a solution to my pathetic situation, I convinced myself that hawking make-up and hair baubles eight hours a day wasn't so bad, and I chanted a mantra as I crossed Market Street: *Not so bad, not so bad, not so bad.* By the cable car stop in front of Woolworth's, an outlandish, funkified beauty had attracted a small crowd. I stopped to check her out. She stood next to a hand-painted sign that read:

Fantazia Laveaux's Petit Circus Hoodoo
Direct From New Orleans
Fantazy! Fate! Fortune! Fire!
$$$$$ Graciously Accepted

Her head was covered by a turban fashioned from a Mexican rebozo, and three or four silver and gold hoops hung from each ear. Her arms were covered with bangles, and she'd tied a sarong of vibrant tropical colors over a gingham granny skirt. Her amusing gold platform wedgies looked expensive. Fantazia may have been hustling, but she obviously wasn't starving.

A curious crowd gathered. "Hey, baby, you gonna tell my fortune?" a teenager with an angry face shouted. His friends laughed uneasily. Fantazia ignored them. "Maybe she don't speak English," one of them said, "or she deaf."

When she moved, her sheer embroidered peasant blouse revealed small, perfect, braless tits under her black velvet bolero vest. It was a chilly, windy day, the beginning of winter in San

Francisco. Wasn't she cold? "Mama, mama, mama," someone behind me groaned. More nervous laughter. Fantazia smiled wickedly, silencing us. Staring at this flamboyant, beautiful creature with the silly, made-up name, I felt a weird mixture of irritation, envy, and desire. She couldn't have been much older than I. *Wasn't she cold? Who was she? How dare she?*

She never uttered a word, and began by making a grand, sweeping gesture with her braceleted arm as if to move us out of the way. Obediently, we stepped back to give her room. Fantazia brandished something resembling a giant Q-Tip, sprinkled it with lighter fluid, and set it ablaze with a Bic. She tossed her head back, her aubergine mouth falling open. *Swoosh.* Flames shot out. We gasped in wonder. It was over in a matter of seconds. Fantazia bowed and curtsied to a smattering of applause, her expression grave. A bowler hat was passed around. I threw in my last dollar. "Is that *it*?" a disgusted tourist muttered loudly to her companion.

I stayed behind when the crowd finally scattered, unsure of what to do and feeling like a fool. My future at Macy's was beckoning on the grim horizon. Fantazia Laveaux must've read my mind. "Gotta keep your head back when you eat fire," she said, sidling up to where I was standing. "Otherwise, you're in big trouble." I watched while she smeared her blistered lips with gobs of ointment. "You do this often?" I asked. "When I have to," she answered. Up close, Fantazia looked exhausted and older. Strands of nappy hair stuck out from under her head wrap. I inhaled the sharp scent of her jasmine perfume mixed with gasoline. "Hey, girl. Lighten up. You look like you could be my sister. Wha's your name?"

I told her. Her smile was broad and intimidating. "Rocky Rivera! *Tú eres Chicana?* No? You in theater? I mean, with a name like that."

Emboldened and annoyed, I mimicked her tone. "What about you? *Tú eres Chicana?*"

"You never know," she said. "Do you?"

I blushed.

I helped Fantazia pack the fire-eating gear into a duffel bag. A Cab Calloway look-alike with stiff, straightened hair and blood-shot eyes danced around us. He clutched a pint of Thunderbird wrapped in a brown paper bag, bobbing and weaving to his own, private music. Ignoring my dirty look, he made excited mmm-mmm sounds, smacking his lips at my new friend. "Fantazia, the way you dress is criminal —"

"Get lost," she said, not even bothering to look at him.

I recognized that low, theatrical groan. "Mama, mama, mama, you breakin' my heart —" Then he decided to give me a try. "Are you a model?"

"Leave her alone," she said. "She's married."

"Baby tha's no problem. I'm married too."

We walked quickly away from him. The sugary, slurred voice now shook with rage. "Whatsa matter, Fantazia? You just into pussy?" He sucked on his Thunderbird and fondled himself defiantly, yelling, "Why don't you girls give *this* a try?" I turned around to give him the finger, but by then we were blocks away.

"Don't mind him," she said. "Tha's Jimbo, practically an insti-tution on Market Street. Usedta be pretty famous."

I was livid. "Famous for what?"

She shrugged. "The usual. Singin' the blues, playin' the blues, pimpin'. Jimbo's basically harmless. Come along, little darlin'. Don't fret. We'll sashay over to North Beach, and I'll treat you to espresso with a twist. You ever had espresso with a lemon rind floatin' in it?"

I shook my head.

"Is very sexy, trust me. An acquired taste, but very sexy. I learned to drink it in New York. You ever been to New York? My name, by the way — my *real* name — is Keiko. Keiko Van Heller."

She lived with her mongrel cat, Scheherazade, in a cramped studio on Divisadero Street, not far from where Elvis and I lived.

There were photographs tacked on the walls, carefully composed black-and-white portraits of expressionless people sitting in empty rooms, or more kinetic shots of strangers on the street, caught by surprise. "Works in progress," she proudly called them. The studio was decorated the way she was dressed, with odd, calculated touches. Coke bottles were lined up on a windowsill and filled with dried roses. A frothy ivory lace gown hung on a tailor's dummy.

"My wedding dress," Keiko explained.

"*You* were married?"

"Absolutely," she answered.

It was getting dark outside. "Hungry?" Without waiting for an answer, she rummaged around for something to cook. "Well, darlin', that was futile," she drawled, emerging from the kitchen with a gallon jug of white wine. It was the sweet, cheap kind, without a cork. I decided to stop worrying about my missed job interview. A few drinks later, I made an attempt to track Elvis down, but he was nowhere to be found. "Your lover?" Keiko asked, when I hung up the phone.

"Yeah. We were supposed to meet for dinner."

"He'll no doubt be pissed," she observed dryly.

Keiko told stories of her childhood, stories that kept changing the longer I knew her. Her mother, Gwen, was the first Japanese American trapeze artist ever hired by Barnum & Bailey. Her father, Franklin Delano Van Heller, was an artist. "Unfortunately, they died when I was —" five, six, seven, eight, nine, ten. The fictional story of Keiko's parents varied along with Keiko's age on the day they supposedly died. Sometimes her mother was a social worker, the first Japanese American to graduate with honors from Barnard. ("I thought she was a trapeze artist," I said. "Yeah, but she *went* to Barnard," Keiko snapped.) Sometimes her father was a respectable black doctor. Sometimes he was more exotic — a blue-eyed, black Cuban boxer who died in the ring, or a blue-eyed, black Cuban artist tortured and killed by Castro's secret police. "You know about Santería?" Keiko asked. I shook my head (I was always shaking my head and feeling ignorant around her). "Santería's close to being Catholic," she explained, "but funkier."

"What about the name Van Heller?" I asked. "That's not Cuban."

"Yes it is," Keiko said. "Remember Frida Kahlo?"

"Frida Kahlo's Mexican."

"Same difference," Keiko retorted. "She was Mexican *and* German. They got everything in Cuba too, even Jews. *Cuban Jews.* Did you know that?"

There was this yarn she later told my mother and Zeke. "Papa managed the Royal Hawaiian Hotel on Waikiki, and Mama was one of the hula dancers. You know that hotel, Mistuh Zeke?"

"I know it's de ugliest, pinkest thing I've ever seen," Zeke replied. He and my mother were on their second round of cocktails by then.

My mother was leery of Keiko. "*Keiko Van Heller* — that's quite a name."

"She's *hapa*," Zeke said.

My mother bristled. "Speak English, Zeke! Do you mean half-breed?"

Keiko was enjoying herself. "Zeke's right. I'm *hapa*. My father's Scottish Dutch, my mother's Japanese Hawaiian. Can you guess why they disowned me? For going out with a Filipino!" She burst out laughing at her own joke. My mother and Zeke sat there, stony-faced.

It never occurred to me to call her a liar to her face, or to ask Keiko why she felt the need to embellish her life. She was my best friend, my teacher. I had often dreamed about meeting someone like her, someone more reckless than I could ever be, someone who would eat fire. Someone unnerving, with Frida Kahlo's caterpillar eyebrows and piercing, black eyes, and that sly black smile, hinting at a thousand more lies and secrets.

Voltaire was just as infatuated when he met her. They hung out a lot, just the two of them. Voltaire dragged her to hear bands at Mabuhay Gardens; she took him to see *The Realm of the Senses*. Very Japanese and very kinky. Voltaire described to me, in excruciating detail, how this woman with a tattooed earlobe makes a pact with her lover. First she fucks him, then she strangles him with a silk cord, then she cuts his dick off, all in the name of great passion. Keiko said it was based on a true story. The real woman wandered in shock around Tokyo or some other Japanese city for days, carrying her lover's severed penis like a trophy. "Isn't that absolutely sick?" Voltaire pretended to shiver.

"Definitely freaky," I agreed. I took Elvis to see it that same night. He hated the movie, but we came home and fucked brutally on the floor for hours, without making a sound.

Keiko invited Voltaire and me to a drag spectacle in North Beach. Everyone had to go in costume. I went as Anna May Wong in *Daughter of the Dragon*, my face powdered chalk-white, my lips the color of dried blood. Keiko wore her Cleopatra Jones Afro wig, completely naked under a chain-mail, micromini gladiator dress. Voltaire went as — who else? — Jimi Hendrix. The black diva Sylvester made a sensational entrance in a Joan Crawford evening gown, carrying a picnic basket and flinging cottonballs at the audience. He crooned "Summertime" in his lush, Nina Simone voice. High above us, a naked young white boy, as pretty as a faun, swung languidly on a trapeze entwined with artificial flowers.

I started dressing like Keiko, haunting the big Salvation Army outlet on Army Street. Bought slinky crepe dresses with ratty shoulder pads, from the thirties and forties. Beaded pillbox hats with net veils. Satin elbow-length gloves. Moth-eaten velvet capes. I sprinkled patchouli oil on a disintegrating ten-dollar squirrel coat, which I proudly wore all winter. My skin broke out in a rash. My mother was upset by my transformation, my brother tickled. "I'd fumigate that coat if I were you," my mother said. She offered to give me her old gowns — "at least they've been dry-cleaned" — which I gamely tried on. They were opulent and wonderful, but all wrong for me. "Ma, I don't have your Coca-Cola body."

She gave me the silent suffering martyr treatment for days after that, frowning whenever Keiko's name came up.

I was truly perplexed. "Would you speak up and tell me what's eating you? Don't you like her?"

She responded with her usual, "You never listen to your mother."

She was right, of course. My mother's power was diminished, and Manila with all its taboos and obligations seemed a million miles away. Keiko was much too fascinating. Her friendship made me feel powerful. I loved running away to her studio apartment, which I did as often as I could, staying with her when Elvis was on the road or at an all-night recording session. I told myself that if Elvis and I ever split up, I wanted a place of my own, just like hers — except mine would have a typewriter, a piano, and a thousand more records and books. I wanted a queen-size mattress set in the middle of the floor, just like hers, strewn with mirrored pillows and covered with a paisley fabric from India, the kind you could still buy on Haight Street. The bed was the center of Keiko's decadent universe, the first thing you noticed when you entered the room.

When I told Elvis about Keiko, he was silent. "Don't you want to meet her? She's an artist."

"Everybody in San Francisco's an artist," Elvis said. He threw his hands up in a gesture of surrender when I started mop-ing. "Okay, okay. You win. Let's go meet your friend and have some fun."

Keiko kept us waiting for over an hour while she got dressed. Then she decided to show Elvis some of her latest photo collages — which took another hour. I could tell that Elvis was trying very hard to look impressed. Finally, at Elvis's suggestion, we went to a boring jazz club in Berkeley. He proceeded to act totally engrossed in the bleak, atonal music played by a quintet of earnest professorial types. The saxophonist bandleader puffed on a pipe while his sidemen took turns torturing us with interminable solos. I drank double shots of tequila to keep from screaming. Elvis fended off Keiko's attempts at conversation with curt answers. *Yes. No. Maybe.* Keiko retaliated by spilling a drink on him. It was all very childish, but it worked. She outdrank him, she outsmoked him, she embarrassed him by flirting with our waitress, flirting with me, and flirting with the musicians while they played. She went home early with this young dealer she met who'd been lurking outside the women's room.

I was depressed. After she left, Elvis ordered another round of drinks and offered his snide, unasked-for critique. "I must admit, Rocky. Your friend's cute. Those gold platform shoes and that Carmen Miranda outfit's cute. Her work's actually *interesting*. But that diamond stud in her nose . . ." He shook his head in mock dismay "Ugh. Very distracting. Looks like a booger."

"You should see when she has a cold," I said, trying to control my temper.

"What's she trying to prove with that Mammy getup?"

"Gimme a break. What're you trying to prove?"

"She doesn't like herself. All that phony shit you told me about Keiko being mixed — one day she's Japanese and black, the next day she's Dutch and Hawaiian. *Boring.*"

"She's an artist," I said, getting up and putting on my coat.

"That's what you say —"

"You're jealous."

"Bullshit."

"She's an artist. Who cares where she came from and what she is?"

"She cares," Elvis said, with contempt. "That's why she lies so much about everything. Hey, Rocky, where you going?"

Even in our bed, Elvis wouldn't let up about Keiko.

"Are you lovers?"

"We're best friends," I said. "Sisters."

"Yeah, yeah, yeah."

"I'm not kidding. We do everything together."

"Is that why Keiko's following us to New York?"

"Why not? She's from there —"

"She *says* she's from there."

I ignored his remark. "— so when I told her we were going, she said it sounded like a great idea."

"I thought she *loved* San Francisco."

"She does. But it's time. She's tired of being a big fish in a small pond."

Elvis flashed his irresistible smile. "Fess up, Rocky. Keiko can't live without you."

I exploded. "Why do you keep bothering me about this? If you wanna fuck her, go ask her yourself."

How could I explain? We were better than lovers. Keiko serving me coffee sweetened with Magnolia brand condensed milk. Coffee thick and sweet as caramel. Sometimes she'd just sit there, licking the milk off a spoon. Content. We'd talk and talk. Never move off that bed. The cat would nap, curled up between us. The light would change. Day into night. Night into day. "More coffee?" Even when her landlord was threatening to evict her, Keiko always managed to scrounge up money for "basics," a can of Bustelo, a can of condensed milk, a carton of Kools.

Keiko prided herself on her fiery gumbo, which she cooked at least once a week. We'd eat on her bed, nonchalant about the mess we made. The cat ate off our plates. We were smug and pleased with ourselves. *Happy.* I was, anyway. Voltaire often joined us for dinner, and we'd watch cheesy, all-night horror movies on Keiko's little black-and-white TV. *Carnival of Lost Souls. White Zombie.* Our absolute favorite was *Vampire Women from Outer Space* — not a vampire in sight, and one of the worst movies ever made. I could've sworn all the extras were Filipino, and the supposedly alien language they were speaking a combination of Tagalog and Ilokano.

Keiko's lovers used to show up unexpectedly, ringing her doorbell at ungodly hours. The men were handsome and hostile, with names like Sekou, Giovanni, Antonio, or The Captain. The women had names like Ambrosia and Ling Ling. Keiko introduced every last one of them as poets. "God, I love her," Voltaire sighed, when we were alone. "You don't love her. You just want to be her," I said.

No matter how late it was or how tired we were, my brother and I always got the hint. We'd bid Keiko and her current poet good night and return to where our angry, lonely, insomniac mother was waiting. She'd be stationed at the sofa, munching on salted watermelon seeds and roasted chestnuts from Chinatown, staring at the same horror movies on her TV and pretending not to notice we were there.

"I know your mother isn't too crazy about me," Keiko once observed.

"She's a little jealous," I admitted.

Keiko smiled. "Your mother's fierce. You know I love her, no matter what." When I didn't respond, she went on. "When my daughter's born, I'm-a name her Milagros Magnolia."

"Are you pregnant?"

She made a face. "Of course not."

"So . . . what if you have a boy someday?"

Keiko looked impatient. "Rocky, please. I'm not innerested in boys." She lit up a Kool and stroked her exposed belly. "Lookit this, Rocky. This-a daughter-bearin' womb." A light patch of kinky hair spread from her belly button down to her crotch. It was oddly erotic, since the rest of her body was so hairless. "Are you innerested in anything but having a daughter?" she asked me.

"I'm not interested in babies," I said.

Keiko was photographing me sitting on the toilet, wearing a serious fifties prom gown. Here we go again — *Rocky Redux*.

"Elvis doesn't get it," Keiko insisted, "and he never will."

"He loves me," I said.

She switched lenses. "He thinks he's the only artist in the relationship. He doesn't appreciate you or your writing."

"He does, in his way. Can we stop now? This tulle dress is itchin' me."

"Rice boys," Keiko said, dismissively. "I almost married one."

I chuckled. "C'mon. You've got to admit: he's hot."

Keiko's voice oozed with contempt. "What, 'cause he's named after that hillbilly and plays the git-*tar*? Rice boys don't talk."

"They don't have to."

"Silent waters. Ha. What's he hiding?"

"Silence can be sexy."

"We scare him," she said. Then, lying back on the floor, Keiko hissed, "Don't move." She focused the camera lens up at me. "Just a few more."

"That's a bad angle," I said. "All chin. I'll look fat."

"You're my subject," she said. "Trust me."

I'd been sitting on that damn toilet of hers for hours. I started to fidget and squirm.

"Don't move," she begged. "Please."

"I hate this dress," I complained again. "This dress is itchin' me."

Keiko sang, "Love is like an itchin' in my heart . . . and, baby, I can't scratch it . . ."

Five more minutes, she promised. Five. More. Minutes. I started to feel sorry for myself. What was this shit Keiko meant about being an artist, anyway? Elvis had his Stratocaster, his very obvious talent, and a growing musical reputation. All I had were my black journals: unpublished, unsung, inconsequential. Poor me. Keiko must be dreaming.

While she was changing film, Keiko uttered his name out of nowhere: "Elvis Chang. Ha. New York'll eat him alive." She said it like she couldn't wait for it to happen.

There were days I got so tired of them both, pushing and pulling on me like they did. I'd run away to my mother's flat, drink Scotch with her and Zeke, write stupid songs about love being stupid, go to the movies with Voltaire, make myself sick with food.

"I wish I were in love with love like you," Voltaire said on one of these evenings.

"Really? I thought you were in love with Keiko," I said, in a vicious mood.

Elvis left banal phone messages: *I met a new drummer.* Or: *That other bass player has potential.* Or: *I think I got us a deal on rehearsal space.*

He never asked me to call him back or begged me to come home. He just kept leaving more messages, enticing me with inquiries like, "What about that music thing you want to try?"

Music thing. Fuck you, Elvis. I asked Voltaire to take me to the Animal Shelter, this notorious little club in an alley south of Market. Monday nights were open mike, hosted by a witty speed freak named Wild Bob. Anyone could get up and call himself a poet, and unknown bands could test out a song or two. The place was smelly and packed. Nervously, I signed up to recite a piece called "My Little Darling," something I'd always thought had potential as a song. When it was over, Wild Bob and the audience acted like they enjoyed it, whistling, clapping, and stomping their feet, but they seemed to enjoy everyone else that night, too. I didn't mind sharing the applause; I'd survived. When Voltaire helped me off the stage, I was shaking with relief and so exhilarated that I forgot Elvis wasn't there.

* * *

Elvis stopped leaving messages; if anyone else but me answered the phone when he called, he'd quickly hang up. My mother was incensed. "What a rude bastard." She gave me a pitying look. "I hope you do better next time." Keiko left carefully mounted photo collages enclosed in padded envelopes on my mother's doorstep. Addressed: "To R.R. You Know Who You R." There I was, the tacky prom queen on her toilet throne, with smeared lipstick, chipped paint on my toenails. In every frame, my wasted expression never changed. Sometimes Scheherazade was in the picture, rubbing up against my legs. Once Keiko posed me with a handgun borrowed from some lover of hers. She scrawled passages from Sei Shonagon's *The Pillow Book* and lines from Neruda and Sonia Sanchez poems across the lurid images.

What did it all mean? I was titillated and flattered by my portraits.

My mother studied the photographs, slipped them back into the envelopes, and returned them to me without comment.

Voltaire said: "You look like a junkie."

Then he said: "Ma's right. I don't think Keiko likes you very much."

It got to be predictable. I'd move back in with Elvis after a few weeks at my mother's. Keiko would show up at our apartment as if nothing had happened. She and Elvis would try to get along. Keiko would invite us over, along with Voltaire. We'd eat gumbo. Listen to music. Go dancing. I'd start posing for her again. "Why do you jump whenever Keiko calls?" Elvis grumbled.

It's a complicated thing, I finally said to both of them. But don't make me choose. If you love me, put up or shut up.

The song I wrote went like this:

MY LITTLE DARLING
*I just wanna put you in a cage. / I wanna lock you up /
and make you mine, / my very own, / my latest rage, /
my exotic pet, / my little darling, / leopard on a leash. /*

I don't care if I'm offensive / or put you on / the defensive. /
I just wanna make you mine / my very own / my little darling /
leopard on a leash.

The bridge:
I'll walk you down / the Champs Elysees, / 42nd Street, /
or Lenox Avenue. / I don't care. / The world is ours, /
my little darling, / leopard on a leash.

And the chorus:
I love you. / I hate you. / What's the difference?
(Repeat chorus 2x.)

Keiko cheerfully initiated my virgin consciousness with a blot of what she called "pure Owsley LSD." "Time to wake up," she declared. She never did explain who Owsley was, or where she got her drugs. I don't think I really wanted to know. I was in a shitty, reckless mood, having left Elvis again. The acid hit me fast, and hard. "My God," I moaned, writhing in psychedelic agony on her floor, "my God." The insides of my skull felt wet and scrambled. I crawled on my hands and knees into Keiko's bathroom, stuck my head into her toilet bowl for an eternity. I was hypnotized by swirling, blue currents of water. I forgot where I was. Keiko grabbed her Nikon, taking my picture. Tears streamed down my face. I began retching. "Don't panic, Rivera," Keiko murmured, as she gently massaged the small of my back. She took another picture. "After this part's over, you'll be fine. *Glorious.* Don't worry. The good stuff's about to begin."

I was spewing up my guts, sure I was dying. The floor beneath me was erupting. At any moment, a big fat intestine was going to fly right out of my mouth. I was sure of it. "Oh God," I kept groaning, "God, God, God." Such strange, unbearable, cosmic pain. Such sadness. I could taste the suffering of the world, sour and searing on my tongue. Into the abyss I plunged, tasting the sadness of my father, my brother, my sister. I was sobbing wildly. "I want a doctor. I want my mother. I want this to stop." Where was my mother, fierce white tiger, the only one who could protect me from this terror? What was I afraid of? Bitter, bitter. I couldn't stop spitting and weeping.

"Shhhh," Keiko said. "Calm down, Rocky."

"Mama!" I wailed with abandon. An *aswang* with pterodactyl wings swooped down from the ceiling and perched on top of the sink. Flaming blue coals for eyes. A sorrowful, feminine, blue vampire face. "It's your fault," the vampire eyes accused me. Familiar eyes. "Sink your teeth into me!" I thought I shouted, but I was just thinking it. The silence was heavy, almost tangible. I hung on to Keiko's toilet bowl for dear life. Whatever I touched gave off electric sparks. The *aswang* covered its face shyly with one of its wings. Was it Milagros, my divine mother *aswang*, or Keiko doing that ridiculous hoochy-coochy dance of the seven veils in the bathroom that night? "Don't panic, baby, it's just your ego dying." Keiko's disembodied voice assured me. Smooth, cool, friendly, professional. Articulate. I must always be articulate. Is the radio on? There's a song in that line. There's a song, isn't there? Gravestones toppled over. Someone flushed the toilet. Thank God. Thank Keiko. The blue water swished. I lifted my head from the vibrating toilet bowl in time to catch my shy *aswang* transforming into Voltaire, into Elvis, then into Minnie Mouse, my mother, who evaporated into Keiko — at last. The toilet flushed. The *aswang* vanished. The floor became a floor. I collapsed with relief, laughing. I laughed and laughed. I choked with laughter. Keiko clicked away at my devastated self with her goddam camera.

"I've seen the glory of God. It's in the fire, the smoke, the vapors." Voltaire prays in his darkened room. I hear the sound of thumping through his locked door. "Voltaire? *C'est moi, kuya.*" He ignores my soft knock. Another thump. "I've seen the glory, O Lord. I have seen. I have borne witness to the grief and the suffering, the fire, the smoke, the vapors."

"How long has he been in there?" I ask my mother later in the kitchen. She dismisses my question with an impatient shrug of her shoulders. "Got to Give It Up" by Marvin Gaye is playing on the beat-up transistor radio I brought all the way from Manila, the radio I left behind when I moved out. I love the song's low-down rhythms and can't help but sing along as I help my mother stuff her lumpia wrappers with ground pork, shrimp, tofu, and bean sprouts. "Raquel, you're putting too much in," my mother complains. "Pay attention. Never mind, I'll finish the rest." Waving me aside, she starts chopping more ingredients for another round of frying. The aroma of garlic and oil pervades the drafty kitchen. "Voltaire was waiting for you all night."

I glance at her, puzzled.

My mother's tone is bitter and condescending. "When Voltaire's off his medication, he doesn't sleep. Of course, when he's on it, he sleeps too much. *You* know that. *You* and Elvis and your pal Keiko promised to take him to something. He waited all night. All night! Must be the full moon. He's starting one of his binges again. I stayed up with him, of course. How was I supposed to sleep? He read to me from the Bible and lit all the candles in the house. He could've started a fire. *Dios ko,* I was so terrified, I almost called your Auntie Fely to come over. What was it you promised him, another stupid movie?"

I groan, remembering what I thought of as a trivial phone call to Voltaire the day before. "Oh God. We forgot."

My mother keeps up the steady, angry rhythm of her chopping. "That's right," she says, "*you* forgot."

Milagros Rivera fumes as she cooks, her face tight with fury and concentration. She blames me for being fifteen minutes late getting here today and for driving Voltaire to the brink of another nervous breakdown. To add even more insult to injury, the banker Rick Foss is half an hour late for lunch. You'd think she'd be used to it — Filipinos are notorious for their casual timing — but my mother considers lateness a personal affront. "*Men*. Between your crazy brother and —" Chop, chop. On the stove, the oil in the pan sizzles.

I help myself to one of the fried lumpias from the platter she's set down to cool, dreading the familiar, self-pitying monologue that is sure to come. My father, my brother, my sister, Zeke, Rick, me and my friends: we are all guilty.

Instead, my mother suddenly falls silent. Nervous, I reach for another lumpia and wolf it down. This one's overdone and leaves a charred aftertaste. The doorbell buzzes. My mother's frown deepens.

Rick Foss is one of those guys from a TV sitcom, plump, conservative, born middle-aged. Timex watch, flashy college signet ring, nondescript off-the-rack suits and matching neckties, brown or gray or navy blue, pinstripes or plaid or polka dots, I can never remember which and it doesn't matter. He isn't much older than I, but you'd never know it. "Aha," he says, brushing past me as I hold the door open for him.

"Fine, thanks," I mutter, loud enough for him to hear. Rick drops his briefcase on the sofa, then hands me a grocery-store bouquet of green carnations. "St. Patrick's Day," he announces, wincing as our fingers accidentally touch. I feel a terrible urge to laugh. "Ma," I call out gaily, heading into the kitchen. "Guess what?" I can't wait to see the expression on her face. My mother despises carnations.

He slides his boxy butt onto a chair at the head of the table, which is formally set for four. *Cloth napkins*. Since when does this bore rate cloth napkins? "Well, Rachel. What a surprise.

How's the new apartment? And . . . ahhh . . . how's . . . ?" He can't bring himself to utter Elvis's name.

I start counting the pale brown freckles on his face. "Your mother tells me you're looking for a job," Rick continues. "We've got trainee positions open at the bank. I could put in a good word, if you're interested." My smile is noncommittal. Maybe my mother needs another loan. That explains the embroidered linen napkins from Manila, the gleaming silver, the lavish lunch. Busying herself going back and forth from kitchen to dining area, my mother pointedly ignores the sorry flowers I've stuck in a vase at the center of the table. "Sorry I'm a little late," Rick finally apologizes, after the atmosphere grows too tense even for him to bear. "There was a crisis with our computers. I had to stick around and oversee . . . make sure we didn't lose important files." My mother glares at him.

From his apartment below I imagine Zeke Akamine pacing around in a heartbroken rage. Zeke's been on my mother's shit-list again, and she won't let him inside the apartment. He knows Rick Foss is over for one of his visits. Maybe Zeke spied on Rick through the grimy venetian blinds as Rick tapped his foot impatiently on the front steps, waiting for us to let him in.

They'd met a few months back, one of those quick chance encounters when Rick was heading upstairs to my mother's apartment and Zeke was on his way out. Zeke immediately smelled a rat. He later tried to pry information out of Voltaire and me, but we weren't in the mood to give anything up. Poor Zeke wouldn't stop trying, but he got nowhere with us. Anyway, Voltaire and I agree: fuck Zeke and all the rest of my mother's victims. They deserve everything they get.

Ten, eleven, twelve freckles. Rick Foss has the bland baby face of a serial killer.

"Incredible," Rick murmurs between bites. "Just incredible."

My mother can't resist his flattery. "You like it?"

"I don't know how you do it," he says, laying it on thick.

"I've been *so* busy," Milagros brags, softening. "Two parties to cater this Saturday — one baptism, then a wedding. One right after the other! And next month is all booked."

Rick Foss is relieved by the change in her demeanor. He even manages a small, cautious smile. "What can I say? You're a success, Mil."

Mil. What a ridiculous name for my mother. The fact that she allows it is bad enough, but I guess it's all for the sake of her precious Lumpia X-Press.

Rick turns to me. "Didn't I predict your mother would succeed?"

"Oh, RickFoss, please. Where would I be without you?" My mother's pretense at modesty is an act I've seen before, and this pudgy banker isn't the first to fall for it. Sixteen freckles so far.

Her mood brightening, Milagros hovers over us like some culinary guardian angel. *More rice? More pancit? More lumpia?* You're not eating enough, she scolds us. *Kain na,* she pleads in Tagalog. *Come!* she orders in Spanish.

"I'm going to explode." Rick beams with happiness.

Try this, she says. Tell me what you think. Chicken wing adobo. Cassava cake. More lumpia, and an assortment of her wicked dipping sauces and condiments.

"I've got to get back to the office, really, Mil." But Rick never stops stuffing his cherubic, freckled face.

The telephone rings. Milagros picks up the extension in the kitchen. From her guarded tone of voice, I know it's someone for Voltaire. Maybe Dr. Love Love again, the one who lent Voltaire all that money. "He's out of town on business. That's right. *Bizness.*" Exasperated, my mother tries Tagalog. "*Sino ka ba?* Ayyy — *walanghiya!*" In the midst of banging down the receiver, she catches us staring at her and smiles innocently at Rick. "Ready for dessert?"

Voltaire suddenly appears, an unshaven apparition in his rumpled pajamas. "Just in time," my mother says, in a fake cheery voice.

Rick Foss can't wait to flee. "Mil, I wish I could stay. But it's past three-thirty —"

"Mr. Foss, how nice." Voltaire hasn't made any moves to join us at the table and remains standing in the doorway. "Mr. Foss," Voltaire repeats, then adds, as if seeing me for the first time, "Raquel, how nice."

"Sorry you missed such an extraordinary meal," Rick says to my brother, not sorry at all. I make Rick uncomfortable, but Voltaire scares him to death. Rick makes a show of looking at the gold-plated watch on his hairy wrist and clucking with disappointment. "God, time flies. I'll be in big trouble if I don't get going. Gotta run, Mil."

Overcoat on and briefcase in hand, Rick Foss promises to call my mother and discuss her plans for expansion. "First thing in the morning, I swear." Then, without saying thank you or goodbye, he scurries out of the apartment.

Voltaire sits down and studies the clutter of dishes before him. He begins by picking halfheartedly at the food, then suddenly accelerates into stuffing his mouth as if he were desperate and starving.

"You see? You see what you've done?" Milagros yells at him, fighting back tears. "*You did that on purpose.*" Voltaire chews noisily.

From Zeke's apartment below, the sad, sinuous strains of a slide guitar float up through the worn floors and threadbare carpets. Faint male voices croon dark harmonies. My mother reaches for a broom in the pantry, pounding the floor with one end of the broom handle. "Goddam Zeke," she mutters, pounding away. As if to mock her, Zeke turns up the music louder. The languid melody clashes with the song playing on the transistor radio. "You . . . light up . . . my life," a woman belts out. Her voice is nasal and powerful. The DJ informs us that we are listening to San Francisco's favorite station, "Easy on the soul. Lite is right. Mellow right. Lite rock, FM."

I get up and turn off the radio. "Don't!" My mother hisses, but she makes no move to stop me. The silvery music floats up from Zeke's apartment below. I can hear it now with a bit more clarity. A solo voice laments his long-gone lover in a flowery, fluid mix of English and Hawaiian. I decipher the lyrics for myself: "Why did you toy with me so? Woman of the sea, how could you be so beautiful and yet so heartless?"

My mother gives up her pounding and collapses with exhaustion on the sofa. The woeful song goes on and on; it is one of the longest songs I have ever heard. "Goddess of the moon, the desire for you is eternal and feeds my soul. How could you toy with me so? How could you be so heartless and yet so beautiful?"

Voltaire puts down his fork and knife. Pushing his plate away in disgust, my brother wakes from his trance. I dab his clammy, sweating face with one of my mother's prized napkins. "I'm sorry I forgot," I say. Voltaire shuts his eyes but doesn't cower from my touch. His body, electric and taut only moments ago, relaxes. For this, I am grateful. The song downstairs fades away; a door slams shut. Perhaps Zeke has run off to the corner bar to drown his sorrows in Scotch. He'll be back, to try his luck with Milagros again. And again.

With her mouth gaping open, my mother snores loudly on the sofa. The broom lays across her lap. I am unable to leave, overcome by helplessness in the face of family, blood, and the powerful force of my own reluctant love. Family sickness, homesickness. Manila, our dazzling tropical city of memory. The English language confuses me. What is at the core of that subtle difference between *homesick* and *nostalgic*, for example? Why is one preferable over the other? I don't get it. Or I just don't want to get it, as Voltaire says. When he is well, when his mind is sharp and free from the din and clutter of demons, I tease and torment Voltaire by asking unbearable questions. "What's Filipino? What's authentic? What's in the blood?"

"Ties to the spirit world, fierce pride, wounded pride, thirst for revenge, melodrama, fatalism, weeping and wailing at the graveside. We're blessed with macabre humor and dancing feet — a floating nation of rhythm and blues," Voltaire answers, repeating what this old guy known as the Carabao Kid used to say: "We're our own worst enemy."

The sun has set and the apartment is gloomier than ever. I don't bother turning on the light. My mother snores on. She'll probably sleep for a few more hours. I decide to stay a little while longer and keep Voltaire company. Elvis can wait. Keiko can wait. I sit with my brother in the dark. Oblivious to my presence, Voltaire hums a dissonant tune softly to himself, hunched over the battlefield that is my mother's table.

Cross-Country

Elvis bought a sixty-three Ford pickup from a rail-thin, six-foot seven-inch cowboy. The truck was dirty white and rust-blotched. One aquamarine fender. Three speed on the floor. The cowboy had driven it cross-country from Cut And Shoot, Texas, to San Francisco, where he enrolled in acting school. Elvis claimed we couldn't do better. The truck was a steal. She'd be perfect, he said. Perfect for lugging our imaginary band's imaginary equipment, perfect for loading up and driving to New York.

The Gangster of Love. The band was just Elvis and me, at first, the name inspired by a dream I'd had after taking Keiko's acid. A choir of fat, menacing angels wearing yellow satin robes sang this song by Johnny Guitar Watson called "Gangster of Love." The choir slowed down Watson's upbeat melody, infusing his boastful, macho lyrics with ominous mystery. I decided the dream was some sort of sign, like, Rocky, either shit or get off the pot. Since my Animal Shelter debut, I'd been writing more poems, which Elvis set to music. He seemed to like what was happening musically. We toyed with the idea of bringing in a drummer, but didn't. Then our fantasies became grander and more ambitious. Should we stick to a streamlined, hard-edged sound (lead guitar, bass, drums, vocals), or go for a powerhouse soul revue with horns, backup singers, intricate Motown choreography, the works?

"When? When when when are you going to form a *real* band?" Voltaire nagged. His question didn't surprise me. It was a question typical of all the other questions that kept popping up and wouldn't go away. Real band? Real singer? Real music? Real lyrics? Real record? Real deal? Real life?

But even Voltaire had to admit. Acquiring the truck was a start. She looked like shit but ran like a dream. We called her Lucille, in honor of Little Richard, B. B. King, and the rail-thin, Shakespearean cowboy from East Texas. We decorated Lucille's dashboard with a glow-in-the-dark magnetic Madonna and strung silver milagros across her windshield for good luck. Her ripped-up seats we covered with leopard-print velveteen scraps I found in my mother's trunk.

Elvis fussed and tinkered with her daily. Bought used or stolen parts to replace whatever Lucille needed replacing. Rebuilt the engine. Changed her muffler. Watered her, oiled her. Recharged her batteries. Loved her more than he loved me. I didn't mind. In those days, all I cared about was getting from here to there. Funky Lucille suited me fine.

The thing I resented was not being able to drive her. All I knew how to drive were automatics. I was sure Elvis had deliberately and perversely chosen a manual truck to prove he was indispensable.

"A Ford? Hmmm." Keiko's reaction was bland and noncommittal. A few days later, she drove up in a chocolate brown Toyota Corolla. "My ex-husband's," she explained, beaming. "He showed up last night." The car was not only luxurious — with air conditioning, AM/FM radio, and tape deck — but automatic. Perfect for grueling cross-country journeys. I groaned when I saw it. "You could ride with me," Keiko teased. She practically purred, she was so smug — and went on to make me feel worse, bragging about how her ex-husband, this suave, successful painter named Arnaldo Ruiz, would be driving to New York and sharing expenses with her. "Isn't it a lovely surprise? He's being so generous, and even offered to pay for the whole trip," Keiko said, "but I thought *that* was a setup."

"Are you sleeping with him again?" I asked. (Just as Elvis would, in that pretend, casual way of his that was so transparent.)

Keiko smiled. "I'm considering it."

They were going to take their sweet time driving cross-country, she informed me, because Arnaldo wanted a chance to experience the *real* America. Whatever that means. They were thinking about the slower, more scenic southern route. "Take two fucking weeks if we have to. See the Grand Canyon, the Mississippi River, the Tsankawi ruins. Stay in motels . . ." Keiko gave me one of her droll, suggestive winks.

Elvis tried to warn them. "Remember *Easy Rider?* Watch out for those rednecks." We were at a farewell dinner that Keiko threw for us. We feasted on her spicy gumbo and drank too much of Arnaldo's dangerously smooth tequila Sauza. Voltaire had been invited, but never showed up.

Feverish, and uncharacteristically verbal and effusive, Elvis proceeded to tell a cautionary tale, one I'd heard him tell a thousand times before, about being in the wrong place at the wrong time. The wrong place happened to be an isolated little gas station off the highway near Cheyenne, Wyoming. When I first heard him tell it, I had asked, "What the hell were you doing in Cheyenne, Wyoming?" But Elvis never answered my question.

"I was with Sly," Elvis began, directing his story to a drowsy Keiko and a rapt Arnaldo. They were drunk too, but not as drunk as we were. "Have I told any of you about my friend Sly?" Elvis said, then shrugged when no one responded. "Well, anyway. Picture this: Sly's driving. He pulls up, and we can see that no one's around. Sly honks the horn, not too loud, 'cause we're not stupid. I mean, shit, this is Cheyenne, Wyoming. We sit there, waiting and waiting. Five, six minutes go by. 'Maybe this is a ghost town,' I say to Sly. 'Let's get the fuck outta here.' We're both kinda nervous, but the tank's damn near empty. Who knows if we can make it to the next stop? Suddenly from back behind the main building where maybe he'd been hidin' and checkin' us out, this teenage attendant appears. He approaches us like he's walkin' on a minefield. Starin' at us in awe, more nervous than we are. I can hear his knees shakin', and his walnut brain workin' overtime. Click click: *Uh-oh, here comes some hippie Chink and his sidekick, Super Spade!* He don't say nothin', too scared I guess, and fills up the tank like I asked him. Click click: *Goddam! The hippie Chink speaks English!* Then this pickup truck pulls up, out of nowhere. Three very angry peckerwoods in it. Maybe the kid had called them, who knows. It all happens very fast. 'What the fuck?' I hear someone say. The driver jumps out and lunges at us with a tire iron. 'We don't need Injuns and niggers 'round here!' he yells. Tries to bash in the windshield of Sly's car, but Sly manages to get us out of there. How, I still don't know." Elvis peered closely at Arnaldo. "Are you with me, man? *Entiendes*?" Arnaldo nodded, frowning. I could tell he was insulted by Elvis's patronizing tone. Elvis grinned at him, oblivious. "Peckerwoods even followed us on the highway, but we lost them." I brace myself for the punch line. "Ever since then, I've wanted my own pickup truck."

Keiko smirked. "Ahhh, Mr. Chang. What an extraordinary reaction."

"Mr. Chang's a very sick boy," I agreed.

Arnaldo had been listening intently. "*Por favor*, my friends. *Qué significa, peckerwood*?"

Arnaldo reminded me of my father, with his aura of melancholy charm and his aloof, gallant ways with women. I loved his growl of a voice and the happy accidents with language which occurred whenever we talked. It was like I had audio dysplasia. Instead of seeing double, I heard double, something besides what Arnaldo was actually saying. "Trouble" when he said "travel," "gender" when he said "genre," "fold" when he said "fault," or "grammatic fever" when he said "rheumatic fever." But after laughing and sorting it all out, we'd come to the ironic conclusion that it wasn't a case of miscommunication at all, but understanding.

Keiko was lucky, and I could tell he adored her.

"He's too old for you," I said to Keiko.

I don't know why I said it. After all those vain, pretty adolescents panting after Keiko, Arnaldo was a relief. Perhaps I was jealous, wanting him for myself or my mother. Milagros would have to admit that Arnaldo Ruiz was irresistible, especially with that big, fierce Olmec face of his. "You must meet my mother," I said to him.

Arnaldo took my hand. I was afraid he'd kiss it, but he didn't. "Rocky, I would be most honored and, how you say, *enchanted.*"

But of course, it never happened. Keiko and Arnaldo seemed to be in a great hurry and left San Francisco a month before Elvis and I did. "Maybe Arnaldo and Keiko are reconciling," I said to Elvis, trying to sound enthusiastic.

"That'll be a hoot," Elvis said.

Keiko traveled light. She took her portfolio, her equipment, one suitcase of her favorite clothes, and Scheherazade. Everything else — the mismatched china and silverware, books and record albums, the frayed wedding gown, the tailor's dummy, the paisley bedspread and queen-size mattress — she sold or gave away.

In her rush to leave town, Keiko had neglected to say goodbye to Voltaire and my mother. "What do you expect?" My mother shrugged, dismissing her once and for all. Voltaire suffered in silence, much too proud to let anyone know how much he hurt. He wandered the streets, not sleeping or eating. In desperation, my mother called my father in Manila. "I'm sorry I can't help you," my father said, "but I'm broke." My mother called the police. "Do you suspect foul play?" a detective asked her. She persuaded Elvis and me to go looking for him. Two weeks went by. Voltaire finally appeared on my mother's doorstep, barefoot. My mother ranted at me on the phone. "He lost his shoes! Can you believe that? His shoes. And his keys and whatever money I gave him. *Pobrecito, talaga.* I don't even know how he found his way home. Fely and I discovered all his medication hidden under the bed! Lord knows how much more he flushed down the toilet. What am I supposed to do? I wish that cheapskate father of yours would bring him back to Manila, but no! He couldn't be bothered. And your sister, with all her money —" I could hear my mother's sharp intake of breath. "Your poor brother's going to snap one of these nights and kill me in my sleep, I just know it."

Of course, we were all to blame for leaving him behind.

What was it he was taking back then? Thorazine. And something else, something insidious that made him break out in hives and scratch until he bled. Mood modulators. Mood elevators.

My mother begs Voltaire to check himself into San Francisco General for psychiatric observation. She's too upset to take him herself, so Uncle Bas and Auntie Fely drive him there. Elvis and I visit him later in the week. Bloated, bored, and heavily sedated, Voltaire sits with us in the grim visitors' lounge of the locked ward. The light is fluorescent and unkind. The chairs are orange plastic and bolted to the floor. Voltaire gives off a pungent smell. "When are you leaving for New York?" he asks, staring dully at me. I force myself to smile. He can't be that crazy if he's remembered that Elvis and I are going away. *Manic-depressive, mild schizophrenic.* Could those poker-faced American doctors actually be right? They are all so young, my mother wails, how could they know? The doctors back in Manila used to shrug and say, "He's just been coddled too much as a baby."

I touch the furious red welts on Voltaire's arm. He jerks away. "Did you bring any cigarettes or candy?" Voltaire's voice is loud and jarring, but his demeanor remains placid and his eyes vacant. "All I want is sugar."

"I'm sorry," I say. He terrifies me.

A feral young man paces back and forth in his paper slippers, shaking his head uncontrollably and mumbling to himself. I try to pretend he isn't there. An orderly sticks his head in the lounge. "Time for your bath, Aaron," he says. Aaron keeps pacing. "Aaron, Aaron, please." Aaron shakes his head and cackles. I want to flee. Sighing, the orderly enters the lounge and takes Aaron gently by the arm. I am surprised by how meek Aaron becomes. The orderly catches me staring and leads Aaron quickly away.

"Why don't you come on the trip with us?" I say to Voltaire. "It'll be fun." Elvis seems taken aback by my offer, but during the entire terrible visit he remains calm and doesn't interfere. I won't let go of his hand.

Voltaire's voice is muffled, as if he were speaking to me from one end of a long, dark tunnel. "No."

"No?"

"No," Voltaire repeats.

Weird. My mother was stoic about my departure, which made me uneasy. I started babbling. "You'll visit us after we settle in New York, won't you? When Voltaire gets better." She smoked and stared out the living-room window into the foggy street. I had expected the usual high-octane melodrama full of tears and accusations, but this time, my mother kept her misgivings all to herself. I figured she had her hands full with Voltaire in the hospital, the new, rowdy neighbors upstairs (the Greens had long since moved out), and her faltering catering business. She was still trying to do it all by herself. "Why don't you ask Auntie Fely or Uncle Bas to help you?" I suggested. "Uncle Bas could at least help with deliveries."

My mother was indignant. "Auntie Fely has a full-time job, thank you. And for your information, I'd rather drown and be eaten by sharks than ask that sex maniac to drive me anywhere."

"Why don't you hire someone part-time?"

She snorted with disdain. "Are *you* going to pay for it?"

I decided not to fall into her trap. "What about Zeke?"

"He's worse than Bas."

I burst out laughing. "Zeke worse than Uncle Bas? Come on, Ma, have a heart. Zeke loves you."

My mother showed no mercy. "That's his problem," she said.

I couldn't wait to escape.

Elvis and I planned to stop in LA and visit my uncle.

"Maybe we should stick around LA," Elvis said, "then move on to New York when the weather gets cooler."

There was a musician in LA Elvis knew — the infamous Sly — who kept calling late at night to ask when we were coming. Sly was house-sitting some aspiring screenwriter's Malibu cottage for the summer. "We'll crash at Sly's," Elvis said. "Rent-free and right on the beach."

Things were shaping up without much effort on our part. Or so it seemed. Elvis said it was all about good karma. What good karma? I burned with guilt about leaving my brother and mother behind, but said nothing.

"Heyyy. Wha's hap-nin'." The persistent and unrelenting Sly phoned at midnight to announce he'd just been hired as the new drummer for a working funk band. "We do covers, but only the hip shit," Sly assured Elvis.

"Speak up, man. Are you calling from a bar?" Elvis shouted.

Sly dropped a bombshell: the band wanted to replace their lead guitarist (who'd OD'd) and add a *chick* singer, for sex appeal. Those were Sly's exact words: Sex appeal. Chick singer.

"You'd better get your ass down here," Sly said, laughing and hanging up. Sly's low, insinuating laugh was his signature, heh-heh-heh.

"Looks like we're on a roll," Elvis said, staring at the receiver in his hand.

"Who is this guy, anyway?" I asked.

"Sly the Stone Washington. Kinda loud and sometimes offensive, but the only drummer I want to play with."

"I never said I was Aretha Franklin."

"Relax. Sly doesn't expect the Queen of Soul."

"I don't know, Elvis. You sure we'll get along?"

Elvis said, "He'll try and fuck you, that's for sure."

The Roxy. Madam Wong's. Whisky A Go Go. Sunset Boulevard. Crenshaw Boulevard. Topanga. I liked the sounds of the names. La Brea. Silverlake. Echo Park. Pasadena. Tarzana. Santa

Ana. Santa Monica. Watts. Century City. Hollywood. The Valley. Endless possibilities. Options. Openings. Agents and record companies. Contracts. Connections. Here was industry, the only kind we cared about. Music, movies. Suntans. There was also my father's brother, my kind of famous, very cool uncle Marlon. He'd take care of us.

"Be nice to Marlon," my mother had said. "He's a good man, unlike your father."

"Maybe we don't need New York," Elvis said. "Maybe not right away."

"Maybe you're right," I said.

We were very agreeable and lovey-dovey the closer we got to leaving town. Big, scary, unknown New York had been temporarily postponed in exchange for the proximity of La-La Land. "See? I won't be far from you," I said, kissing my mother goodbye and feeling much less guilty.

Swimming pools, palm trees, smog, and the Mexican border awaited us. Our stylish and dangerous future awash in the white light of the Pacific. Blazing, white, tropic light. Zoom lenses and prehistoric freeways. Incinerated guitars.

Highway 1. Like a man possessed, Elvis drove all night. Windows rolled down, me singing along with the AM radio and cracking jokes to help keep him awake. Only eight hours driving time from San Francisco — divine, aquamarine blue destiny. Los Angeles glowed in the distance, a celestial mirage of infinite, crass possibilities.

Lost in Translation: Rocky Tells Elvis a Filipino Joke

An old Filipino man goes before the judge for his citizenship papers. The *manong's* really nervous. He's been in America since 1930, waiting for this Big moment all his life.

The judge isn't too friendly. He says, "Excuse me, Mr. Manong, but before you can get your citizenship papers, I must order you to compose a correct sentence in English, using the following words: *deduct, defense, defeat,* and *detail*."

The *manong* jumps up and down with excitement. "Ay! Very easy, judge! Very easy. See? De duck jump over de fence. First de feet, den de tail!"

Lost in Translation: Another Filipino Joke

The same judge decides to test the *manong* even further.

"Mr. Manong, I'd like you to use the English word *persuading* correctly in a sentence."

The *manong* is once again eager to please. "No problem, judge! Last month I went to my sister's pirst wading anniversary party."

The judge is appalled, but gives the old man another chance. "Mr. Manong, do you know the word *devastation*?"

The *manong* smiles. "Of course, judge! I know that word! De-bas-tay-shon. That's where I go to wait for the bus."

Joke Not So Lost in Translation

Why did the Filipino cross the road?
   Because he thought America was on the other side.

He Was a Big Freak

I was shocked to learn that we had club dates practically the moment we arrived in Los Angeles. Sly had a gig waiting at Club Brassiere, a warehouse on Industrial. The club was rented on Friday and Saturday nights by two snooty, painfully stylish South African brothers named Dirk and Kirk Roedder. The Roedder brothers were primarily "promoters," but they were rumored to dabble in dope, porn videos, and art. They owned a gallery on Melrose, and would only be seen with black and Asian model types. We ended up working for them at the Brassiere pretty regularly, calling ourselves Sly & Co. I surprised myself. I was actually making a marginal living and learning how to sing.

"I'm calling this band The Gangster of Love," I announced to Sly one afternoon. Sly gave me a groggy look, swinging idly on a hammock strung across the porch of the ramshackle oceanfront bungalow. It was almost four, and he'd just woken up. "Uh-huh," he grunted noncommittally. "Bitches Brew" was blasting from somewhere back inside the house. It was a strange LA day. Smog-free, balmy, almost too bright and perfect. The summer was just about over, and I still couldn't make up my mind about Sly. Sometimes I thought he was stupid and callow, sometimes I thought he was a brilliant trickster, afraid of nothing. Elvis was right about him musically — Sly was an awesome drummer, fierce and unrelenting. In the groove, under the groove, he was exactly what we needed. Elvis urged Sly to come with us to New York, which I half dreaded. Let's just say that Sly brought out my worst instincts. We enjoyed an edgy camaraderie, and I loved getting high with him. Sly didn't know the meaning of guilt. Because I was Elvis's lover, and only because, Sly was generous with his drugs and connections. He was actually a stingy man and gave freely only when there was something to be gained. When it came to women and not getting his way, he could be vindictive and belligerent. I'd seen it with my own eyes. But for some sick reason, I had a soft spot for him, and he for me. Life with Sly was about finding the next party, and never growing old.

"Pharaoh's Dance." A comfortable silence had descended upon us. We drifted off into the bleak, pulsating music. Sly used to call Miles Davis the devil. He once described to Elvis and me getting high with Miles in a backstage freight elevator right before a concert. "Motherfucker snorted up all my shit in one go."

"Did he pay you for it?" Elvis wanted to know.

"You kidding?" Sly laughed, breaking into his uncanny imitation of Miles's hoarse whisper: *"You got any more?"* Sly paused for dramatic effect. "I said to Miles, 'That's some freaky *nose* you got, my man.'" Of course, if you believed Sly, after that little episode, he and Miles Davis were as tight as thieves.

Sly shifted his body in the hammock. "Ever wonder what would've happened if Hendrix had lived to play with Miles?"

"My brother wonders that too," I replied.

"Yeah, well. I'm asking you, Rocky. Miles and Jimi. What do *you* think?"

"Spontaneous combustion."

Sly's gaze was carnivorous. His voice thickened. "You're *smart*, Rocky. Smart and *fine*. A Mercedes-Benz of a woman. I wish I were the one —"

My skin crawled. "Shut up, Sly." I gave him a pointed look. "So what about the band's name?"

Sly feigned indifference. "Call it whatever. Whatever makes you and Elvis happy. Names ain't my thing." His attitude turned serious. "We're playing opposite White No More at the Brassiere this weekend. I negotiated sixty percent of the door, plus I'm trying to get a cut of the bar."

I couldn't imagine Dirk and Kirk Roedder giving us a cut of anything so lucrative. They were too sharp and ruthless. All of their "ventures" turned out to be extremely profitable. "No kidding," I said, genuinely impressed. White No More had everything we needed: a manager, a cult following, a briskly selling, self-produced dance single, a major deal in the works.

"And since I've been acting as our temporary manager," Sly continued, "I need double-duty pay."

Today was Thursday. Our new bass player, E. Sharp, was still a shaky bet. "I'll call another rehearsal," I said, frowning.

Sly chuckled. "Relax, Rocky."

"Yeah, but —"

"We'll smoke 'em. We got Elvis, remember? Fuck White No More."

I wasn't particularly interested in competing with White No More. I knew who'd win. They were a tight funk band fronted by a spastic lead singer in skinny ties and porkpie hats who called himself Johnny Unforgettable. He wrote paranoid lyrics and lived up to his name. The band's horn section was formidable. Plus, they were from New York, a fact that in itself commanded some kind of grudging respect. Just like me being from Manila, or Elvis growing up in Oakland, or Sly in Detroit. It had to count for something. "They're pretty good, you have to admit," I said.

"Fuck 'em," Sly said. His tone became whiny and self-right-eous. "You're too kind to those white boys, Rocky. They're fuckin' copycats. They steal shit. *Our* shit. And they get press coverage, record deals, and we don't."

"Enough," I shot back, glaring at him. "We do the same thing, don't we? We cop from Jimi, from Sly Stone, from George Clinton, from Miles, and Betty Davis —"

At the mention of Miles's ex-wife, Sly's eyes bugged out. "Okay, okay, I hear you. Nothing's original. But please . . . Betty Davis?"

I happened to be a fan of Betty's song, "He Was a Big Freak." ("He usedta beat me / with a turquoise chain.") Some said it was an ode to Miles, some said to Jimi Hendrix. I'd seen her band open for Bobby Blue Bland once. A total disaster. She slithered onstage in her underwear, and most of the audience cringed. Betty was ahead of her time, a narcissistic amazon who wrote gritty, witty songs. No one in the music world took her seriously.

All warmed up and wide-awake now, Sly said, "I mean, the bitch is *fine* and all that, but she should stick to —"

"Don't say it!" I growled, taking him by surprise. Sly cracked a conspiratorial grin. I grinned back.

"Fuckit," he said, sliding off the hammock and disappearing into the house. He returned a few seconds later. "Life's too short. Let's get high."

Sly's on the phone. "Hey, baby. Sly here. Whazzup?" I hear him through the screen door sweet-talking some unsuspecting woman and making plans for the evening. I stay outside on the porch, taking his place in the hammock. Elvis should be home soon, frustrated and tired after tinkering with Lucille's engine all day. Since we got to LA, Lucille's been giving us nothing but trouble. Yesterday she wouldn't start at all. I hear Sly hang up, then dial someone else. "Hey, beautiful . . . Sly here. You miss me?"

The ocean is flat and still. A lone surfer in a wet suit paddles out from shore. An agitated black Labrador appears out of nowhere, scampering to the water's edge. The dog turns to bark at a woman behind him. I don't know why, but I assume the dog is male. The woman says something inaudible. The dog keeps barking. She picks up a piece of driftwood and hurls it into the water. The dog swims after it. He emerges from the ocean, victorious, proudly dropping the branch at the woman's feet. Wagging his tail expectantly, the dog waits for the game to begin again. The woman pets him before attaching a leash to his collar. The dog resists, but she is firm and leads him away. Woman and dog disappear farther up the beach behind some dunes.

I hear the low, caressing tone of Sly's voice. "Yeah, baby." More plans are made. I hear the words Club Brassiere. Is he talking to yet another woman? There is no one left on the desolate beach. My solitary surfer paddles farther and farther out, undaunted by the eerie calm of the ocean, waiting for waves that never come.

Our Music Lesson #1, Or How We Appropriated You: An Imaginary Short Starring Elvis Chang, Rocky Rivera, and Jimi Hendrix

[*Interior of an empty nightclub. Midafternoon. A tape loop of "Voodoo Chile" plays on the sound track. A young couple kissing passionately, ensconced in a booth. The male is Chinese American, with very long black hair and a wary, tough look about him. His smile is electrifying. The woman's ethnicity is slightly more questionable. She could be Mayan, Malay, Pinay, or Gypsy. Her hair is cut very short; she wears heavy eye make-up and has a wary, tough look about her. Sitting across from the kissing couple is a bemused Jimi Hendrix. As he looked in 1970, the year he died. He wears all black Western gear: a silver conch belt studded with turquoise, a black sombrero and sunglasses.*]

Elvis: It was always you, old man. Kinda obvious, isn't it? Listen to your own words. "Oh, the night I was born, the moon turned a fire red." You were in sync with the times, but ahead of it too. Before you, there was no one. Maybe Chuck Berry. Maybe Little Richard. I was into Chuck Berry, just like every other guitar player in the world. I memorized all his licks. And that jagged chunka-chunka thing in all them James Brown classics. Juicy horn riffs.

Jimi: Maceo.

Rocky: That groove on "Cold Sweat." You know it?

Jimi: Say, beautiful. Don't patronize me. Of course I know it.

Rocky: [*trying to appease him*] I meant "you know it." Like you know it. Not you don't know it. Know what I mean?

Jimi: Gimme a kiss, Tweety Bird Lips.

Rocky: Now it's my turn to be offended.

Jimi: Sorry, beautiful. I'm feeling blue. Desolate and blue.

Rocky: Take off those glasses. Let me see your eyes.

[*Jimi takes off glasses, slowly.*]

Listen to the wail of your lead guitar, feedback so fierce against the drummer's desperate flailing and bashing. What was his name?

Jimi: Noel. [*puts glasses back on*]

Rocky: Whatever. He can't keep up. He's drowning. The song winds down, the song's about to end. Hey, it was Mitch Mitchell on drums, wasn't it?

Jimi: You mean *whomever*, don't you? God, I am so bored with that song! Keyboards like a funhouse circus, the bass thumping. Aren't you sick of it? And I'm singin' so earnestly! They never said I *couldn't* sing, but shit. I hate *earnest*. God in a roomful of mirrors. Music is strange like that. Do the old man a favor and *turn the goddam song off!* [*pause*] Save your soul, baby.

Elvis: Three things to remember, old man. *Uno*, hindsight is easy. *Dos*, that was Stevie Winwood on organ. *Tres*, Rocky is saved.

Rocky: But on that blues session, it was Billy Preston. And I had a question about this very song —

Jimi: Put anything else on. I don't give a fuck. Funkadelic! The goddam Beatles! Prince!

Rocky: I was fourteen years old when you died. My brother was seventeen. He wanted to play guitar like you so bad, it paralyzed him. [*pause*] If you listen carefully, the "Voodoo Chile" melody is exactly the same as "Catfish Blues" —

Jimi: Aha! We've got a musicologist here —

Rocky: Is that why one song follows the other?

Jimi: Are you accusing me of plagiarizing? Do this old man a favor and *turn* that fucker off! [*looks around, agitated*] Garçon! Garçon! Goddamit, where's service when you need it, *s'il vous plaît!*

Rocky: I believe we're in Spain.

Elvis: We're in LA. [*embarrassed*] Sorry. We'll come back later. [*gets up to leave, but Rocky pulls him back into his seat*]

Rocky: [*to Jimi*] Don't fret. We're in Barcelona or West Hollywood, eternally twenty-seven years old, in honor of you. Why are you afraid? This is a beautiful song. You wrote it. You sang it.

Before you, there was no one. Accept your role in history. Flames bursting out of your skull. Salvation funky. Redemption funky.

Jimi: Redemption? [*laughs*] I sure as hell can't relate to that, sister.

Rocky: Forget your troubles. Let's dance. That groove on "Ants in My Pants." Know that one?

[*Jimi chuckles. Rocky climbs up on the table and starts to dance wildly. Just as abruptly, she sits back down.*]

Elvis: I couldn't resist the lure of Vegas. Had to play catch-up. With you, old man.

Jimi: "Not enough grease." "Too much grease." I got tired of being critiqued. Do I play like the white boys? Do I fuck too many white women? I always wanted some of that white boy money. What a dilemma. Shit. I'm just a country boy.

Elvis: I'm just a country boy, too, Oakland country. My pop taught me to love the blues. Sounds just like Chinese music, he said. He don't talk much, but my pop's always been a visionary. He gave me my name, didn't he? And I took a lotta shit for it.

Jimi: Your father named you after a clown and a thief. You know what Elvis once said? "Ain't nothin' a nigger can do for me but shine my shoes."

Rocky: [*to Elvis*] Your father named you after the Elvis of his perverse imagination. You got your shufflin' walk, that thing I call the chicken strut, from Chuck Berry. Your musical ideas, your visual style, that came from Jimi here.

Jimi: And what about you, beautiful? What's my gift to you?

[*Rocky doesn't respond.*]

Why you try so hard to be a man?

Rocky: You sound just like my mother.

Jimi: Fuck me, then. Save my soul.

Rocky: Let's get one thing straight. You can't fool me. I know all about you. I was fourteen when you died, but I'm not stupid. I've been to your museum in Amsterdam. Heard all the stories. Seen all the boring documentaries. Watched tapes of you on Johnny Carson. Or was it Dick Cavett? Then there was my dream. A young girl trying to get in backstage at the Fillmore West. She was crying. She was maybe Japanese or Chinese. Very naive and pretty. Hair down to her butt. Dime a dozen, right? She was clutching a note in her clammy hand. Trying to give it to the security guy so he could pass it on to you. She begged him. "Suck my dick first," the guard said. He was smiling. She was crying. I dreamed about standing in line, watching the whole thing go down. We're all in line behind the poor little lost yellow girl, trying to get in backstage, to the inner sanctum, so we can pay our respects to the pope. King Kong was the keeper of the flame, and I did not wanna be that poor little yellow girl. She sucked King Kong's dick to get to you —

Jimi: Have you any idea how much pussy was thrown at me?

Film Noir

The scorched yellow sky burns high above as Marlon Rivera waters his tiny, perfect garden. His sweat-stained basketball shorts and fishnet tank top cling to his brawny dancer's body. *Squish, squish.* His rubber thongs are streaked with mud. Marlon sprays his garden hose on ferns, wild tiger lilies and roses, cactus, the roots of a jacaranda tree. Violet cattleya orchids — his pride and joy — thrive in a bamboo grove in the breathtaking heat.

"*Magandang umaga*, Señor Rivera." Marlon's neighbor, Isabel L'Ange, greets him in today's rich, mellifluous voice. Besides teaching the old woman how to say "good morning" in Tagalog, Marlon has also taught her how to say *putang ina mo*. Literal translation: your mother's a whore. Marlon's translation: motherfucker.

Is she Peggy Ashcroft, or Deborah Kerr? A few nights ago she was somewhere within the melodious regions of Brazil, all o's and swirling j's, and a purring, sardonic Eartha Kitt. But then, she'd been drinking.

After several tries and muttered curses, Isabel yanks her key out of the rusty lock on her door. She turns the knob once to check it, lets out a deep breath. "Damn heat. My keys always get stuck."

"Up so early?" Marlon Rivera smiles. She is one of his favorite people, an authentic grande dame, he likes to tell his friends. Very chichi.

"At my age, sleep is a damn waste of time. You'll be home the rest of the day? Keep an eye out for me, will you?" Isabel and her family had been robbed once, years ago, in their Spanish villa in the valley. There were three men. Her trembling husband was made to lie on the cold tile floor, bound and gagged. Their only daughter, who was four at the time, had a gun aimed at her head while Isabel led the other two thieves to a safe in the library that contained cash and Isabel's jewels. "It was such a cliché," she said to Marlon, "that safe. Hidden behind a mediocre impressionist painting! They knew exactly where to look. They had us all figured out."

And now, having outlived her husband and daughter, Isabel L'Ange lives next door to Marlon in West Hollywood, with five cats she calls "my children." All the windows to her cottage are nailed shut, except for one. "An old woman like me," she says, without bitterness. "I'm easy prey."

Marlon knows how much effort it takes for Isabel to groom herself. If she could get away with it, she'd wear that silk kimono of hers until the day she died. He wouldn't be surprised if she asked to be buried in it. Hell, why not? She has her ratty robe and *tsinelas* — Marlon has his endless supply of cotton T-shirts, basketball shorts, and eighty-nine-cent flip-flops. Neither of them has anything left to prove.

Isabel L'Ange has thrown on her classically chic uniform for facing the public — khaki safari pantsuit, espadrilles, and a rakish Panama hat that had once belonged to her husband, Fritz. Part black, Mexican, and Filipino, Isabel at seventy is still a beauty, with her wiry, white hair pulled back in one simple braid, her glowing bronze skin unmarred by lines.

A former Forbidden City chorus girl and starlet, Isabel's rivals had been Anna May Wong and Dorothy Dandridge. Her acting career was short-lived, but her marriage to the legendary expatriate director guaranteed her an uneasy place in Hollywood history. "Those studio guys had no use for me. I was an uppity nigger, always shootin' off my big mouth," she says to Marlon the first time they drink together. "But when I married Fritz, well, they couldn't exactly ignore me, could they?"

"You shouldn't have given up acting. You were amazing in *Harlem Rhapsody.*"

She looks bored. "Bullshit. I was a passable dancer. That was it. As far as acting goes — ha! I sleepwalked through most of those films. Thank God for Fritz."

"What about that bit in *Shanghai Deadly*? Pure sex. You and Mitchum practically burned up the screen —"

"Absolute bullshit. Darling, you should know — you've made more movies than me. The camera picks up everything — and the less one does, the better. I knew how to do as little as possible."

It amuses her that he's seen her movies. "You mean all four of them?" Isabel's laugh is light and airy, but her eyes are guarded. "You must be the only one —"

"No," Marlon insists, "you were a very popular star in Manila, believe it or not. There were fan clubs. Movie magazines devoted to you."

"I was a romantic prop, for godsake. Second banana."

"There were contests," Marlon says, "for the Isabel L'Ange of the Philippines. You were proudly referred to as Filipina, one of our own. There was a take-off made in your honor called *Manila Rhapsody*. My mother took me to see it twice. She adored you. She was heartbroken when you retired from the movies."

Isabel L'Ange is silent. "My mother . . ." Marlon stammers, not sure if he's offended her, "looked a little like you."

Isabel sighs. "Poor darling. Who'd have thought we'd be neighbors one day?"

Marlon Rivera watches Isabel L'Ange limp slowly toward the curb, where her car is parked. He knows better than to offer his help. She clutches a briefcase and grimaces in pain. "Where's your cane?" Marlon calls out to her. "You need a walking stick, one of those elegant things with an ivory tip."

She waves to Marlon. "Off to the lawyer's," she informs him in today's lockjawed rendition of Katharine Hepburn. Tomorrow she could sound husky and growl. Tallulah Bankhead. "Join me for tea later?" She stares warily at Marlon with cat's eyes that are a speckled brown. She always expects him to say no, though they've been meeting every afternoon for tea ever since Marlon moved in.

"Love to," Marlon says.

It is their daily ritual, broken only when Marlon is on tour, dancing with road companies or choreographing the millionth run of *Flower Drum Song* or *West Side Story*, playing the Yul Brynner part in a second-rate dinner theater production of *The King and I*. Tampa, Jacksonville, Orlando, Gainesville. He's been to every stop in Florida, it seems. The role is Marlon's current favorite, his only chance to play a lead. He refuses to wear a latex cap and instead shaves his head during the run. While four hundred senior citizens chew leathery prime rib and overcooked broccoli, Marlon bellows "Shall We Dance?" and hams it up. Most of the children in the cast are Filipino and call him "Tiyo" or Uncle. They join Marlon onstage for carefully choreographed bows. Their parents hover in the wings, inviting Marlon over for home-cooked *adobo* dinners and introducing him to their aging, virgin daughters and embarrassed, giggling nieces. "Meet the king of show business," they'll say. "Remember how wonderful? He was Chino in *West Side Story*!"

After the show, several members of the audience inevitably approach Marlon for an autograph. "You speak such good English!" a woman with cotton candy hair exclaims. Her face is painted like a Kewpie doll's, rouged cheeks and terrifying eyes caked with mascara. She shoves a notebook at Marlon and he thanks her in spite of himself, thanks everyone clustered around him backstage, peering, shoving, poking at him. He is still in full make-up and costume, and obligingly poses for snapshots with his fans.

Isabella Arabella. B-movie temptress and reclusive widow. Marlon Rivera's neighbor and fantasy mother. Isabellina the bankrupt martyr. "He blew all the money," she once said about her husband in a drunken confession. She hiccupped while she laughed. "All our fucking money."

Marlon watches the old woman as she gingerly maneuvers herself into her dusty beige Honda. It seems an eternity, but she finally drives off, disappearing in a white film of heat.

"It's pretty quiet and residential around here," his surly niece Raquel observed wryly when she arrived.

"Don't be deceived by our cozy neighborhood," Marlon said. "Victor Mature's my landlord, Troy Donahue rents my garage, and Anna May Wong lives next door."

"Anna May Wong's dead." Raquel inspected Marlon's altar in the living room. "Isn't she?"

"I'll show you Troy's motorcycle later if you want."

"Who's Troy Donahue?" the young man with Raquel asked.

They ignored him. Raquel made a gesture as if to pick up one of the black angel figurines on the altar, then changed her mind. "Tiyo Marlon, how long have you lived here?"

"I dunno. Long enough. Go ahead, pick it up."

"What's all this?" Raquel indicated the cluttered altar with her chin. A Filipino gesture, Marlon observed, pleased.

"Santo Niño from Cebu, a cross from Peru. Hey, it rhymes." Marlon went on. "La Virgen de Guadalupe from Mexico, another one from who knows where, except I bought it in Manila. They told me it was from the diggings in Panay, overcharged me. 'Antique.' *Daw!* You know they got factories in Cebu that turn these out, perfect antiques with broken noses! For the tourist market, *siempre*. I knew better, but I bought it anyway. The vendors were laughing behind my back. Tourist Pinoy!" He shrugged. "That's what I deserve for being gone so long. Isn't it ugly? Look at her hair. It's real. I love this ugly Virgin, I really do."

Raquel made a face at the crying madonna. "Spooky."

"Our Lady of Bad Dreams," Marlon agreed.

* * *

"Are you lovers?" Marlon asked his niece. She was stretched out on his sofa, lost in thought. She ran her fingers through short, magenta-streaked hair, yanking it upward into spiky clumps. The young man was out of earshot, on the phone in the next room.

"Sometimes. All the time." She gave Marlon a coy look. Then, after a moment's silence, "We're moving to New York."

"New York? But how are you going to manage? And how are you surviving Malibu?"

Raquel blushed. "His buddy Sly house-sits this wreck of a house on the Pacific Coast Highway. It's wonderful and awful, the termites have eaten away the foundation. I love it. The beach is right across the road. We don't pay any rent, so we've got a little bit saved from our gigs. As soon as the owner comes back, the three of us are heading east."

"What does your mother think?"

"What do you expect? She's pissed."

"Forgive me for nagging, but that truck of yours —"

"Don't worry, Tiyo M. Elvis is ready to sell Lucille. She's been acting up."

"New York is tough. You'll need a real job —"

"I know that," she snapped irritably. She started to say more but stopped herself. An awkward silence settled between them, and Marlon wondered if she regretted her visit.

The young man loped into the living room. "I'm hungry, Rock."

"You're always hungry." She made no move to get up from where she was sitting.

"Let's go over to Danny's Diner."

Marlon wouldn't hear of it. "You'll stay right here. I'll cook up some of my famous *adobo*. Have you ever tried *adobo*?" he asked the young man.

"Rocky's mom made it once."

"Well, I'm sure it was good, but I'm the better cook. You haven't had the real thing until you've tried my *adobo*."

"The best," Raquel Rivera agreed.

Marlon studied Elvis Chang — his niece's lover, boyfriend, whatever. Tall and maybe a little too skinny, but pretty enough with that gold hoop in his ear. Elvis Chang, Marlon thought to himself, amused. Elvis Chang in the home of Marlon Rivera. Fucking ridiculous. "When you cook *adobo*, make sure there's plenty of black peppercorns and the right kind of vinegar. Plain white vinegar, nothing fancy, that's the key. Use lots of it," Marlon emphasized, "and garlic — the more, the better. You got anything against pork?"

"Nah," the young man said. "I'm Chinese."

"Ahh." Marlon smiled. "Of course. How could I forget?" He winked at his niece, got up from where he was sitting, and sauntered off into the kitchen, the largest room in his stucco bungalow.

They watched him cook.

"What was it like . . . ?" The young man hesitated, suddenly shy.

"What 'it'?" Marlon was still smiling.

"*West Side Story*. Weren't you one of the original cast members?"

"Both the Broadway and movie version, isn't that so, Tiyo Marlon?" Raquel sat at the kitchen table and pulled out a cigarette from her leather jacket. "Mind if I smoke?"

"Yes," Marlon said, "and yes to your other question." He opened the refrigerator and pulled out a large plastic bowl. He dipped his finger in the marinade and licked it, making a face. "Needs more," he murmured to himself, pouring vinegar on the cubes of pork and beef mixed with chicken wings. "Hmmm." He added a teaspoon of sugar then tasted it again, perplexed. "Have you seen the movie?" Marlon asked the young man. Raquel held the unlit cigarette in a disgruntled pose, not sure whether to defy her uncle.

"Yeah, on TV once. But Rocky says I should see it in a movie theater."

"She's right. There's nothing like a big screen, especially for that opening sequence. Aerial shots of New York City, remember that?"

"Oh, yeah." Elvis Chang smiled faintly.

"Stunning. And remember, the first fifteen minutes of the movie had absolutely no dialogue! Very innovative for its time, *di ba*? Only music and street dancing." Marlon plugged in his always dependable, industrial-size I-want-to-feed-the-world Hitachi rice cooker. "You like rice, I presume?" He was flirting, Elvis was aware of that. It made him uncomfortable. Rocky's uncle was an attractive man. In spite of his graying hair, he still had the body of a twenty-year-old dancer. And his face, too. Hard, brown, smooth.

"That chick was no Puerto Rican," Elvis said.

"And her accent was gross," Rocky added.

Marlon's tone was mocking. "*That chick.* You mean Miz Natalie Wood? But she was a *star*, and that's what they thought was important, you see." He paused. "And what about me? Did I pass for Puerto Rican?" Elvis Chang shrugged, his face closing off and taking on the same sullen cast as Marlon's niece. They both sat there frowning at him.

"Ay, *puta*!"

Raquel looked up as her uncle cursed.

"Bay leaves," Marlon Rivera wailed. "I forgot the bay leaves!"

Marlon packed the leftover *adobo* and rice in Tupperware containers for them to take back to Malibu. After thanking Marlon for his hospitality, Elvis went ahead in the darkness to warm up Lucille. Raquel lingered on Marlon's front steps. She seemed reluctant to say goodbye. "Don't be a stranger," Marlon chided her gently. "How come you've been here all this time and I've only seen you once?"

"I'm sorry," Raquel said. "We've been rehearsing nonstop and working a lot."

"You enjoy it? The music, I mean."

"I guess." She smiled at him finally. An open, radiant smile.

She could be quite pretty, Marlon decided. Like her mother.

But so many walls up. "I'd love to hear the band sometime," Marlon said.

"I want you to," Raquel said. "We're getting better and better." She smiled again, shyly. "Funny. I'm not good at any of those things you or Ma do. I'm not good with my hands." She smoked her clove cigarette with studied gloom. "Your garden is incredible," she said. Marlon gazed at his niece with deep affection. She was reinventing herself moment to moment, day by day. Los Angeles suited her. He wished she'd give up her crazy New York plans and stay around.

"How's Voltaire? You know he calls me from time to time. Collect. When I don't hear from him, I worry. Your father worries."

Raquel spoke with unconcealed bitterness. "Pa worries? That's interesting. We never heard from him or Luz the whole time Voltaire was in the hospital." She paused. "He's been released. You remember the last job fiasco? At the bank? Now Ma's got him working at Harry Fong's grocery. Pity Mr. Fong. That should last about a week."

It was too depressing even for Marlon, who quickly changed the subject. "Elvis seems very talented and smart."

She turned her head away to exhale clouds of perfumed smoke. "We've got a great band," she said. She didn't bother saying goodbye. Zipping up her leather jacket, she started down the flagstone steps of the path that led to the street. Abruptly, she turned to address him. "Tiyo Marlon, he's got the most incredible tattoo," she whispered. Her eyes shone with lust. "A dragon wrapped all around his belly. Do you know how that must've hurt?"

Isabella of Spain, Marlon calls the old woman when he's high.

"What happened to that lover of yours? He was such a sweetie." Isabel is in good spirits today. The meeting with the lawyers must've gone well. Her eyes are darting and alive, she sits with her back straight in spite of the pain.

He lies and says Stephen is in Mexico on an assignment. They are drinking rum and Coke in the garden. "Let's have tea at my place," Marlon had insisted. On days like this, Marlon couldn't stand being inside her cottage, with its carpets and furniture covered with cat hair and lint and the airless rooms reeking of piss.

"Oh yes," the old woman had said with enthusiasm. "Let's! Balthus! Ginger! Demian! Marmalade! Thelonius!" Isabel crooned for her cats. "Mama's going next door for a bit," she informed the one-eyed Balthus, the biggest and oldest of the neutered bunch. The others were out back, hunting rats and snakes in her weed-choked yard. Marlon had heard them fight, a burst of screeching and howling in the distance.

She'd come over with a bottle of Haitian 5-Star Barbancourt rum and a wrinkled lime that had obviously been in her refrigerator too long. Marlon supplied the Coke and the ice. They are sitting on canvas beach chairs, with a rickety card table between them. "Are you hungry?" he asks. But she's never hungry, and eats only when he cajoles her. "Just a little bit," he says, "otherwise you'll get drunk too fast."

This always amuses her, and she allows him to serve up leftovers on a paper plate, delectable leftovers that she picks at to please him while she sips more rum and Coke. "Your food is too good," Isabel L'Ange admits, "but I couldn't care less."

"Eat."

"And that niece of yours? Let's see." The old woman is being playful. "She must be in New York by now. I'm sorry I never got to meet her. Dear Stephen is in Mexico and dear Raquel is in New York."

He doesn't respond. It is almost seven in the evening, but the sun refuses to set and there is still no breeze.

"Tell me again," she pleads, "about your mother choosing your name."

"I chose my name," Marlon reminds her. "After I saw *The Wild One. My mother* called me Epifanio Sebastian for two reasons — after the feast of the Epiphany, which was my birthday. And after her favorite saint."

"Ahh, yes." Isabel beams at him. "You told me once. Se-bastian. Your mother considered him the most handsome." She has put on her bracelets for this special occasion. Heavy gold bracelets, with miniature charms dangling. A conch shell, a jade heart, a coolie hat. A bicycle, an abacus, a pair of slippers. Isabel's face is glowing. The liquor has taken effect, softening her features. "You're very lucky," she says.

"I never thought so."

"But you are. To be born Catholic, it's quite a legacy, in spite of what you think. And I know what you think."

He says nothing, gazing at her with his angry little smile.

"That it is a burden. Some hideous burden that has been imposed upon you . . . and your people." Isabel smiles back at him then pours herself, this time, a glass of straight rum. They talk in shorthand. "*Our* people. Do you know I've never been to Manila? My mother's folks were from someplace called Samar. Beautiful name, isn't it? All I knew. Fritz was invited once, for one of those festivals. Back when . . . that woman. But I never wanted to go. That woman, I said. You can't. So he went alone." She giggles. "Had a ball, he said. Great parties, that woman. Not politically correct, I scolded him. Couldn't give a shit, dear Fritz." A smile pasted on her face, she toasts Marlon with her glass, "To the people."

Now shy, now sad, she waits for him to speak. When the silence becomes unbearable and there is no more to drink, Isa-bel L'Ange makes a motion to leave. "I've talked too much, haven't I?"

The night is too young and there is no breeze. Should he go back inside and find . . . Stephen used to forget hiding bottles of tequila or rum way back behind the pots and pans stacked inside the kitchen cabinets. Weeks would go by, then Stephen would unearth some forgotten treasure. Should he bother look-ing? Marlon Rivera shrugs and makes a gesture with his hand. He is angry but not drunk enough yet. He collapses into him-self and broods. Isabel sits back down. She stares at the street, unsure of what to do next. Marlon knows she is afraid of his temper, and this saddens him. "I'm okay," he says softly to her. "Don't worry."

She is memorable in the fading light. The heavy lids of her almond-shaped eyes, her cheeks sunken with age. In profile, there are still elements of this and that. Marlon considers this and feels blessed.

Isabel L'Ange in *Harlem Rhapsody*. Garbo in *Ninotchka*. Lena Horne in *Cabin in the Sky*. Dorothy Dandridge in *Carmen Jones*. And his favorite. The laundryman's daughter, Anna May Wong. In her first. Was it *Lotus*? *Jade*? Or *Dragon*? Something really obvious. *Jade Lotus Blossoms*? Or that Dietrich movie whose title temporarily eludes him. Yes. That was it. Probably her best. A definite vehicle for Marlene, but Anna May stole the show. *Shanghai*, wasn't it? It was always *Shanghai* something.

Big Apple

The night we arrived in New York, Sly, Elvis, and I took a cab from JFK. I couldn't quite digest the fact that we had actually landed. We'd been up for days partying, saying our long goodbyes to Uncle Marlon, the Roedder brothers, and the gang at Club Brassiere. Wired and exhausted, I blinked in wonder at the awesome and sprawling airport. Sly described JFK as "So big and baaad, they had to let the Concorde land here."

I gave the driver Keiko and Arnaldo's address on Canal Street. "Which way you wanna go, lady? Which way?" The cabbie's voice was gruff, and he didn't bother turning around to look at me when he spoke. His license read: DENNIS SEPULVEDA.

I tried sounding like a native. "Manhattan, West Side."

His voice became impatient. "I said, which way you wanna go, lady?"

"You're driving, dammit. Figure it out."

Elvis gave me a warning nudge with his elbow, but it was too late. Dennis turned his head to gaze at me. He was younger than I'd expected, with haughty Roman features, a trim goatee, and piercing eyes. "What is wisdom?" he asked, mysteriously. Without waiting for an answer, he stepped on the gas, taking us on a wild, extended tour of the outer boroughs. He drove us into the heart of Queens and out again, up the Grand Central, past another airport ("LaGuardia," Sly whispered), across the Triboro Bridge, into Harlem, then finally, all the way downtown. None of us uttered a word of protest, enduring Dennis Sepulveda's vengeance in stunned silence.

We'd been held hostage. The ride ended up costing us close to seventy dollars. When it was over, Dennis Sepulveda sat morosely in the front seat, waiting to get paid. He didn't lift a finger, staring straight ahead while we hoisted bags, Elvis's guitar case, and Sly's entire drum set from the trunk on to the curb. Outraged, I watched Elvis hand him four twenties. "You mean we *tipped* that asshole?" I groaned as Dennis drove away.

"You do what you gotta do," Elvis muttered, shrugging.

"Welcome to the Big Apple." Sly chuckled.

In front of Keiko's building, a man lay sleeping on a large square of cardboard, his head on a battered suitcase. It was late September, but muggy and hot. The sidewalk reeked of wet ash, spilled beer, and urine. I took a deep breath, cautiously stepped over the sleeping man, and rang the doorbell.

"*Buenas noches*, welcome, welcome," Arnaldo bellowed effusively, opening the heavy metal door. He helped us load everything into the freight elevator. "There are many artists living here, and sweatshops on every other floor," Arnaldo informed us as we went up. "You see the women during the day going to work with their children. Is very sad."

Keiko was waiting in the hallway, cradling Scheherazade in her arms. She nodded at Sly in acknowledgment and offered up her cheek for Elvis and me to kiss. "I was starting to think you were never going to come." She pouted. "What took you so long?"

"The cabdriver literally took us for a ride," I said.

Keiko laughed. "No, silly. I meant, you were supposed to be here *a month ago*."

Sly leered at Keiko and made the mistake of saying, "Well, well, well. I don't know about anyone else, but I'm *really* glad to be here."

Keiko gave him a withering smile. "What did you say your name was?"

Elvis and I were to sleep in the tiny guest room. Sly was shown the futon in the living room. "Not much privacy," Sly observed rudely.

Keiko's tone was icy. "Sorry, hon. It's the best we can do."

The cat pounced on Sly's lap and started licking herself. Sly panicked. "Oh shit. Get her off me! I'm allergic —"

Keiko smacked herself on the forehead. "Oh dear, oh dear. Maybe you need to move to a hotel!"

Arnaldo, ever the gentleman, intervened and invited Elvis and Sly for a stroll to Chinatown and a late-night meal. I opted to stay behind and play catch-up with Keiko, much too excited to eat. She toured me around the dingy loft. "We're still in the process of settling in. Everything's a mess, or in boxes. I hate unpacking. We're installing track lights over there." Keiko and I stood, bent over, in the walk-in closet that served as her temporary darkroom. Keiko seemed different somehow, preoccupied and anxious. "That drummer of yours — what's his name again?"

"Sly Washington. I know, I know —"

"What an asshole."

"I know. But he's a really good musician, and pretty funny once you get to know him. I'll make sure he finds another place. Like you said, a hotel or something."

Keiko scowled. "Elvis has bad taste in friends." She added hastily, "Not counting you, of course."

We wandered into the kitchen area, which wasn't much of a kitchen at all. Hot plate, minifridge, plain wooden table and four mismatched chairs. Out of the minifridge came a jug of white wine. She poured me a glass, then refilled hers. "Arnaldo wants us to get married again and take me to Mexico. What have I gotten myself into? He's driving me crazy."

I didn't know what to say, so I said nothing.

"Shit, Rocky. I know what you're thinking. Such a nice man, such a generous man, such a fine artist . . ."

"Arnaldo loves you, no doubt about that."

"Yet he criticizes my work for being shallow and obvious! Always couched in kind, careful language, of course. Arnaldo's such a *gentleman*. He'd never just come out and say what's on his — ah, fuck it. You know what I think? His work isn't selling right now, and he's jealous of all the attention I'm getting." Keiko paused for effect. "His dealer's dying to represent me."

The tension between Keiko and Arnaldo made everyone uncomfortable. Even Sly was moved to comment. "What the fuck's goin' on with your friends?" He and Elvis stayed out as much as possible, clubhopping and jamming with other musicians. I spent time at the loft, trying to make sense out of what was occurring between Keiko and Arnaldo. It was just the three of us at dinner one evening. We'd all been drinking too much, ignoring the elaborate seafood curry Keiko had painstakingly prepared. Arnaldo began by asking, "Have you heard? Our Keiko is being touted by the critics as a 'rising feminist artist of color.' *Qué significa*, 'artist of color'?" When no one responded, Arnaldo persisted in his attack. "Such American bullsheet! *Coño*, are we not all of color? White people, black people, brown." He caught my eye. "What do your ears hear, my friend?"

Keiko threw her wineglass at him but missed. Glass and wine scattered in all directions. "Why don't you shut up with your goddam sanctimonious Mexican *bullsheet*? I am so sick of you!" Keiko shrieked. I didn't know what else to do, so I poured myself a shot of Arnaldo's tequila and drank.

Arnaldo rose from his chair. "All right, then I shall go," he said with quiet dignity.

"No!" Keiko sobbed, flinging herself at him. Arnaldo comforted Keiko, a gloomy, resigned expression on his face. He stroked her disheveled hair and whispered to her tenderly in Spanish. He'd been through this with her before, I could tell. He led her, staggering, into the bedroom and shut the door quietly behind them. I sat in the kitchen for some time, listening to the sounds of weeping and fucking going on in the next room. When I'd had enough, I threw on my jacket and went out into the streets, determined to find Elvis and Sly.

We moved out. An aspiring rock critic and NYU law school student who Sly met at Club 57 let us crash on the floor of his overheated tenement apartment on St. Mark's Place, in exchange for an endless supply of Sly's reefer and coke. His name was Glen. The tub was in the kitchen, the toilet barely flushed, there were too many locks on the door, and the sweet, toxic aroma of Black Flag was the first thing that hit you as soon as you walked in.

Glen had a habit of spying on me whenever I bathed, which wasn't that often because there was never enough hot water. Once I actually caught him jacking off. "You're pathetic," I said, climbing out of the tub and drying myself furiously with a towel. He came all over himself, just as I finished getting dressed. "*Baboy,*" I snarled, calling him pig in Tagalog. "*Baboy ka talaga.*" The creep later accused me of stealing money from him and kicked us all out.

Thank God Sly was such a social animal. His new girlfriend Severine, a femme fatale from France whose visa had expired, invited us to move in with her. Severine had an illegal sublet on Grand Street. The previous tenant had left behind a busted vintage jukebox, a pool table, and an empty fish tank. Useless stuff, but interesting enough to keep around. Enterprising Severine, using old bedsheets, had blocked off what had once been a spacious, sunny loft into cramped hovels she rented out to foreign students at exorbitant prices. No one seemed to mind being exploited by her. There was Rodrigo, a hunk from Brazil who studied graphic design at FIT, and Yoshiko, a video artist from Tokyo who was enrolled in cultural studies at The New School. The two of them loved eating out and going dancing together. Rodrigo and Yoshiko were perfect tenants — they came home only to sleep and change clothes.

Severine and Sly seemed like a match made in heaven, two scam artists in love. Charm ran in Severine's blood. It was hard to stay mad at her even when she overcharged us for the rent and invited her parasite friends over constantly for impromptu parties. Getting high with Sly was their ultimate goal. Elvis and I ran past a gauntlet of trendy burnouts every time we went to the bathroom. Privacy was unheard of at Severine's. "We've got to get out of here," I said to Elvis.

Keiko called once a week to relay my mother's increasingly emotional messages: "Why haven't you returned my calls? We're all worried. When are you coming back to San Francisco? When are you going to get your own phone?"

The last straw was Sly's proposal to swap partners. "We'll have big fun," Sly murmured, as we freebased the night away in the garbage-strewn living room. "Big fun. Severine's got a thing for Elvis. Right, babe?"

Severine purred. A dull explosion went off in my head and my chest. Where was Elvis? Ah, yes. Off to the liquor store for replenishments. And Yoshiko and Rodrigo had gone to Kid Creole's concert at The Ritz. Kid Creole and the Coconuts. My God, I was a coconut. Co-co-crazy. My spirit flew out of my body and snapped at my heels. Sly grinned at me, his teeth bared and sparkling. I chased myself, only I was a shell, with no self left.

"Knock, knock. Rocky? Anybody home?" Sly cackled. Always cackling at some secret joke. "You are gazing upon the best pussy eater on the planet," he bragged, his face a vibrant blue-black, the cobalt-blue-black of Madagascar. The blue-black Berber women of the desert. Shit. I'd seen too many National Geographic specials. *Qué significa, azul?* I missed Arnaldo. Whoosh. There I am, Velcroed to the ceiling, gazing down on our sordid tableau. What year is this?

My voice sounded muffled, underwater. "When are you going to get it through your thick skull that you are just not my —"

Severine crossed her sleek legs and stretched her arms. Was she teasing me? She had sprinkled her exposed, hairy armpits with gold dust. She looked splendid, really. Toned and tanned. So French and hip. With her little tight face, little black dress, and little black pumps. Splendid.

Sly blah-blahed. Blah-blah-blah. "They call me the blue-tongued skink, the true blue gangster of love. I take my sweet time, know how to make grown women howl. Ask Severine. Test out your goose-bump meter with my tongue. Now's your chance, Rocky. Beauty isn't everything. Sly Washington guarantees he'll put all them lazy, pretty boys you like to shame." Severine and I cracked up as Sly got down on his knees to demonstrate. Severine slowly pulled up her skirt.

"What the fuck's goin' on?" Elvis stood at the door — God knows how long he'd been standing there — and stared at us.

Rodrigo went back to Rio de Janeiro. Yoshiko paid someone to marry her, got herself a green card, and her own place. Sly stayed with Severine. Elvis and I moved around a lot those first few months. No fixed addresses or phone numbers, a great excuse to be incommunicado. My mother left more messages on Keiko's answering machine. "This is your *nanay* calling. I'll be home all day, hint hint." Elvis and I sublet a studio way down on Gansvoort Street, above a private after-hours club called The Rack. I hated and loved our new neighborhood. Butchers wearing stained lab coats noisily unloaded animal carcasses from the backs of trucks and vans. Warehouse signs advertised ox tongues and lamb brains. The stench of blood and raw meat pervaded the mornings. Brawny, garish transvestites displayed their wares after dark.

We passed The Rack's black door on our way up the narrow, grimy stairs to our studio. A discreet sign was posted: MEMBERS ONLY. A middle-aged pit bull of a bouncer named Russ guarded the entrance, arms folded across his massive chest. Russ was actually rather sweet. "How you kids doin'?" he'd greet us. "Cold out tonight?" I got the feeling it was a lonely, tedious job. All the interesting stuff was going on inside, while Russ had to stand outside, from midnight until six every morning. Curious about the club, I once got pushy and whiny with him. "Won't you let us in? Please, Russ. Please? Just for a second. Promise we won't bother anybody."

Russ glowered at me. "Are you kidding? No way, girlfriend."

Elvis and I subsisted on peanut butter and grape jelly sandwiches, black coffee, and Indonesian cigarettes. I was down to my last fifty dollars, but I didn't panic, reminding myself there would always be jobs, minimum-wage and mindless. Being in New York was an adventure, fresh and filled with an assortment of witty, noble characters and the perverse high of near violent encounters on subways and streets. New York was a source of intense inspiration, a daily barrage of worthy movie moments. How could I dream of living anywhere else?

I was willing to try anything to survive. The first job I found was waiting tables at Mekong, a pricey Tribeca restaurant owned by a coke hound named Gustav, one of Severine's pals and Sly's regular customers. Mekong was famous for its chic, willowy Asian waitresses and French Vietnamese nouvelle cuisine. I had zero waitressing experience, and I'm sure I was much too earthy-looking for Gustav's ethereal taste. But armed with Severine and Sly as references, I was given a chance. Poor Gustav. I never could remember who ordered what, spilled drinks, cursed at customers who were rude, and spent too much time chatting with the underpaid, overworked, but amazingly good-humored busboys from Ecuador and Guatemala. I was politely dismissed before the week was out.

I signed up with Trail Blazers Temp Agency and moved on to proofreading and coding at a hoity-toity Madison Avenue law firm, Woodrow, Woodrow, and Knapp. Trail Blazers took twenty of the twenty-five dollars an hour I was supposed to be paid, but I didn't know it. I managed to go unnoticed for months, just one of many lost in the pool of misfit, black-clad paralegals working the graveyard shift. There were a lot of struggling artistic types working nights, furtively agonizing over poems and novels while pretending to be immersed in proofing and typing legal briefs. To compensate for the utter meaninglessness of our jobs, we hijacked the Xerox machine for personal business, stole stamps, and made a daily habit of stuffing our knapsacks with reams of fine-quality paper and other assorted office supplies. A suspicious supervisor demanded that I open my bag as I waited to punch out one morning. "What about my right to privacy?" I stammered sheepishly.

"I could have you arrested," she sneered, "but you're not even worth it." Quite a few of us were fired that morning. I was back to zero, dropped from the Trail Blazers roster of eager temps. I can't say I was sorry.

I found my next job through the want ads. Located in Times Square, Ding-A-Ling Switchboard ("twenty-four hours a day, seven days a week, including Christmas") catered primarily to actors, and also to call girls, drug dealers, and other shady entrepreneurs. The pay was shit, but the hours were flexible. I assumed it would be a fun and easy job. After all, how much brains would it take to answer phones and write down messages?

Ding-A-Ling's distinguished CEO was a former child actor named Dickie Drew. Dickie monitored all calls from his office. He was a rare bird, who believed in giving people what they paid for. We were instructed to say "Ding-A-Ling, please hold" in the cheeriest voice we could muster. We were also expected to answer as many as five calls at the same time. "At Ding-A-Ling, our goal is to provide fast, efficient, and courteous telephone service," Dickie Drew informed me. In spite of his prim, zealous manner, Dickie was an okay boss. Of course, I lied about my previous experience, which again amounted to nothing. It helped that I was blessed (as Dickie Drew said admiringly) with a "mellifluous voice" and had lived in San Francisco. Dickie Drew got positively starry-eyed, waxing eloquent about leaving his favorite city. "So romantic, isn't it? So clean, so civilized, so cosmopolitan . . ." He sighed. "I hope to retire there someday, buy myself one of those Victorians. Miss Rivera, I hope you don't mind my asking, but whatever possessed you to move here?"

We got along famously, at first. I called him Dickie, though he persisted in calling me Miss Rivera. During my breaks, he'd wander over and start gossiping about the movie business, usually about actors who were unfamiliar to me, actors who were old or dead. My stories about Uncle Marlon intrigued him. But by the end of my first week at Ding-A-Ling, Dickie stormed into my station. "Miss Rivera, I regret having to say it, but your performance is totally unacceptable."

"But Dickie —"

"Forget that Dickie crap! It's Mr. Drew." He pursed his thin lips and waved a bunch of pink slips in my face. "These messages are totally illegible! My clients are very upset. I trusted you, Miss Rivera, but you've cost me plenty." He paused. "You incompetent bitch."

"There's been some mistake," I said, my thoughts racing. The Gangster of Love had started rehearsing again. E. Sharp, our bass player, followed us out from LA and got himself an apartment in Alphabet City. He and Elvis stumbled onto an affordable rehearsal/recording studio right around the corner. As the newly acknowledged leader of the band, I was stuck with paying for studio time. I couldn't afford to let Dickie Drew fire me. If I had to kiss Dickie's preppy suede loafers to keep my job, I would.

"Dickie, Mr. Drew, I'm sorry, I swear, I'll fix it."

"Ha! Over my dead body."

The phones were ringing off the hook, but the other receptionists were transfixed by our confrontation and didn't pick up. I went to answer one of the phones, but Dickie practically lifted me off my chair, grappling for the receiver. "You've done enough damage, Miss Rivera!" he roared, keeping the precious receiver out of my reach. "Don't you dare, don't you dare, don't you dare!"

Voltaire used to tease me about being the most uncoordinated and physically inept female in the world. Here I was, descendant of a yo-yo master, and I couldn't tie shoelaces properly, wrap packages, roll joints or lumpias. And living in New York brought on more harsh revelations. I couldn't answer more than one phone at a time, shut the fuck up, or make nice. How was I going to support myself and my band? I considered writing my tightfisted sister a gushy letter begging for a loan, but remembered that Luz had just given birth to another child. I called Uncle Marlon after eleven, when the rates went down. "Sorry, Tiyo Marlon. I hate to do this, but I'm broke."

"No, no, I'm glad you called me. Are you in trouble?"

"Not exactly."

"How much do you need?" He started coughing. A small, gurgling, distinct cough.

"You okay?"

"Just a stupid cold," he said.

It was because of Uncle Marlon that I got my next job. "Go see Sandy Oppenheim," he urged, "my former acupuncturist. She moved to New York from LA a few years ago. A great gal, did research on holistic medicine and herbal remedies in the Philippines. Runs a clinic in the Village. Or is it SoHo? She may have an opening. Here's her number."

He probably called her right after talking to me. Uncle Marlon was that kind of person. I never did find out, but when I walked into her office the next morning to inquire about a job, Dr. Sandy Oppenheim acted like she'd been waiting for me all her life. "Marlon's niece, how marvelous!"

"I'll do anything," I said, trying to make light of my situation. "Sweep your floors, mop the toilets, make coffee. I make great espresso." I noticed, with some envy, her display of Philippine Ifugao baskets, the fertility gods and crouching *bulols* carved out of wood, the brass gongs and bamboo nose flutes, the dazzling *ikat* tapestries. I felt as if I were in the Museum of Natural History. "I'll be happy to dust your collection."

"Don't be silly. I've got a cleaning service for all that. May I call you Raquel?"

"Call me Rocky."

"Rocky. How unique! At least you weren't nicknamed Baby or Jing Jing," she said in a bemused tone. "I should've known, since you're related to an extraordinary artist like Marlon. He tells me you're good with the public."

"He did?"

"You know. Making appointments, answering phones, filing."

Visions of Dickie Drew raging loomed before me. I toyed briefly with the idea of getting the hell out of Dr. Sandy's office before I got in too deep. No sense ruining Uncle Marlon's friendship with her. Then it occurred to me that I had no choice. "He did?"

She must have loved my uncle a lot, because she hired me on the spot. I became one of several part-time receptionists at Dr. Sandy's SoHo Pain and Stress Center. A dead-end job, but I didn't mind at all. The environment was more than pleasant, the hours and the pay were reasonable. No chance in hell for climbing up that corporate ladder; we receptionists would remain receptionists until we died or quit. But who cared? Besides me, there was Mamie, a retired librarian in her late sixties who worked part-time to keep from dying of boredom, and Anna, a somber cinema studies major from NYU. It was a perfect job for all of us, undemanding, with lots of dream time thrown in. I called my mother with the first good news in months: "I've got a great job. Don't worry, don't worry."

I called Uncle Marlon, thanking him profusely in three languages: "*Maraming salamat. Muchas gracias.* Thanks for saving my life."

"Isn't Sandy a great gal?" Uncle Marlon chuckled knowingly.

"Kinda like Margaret Mead," I said.

When I wasn't working at the Center, rehearsing, or performing, I tagged along with Keiko to swank parties and art openings. While she networked and gabbed with her svelte new friends, I stuffed myself with canapés and drank.

Elvis was lucky and never had to get a "real" job. Somehow he always managed to scrape by as a session musician, and on what he made from our gigs, taking an extra cut off the top because he composed and arranged all the music. "Then I should take a cut for writing the lyrics," I argued. He insinuated that my songs wouldn't be songs without him. That's what our fighting was usually about these days. I brooded about getting my own apartment, but I wasn't ready yet.

When he needed extra cash, Elvis moonlighted as delivery and backup boy for Sly, delivering what Sly called "product" to his regulars, or going with Sly on his riskier runs. The bodyguard role was kind of a joke: it was Sly who carried a gun. Elvis was also starting to get quite a bit of session work, and a couple of big names had been leaving cryptic messages on our machine. I was sure they were trying to lure him away. I was happy for him, and threatened. Could The Gangster of Love exist without him?

"Let's go eat some meat," Elvis would say whenever he was flush and in a playful mood. Money burned a hole in his pocket. We'd check out rival bands at clubs where we got in for free, then finish off the night at Shine's on Lafayette Street, a hole-in-the-wall that Keiko had turned us on to. Shine's had the best jukebox and juiciest cheeseburgers in town and was run by a part-time opera singer named Shine and her bartender-husband, Angelo. Sly used Shine's as his headquarters, but Shine and Angelo didn't seem to mind. They were coke hounds, too. Sly and Severine could always be found huddled at the bar, or in the ladies' room partying with the big-nosed, big-hearted proprietors.

The Gangster of Love was starting to build a following downtown. CBGB's, Squat, Armageddon, Mudd Club, Danceteria, A7. The band grew: Eddie "E" Sharp on bass (who, depending on his mood, sometimes added an *e* to his last name to make it Sharpe), Jamal Wilkins on keyboards and synthesizer, Ray Vasquez on alto and tenor saxophone. Frankie Ford, this laconic white boy who thought he was Miles Davis, sometimes sat in on trumpet. If the gig paid really well, we'd hire the LaStrange sisters, Darlene and Fanny, to sing backup. They were from New Orleans, gawky and blue-eyed, with soulful voices. Darlene and Fanny inspired me to sing better and act wilder. I wanted to make them a permanent part of the band, but Darlene refused. "You know we love ya, Rock, but as long as that Neanderthal's around, you can fuckin' forget it."

She meant Sly, of course. Sly, who was always pawing at Darlene, Fanny, and any woman under the age of sixty. "He raped me," Fanny blurted out, her face and voice devoid of any emotion.

"He what?"

"You heard her," Darlene LaStrange said.

I confronted Sly at Shine's later that evening. He was holding court at the bar, one paw proprietorially placed on Severine's golden thigh. "I'm surprised at you, Rocky. Fanny's nothin' but a coke whore, and so is that dog-faced sister of hers. How can you take that white girl's word over mine?"

I gestured toward Severine in disbelief. "What the fuck do you mean? *She's* white." With a look of disgust, Severine slid off her bar stool and sauntered over to the jukebox.

"What the fuck do you mean, what do I mean?" Sly was coiled up and tense. I had never seen Sly really angry, ever. Certainly not in LA, and certainly not at me. Sly always managed to turn a bad situation into a joke. "It ain't worth dyin' for," he used to say. He had a pretty even temper, except when it came to pussy. I knew I had definitely crossed some line with him now, but I wasn't sure why. "What the fuck do you mean?" Sly repeated. From the jukebox came Bob Marley's "One Love." Soothing. Optimistic.

She'd say, "C'mon, Elvis Chang. Make me laugh. I want to laugh."

So I thought of all kinds of things to amuse her.

I'd bring angelic women home who pretended they were stupid, skanky, dangerous-looking, women she thought were potentially more beautiful or interesting than she was.

Rocky liked to compete.

She taunted me. "You better watch your step, Elvis. I'm the diva of Manila. I'm the Blessed Whore Mary of divine suffering."

"You sound just like your buddy Keiko," I said.

Sometimes she didn't like being touched.

She'd never seen snow before coming to New York.

She was always cold.

I'm leaving you, she said. I've found my own place.

Why? I asked.

I love you, but it's over.

What's over? I asked. If you love me, then what's over?

Keiko called after midnight. Slurring her words, spouting her usual preposterous shit. "I've finally met that special someone who'll change my life." She'd put some embarrassed jerk on the phone, and Rocky would be forced to make small talk. There'd been quite a few special someones since Arnaldo left: a mortician who wanted to be an actor, several jazz musicians, and Olga, an ambitious, jittery painter from Barcelona who stole money and dope and ran up enormous phone bills. This is the one, Keiko would insist. *The One.* She loved to speculate: "I'm sure I'm pregnant." Or she'd make casual, drop-dead announcements like "I just got another abortion."

I didn't believe any of it, of course.

I begged Rocky not to go over there so much. Why bother?

She always came back from Keiko's in a funk. But Rocky was loyal to her. All Keiko had to say was, "Save me, I'm drowning," and Rocky would drop everything, borrow cab fare from me, and run off to Canal Street. I think she was flattered by Keiko needing her. I imagine the two of them — Keiko rambling all night about her escapades as she painted or worked in the darkroom, Rocky trying her damndest to stay awake, snorting what Keiko blithely plundered from Arnaldo's steadily diminishing stash of coke. Rocky chased the coke with Keiko's usual beverage of choice, fruity-sweet California white. Keiko bought the same cheap wine she'd been drinking in San Francisco, even when she became a famous rich artist, and never slept. "How can you drink this rotten sheet?" Arnaldo used to say. Arnaldo was pretty much out of the picture by then, although you could always count on him to fly in from Mexico and engineer another temporary, tearful reconciliation.

Rocky would straggle back to our apartment at noon the next day — all hyped up on another pie-in-the-sky project that Keiko promised her, or angry and depressed about wasting her time. She'd grind her teeth, wired and on the verge of tears. The best thing was to let her talk. I'm a great listener, just like she is. I never interrupt. Unless somebody gets me real pissed off, that is.

Keiko was a hustler, no question. New York was the perfect town for her. Those early out-of-focus photographs she took of Rocky back in San Francisco? Puh-leeze. In my opinion, Keiko was a careless, sloppy photographer who got lucky. "Focus is not the point!" she once snapped at me, self-righteous and indignant. Keiko had expanded her so-called "visions" and vocabulary by the time we all met up in New York. She landed in a couple of big group shows and kept getting singled out by the critics. Buzz, buzz. As the hype went, Keiko was some kind of funky urban mystic.

She took pictures primarily of women, women she met or saw on the street. She called them her "friends and curiosities," which even Rocky thought was patronizing. Keiko blew up the

photos real big, painting or writing over the images until you
could barely make out what was there. This German critic referred to her process as "hybrid manipulations," whatever the
fuck that means. Keiko went further, painting separate versions
of the distressed photographs on canvas; you could buy just the
photograph, just the painting, or both.

None of us was prepared for Keiko's overnight success, and
that sudden influx of fresh new money. Her timing was impeccable. The three big C's as she called them — curators, collectors,
and critics — ate her shit right up. Through Arnaldo, Keiko acquired a hawkish dealer named Alex, who wore bold red suits
with matching lipstick and pumps. She was severe and sexy
and wouldn't let anyone near Keiko. Alex couldn't stand me, and
was threatened by Keiko and Rocky's friendship. Keiko called
Alex "Mommy" and couldn't scratch her ass without consulting
Mommy first. Mommy made Keiko very rich.

When Keiko's unsmiling mug was on the cover of *Newsweek*,
even Sly was impressed. "Hey, let's ask Keiko to direct our video."

"I didn't know we were doing one," Rocky said.

For "Outside/In," her first solo show, Keiko photographed
drag queens, transsexuals, and real women who looked like drag
queens and transsexuals. Sort of reverse psychology, you know?
Kinda obvious, but the show was a smash. Some best friend
Keiko turned out to be. Rocky practically had to get on her hands
and knees for an invitation to the private reception before the
opening. When we got there, the only one who bothered speaking to us was Arnaldo. He seemed relieved to see us. "Would you
believe this, my friends?" He pointed to the limited-edition cof-
fee-table book published in Japan to coincide with the exhibit. I
couldn't tell if he was outraged or pleased. The damn book was
priced at a hundred dollars.

Rocky and I were at Shine's the last time Arnaldo and Keiko
fought. Who knows how it started? They'd been arguing by the
jukebox, and Keiko defiantly put on some Prince. They argued a

little louder. "Oh God," Rocky said, "there they go again." We were sitting at the bar with Sly, watching. Keiko threw a drink in Arnaldo's face. He slapped her. She slapped him back. Shine and Angelo called the cops, who showed up and hauled Arnaldo away. Keiko was sobbing furiously, drunk out of her mind. Rocky peeled her off the jukebox. "Let's go home," Rocky said, steering her toward the door. Keiko lurched toward the bar to confront Angelo and Shine.

"Why'd you call the fucking cops, you stupid guineas?" Keiko screeched.

Shine was stunned by Keiko's ugly outburst. "Get her out of here," Angelo said to me, real quiet.

Rocky and I struggled to get Keiko inside her coat and up the stairs to the street. She wobbled uncertainly between us, one side of her bruised face starting to swell. "You're my saviors," she moaned. "My dearest darling saviors, my only friends." She turned her glassy eyes on me. "I know you detest me, Elvis. But promise you won't leave me alone tonight." When I didn't respond, she turned to Rocky, becoming frantic. "Promise!"

Rocky's tone was soothing. "Okay, Keiko, okay."

Without warning, Keiko broke free from our grip and squatted down between two cars parked curbside. She lifted up her voluminous, tiered skirt and began to pee. Noisily. She'd been drinking quite a bit all night, so she peed for a long time. Guess she wasn't wearing any panties. I found the whole thing kind of funny. Rocky had a grim look on her face. "Ow!" Keiko yelped, as Rocky yanked her roughly back on her feet. Lucky for us, it was very late, very dark, and Lafayette Street was deserted.

During the next eighteen months, Keiko suffered several very public and extravagant nervous breakdowns. She checked herself in and out of celebrity rehab centers and private clinics, making everyone around her, especially Rocky, worried and crazy in the process. I don't think there was anything wrong with Keiko at all, except for her money and fame.

"She's going to kill herself," Rocky would say, "I just know it."

"No way. Keiko's having too much fun," I said.

I went with Rocky to the Payne Whitney Clinic to visit Keiko, after one of her wine, coke, and Valium binges. "Hurry," Keiko gasped to Rocky on the phone. "I'm all alone and I need you." When we arrived, there must've been at least twenty people there. The room was filled with flower arrangements and get-well cards. Arnaldo had flown in from Mexico, and stood forlornly next to the doting Alex. Keiko's fawning supplicants — her press agent, her studio assistants, her lawyer, her current love object, even the guy who did her hair — hovered around her hospital bed. She never even noticed we were there.

Rocky was a lot more tolerant than I was, still accepting whatever invitation Keiko threw our way. Going over to Keiko's renovated, overdecorated loft for boring dinner parties with her new, upscale pals was absolute torture. Real estate was the usual topic of conversation. And food. They'd sit there gushing about what they were eating, how fresh and fabulous it all was. I always left hungry. How could Rocky just sit there like she did, grinning like the Cheshire cat? What did she want? Me — I wanted to fuck them all and teach them a lesson.

"I'm not goin' there again, ever."

Rocky needled me. "Where's your sense of irony, Elvis? They aren't *all* that bad. And pardon me for sounding crass, but it's a free meal." She paused. "Think of it as a Woody Allen movie. *Manhattan.* I thought you liked *Manhattan.*"

"No soul," I said. "Vacant lots for eyes."

"Great line for a song," Rocky said, writing it down in that journal of hers.

There were women on the street who got pissed off when Keiko took their picture without first asking permission. This homeless woman attacked her once, grabbing at her camera. "Who the fuck you think you are?" Keiko never asked anyone's permission, but most of the time, the women she approached were thrilled to be the object of her attention. The results weren't always flattering. This collector who'd commissioned a portrait started to complain about the transparent plastic sheet draped over her face. "I look like a bloated corpse. And my skin — my God. Is this necessary? I mean, is this really necessary?" Keiko just kept shooting away. The unhappy collector did everything she could to ruin Keiko's reputation after the sitting, calling her a misogynist and a fraud. Then the collector saw her morbid, blown-up portrait prominently displayed at Keiko's opening and bought it. Gets them every time, I guess.

Rocky and Keiko used to fantasize about growing old together — decked out in hats and veils and rockin' on the porch of their . . . sometimes it was a cottage in Wales, sometimes a shrimp farm in the Philippines, sometimes a run-down villa in Tuscany. Even when Keiko became more famous and more unreliable, Rocky acted like nothin' had changed between them. Elvis Chang didn't matter in the long run, and phony Keiko was her one true love. "Why don't you move in with her? It'll be an excellent career opportunity," I said. Rocky acted like she didn't hear me. We weren't getting along, and she accused me of sabotaging her band. I was sick of her shit. "*Your* band?" She'd glare at me with that dark and smoldering look of hers, like yeah, right, sure. Fuck you, Elvis, I'm just as bad as you. Like everything was my fault. The band breaking up every other month, no money and no prospects, Sly strung out, her crazy brother, her destitute mother. She whined about being trapped in New York City: "Why the fuck did I come here?" But I knew it was bullshit. She'd never leave.

Rocky was probably right. Keiko was on my mind more than I cared to admit. "I wish you'd both get in bed and get over it," she once said.

Keiko took me by surprise and called one night, when Rocky was in San Francisco. I was on my way to work at The Ritz with this other band, White No More. Their lead guitarist happened to be temporarily detained at the Betty Ford Clinic. It promised to be a lucrative and prestigious gig, and I was in a big hurry.

"Rocky's in Frisco," I said.

"I know *that*."

"Wanna leave a message?"

"I was actually callin' *you*, Mr. Chang."

"Oh."

She giggled, then fell silent. I wondered if she was high. I was anxious to hang up and get movin', but I also felt this weird, tingling excitement. *Bitch*. I waited for her to speak. "Elvis?" She said my name kinda sweet and uncertainly, then fell silent again, and I knew.

I invited her to the gig, even put her on the guest list. Bitch never showed up.

Rocky got her own place around the time my parents, Edison and Ruby Chang, proprietors of the Lucky Phoenix Noodle Palace in Oakland, paid me a surprise visit. They brought my younger brother, Dwayne, a forensics major at Berkeley. It was Dwayne's semester break, a good excuse for them to check on me. They stayed at the Holiday Inn in Chinatown, spending their days doing all the tourist shit and complaining: Statue of Liberty (too tiring), Empire State (too windy), and all the museums (too many). Dwayne was fascinated by the Guggenheim: "Looks just like a parking garage."

We ate at a different restaurant every night. Pop and Mom referred to their little excursion as "comparative culinary research," and therefore tax-deductible. I ate better than I had in years, though I had to endure their endless whining about the pasta and fish in Little Italy ("not as good as North Beach"), sushi in midtown ("overpriced"), and gooey sweetbreads at some French bistro in the Village ("overpriced *and* overcooked"). At the end of their stay, I invited Rocky and Keiko to join us for my family's farewell dinner at the Silver Palace on Bowery. Don't ask why. Maybe I was just in one of my perverse moods. Maybe I just needed an excuse to see Rocky. They came late, dressed like they were going to some United Nations ethnic costume party. A pint-size white guy in a velvet suit scurried along behind them. Mom and Dwayne were nursing Diet Cokes while Pop and I were on our second vodka martinis.

Pop and Dwayne stood up in greeting, bowing and scraping and pulling out chairs.

"God, I hope we haven't kept you waiting too long," Rocky said.

"You remember Rocky," I said, without getting up.

"Of course," Pop said, giving me a baffled look.

I ignored him. "And this — is her best friend, Keiko."

"Ahhh," my mother murmured, studying them intently. She was probably trying to figure out if I was fucking them both.

"Ahhh," my father echoed, his eyes twinkling behind horn-rimmed glasses. "How are you, Rocky?"

"Excellent," Rocky answered, all sparkly and shit. The little white guy cleared his throat. "This is Brian," Rocky said, nudging him forward. "Brian Goode. He's going to manage our band. Aren't you, Brian?"

I forced a smile. "He is?"

Brian looked uncomfortable. "I don't mean to barge in on a family gathering," he said, with an accent right out of "Masterpiece Theatre."

"We just came from an opening and ran into Brian here," Keiko explained. "He's an old friend of mine, from my London days —"

"That's right," the Englishman said, nodding. "London."

"How ya doin', Byron." I stuck out my hand.

"Brian," he murmured, shaking my hand vigorously. His stringy hair, close-set eyes, and long nose reminded me of a melancholy ferret.

"Please, sit," Mom said.

"I shan't be joining you for dinner," Brian said. "But thank you, anyway."

"Nonsense!" Mom declared. "We've ordered plenty of food. Sit."

"Plenty," Pop agreed. "*Sit*." Brian sat.

Dwayne couldn't keep his eyes off Keiko. "I've seen you in *Newsweek*." He finally realized, astonished at who she was.

"Oh, *that*. Such an unflattering picture." Keiko gave a theatrical shudder. "The photographer hates women."

"Oh . . . ah . . . no," Dwayne stammered. "Actually, I thought it was . . . rather *powerful*."

Keiko addressed me coyly. "Elvis, how come you never told me you had a baby brother?"

"You never asked," I said.

My earnest, intellectual brother was ripe pickings for a seasoned predator like Keiko. She could smell the sexual freak buried deep beneath his permed locks, jade pendants, Geoffrey Beene cologne, and L. L. Bean wardrobe.

"How's your mother's catering business?" Mom asked Rocky.

"Up and down." Rocky sighed. "You know how it is."

"We do." Mom smiled sympathetically. "It's been a tough year. Hasn't it, Ed?" She turned to Pop, who grunted his assent. He signaled the waiter for another round of drinks. "What are you having, kids?"

"Whatever you're having," Keiko responded, avoiding my eyes.

"You from Frisco?" Dwayne asked her. Boy, was he smitten.

"Sort of," Keiko said.

"What high school did you go to?"

"Guess," Keiko said.

"Bet you're a Lowell girl," my poor brother said.

"You're absolutely brilliant," Keiko said with a straight face.

I decided to interrogate the Englishman. "So how many other bands do you manage?"

"Well, uh, actually — none. I'm a painter."

I thought maybe I didn't hear him correctly. "A *painter?*"

"He hung out with Jimi Hendrix," Rocky quickly said.

"In London," Brian said. "That's right. Right before he died."

I was pissed. "So what does that prove?"

"The art market's on a downslide," Rocky said cheerfully. "Brian's looking for a new challenge. I think he'll be perfect for us. Won't you, Brian?"

"Crash, ka-boom," Brian agreed, morosely.

Pop had a dopey grin pasted on his face. He pretends he can't hear too good, so he doesn't have to talk. He grunts and nods, takes his glasses off from time to time and rubs his eyes like he's tired. That's about it.

"Everything okay, Mr. Chang?" Rocky asked.

"Fine, fine," Pop said, one hand waving away invisible flies.

"New York's too noisy and too chaotic," Mom said. "Just like Hong Kong. And *dirty*. I don't think we'll be coming back."

"Reminds me of Manila," Rocky said, "I love it."

"I was born in Hong Kong," Keiko said to Dwayne. "Did Elvis tell you?"

"We saw *Les Miz*," Mom announced to the entire table. "A little too busy, but we enjoyed it."

Keiko leaned closer to Dwayne. Her oversize, thousand-dollar Japanese designer jacket fell open, giving Dwayne a nice view of her tits. "I'd love to take you to something less banal, Doo-wayne."

"Gee, that's too bad. They're leaving tomorrow," I said.

Mom admired Rocky's porcupine hairdo. "So amazing. How do you get it to stand up like that?"

"Motor oil," I said.

Rocky tried not to smile. "Have you been to Bloomingdale's yet, Mrs. Chang?"

Mom nodded enthusiastically. "Bloomingdale's, Bendel's, Bergdorf's, Barney's."

The waiters were rude, and the food came much too slowly, one mediocre dish at a time. We were punchy.

"Food's not bad," Rocky said, trying to be polite. She'd always been fond of my family.

"Pedestrian," my father grumbled.

"Too much cornstarch," Mom added.

"You've hit the nail on the fuckin' head." Keiko laughed.

Mom and Dwayne blushed whenever Keiko or Rocky swore, which was fairly often, punctuating every other sentence with *fuck*, *damn*, and *shit*. My father didn't seem to mind and just kept eating.

"Fuck!" Rocky barked, spilling soy sauce all over the table. She saw Mom and caught herself. "Oops. Pardon my French."

"No, no," Mom said. "No problem. Elvis is worse."

"Definitely," Dwayne agreed. "The worst."

Rocky slipped her hand under the table and rested it on my dick. "I miss you," she whispered in my ear.

I gave her one of my what-the-fuck-do-you-think-you're-doing looks.

"You still in love with her?" Mom asked in Cantonese.

"We broke up," I answered. I hated when she talked to me like that. My Cantonese was lousy. Pop looked disappointed, Mom looked relieved.

"You doing okay?" Dwayne asked with concern, also in Cantonese.

"Always okay," I answered in English.

Keiko gave me a big phony smile. "Aren't you going to translate?"

I glared at her.

Cut your hair! Get a job! Marry Chinese! Stop dreaming!

"Whatever happened to Doreen Chu?" Mom continues to address me in Cantonese.

"I dunno," I say in English, "I think she's dead."

"Doreen Chu was a catch," Mom says, unfazed. "So beautiful and smart . . ."

Sure, I want to say, Doreen was a catch, all right, a member of the Oakland Black Dragons who turned me on to dope when I was thirteen. When she needed to, she could act like a nice

Chinese girl. Too tough, too sexy Doreen, bad to the bone. She loved to strip to Marvin Gaye's "Let's Get It On." And we did.

Mom turned to my father. "Lily Chu's youngest, you remember. When we lived in El Cerrito." Then she declared in English, "Elvis, you are the bane of our existence."

Dwayne groaned. "Not here, Ma. Please."

Rocky kept her hand under the table, on my dick. She and Keiko exchanged amused glances. Brian looked even more uneasy. "Ma," I said, trying not to lose it, "Doreen Chu OD'd. Remember?" Mom didn't respond. "Doreen was a bona fide junkie," I continued. "You know. Heroin. Cocaine. Methedrine. Dilaudid. You name it, she shot it." Then I said, "She was in love with a black pimp, and the only Asian boys she'd fuck were Filipino. The closest thing to black, she used to say." I was drunk now, excited by Rocky's presence. Mom's face got all twisted. "She gave me hepatitis, remember? You were pissed. God, you were pissed. Ask Lily Chu. She probably still lives in the same tacky house. She knows about her dead daughter."

Mom turned away from me in disgust. She glanced at my father, then my brother, then down at her food, humiliated. Everyone at the table stopped eating. I pushed Rocky's hand angrily away from my lap.

"That wasn't necessary, Elvis," Dwayne said.

"Fuck you," I said.

Why did I bother with any of them? Family = pain in the ass.

This whole stupid visit was bound to end up ugly — it always did.

"Try conking your hair next time," I snapped at Dwayne, as our teary-eyed mother rushed off to find the ladies' room.

"Fuck you too," Dwayne said.

Pop finally spoke, very quietly, in English. He savored each delicious word, not taking his eyes off me. Contempt made his voice quaver: "She came — all — the way — just to see — you — how can — you talk to her like that — don't ever — again

— you hear me? — stupid — cruel — selfish — mother— fucking son."

I got up from the table, fists clenched. Rocky reached out to stop me. "Don't," she whispered. We left the restaurant together, and I never looked back.

There was this dark, snooty midtown hotel bar Rocky loved, with a serious monkey motif and a piano, where Tennessee Williams used to hang out before he died. She took me once. The uptight manager made me put on a cardboard jacket and a tie, but for once I didn't mind. We were celebrating the release of our extended dance single, "Greed." One of her best songs, produced by The Gangster of Love with the help of Sly's dirty money. Throbbing, low-down funk groove, sparse guitar riffs, exotic horn lines. The jerk rhythm of James Brown, only much more wicked. Rocky's wispy voice in a cruel, reverb whisper: "Need. Greed. Fuck me till I'm freed." Or maybe it was: "Bed. Head. Fuck me till I'm dead." We hung out for hours, just the two of us, munching on peanuts, sipping Manhattans. We spent every last dime we had.

"I love you," I said to her, the only time I ever said it out loud.

"Baby baby baby," she cooed.

From there we went to Keiko's loft, so Keiko could pierce another hole in my ear. She greeted us in a high-necked, long-sleeved gown. "Yesterday I was Josephine Baker," Keiko blithered, "but that got too obvious. Tonight I'm Edith Sitwell, and Rocky's Marpessa Dawn. We can be them forever. Anytime we want."

"You're fried," I said, but she ignored me.

"I prefer Sonia Braga," Rocky said.

"Okay," Keiko said, "you can have wet dreams about Sonia Braga —"

"*Being* Sonia Braga," Rocky corrected her.

Keiko dabbed my earlobe with alcohol. "How many holes you want?"

"Just one," I said. "Sure you can manage this?"

She jabbed the sewing needle in, hard.

"I have wet dreams about Jeanne Moreau in *Jules and Jim*," Keiko murmured, pulling the needle out slowly. "It's that mouth of hers. The downward curve of it I love. I want to grow old like her. Done!" she announced, with satisfaction. She inserted one end of a tiny gold hoop into the raw wound, and I almost passed out. Rocky, who had shut her eyes when Keiko stuck the needle in, now opened them. "Purrr-fect," she said, surveying the damage.

Who the fuck's Edith Sitwell? Marpessa Dawn?

Rocky showed me photos of dead, homely poets in books. On another day, she took me to see a revival of *Black Orpheus* at Film Forum. "See?" she said. "Isn't she breathtaking?"

"Those ugly poets I can live without," I told her.

The night we left my parents behind at the Silver Palace, Rocky and I ended up at Shine's. Sly and Severine introduced us to a young cellist from Paris named Baba. I think Sly was fuckin' her too. Baba spoke just enough English, and she seemed willing. It was an electric, edgy night, and Rocky and I were full of wild ideas. We invited Baba back to my studio. I lived in one big room, with a bed, a desk and chair, and a sink. The shower stalls and toilet were down the hall, and you needed a special key for both. When I didn't wanna be bothered, I used to piss in the sink.

I offered Baba wine. She sat on the chair by the desk, very prim and proper. Rocky and I sat on the bed. We drank and talked music for the longest ten minutes I'd ever experienced. Baba was too shy about her English to say more than yes, no, or I think so. I was asking all the questions, really deadly stuff like, Do you like Ornette Coleman? Jimi Hendrix? What about that guy, Pierre Boulez? Finally Rocky yawned and said, "What are we waiting for?" She took off her clothes and started ordering us around. Bovine Baba straddled me on cue and went along with everything. I'd copped some shitty coke from Sly, and was alternating between anxious flashes of insane pleasure and my mother's grieving face. Rocky wouldn't allow me to come inside Baba. She pushed her aside and pulled me toward her, murmuring in very bad French, "He is mine, after all." I started to laugh, but stopped when I saw the intense look on Rocky's face. Rocky and I couldn't get enough of each other that night. Insulted, Baba threw her clothes back on and left without saying goodbye.

Two months later, Rocky told me she was pregnant.

She made me promise not to tell anyone about the baby. "Not even Sly." Only Keiko knew. Keiko kept her distance from us, like she thought Rocky and I had made some terrible mistake. She suddenly decided she needed a vacation, and flew off to Bali with Alex.

Rocky kept buggin' me. "Should we keep it?" Your body, your decision, I said. *The baby.* It was hers more than mine, I knew that from the start. Never real to me, ever. *Blam de blam blam. While my guitar gently weeps.* I convinced myself that Rocky and I were right not to live together. It hadn't worked before, and we were both too crazy. Look at the jam we were in.

"Is she pregnant?" Sly asked, after a particularly bad rehearsal one day.

Rocky was about three and a half months along when she miscarried. She woke up in the middle of the night, vomiting, bleeding, shitting all over the place. I rushed over in a cab to her apartment. "This baby," she said, smiling a spooky little smile, "this baby's tryin' to kill me, Elvis." We had never made our decision. I guess we just kept hoping the baby would go away by itself. So it did.

I called 911.

Dr. Moreno, the doctor on duty in the emergency room at St. Vincent's, asked her if she wanted the baby saved. Rocky looked at me, petrified. What did she want? What could I do? All these other doctors came in, ignoring me, talkin' about her in the third person, like she was invisible, or some lab specimen. They poked fingers up inside her to see if the baby was still in one piece, still salvageable.

"I'm afraid . . ." Dr. Moreno murmured. Rocky kept her eyes on me. "Are you the father?" Dr. Moreno asked me. I felt really tired and really sad. Rocky was anesthesized, wheeled away, and given a D and C by Dr. Moreno. In the morning, euphoric from the Demerol they'd given her, Rocky said "I love you" as soon as I walked into the room. She kept repeating it, like it was supposed to make her feel better.

Her euphoria wore off pretty fast. I brought her back to my apartment to recuperate. Dr. Moreno had said all she needed was a day or two. Rocky stayed in my bed watching television. Stayed in the same flannel nightgown for weeks. Stank. "You want me to call your mother?" I asked in desperation. She wouldn't respond. It's like she curled up inside of herself and died. She wouldn't return calls, not even Keiko's. She cried at the drop of a hat. Cried as soon as she woke up. Cried when she ate, and in the middle of the CBS evening news. She'd weep and wail at anything to do with violent deaths, especially when it involved children. And this being New York, there was plenty for her to cry about. "Shit, baby, that's life," I said. She'd sit there like a zombie with bloodshot eyes. She'd sit there for hours, not moving. I'd get so spooked I'd stay out with Sly. Sometimes she'd beg to get high with me, beg me to fuck her. She was scary. Then at the best part, when I got a fix on it and we had a rhythm going and it seemed like all the bad stuff was forgotten, she'd push me away or slap me, scratching and biting and trying to draw blood. The crying would begin all over again. Then one morning she just looked at me real calm and said it was over, it was time for her to go. She just didn't love me that way anymore.

Somewhere in Hamtramck, Michigan, Keiko and I are getting stupid drunk on tequila. *Hamtramck.* I relish the sound of it, the way I relish the anonymity of this corner saloon. What is it called? Something Polish. Darkness inside. Easy on the eyes. Except for the bartender, there are no other women or authentic exotics for miles around. The men's stares are openly curious, with a touch of hostility. We've been drinking since noon; we are loud and dirty. Keiko and I shed our skins, turn into a couple of sweaty banshees. The burly bartender stays as far away from us as possible.

"Blockhead," I mutter. "Cauliflower ears."

"Shut up, you fucking racist," Keiko says. "Or she'll throw us out. Want another drink?"

I slur my words. I haven't felt this good in a long time. "Nah. She wouldn't dare. Never. Need. Money."

What year was it? As far back as 1979? Or something more like 1981? The only thing sure is that the numbers involved are odd. But I remember everything else: the oversize Boy Scout shirt Keiko was wearing, the bar's stale air-conditioned smell, a few sad old men with watery eyes and bulbous noses, the glaring sunlight every time someone pushed open the door. But the exact date eludes me. Only a Sly Stone oldie fading in from the street gives me some sense of how past is past. *Hot fun in the summertime.* Back then, Sly's melancholy funk gnawed away at me with its pretty melody, but now even the music provides no clues.

Keiko's hazel eyes narrow, her face a crimson blush. "Whatsa matter, Rock? You okay?"

"I gotta gig tonight. But I'm gonna get sick first." Then I sang: "Mama was a dancer, Papa was a gambler. Grandma was a shaman, Grandpa yo-yo champion of da world."

Keiko chuckles, then calls out gaily to the bartender in her gravelly voice, "Another round, *por favor*."

"Wanna try a boomba?" the bartender asks, suddenly friendly.

"What the fuck's a boomba?" Keiko asks in a whisper.

"Some kind of native drink," I whisper back. "We'd better stick to our usual," I say out loud to the bartender. "Thanks anyway." She pours us two more shots of Cuervo Gold and skulks away. "I love — I absolutely love the way you use — the most —" My brain is fried. I struggle to finish the sentence. Why did I even begin? "The most *ordinary* words."

"You crazy. Like what?" Keiko acts paranoid whenever she drinks. I've gotten used to it.

Time to go home. But where? Back to the Motel 6? My sister's villa in Manila? My chest constricts in pain. "Like *bullshit*. I love the way you say *bullshit*. Like *nice*."

"I haven't said *nice* all day," Keiko pretend-pouts, the tequila kicking way in. "You makin' fun of me? You always makin' fun of me, Rocky." She leans in closer so the curious men won't hear. I can smell traces of her perfume gone sour. "You know what I'd really like to do? Right now, Rock. Right now." Between her fingers is an unlit cigarette. I imagine her hand is trembling, ever so slightly.

"What." I shut my eyes, inhaling through my nostrils and exhaling slowly like Elvis Chang taught me to do whenever I went off, like I felt I was about to do any second. Go off and scare myself mute. Take a deep, deep breath. Let the air slowly out. Don't hyperventilate. Release those toxins! Elvis said, Whoever lives by breaking the rules, lives.

I am close to blowing my first out-of-town gig with the band, too wasted to remember the lines to any of my songs, sure I am suffering a heart attack from too much tequila. Elvis's yoga exercise isn't helping me one bit.

"I wanna make love to you. Let's go to the toilet," Keiko whispers. "Right now."

"You're the one who's crazy." I have to smile. We're in one of those bars where hard-boiled eggs are sold for seventy-five cents as "chicken lunches" and you have to beg the bartender for a key to the john every time you needed to go. The old girl would probably call the vice squad on us. She's been waiting all damn day for just the right reason.

"Don't be such a pussy." Keiko realizes what she has just said, then bursts into laughter.

"Mama was a dancer. Papa was a gambler —"

"You're scared," Keiko accuses me. She's about to pass out.

"Come on, time for me and you to go." I try dragging her off the bar stool. "Sound check's at five."

"One more drink, *por favor.*"

I start pushing her gently toward the door. "Good afternoon, *ladies,*" the bartender says, with a weary smile. I manage a lopsided grin. Keiko stumbles out into the afternoon sunlight with me. "Let's go find Elvis and the boys," she mumbles, "*por favor.*" The liquor burns holes in my empty stomach. Like a fist, my heart tightens again, then again.

Tonight we play Detroit. My band is last on the bill of the First Annual Detroit New Music Festival, an event that has definitely already run its course. "I hate this town," Sly grumbles, as he lugs his drum kit up the flight of stairs to the motel room he is to share with Elvis. "Why are we here?" Sly, a.k.a. Dwight Washington, a.k.a. Sly The Stone, was born in Detroit. Being back makes him anxious. Nobody knows why. "Why'd we take this gig?" he keeps asking B. Goode, our manager. "We're barely making expenses."

"Would you quit whining and shut the fuck up?" B. Goode growls. "You should be proud of your hometown. Martha and the Vandellas, Diego Rivera, General Motors! Fuck money. This is Detroit. Maximum art-rock exposure."

I applaud his welcome tirade. "We love you, Brian!"

Sly rolls his eyes. "Art rock? Is that what we're calling it?"

Elvis and I jump on one of two narrow beds. "Motor City,"

Elvis howls into an imaginary microphone. "Praise the Lord Jeez-us. We're in Motor City!"

"Don't break the fuckin' bed," B. Goode warns. "We can't afford it."

"This'll be a great gig," I assure Sly. "We'll play ugly music. Ugly music inspired by Motel Ugly, the only motel in America designed to push you over the edge." I look around. Everything is orange and brown, except for the ugly off-white bathroom. B. Goode, Keiko, Ray, and Eddie are gathered in the doorway, watching our performance. Keiko's the only one who seems amused. Sly collapses on the other bed and groans. Elvis jumps down, then draws back the ugly curtains of the ugly motel room. "Cheer up, everybody! A parking lot!"

Which is why Keiko and I had run away and ended up at the bar around the corner. It was all too depressing. "I'm checking the bed for ticks and taking a shower with my boots on," I said.

Tonight, we play Detroit. Tonight, everyone is angry. There are two thousand surly people hanging off the rafters of the once elegant, but now seedy art deco, neo-Mayan Fox Theater, which seats half that number. There is nothing Elvis or I can say or do to relax the band. And it doesn't help to have Sly reminding us over and over again that we made a big mistake in coming to his hometown. "Welcome to Detroit," Sly drawls in mock homage to Elmore Leonard. "City Primeval. Capital of Ugly and Unknown Man Numbah 89."

E. Sharp can't take it anymore and snaps. "Better watch it, motherfucker. Yo' mama's in the audience." Styrofoam cups of beer and sticky soda are hurled down from the balcony; the stage is littered with trash. Musicians in band after band duck the barrage and keep playing. White No More, Bad Karma, Rimbaud's Beaux, F**K, Stupid Junkies.

And then there is us.

Enthusiastic boos from the eternally restless audience. "And now, from New York — The Gangster of Love!" Boo . . . boo . . .

booo . . . "Who the fuck are you?" a woman screeches in the dark.

"I don't know about your band's name," Brian Goode said the first time he came to see us. "A bit too lyrical, don't you think?"

"What do you mean?" I asked, taken aback.

"I dunno. *Gangster of Love*. A bit precious. A bit too . . ." He shrugged, in that world-weary, English way of his. It always seemed a good idea for bands to have managers with foreign accents, even if they were incompetent. Especially if they were from England. The English were supposed to be in the know, musically. Ahead of their time. Like Mick Jagger copping dance moves from James Brown and Tina Turner. The English knew exactly who and what to exploit. Whereas Americans missed out on what was right under their noses. Hicks about their own fucking culture.

So if you had a manager like Brian Goode, even if no one's ever heard of him, even if he's only got one band on his roster, even if the biggest gig he can get us is a nightmare . . . Well, do I have to finish the sentence for you?

I blame myself for the band's stupid name, I blame myself for Detroit. We were scheduled to go on at eleven and it is now two in the morning. The DJ plays Parliament/Funkadelic in between sets, yelling over the speakers, "All right, Detroit!" every now and then. The screeching woman in the balcony yells back, "Fuck Bootsy! Let's go!"

We are heckled mercilessly. My lips are stuck to my gums, dry from all the coke I snorted waiting around backstage. By the time the spotlight hits me, I'm frozen stiff and can't remember what comes next. I frantically try to improvise lyrics to one song after another. Elvis bores everyone to death with his deafening, meandering solos. Sly tries to compensate by abruptly switching rhythms. The songs are played at super speed. No one in the band seems to care whether I can be heard or not. Eddie and Ray retreat into their own private reveries; they keep up with the craziness as best they can. Jamal stops playing and rests his fingertips on the edge of the synthesizer keyboard, looking baffled. I eventually give up trying to sing and just stand there, staring at the sea of faces before me. Elvis and Sly compete for who can play the loudest and the baddest, and I imagine this terrible night will never end. When it is finally over, B. Goode hustles me offstage. "Stupid, stupid girl." He practically spits in my ear. He looks like he wants to cry. If he could get away with it, he'd hit me. Like a father would, when he can't believe what his daughter has done. I give him the same lopsided grin I gave the bartender this afternoon in the Polish bar in Hamtramck.

I try to convince myself and the band that we are too advanced for Detroit. I am the leader, after all, doomed to keep up a good front. And B. Goode works for me. Who was he until Keiko and I found him? A failed artist with an accent, a middle-aged man in a slump. Eurotrash. The galleries weren't interested in his work. Not even nonprofit *alternative spaces*. No one gave a shit about landscapes and still lifes in the eighties. No one gave a shit about paintings, period. He couldn't give them away.

"We sucked." Elvis packs up his guitar and leaves the filthy dressing room without waiting to get paid. That's how mad he is. Keiko chain-smokes and leans against the smudged mirror on the wall, waiting for my next move. Someone from another band — Rimbaud's Beaux? — comes in to get something, but he thinks better of it, mumbles "Sorry," and shuts the door. Exhausted and depressed, the rest of us sulk in silence.

Even with Brian B. Goode in the picture, I thought I could do everything myself: write songs, perform, hire and fire musicians, pay the rent with my part-time jobs. A record deal would materialize soon, I was sure of it. A record deal would get me out of this hole, solve all our problems. I thought all this even though I am more cynical than my mother, Milagros, the Queen of Cynics. I think I am special and that in spite of the odds and what I've been carefully taught, special things are therefore due me. I am talented. I work hard. And, in spite of the drugs I occasionally take, I am not particularly self-destructive. Like Keiko says, I look good and act good. I try real hard. A good girl. But of course, I am wrong.

On one of my visits back to San Francisco, my mother asks me why I try so hard to be a man. "Look at your Grandpa Baby. So-called inventor of the yo-yo. And what did that get him?" She blames it all on coming to America. Grandpa Baby was a renowned wood-carver in his hometown back in the Philippines, but he gave it all up to come to California. First he broke his back picking asparagus in the fields, then he worked as a bellhop in some hotel in Santa Monica, where he ended up whittling a yo-yo and starting his own company. The rest, as they say in my cynical family, is the same old shit history. Grandpa Baby sold his rights to the yo-yo for a lousy thirty thousand dollars. He later went on the road and did yo-yo demonstrations with a bunch of other Filipinos. Besides Grandpa Baby, there was Baby Manila, Nemo Concepcion, Aniceto Fabionar, Eddie Coo, Gus Somera, Fortunato Annunciacion, and Tico Lico. Names like Regal, Deferino, Anacleto, Flor. There was also Patty Stewart and Selma Sardilino. I never met Grandpa Baby or any of his friends. He died before I was born. I know from faded photographs that like the other men, he slicked his hair back with pomade and wore beautiful shiny suits. He danced the yo-yo dance. He was the best, according to my mother and Auntie Fely. Brain twister, loop-the-loop, walk-the-dog, rock-the-baby.

My mother compares me to Luz. "She's not like you at all," she observes, tapping her long, manicured nails on the dining room table. "Perfectly content to stay in Manila and run things. Ha." Tap-tap-tap, my mother goes.

"I'm more like Voltaire," I say.

"Your brother's a certified nut," my mother says. "At least you've got ambition."

I don't know why I say it, but I do. "You say you hate her, but you bring her up constantly. Luz, Luz, Luz. She probably still believes in the literalness of heaven and hell. I dream about her, just like you do. Her fear of water. Her swimming pool. Her husband, her children, her servants, her dogs. Her father, my father —"

"Don't bring him into this!" My mother takes a moment to calm down, then sighs. "Ayyy, Raquel. At least Luz is financially secure. I worry about you, living in that violent city, so far away. You and your brother. What's going to happen?"

I hate this moment. We always get to this awful moment, no matter how my visits begin. I could show up with a big smile, laden with expensive gifts and wads of cash, but we'd always end up in some grand Filipino fatalistic funk, with my mother asking this same stupid question and me not being able to answer. *What's going to happen?* I decide to lie. "There's a record guy hanging around. He loves my demo. I think he's going to sign us," I say. My mother stares at me long and hard, desperately wanting to believe. I meet her gaze. Finally, my mother goes off to the kitchen and starts clanking pots and pans. "Ready to eat?" she calls out, her voice lightening.

"Sure," I say. "I haven't eaten since —" I don't finish my sentence. Actually, it had been a few days since I'd had a real meal.

Keiko helps carry our equipment back to Motel Ugly, where all the bands are staying. She decided to travel with us to Detroit the same week Arnaldo left for Mexico City. This was the fifth or sixth time they'd broken up.

"We'll end up killing each other if we stay together," Keiko said. "Can I hang out with you? I'll help drive the van —"

I'm relieved to have any woman along for company. I've had to make do in the past with someone's hostile wife or druggie airhead girlfriend-of-the-moment, but I'm always grateful for their whiny female presence. (Rock 'n' roll's such a boys' club, and I'm sick of it. Whose guitar/dick/tongue is the longest and loudest?) Keiko is more than just any woman, of course. She is the only one I can face after my failed performance.

We are in my motel room, sharing a pint of Cuervo Gold. It is six in the morning, the equipment is stacked in the bathroom, and I am weeping with exhaustion. In a few hours we're off to Ann Arbor.

"Elvis wants to fuck me," Keiko says. "Sly wants to eat my pussy."

"Elvis and Sly want to fuck everybody."

Keiko's face is wistful. "Sly and Elvis want to fuck me, but I want to fuck you."

"Men are easy, aren't they?"

"Are you still in love with Elvis?"

I shrug.

Keiko's smile is ironic. "You are."

Here I am, Keiko. I slip off my T-shirt, lay back on the bed, unzip my jeans, pull my pants down, and wait for her to do something. She starts to laugh. I laugh with her, a laugh tinged with bitterness. "You're so lazy," she says. She practically swallows my tongue with her kiss, and we make love. I am angry, but she doesn't seem to mind. It seems like a long silence, her kissing and touching me, my touching her back. I am terrified by my numbness but don't know how to tell her to stop. She is beautiful in her scowling intensity, her hair a black veil falling over me. I fade in and out of being there with her. I resist our pleasure, and she knows this. She is furious with me but says nothing. Finally, we fall asleep curled against each other.

I think now we were both cowards.

Maybe I let my Catholicism get the best of me. Maybe I'd rather fuck in my imagination. I allow myself to run wild and wallow in my own private kitsch. I dream of hermaphrodite angels with bronze skin floating alongside the naked, bleeding perfection of my tormented Saint Sebastian. Arrows pierce his bony ribs as he arches his back in anguish. In my dream, Tagalog is not spoken, nor English, nor Spanish. The silence of penance prevails. My perverse angels ascend before disappearing into the cotton ball clouds of heaven. Orgasmic bubbles burst in my vast, baby blue void. A hundred more arrows sail through the air. *Whoosh*. Flames erupt from a gaping, aubergine mouth. Saint Sebastian rolls back his eyes in ecstasy.

My mother's right. I am just like everyone else in my family. I believe in heaven and hell, the pleasures of denial, and the rewards of sin. I want to tell Keiko the truth. "I enjoy this only because it's forbidden."

I know what Keiko did that morning, while I slept. She crept next door to where Elvis lay waiting. Sly watched them fuck from his bed. That day, I sat up front with Sly as he drove our van to Ann Arbor. Elvis cuddled in the back with Keiko, and everyone acted like everything was normal. Snickering at the memory, Sly proceeded to tell me about Elvis and Keiko, gloating over every detail in a low voice. What he saw, what he heard. Heh-heh. How he wanted some of it. He can be crude and cruel like that.

I could call Sly a jealous motherfucker, which he is. I could ask Elvis to beat him up, which he would. But Sly has a gun, so I don't. I'm too tired to fight, so I listen sleepily as Sly talks nonstop, wicked and edgy from all the coke he's had for breakfast. Music from the tape player is blasting. *"One nation under a groove, / gettin' down . . . One nation, / we're on the move."*

Carabao Dreaming

"The yo-yo was once a jungle weapon."
— *Milagros Flores Rivera*

Los Blah-Blahs: One

Last night I dreamed that Fidel Castro was driving a Jeep Wrangler, crossing Sixth on Twenty-eighth. High noon, traffic backed up. The whole world on a lunch break, even the unemployed.

When I dream, I dream dreams in nocturnal settings. Sometimes they're very specific: deserted mariachi plazas in Guadalajara, or deserted hotel rooms in Hong Kong, for example. I'm alone in the dream, but I know exactly where I am. It's the haunted house I grew up in, or Paco Cemetery in Manila. Sometimes the settings are more confusing: murky swimming pools suddenly appear in the midst of moonlit generic jungle ruins, which could be anywhere from Angkor to Mazatlán. Or I find myself trapped in bleak kitchenettes lit by twenty-five-watt bulbs, which could either be in Española, New Mexico, or Oxnard, California. I am being threatened and toyed with by someone in the dream. Someone anonymous yet familiar. It's dangerous, sexy, and terribly mundane. You get the picture.

But this dream, this dream was different. The sun was out, the colors turned way up. TV colors. Electric and garish, dirt and dazzle. You couldn't mistake him, beaming and chomping on a fat cigar, dressed camouflage-crisp the way Fidel Castro should dress in a dream. I was a passenger in the front seat of another car, but I don't know what kind. Maybe a 1981 Mazda. Maybe our old truck, Lucille. Elvis or Keiko driving. Look, I said to whomever, astonished. It's what's-his-name. Fidel waves a politico's wave of acknowledgment. Nothing more, nothing less, nothing deep. Disappointed, I lean out the window, and yell, "Hey, I know you. Quit flapping your hand around. I know who you are." The streets are teeming crazy crowded, business as usual. Everyone's too jaded, hot, and stressed out to give a fuck about Fidel in the flesh.

My dream hurts my eyes. "Hola, hombre. *Mr. Castro Señor Sir. We need to talk,*" I say. "Yo habla español, *sort of. Pero, the good thing is, even though* mi español es muy terrible, yo entiende *pretty good. Cough up the dirt.* Habla me. *This may only be a dream, but I demand all your secrets.*"

Homesick

I am panicked by the thought of growing old in New York. Trapped forever in this rent-stabilized apartment, in this city, alone. Borderline poverty and self-pity engulf me. I imagine my ankles swollen. How I'll shuffle up the street to the trendy and overwhelming Food Emporium and buy sale items every week. Jumbo containers of acetaminophen and shampoo, six-packs of rough toilet paper, the carefully clipped coupons and food stamps tucked into the pocket of my secondhand wool coat, which stinks faintly of body fluids and baby powder. I wear it year-round of course, buttoned all the way up to my throat even in the thick heat of summer. I will outlive my family, my friends, my lovers, my band, and be buried a pauper in this same stinking coat. Whatever children I may have will abandon me, I am sure of it.

Once when I was on acid I saw myself age, fast-forward, into a very old woman. Layer by layer of flesh and bone softening, wrinkling, cracking, collapsing. "Look," I said to Elvis, staring in fascination at my reflection in the mirror. "I'm turning into my mother."

I live on Eleventh Street, in a roach-ridden postwar building with a still-grand facade. I live alone on the top floor and have become a voyeur, spying on the enchanted family in the building across from mine. I wake up to the startling beauty of their second-story roof garden, an enclosed oasis of AstroTurf. Sunflowers, Douglas fir, and wild grass sprout out of planter boxes. Begonias and marigolds bloom in clay pots. Ivy and morning glory wrap around the stakes of a bamboo fence. When it is sunny and warm, a middle-aged woman brings out a young man in a wheelchair. Sometimes she stays to chat. He listens carefully to whatever she says. They laugh. They seem very fond of each other. She puffs on her cigarettes but takes care to blow smoke in the opposite direction, away from him. As if it mattered. Or she kisses his forehead and disappears back into the building. I imagine she goes off to her job, as I usually don't see her again until much later. I know she is not the young man's mother. Nothing about them suggests blood. Most of the time, I don't know how the young man gets wheeled back inside. He seems too weak to do much for himself. When he is alone, the young man reads, dozes off, or just sits, slumped over and still. I imagine he is waiting to die.

The woman appears at the sink. Framed in her kitchen window, only parts of her face and body are visible. I imagine her name is Ingrid. Her white blond hair is cut very short. Her arms are muscular and tanned. Today she wears a loose lavender caftan. For a few moments she pauses at the sink, smoking. I imagine she is perturbed about something. Then she walks away. When she returns, she washes out a coffee cup. A black cat leaps from the kitchen window, landing first on the white, wrought-iron table, then on one of the white chairs. The man in the wheelchair is already outside. He reaches out with one arm and slowly strokes the cat's head. The cat arches its back.

I imagine the man in the wheelchair is Voltaire.

Other people come and go, all adults. I imagine they are members of some sophisticated urban commune, with Ingrid as their leader. They have interesting jobs and identities: architect, fund-raiser, advocate for the homeless, curator at MOMA. I imagine some of them do volunteer work. They are not smug, nor are they, by any means, rich. They are well informed, well meaning, and well connected, and have access to important cultural events. They love to talk to each other. That much is evident, even when there is too much traffic noise and I can't make out what they're saying.

There are many nights when a big feast is prepared, and the family gathers under a frayed canvas awning. I hear snatches.

"Jonathan," Ingrid addresses a flawless man with chocolate skin, "how could you?" Someone else interrupts: "Weren't you at the Latin . . ." Jonathan's response overlaps: "God, that was *old*. Absolutely never again . . ." Bronze wind chimes sway in the breeze. Citronella candles are lit, wine is poured. I envy my beautiful family.

Ingrid makes a toast. "To Jonathan," she says. Clinking of glasses. It is Jonathan's birthday, but even then, the young man in the wheelchair remains the center of attention. Ingrid serves him a plate piled high with food. Sometimes he eats without requiring any assistance, but there are times like this when he seems exhausted and distant. All this is apparent from my bedroom window — his appetite, or lack of interest in food and the people around him. With great tenderness, Jonathan spoons him birthday cake.

Since Detroit, I've been meaning to call Elvis. I almost called early this morning, but I didn't.

My enchanted family's cat prowls on the tarred roof of the adjacent building. Back and forth, back and forth, hunting pigeons and rats. Voltaire ignores the cat. He seems more frail than usual. Too many dinner parties, maybe. Too much commotion. He wears a pale blue shirt and jeans. A loosely draped shawl covers him from the knees down; a book lies unopened on his lap. I wish I could see what he is not reading. Suddenly he lifts his head and gazes up at my window. I tell myself there is no way for him to make me out in the shadows. I am elated and ashamed. Perhaps he has felt me spying on him. Perhaps he has known all along.

An older man, someone I've never seen before, comes to take the sick young man in the wheelchair back inside. I pull myself away from the window and head for the bathroom. Wash my face and brush my teeth, make a show of it. Grow up. Shave my underarms, my legs. Head on out the door. Make sure to lock it behind me. Check if there's enough change for the genteel, hollow-eyed woman who begs in front of Chemical Bank, enough change for a coffee to go from the deli downstairs. An energized, clear head is what's desirable. Clear and caffeinated, precise and percolated. *Un café solo, por favor.* Black, brackish, briny, burned.

There's enough change but not enough time. Norberto hands me the Styrofoam cup of boiling java. "How about a bagel with schmear?" he offers. "No thanks," I say. "See you later, alligator. Gotta go, gotta date, I'm late."

Is there enough change for a taxi to SoHo? If I jump in the first taxi I find, I can make it on the dot. On the money, as Sly might say. Beat the clock. Punch in without guilt, without remorse, without humiliation or fear.

But there's not enough change, not enough time. I walk. I hoof it. I gallop. I do what I can. I'm already stinking in this heat. My Shiva of Berkeley Aloe Vera Clove Deodorant is not working, not toxic enough to plug up my overstressed sweat glands.

I pray for myself as I run down Prince to Broadway, make a right, make a left. How am I supposed to meet and greet the public, do my job, do right by Uncle Marlon, do right by Dr. Sandy, who's done right by me.

Lucky me — Dr. Sandy understands. "Good morning, Rocky. Everything okay?" She doesn't care if I'm a few seconds late, if I look frazzled or give off the scent of fear. Dr. Sandy cares only about the big picture, and I am endlessly, secretly grateful to her. Being grateful is nothing I'd care to admit to Keiko or anyone. Filipinos are endlessly grateful, but I'm supposed to be tough.

And the less people know about my job at the Center, the better. It's bad enough that Keiko's become one of Dr. Sandy's celebrity patients and shows up regularly for her colonics and acupuncture treatments. Keiko can't help her pitying looks when she thinks I'm not paying attention.

Dr. Sandy prides herself on hiring frustrated wanna-be artists like me. Chiropractor, masseuse, holistic therapist, acupuncturist, and author of the best-selling *Living with Pain*, Dr. Sandy's a formidable New Age warrior, an earnest brunette armed with diplomas in Western and alternative medicines. She's obsessed with tropical maladies, which she loves to describe, preferably when we're eating. "Did you know there are spiders in parts of eastern Africa that lay eggs right beneath the surface of your skin while you sleep? The arm swells up like an elephant's trunk. I've seen little children afflicted, silent and stoic in their agony. *Imagine the pain*," Dr. Sandy says, awed by the memory. "When these spiders are born, the flesh ripples constantly with their fast, angry movements, as they try to bite their way out from the inside."

I once made the mistake of complaining to her about my weight. Dr. Sandy went on her usual radical rant. "Americans are shortsighted and puritanical. Diets don't work because they're all about denial. Don't do this, just eat that. Exercise, exercise! No fun at all. Instead of all this bland, low-cholesterol crap, what you need is a tapeworm. In South America and Southeast Asia, parasites are a fact of life. You must be suffering from cultural amnesia, Rocky. You're from the Philippines and should already know this. Eat whatever you want. Pork fat, chicken butts, French fries, chocolate cake. Who cares? Embedded in your intestines, the tapeworm eats everything you do. Mother Nature's way — marvelous, and so simple. When you're down to your desired weight, why then all you do is take a few herbs and shit the worm right out of your system."

I get Sly to fill in as one of Dr. Sandy's clerk-receptionists when Mamie goes on vacation. I figure the job will provide a temporary respite from dealing, the only other thing Sly knows how to do besides play music. He's lying low until some people he's burned leave town. "You're gonna get yourself killed," I nag him. "Bad karma."

"Rocky, please, spare me that sixties shit." He's reading some article in the *Times* "Metro Section" and starts guffawing. "Listen to this, Rock. A meter reader found the skeleton of some old Puerto Rican guy in a basement!"

"Where?"

He's laughing so hard he's in tears. "Queens. Where else?" He starts reading the juicy parts out loud: "'The gas company had been trying to read the meter in the Vargas household for two years but could never get a response.'" He laughs again. "'Finally, armed with a court order and flanked by a locksmith and a city marshal, the meter reader gained access to the tidy, one-story brick house in a quiet, residential area of Jackson Heights. The men ignored a request by Mrs. Saturnina Vargas, sixty-five, not to go down to the basement. After pushing their way through a giant cobweb, they found the skeleton of Roel Vargas, sixty-eight, a pharmacist, sitting erect in a chair by a table. The skeleton was still dressed in a brown sweater, blue shirt, blue slacks, and black running shoes —'"

"They're not Puerto Rican."

Sly is dying. He keeps reading to me: "'Beneath the table was a skull that had apparently broken away and was identified as Mr. Vargas's. The police said Mrs. Vargas appeared surprised at their discovery. She seemed confused and said she had not seen her husband for over a month. The couple had lived in the house for twenty years.'"

"They're not Puerto Rican. They're Filipinos," I say.

"How you know?"

"Their names. Roel and Saturnina. Plus, they live in Jackson Heights. Plus, he was a pharmacist. And" — here I paused for maximum Sherlock Holmes effect — "she probably killed him."

Sly shook his head in amazement. "Man, oh, man. Your people are wild."

"I know," I said with pride. "Isn't it great?"

Sly's determined to succeed. He wears star-shaped Bootsy Collins sunglasses and fantasizes out loud about the money we're going to make when our album goes gold. "What album? We can't even get a record deal," I remind him.

"Be patient, darlin'," Sly drawls, "just be patient."

"I think I'm getting too old for this band shit. Maybe I should quit."

"Sure, Rocky. And you won't mind working for the doc forever, right?"

"Why not? I happen to like Sandy. She's decent, humane —"

"Damn. Are you about to have your period, or what?"

It's embarrassing how much he believes in this stardom crap, but at least Sly makes the workday entertaining. We talk band talk when we aren't answering phones, reading trashy news items, filing away patients' folders, getting high in the bathroom, or fucking up accounts on the new computer.

"How's the dynamic duo doin'? Am I late for my appointment?" Keiko beams at us, then introduces a breathtaking woman standing next to her as Gorgeous García Lorca, performance artist, model, and obviously Keiko's latest muse.

"Are you related to the poet?" I ask her.

"But of course," Gorgeous replies.

"Oh, bay-beh!" Sly pretends to pant with desire, licking his lips.

Gorgeous is not amused. Neither is Keiko. "Grow up, Sly."

They glide haughtily away, holding hands. Sly flicks his tongue in and out behind their backs. "Bay-beh, bay-beh," he sings. When they are out of earshot, he asks, "So. What's with you and your pal?"

I lead them into Examination Room 1, which reeks of the cinnamon and orange peel potpourri that Dr. Sandy makes herself and brings to the office. Forlorn whale music pipes through the speakers. I hand Keiko a freshly laundered kimono. "Dr. Sandy will be right with you."

"Join us for dinner later?" Keiko asks me. Gorgeous tries to look nonchalant. I shrug maybe, then pull the curtain shut and leave them to their privacy.

At the front desk, I find Sly scowling at the monitor.

"What? Something wrong?"

"Something's been erased," Sly says.

"What?"

"Something, but I'm not sure what."

"Is there a problem?" Dr. Sandy asks, pausing at our station on her way to the examination room. Dr. Sandy doesn't really like or trust Sly. The only reason she gave him a chance was because of my recommendation. She's regretted hiring him ever since, and needs constant reassurance. "I don't care what he wears, but are you sure that boy's capable?"

"Of course," I say, "he's a computer whiz."

"Is he on crack?"

"My God, no," I say.

There is a threat insinuated into her syrupy voice. "Well, Rocky. If you say so. He's *your* friend. Just remind him to keep his dick in his pants."

"Is there a problem?"

"No problem," I answer quickly. I get busy punching God-knows-what on the keyboard, acting like I can retrieve the deleted account. "No problem," Sly echoes softly. Dr. Sandy gazes at him with suspicion, then hurries off to her waiting client. She thinks "client" sounds more positive than "patient."

"Bitch needs a good fuck," Sly mutters.

"You need one too," I say, sick of his shit. Sly's been unbearable since Severine was deported to France.

It's a busy day for the Center. Dr. Sandy's raking it in, starting at $150 minimum for a brief consultation. The phone rings nonstop. "Good morning, SoHo Pain and Stress —" Sly puts them all on hold. He's scanning the personals in this week's *Village Voice* and can't be bothered paying attention to anything else.

Music, dope, and kinky sex constitute the Holy Trinity for Sly, who could never get used to the concept of responsibility. "Don't be surprised if I don't show up tomorrow," Sly warns me every day when he punches out.

I've got three more hours to go. Should I let Keiko and her new love buy me dinner? Should I let Elvis and Brian know once and for all I want to disband? Fuck this sleazy music business, I'll say, I'm going to devote my life exclusively to the alleviation of physical pain and spiritual misery. Under the guidance and tutelage of the practical yet passionate Dr. Sandy, alleviation seems like a sure thing. Plus I'm guaranteed a steady salary, fringe benefits, and the soothing structure of a daily schedule. Isn't that what we all need? The SoHo Pain and Stress Center. Tapeworms, herbal enemas, slick haircuts, nine to five.

My frantic hysteria gives way to calm. I am like Voltaire in the wheelchair, serene and still. The computer glows back at me. It doesn't matter if the account has been lost forever. Dr. Sandy won't miss it; Sly and I won't be fired. This is New York City, after all. Capital of pain and desire. Dr. Sandy's Center will never want for clients.

The phone keeps ringing. I can't stand it anymore and pick up. "Hello. Sorry to keep you waiting. May I help you?"

Aquamarine. I am mesmerized by aquamarine swirls on the computer screen. Darting lizards, fish blowing bubbles, flying toasters with wings.

Computer lingo, Sly gleefully pointed out his first day on the job, is pure poetry. "Check it out, Rocky."

Cancel. Delete. Erase.
Restart.
Sleep. Shut down.
Quit.
Empty trash.
Help. Go to . . .
Find.

Border. Show. View.
Save.
Save as.
Save.
Don't save.
Don't you have a better idea?

The text on-screen taunts me.

B Train

The train is late, the train is packed, the train stinks of vomit. *I got it bad, and that ain't good.* The junkie sitting across from Rocky is singing, his quivering voice liquid with anguish. The crystal-line alto beauty of Hector Lavoe. *Aguanila. Everyone comes from a small town, even if it's only in their minds.* . . . Next to him, a tense young woman and two frisky little girls in ruffled party dresses. The junkie looks about forty but could be younger. He is shirtless, can barely keep his eyes open, scratching at his bare chest. The girls climb all over him, treating him like a comfort-able piece of furniture. The young woman calls him Bobby. "Bobby, whatchu play games wid me for? I never play games wid you." She's resentful, she doesn't give a shit about anyone else on the train. "Talk to me, *jíbarito.*" The junkie's head rolls around as he sings. *I got it baaad . . . and that ain't good.* The young woman's eyes are blazing. "Muthafucka, talk to me. I'm talkin' to *you.*" The little girls giggle hysterically, scrambling all over the junkie, jumping on and off his lap. The woman swats at them like mosquitoes, yelling, "Be patient! You have to learn to be patient!"

Sly and Elvis keep buggin' me. They want session types to back me up, flashy women in spandex with booming gospel voices, big hair, and plenty of attitude. "Enough of this arty shit. It doesn't work."

"I'm a poet," I remind them.

"People want something they can dance to," Sly says.

We trudge from one dead-end gig to another, bickering and demoralized, and still no record deal in sight. Our indie single never went anywhere, never got picked up. From Manila, Luz writes letters dripping with malice: "So when are we going to get autographed copies of your platinum hit? Better hurry. We have rappers now in Manila. Rapping in Tagalog, can you beat that? Your nephew and nieces keep asking me about their famous auntie. She's not exactly famous, I tell them. She's *notorious*."

This weekend, we are headlining once again at CBGB's — fifty other bands on the bill, no guarantee, no guest list, no free drinks. At three sets a night, it's slave labor. I've heard of clubs where bands actually pay to perform, but this situation isn't too many shades better. I complain to my ineffectual yet strangely loyal manager. "Is this the best you can do?" He doesn't even bother to answer. Maybe it's the heat that's responsible, frying up our brains, what's left of us as decent human beings.

Elvis and I lug guitars and amps in ninety-five degrees of humidity so thick that it hurts to breathe. We are late for rehearsal, distracted by the whooping war cries and mystic babble of dealers on the street. Sonic frenzy, inspiration for more eerie songs.

"Three-five-seven, my kinda heaven." A young, preppy white man in suit and tie crawls through a hole in the wall of a gutted-out building. "Didja see that?" I nudge Elvis. Fuck Galileo. The world is definitely flat. Everyone's tainted and falling off the edge. Reality's finally outdone the movies.

Investment banker. Horn player. Cop.

Elvis dismisses him with a shrug.

"Toi-let, toi-let, China white, China white." We glide past throngs of junkies and crackheads shuffling back and forth in a pathetic ghost dance. A car with Jersey plates slows down and is descended upon by locusts. It's a New York City cliché. What's next? A van of rabbis cruising for transvestites to give them blow jobs?

"Fuckin' too hot. We should've canceled rehearsal," Elvis mutters.

"We got a gig this Friday —"

"Fucking so what." Elvis wipes the sweat off his face with a dirty bandanna, then ties it around his forehead. He blames me for all of it, but I don't care anymore. We are not going to fight today.

"Toilet, toilet." A child in oversize clothes hisses in our direction.

Elvis hesitates, tempted.

"Come on, I ain't got all day." The boy shifts his weight from one enormous sneakered foot to another.

Elvis flashes one of his charming smiles at the boy, who is unmoved. "Don't waste my time, China man."

"It's later than you think," I say, as I pull Elvis away from him.

The child is furious. "There won't be a next time, slant-eyed muthafuckas."

I turn to cuss at him, but he's vanished. His grown man's rage is impressive. "God, what a little shit. He probably had a gun hidden in those baggy pants. How old could he have been?"

Elvis chuckles. "Old. At least eight or nine — tops."

"That was one of the stupidest things you've ever done."

"It was *interesting*. Didn't you think that kid was interesting?"

"Stupid," I repeat, "stupid. *What if? Rat poison! Clorox! Baby laxative! Horse manure!*"

Elvis Chang kisses me, but it is a patronizing kiss, full of hatred. "You're such a nice Catholic girl," he says, "that's why I love you."

I slap him — not too hard, but hard enough.

A spidery woman the color of ash blocks our path. She has the same solemn Modigliani face as the angry child. Perhaps she is his long-gone mother. I brush past her, ignoring the cup she holds out. Elvis exhales a deep sigh. "What's the hurry?" he asks, annoyed. "Did she spook you?" He rummages through his pockets for change, which he drops in the woman's cup. She doesn't react. I set his amp on the sidewalk and plop myself down, sulking. I don't know why I choose to remain in New York, why I don't go screaming back to my fading mother in San Francisco, my lost brother in La-La Land, or to the tropical banshees that await me in Manila. When Elvis and I were lovers, I once asked him, "Is this the country where you want to die?" He admitted, "It's all I know, but I'll take Montana." He was teasing me then, but now he's itching for a fight. People step cautiously around us. "This is the last gig I'm doing," he says, just as we get to the entrance of the studio. Sly is waiting in the unwelcoming, fluorescent-lit room that passed for a reception area. We can hear somebody shouting a song through the cheaply soundproofed walls. "Better late than never," Sly says, without much conviction. "How you lovebirds doin'?"

"Never," I say.

The story of the mysterious ghetto blaster goes like this. A black Lincoln Continental with tinted windows pulls up to the stoplight. The passenger door swings open and a woman falls out, clutching a baby like a shield to her chest. She runs. She's an uptown girl, very young and very pretty, Sly's ideal type. Her name is like a song: *Shaquanna. LaShante.* Her ornately painted eyes are bright with fear. She runs past me shrieking curses in Spanish and English, the baby bouncing in her arms and whimpering in protest. A young man, even prettier than the young woman, leaps with grace from the car and chases after her toward the abandoned building. He is a lithe, menacing dancer and this is the end of a tragic romance.

The way the story goes, the way Elvis liked to tell it much later to anyone who cared to listen, is that he saved my life that day. *Run, my savior, Elvis, whispers in my ear. Run, run, run. Don't look, don't get caught in a cross fire, don't be stupid.* Stupid has never been cool in the king of cool's book. He grabs my arm and pulls me into the ex-priest Don Arturo's bodega. Even from the shelter of the cozy bodega perfumed by rotting mangoes, the bodega cluttered with bags of plantain chips and tins of Argentinian corned beef, the sound of the woman's cries is clearly audible. Her voice crackles: *Never Never Never No You Sonuvabitch Goddammit You Can't.*

Don Arturo recites a prayer in Latin. I shut my eyes tight, burying my face in Elvis Chang's bony shoulder. Five firecracker pops explode in succession. Sharp, festive, and quite ordinary.

We join the swelling crowd gawking at the corpse of the young woman, sprawled on the sidewalk in front of the gutted-out building. Her ornately painted eyes are open in a final, startled gaze. One high-heeled boot has slipped off her bloody foot. The baby in the pink jumpsuit with the pink bunny ears and cotton puff tail is unharmed. I assume it is a girl, with a name like her mother's, a name like a song: *Tanyika, Njeri. LaWanda.* The baby crawls slowly and determinedly away from her mother, toward us. We are horrified and fascinated. We do nothing. Finally, Don Arturo pushes his way through the crowd and snatches up the baby, who settles placidly into his arms.

The legend of the ghetto blaster became a song about a wolf. "*Businessmen junkies seek a caress. / Schoolgirl junkies in Catholic dress, / Unemployed junkies with tropical eyes, / Blond Republicans in slum disguise. / They flock to their savior on the crowded street. / He gives them his sales pitch. / Wolf loves meat.*"

A horn line follows, ragged, funky, and mean. Fingers snapping, menacing and cool. It verges on camp, but we do it with a straight face. That's why it worked. Like Uncle Marlon said after he saw us perform at Madam Wong's in LA: "Very funny. Very creepy. Very, very *West Side Story*." He got the joke, and he was proud of me. After Madam Wong's, it was back to Uncle Marlon's orchid-filled house to heat up a batch of my mother's party-mix lumpia and my uncle's famous *adobo* and rice. We gossiped, laughed, pigged out, until the sun came up. Filipino soul food, Filipino therapy, the best cure for hangovers and general spiritual malaise, according to Uncle Marlon.

"He could be a surgeon, / he could be a stunt man, / A soldier of fortune leading a band, / An elegant hoodlum / On the crowded street / Attracting his prey, / wolf loves meat."

The song ends with Sly and me chanting softly: *"Three / five / seven, / my kinda heaven. / Twenty / twenty, / golden nugget too. / A cheap hit, / A sterile kit. / Do you want it? / Wolf loves meat."*

A Generation of Hairdos

The sympathetic-looking man kills time at the bar until the rest of the band straggles into CBGB's. The man's face is kind — not pretty, not cruel — but surprising. I like looking at him. Apparently he's important enough for Sly to fling his dreadlocks about and try to impress. "Those were tough times in Detroit, man. If it weren't for music, I'd probably be dead. Ever been to Detroit?" The man ignores me, giving Sly his undivided attention. "I like Detroit," he says. Sly's on a roll, name-dropping. "Linda McCartney? Fuck. Paul paid people to buy her photos."

I'm dying to interrupt and say, "My heart is breaking and I sure could use a diversion." Instead I ask, "So, Jake. How much you gonna cost us?"

Sly is exuberant. "Baby, this is an investment you won't regret. He'll deliver the slickest live tape ever —"

I hold out my hand. "Actually, my name's not Baby, but Rocky. Rocky Rivera. And you're Jake —"

"Montano."

"A.k.a. Mr. Acid Mix, hottest soundman and recording engineer in New York City. C'mon, I ain't lying," Sly gushes. "He did Bad Brains. He did Kid Creole. He did Debbie Harry.— who I would not mind doin' myself." Heh-heh-heh. For Sly, the world boils down to one, big, dirty innuendo.

"I know who he is," I say.

Mr. Acid Mix clears his throat. "Where's the rest of your band? Sound check was scheduled for — what time is it now? I can't wait around forever. Got to get back to the studio before your gig tonight."

"Give it another five minutes — please." Sly disappears to make a phone call.

"I worked your gig at Armageddon," Jake says.

"Armageddon was a disaster."

It's his turn to be amused. "I found it very interesting."

"What the fuck is that supposed to mean? I hate that word, *interesting*. Sounds like a euphemism for *shitty* to me."

Sly reappears just in time to overhear me. "Uh-oh. Don't piss her off, man."

Jake keeps his eyes on me. "I meant — the band was ambitious, and I liked that. Like maybe you lived up to your hairdos. And then I thought sometimes you were way over the audience's head, and that was okay too."

"Way over the audience's head? You mean like there were four hundred–something people with one collective head and I was flying right over it?"

Sly does his bug-eyed rendition of Mantan Moreland. "Uh-oh, Massa. You in big trouble now!" Then he gives Jake a reassuring grin. "Don't leave, my man. Relax. Lemme buy you another drink. Word is, the band'll be here any minute."

I find myself making edgy come-ons when our sets are finally over. It's after three in the morning, and we're all packed up. Elvis is sitting at a table flirting with two expensive-looking Japanese girls. Their blond duckling haircuts are more radical than mine, which makes me jealous. The rest of the band is tucked away in the basement, greedily inhaling line after line of Sly's Bolivian cocktails, while I'm stuck upstairs at the bar, waiting to get paid and sparring with Mr. Acid Mix. "So, Jake, did we live up to our hairdos tonight?"

"You certainly did."

"I think I know what you mean about hairdos, but what exactly do you mean?"

"I overheard this artist accuse your generation of being nothing but a bunch of hairdos. A lot of talk, but no action."

I study Jake's own affected convict/POW do and try not to sound defensive. "What about *your* generation?"

"Just as guilty."

I'd like to rub my skull up against his. It's been about, what, six months of self-imposed celibacy? I really should take him home. Sex with a near stranger, oh, boy! He's a perfect candidate. Safe (I trust my instincts), but also mysterious enough to provide the right element of suspense. My apartment's in chaos, but I don't give a shit. I don't think he would, either. "You know, you're like a movie, Jake. *Escape from the Bronx*. Starring That Rugged Vietnam Veteran Soundman With His 128-Pound Kevlar, Bullet-proof Vest."

"Yeah? Did you write the script?"

"Maybe."

"How'd you guess that's what I'm wearing?"

"Elvis told me."

"He played a great last set tonight. You did, too."

"Yeah, well. It might be his last gig." I paused. "His solos were self-indulgent." One of the Japanese girls from Mars lights Elvis's cigarette. "I hate solos, don't you? Ego, ego! Drum solos, especially. Long, loud, and meaningless. I have asked Sly to keep his soloing to a minimum. Flute solos are the absolute worst."

Flynn, the old beatnik manager, surfaces from the basement. He hobbles over and hands me a stack of twenties and tens. I point to the powdery residue coating his nostrils. "Wanna head-line for us on Halloween?" Flynn asks as he wipes the back of his hand across his nose. He pours me a double of cheap, brand X tequila as a gesture of thanks. "I prefer Gold," I say, smiling sweetly and sliding the untouched drink back at him.

I'm glad I'm sober. I count the bills extra carefully, then count them once more, just to be sure. "Damn. Wasn't the club packed for all three sets?"

Flynn shrugs. "You have to split the door with another band, remember?"

"That band sucked. Plus the audience was ninety-nine per-cent mine."

Flynn shrugs again.

"I don't know why you bother with so many bands on the bill," I mutter. The old man hobbles away. "Fuck Jack Kerouac, fuck if

I ever work here again," but I know I will. Halloween, did he say? Headlining? That means a higher percentage of the gross.

How low I've sunk. I should've negotiated a cut of the bar. An impossible concession, but I should've tried anyway. A point of pride. My audience knows how to drink and how to tip. Where the hell is my unreliable manager? He should kick that old scumbag's butt on my behalf, just on g.p.

Jake stares at me with concern. "It's okay if you can't pay me."

I throw two twenties grandly on the counter. "I know we promised you more, but take this for now."

"Thanks," he says.

"I believe in paying my debts," I say, feeling prim and ridiculous.

"What's that Filipino thing? *Utang* . . ." Jake hesitates. His pronunciation isn't bad.

"Don't tell me you picked up Tagalog in Nam." Why do I sound so hostile? Maybe it's Sly's nasty coke. Plus the realization that we have worked all night for a measly forty dollars apiece is bringing out the worst in me.

"Nope."

"Don't tell me. You had a Filipino maid." When he doesn't answer, I keep at it. "Your family had a houseboy. A gardener?"

"Lighten up." Jake turns away from me in disgust. He adjusts the bag of recording equipment onto his shoulder, buttoning up his jacket. "It's been a pleasure," he says.

Words come flying out of my mouth. "Don't. Really. Please. I didn't mean it. Really."

Mr. Acid Mix and I are in my bed. "I hate sex," I say, throwing one leg over his thigh. His penis hardens in my hand. "Don't touch me. You smell bad. I smell bad. What do you think you're gonna do with that thing between your legs?" I kiss him some more.

He adds to my litany of denial: "Sex — overrated. This bed's for sleeping . . ."

I take him up on it. "Let's fuck first, then go to church. Let's go to confession. Talk dirty to me in Latin. I love dead languages. I'd like to see you at the altar, on your knees. Don't whisper 'I love you'—"

He finishes the sentence for me. "Whisper 'Forgive me.'"

"Forgive me," I whisper.

Very interesting. I'm actually enjoying myself. He fucks with a different kind of passion than Elvis, who fucks like he has something to prove. This one's a lot less angry, more tender and cautious. For now, anyway. Maybe it's got something to do with his age. Jake's probably older than I think. I'm confused.

I miss Elvis. Don't I love Elvis? Of course I do! But I'm *enjoying* myself. Jake's body puts me off a little. It's so muscular and mannish. Almost too strong. Elvis was eternally a boy. I like boys' bodies, but I find Jake's worn-out face compelling. "So what are you? Cuban and Sicilian?"

"Who gives a shit?" Jake licks my nipple.

"Don't." I push him away. "My mother once said that some women's breasts hang like old socks." I touch one of mine. "What do you think?"

"You're afraid of your body," Jake says.

"I'm a lapsed Catholic rebel. And you're a Catholic rebel vet with a bulletproof vest," I tell him. He drinks from a bottle, spitting out the icy water between my legs. I burst out laughing.

"Don't talk anymore," he says, entering me again. When I start to protest, he goes "Shh, shh" very softly.

I forget that my cheap answering machine died from abuse just yesterday, and I can't imagine why the phone keeps ringing. Jake doesn't seem disturbed by it. He's buried his face in my neck, lost in the slow, deliberate rhythms of his lovemaking. Poor Jake. As for me — I'm too easily distracted. Maybe this has all been a mistake. I won't fuck him again, but does this mean he won't work with the band? The phone rings five or six times, then abruptly stops. I tense up, anticipating more of that awful jangling sound. There. The phone rings again. What nerve.

Either it's Keiko calling from Cape Town (slut — she's got a new lover), or Elvis checking up on me (slut — probably in bed with those chic Tokyo punkettes). Ring, ring, ring. Jake groans with pleasure. I groan back. What if it's my mother? She never sleeps anymore and phones me at all hours of the day or night, *to chat*. Perhaps my brother's been found dead. That's it. Enough. I turn over and unplug the phone.

Stop Ssscreaming

Jake was a man without a clear history. No family left to speak of. The aunt who raised him had been quite old when she died in a nursing home in Queens. His father abandoned Jake and his mother when Jake was born, and was said to have remarried and retired in Miami. Jake had a vague memory of his mother, a young, broken woman who died when he was five or six.

"Aren't you curious about your father?" I asked.

"Sometimes," Jake said. "Sometimes I fantasize taking a trip to Miami and surprising him. Maybe killing him," Jake added with a chuckle.

"Do you hate him?" I enjoyed asking Jake all kinds of questions. He was a cautious man, but not afraid to reveal himself.

"I blame him for leaving my mother, letting her die like she did. It's easy to blame him. But —" He seemed conflicted and stopped himself.

I finished the sentence for him. "But you're not sure."

Jake sighed. "How could I be?"

After the last gig Jake worked on as our soundman, he came up to me backstage between sets. I was resting on a pile of debris that the club owner called a sofa. "Can I make a suggestion? Stop screaming when you sing, Rocky. Singing isn't about screaming."

God, I was tired. "Maybe that's all I want to do. Scream."

"When you start with a climax, there's nowhere left to go. Think dynamics. Horizontal, vertical, up, down. Soft, soft whisper, then . . . surprise us."

"Just give me reverb, okay? That's all I ask. Superior microphones. Don't let me pop my *p*'s, fleas. You know Filipinos — or Pilipinos, whichever you prefer — are renowned for switching *p*'s to *f*'s, and vice versa."

"You mean like: Are you fucking your suitcase por a pun-pilled holiday?"

"Exactly. I don't go anywhere without reverb on my voice. Just a little, not too much. I know what I need. It's not about my voice, really. I don't claim to be Aretha, but with the right accessories, I can sound like Sade. The writing's mine, though. You can't fake that."

"How come you scream so much? Alienates the audience, damages ears."

My voice dripped with sarcasm. "Talk to Elvis about that. He's the composer. The arranger. He's my melodic half, and he loves it when I scream."

"Have you ever been in love?"

"Like I said. Elvis loves it when I scream."

"That was serious, wasn't it?"

"It's over, but we still work together."

"I lived with a woman for six years. Then she got sick of New York, and me. Moved back to Seattle."

"An artist?"

"No. Does that make her less interesting to you?"

"It could."

"How sad."

"I'm honest about it, at least. So what does she do?"

"She was, *is*, a physical therapist. Works with a lot of stroke victims. That's how we met. She took care of my aunt."

"Do you miss her?"

"She fell in love with someone at her job. Another woman. They live together on one of those islands around Seattle."

"You miss her?"

"She still writes me, you know. These sort of wonderful, detailed letters. I think about her often. You'd like her."

Los Blah-Blahs: Two

I glance over his shoulder: EDUARDO ZUNIGA. *A laminated photo of a solemn man with burning eyes.*

"Should we avoid Fifth Avenue?" I ask him.

"Fifth Avenue? Why?"

"I dunno. Isn't there a parade today? Puerto Rican Day parade."

"Ah, the parade."

He seems amused but says nothing else and keeps driving. My reaction to his nonreaction is stomach-churning anxiety. If he goes the long way, the wrong way, the complicated Lexington-Madison-First-Second-Avenue-across-Twenty-third way, the Broadway-make-a-right-on-Fourteenth-take-FDR-don't-take-FDR way, I'll be fucked. I have enough on me, just enough. Including tip. Fifteen percent, exactly. That's if he doesn't try to fuck with me. I think I know the quick way, but I don't want to be too pushy with this guy. I've had cabbies ask me to get out of their cabs for nothing, for maybe reminding them as politely as I could to slow down, please, I'm not in that much of a hurry to die yet.

And then there are the other kind, the kind who keep gazing into the rear-view mirror and combing their hair, who have eyes only for their blow-dried coifs, who don't care if you fight or fuck in the back seat, as long as you pay.

I try the deferential approach. "What do you think, sir? Should we take Park Avenue downtown, then cross on Ninth?" My father, I want to tell this cabdriver named Eduardo Zuniga, was once so respected that he had no name in the Philippines. Everyone just called him "Sir." I also want to say: Eduardo Zuniga is a poet's name. But I don't.

"You want Park, I'll take Park."

I sink back and relax, just a little. I am so grateful that he didn't bite my head off, I don't even mind the fumes emanating from the strawberry-scented deodorizer shaped like a four-leaf clover and dangling from his rear-view mirror. His dashboard is a shrine to saints, archangels, and virgins. Saint Christopher, Santa Barbara. Archangel Michael brandishing a fiery sword at a prone Lucifer. All plastic and magnetized. My uncle Marlon would feel right at home.

"You know that story by García Márquez?" Eduardo Zuniga doesn't bother to wait for my answer. "This dictator rules the country with an iron hand, see. There's the usual: unemployment, hunger, suppression of civil liberties. See? And the people are getting restless. So the worried military runs over to the palace to seek the dictator's advice. 'General, there's rioting in the streets. What shall we do?' The general is confident and calm. 'No problem,' he tells the army. 'Just give them a parade, boys. Give them a parade.' See?"

"Sí."

"Where I'm from, we read a lot. You from here?"

"No."

"Ah. I didn't think so."

"I'm from the Philippines. You know?"

"Of course I know. Colonized the same year as Puerto Rico, see? 1898."

"And here we are."

"Here we are. Need a receipt?"

"Yeah. Great."

"Remember."

"Yeah?"

"Wherever you go, give them a parade."

"You too."

Chonggo

Keiko rubs her hairy belly. Lights up a Kool. "Pregnant *again*? Damn, Rocky. I guess you as fertile as the fertile crescent."

I laugh. "I don't even throw up."

"Git outta here, no symptoms at all?"

"Thought I had gas or something, except it never goes away. Period's late, of course, but I've never been the most regular person. I can't stand the smell of fried food, and I'm always throwing crap out of my refrigerator, perfectly okay crap, but I can't stand the sight or smell of it. But no nausea, no headaches, none of the regular stuff," I say with pride. For once, Keiko is all ears. I point to my throbbing breasts. "Dead giveaways, hard as rocks. Just like the last time."

"Just think, now you've got cleavage." Keiko smirks. "Whose is it?" When I don't answer: "Does Elvis know? What about what's-his-name?"

"Jake," I snarl. She knows Jake's name all right, even tried taking him home the night she met him. "I think Jake suspects —"

"I think Jake's cool," Keiko says, casually.

"Yeah, I noticed."

"Reminds me of Arnaldo. You gonna keep it?"

"What?"

"The baby."

Dr. Sandy recommends a downtown midwife, Graciela Delgado. Graciela works out of the Harmonic Alternative Ob-Gyn Women's Clinic, a cozy little sanctuary located ten floors up from the Pain and Stress Center. A majestic receptionist spots me tiptoeing out of the elevator. Clearly I don't want to be here.

"This your first visit?" she inquires, as she skillfully navigates the busy phone lines. "Good morning. Harmonic Alternative, please hold." The name ODESSA POUNDS is pinned to her flashy satin blouse. "I'm sorry to keep you waiting." Her voice is crisp and mellifluous, which makes me wonder if Odessa ever did time at Ding-A-Ling Switchboard.

"What day is good for you?" She croons into the phone, while handing me a clipboard with forms and a ballpoint pen attached. I am riveted by her red clawlike fingernails and the impossibly dainty heart-shaped rhinestone at the center of each one. "Make sure you get those back to me as soon as possible." Odessa Pounds gives me a sharp look.

I slip into the only chair left in the waiting area, feeling like a bratwurst encased in my snug leather jacket and bursting jeans. Women with awesome basketball bellies surround me. In a matter of weeks, I'll look just like them, waddling like a penguin, my back swayed and my distended balloon of a belly leading the way. Can I manage alone, or is there still time to abort? A couple of lumpy, husband types are marginally present, their noses buried in Elmore Leonard or William Gibson. What makes me think I can handle the bloody mess of childbirth. What makes me think I'm capable of handling being any sort of mother at all? My own mother hasn't exactly set a warm, loving example. She isn't the least bit curious about the grandchildren she already has, back in Manila. I myself have never spent time mooning over children, nor do I think all babies are automatically cuddly or precious. Luz once sent each of us a snapshot of her middle child, taken hours after she was born. She resembled a hairy, wrinkled watermelon.

A gray-haired, late-fortyish woman with spooky eyes and the biggest belly of them all smiles at me. I make an effort to smile back. A toddler with a runny nose and the same pale eyes crouches by the gray-haired woman's feet. I can't help noticing how the gray-haired woman's sneakers are filthy and worn. Her child clings to a ratty Barbie doll, sucking listlessly on her thumb. "Poor baby's got a little temperature," the gray-haired woman explains to the room. A few women cluck and nod in sympathy, I among them. The men keep reading. The child's face suddenly crumples in despair, and she hurls her Barbie violently to the floor. The women in the room stare at the child with pained expressions. "Have you tried giving her Children's Tylenol?" someone asks.

"There, there," the gray-haired woman murmurs, enveloping her daughter in a huge embrace. "There there."

PLEASE CHECK THE APPROPRIATE BOX

Have you ever had:

(If the answer is yes, please explain below.)

◻ Diabetes	◻ Chicken pox	◻ Allergies
◻ Rubella	◻ Measles	◻ Congenital heart disease
◻ Tuberculosis	◻ Asthma	◻ Venereal disease
◻ Mumps	◻ Cancer	◻ H.I.V./Other

Graciela Delgado is in her thirties. Her closely cropped, hennaed Afro frames her chiseled brown face devoid of any make-up. She peers at me curiously. "Where are you from?"

Here we go again, I groan to myself. Maybe I should act dumb, and say "Manhattan." Why are people always trying to figure out where I'm from? Mexican, Japanese, Lakota Sioux. You name it, I've been it. And Filipinos are just as bad with each other. Excuse me, *Pilipino ka ba?* Polite enough, but nosy. My mother and Auntie Fely used to drive me nuts back in San Francisco. They'd approach their victims on streetcars, at Macy's, at Woolworth's on Powell Street, at some corny souvenir stand on Fisherman's Wharf, give them apologetic little smiles, then, "Excuse me, are you a Filipino?"

"Why is it so important?" I once asked ask Auntie Fely. "So what if they're Filipino?" Auntie Fely frowned. "Ay, *anak*." She clucked. "If you have to ask . . ."

"God, Ma." I'd try to disappear while walking next to her. Or stand there with a bored, patronizing expression as she and Auntie Fely chattered away in Tagalog or Ilokano with their brand-new "friends." They ignored me. If Uncle Bas was around, he'd join in, too. The people my mother and aunt approached never seemed to mind. They were often thrilled and grateful to meet a friendly *kababayan*. Voltaire wasn't around for these confrontations; it was I, Miss Too Cool Teenage Amerikaka, who was always dying of embarrassment.

"I'm from the Philippines," I explain to Graciela Delgado, steeling myself for more stupid questions.

"Ow!" I yelp, as Graciela gently pinches one of my tender breasts. She writes something down on my chart.

She seems mildly disappointed. "Really? I thought you might be Puerto Rican. I'm from Ponce. You ever been there? Lay back."

I do as she says. I hate having my legs wide open and my crotch exposed to the world, my feet stuck in those sinister stirrups. I hate urine tests, blood tests, and gynecological exams, period. There must be a better way to do this. "Relax," Graciela commands brusquely. "Now scoot down. A little lower, please." I flinch. There go those icy, metal clamps. Her gloved hand is inside me. "Gonna feel a little cold, no big deal, I'd say you're about nine weeks." Poke, poke, prod, prod. Thank you, Graciela. A little Vaseline, a little telltale knot in the womb. I recoil and bite my lower lip. I remember other hands, even less gentle, probing my insides. "Okeydokey," Graciela Delgado chirps. "You can get dressed now."

Her office is filled with diplomas and family photographs. An ornate oval pewter frame holds a sepia portrait of a prosperous, formally dressed, nineteenth-century couple. A color five-by-seven of Graciela on the beach is prominently displayed on her desk. She is posed between a handsome man in a Red Sox baseball cap and a skinny little boy with missing front teeth. They are all wearing bathing suits and smiling for the camera.

Graciela studies me with a look of grave professional concern. "Are you trying to do this all by yourself?"

So. I want to call Elvis but I don't. I call Jake instead.

* * *

We meet at Shine's for happy hour. Jake plays Martha and the Vandellas' "Heat Wave" on the jukebox. He knows I love the sound of Martha's compelling voice, and the Vandellas' determined fuck-you chorus. Jake recorded the band's speeded-up version at CBGB's. It's one of the only covers we do, our tribute to Motown — rockabilly clashed with psychedelic funk — very funny, fast, and loud.

He orders us both shots of tequila. "Maybe you shouldn't drink," he says when the shots arrive.

I order another round.

"Wanna have dinner? You should eat."

"Not hungry." All his shoulds are starting to annoy me. I bum a cigarette from Shine just to prove a point.

"I'm here for you," Jake says. "Whatever you want to do."

I was afraid of that. The night is young, but after two tequilas and too many awkward gaps in the conversation, I'm feeling old and tired, probably a lot like the gray-haired lady at the clinic. Jake and I promise to meet again tomorrow. I wonder if I've made a big mistake. I go home and call Uncle Marlon in LA. I can always count on him for sympathy — but all I get is his machine.

After several deep breaths, I dial my mother in San Francisco.

"Hmmm," she says. "A baby."

"I think I'll go ahead and keep it. What do *you* think?"

"Sounds like you're talking about a pair of shoes. Is he black?"

"Goddammit."

"Hoy, don't swear at me. I'm asking you an obvious question."

"Goddammit, Ma. So fuckin' what? We're *all* black."

She hangs up, then calls me back after five long minutes, collect.

Milagros speaks slowly and deliberately, as if to an idiot child: "For your information. *Hija,* darling. *Anak ko.* We've never been black. That's preposterous. And I don't deserve your contempt."

"You asked an irrelevant, offensive question."

"Ha."

"Have you heard from Voltaire?"

"No one's heard from Voltaire."

"I'd like to tell him. How's Auntie Fely?"

"Working like a dog. When are you going to tell your father?"

She surprises me. I haven't thought about, written, or heard from my father in months.

"He's dying," she blurts out suddenly.

"How do you know?"

"I always know. I called Luz and she confirmed it. Then I ran into Patsy Lozano at Macy's in Union Square, just yesterday. She's visiting from Manila —"

"Who's Patsy Lozano?"

"Patsy Lozano," my mother repeats, agitated. "Senator Lozano's ex." She gets agitated when I deliberately act ignorant. "Patsy said your *tatay* is back in the hospital for chemo. Didn't you know Patsy's daughter?"

"That was ages ago," I say.

"She married that Kunstler boy," Milagros adds, trying to be helpful. "The one who was after you. What's his name?"

I haven't forgotten. Baby Lozano was another Baby in my life. We'd gone to the same school in Manila. Our Lady of Perpetual Sorrow. Baby was a very rich girl. Richer than Jose Mari Kunstler. Though she could barely read and write, the nuns kept giving her passing grades. We had nothing in common, but poor Baby must've found me amusing. She invited me over to play when she was bored, which was often. I knew better than to invite her over to my house, which would be much too modest for her tastes. I didn't mind her in small doses. The vulgar grandeur of her life fascinated me.

The Lozanos had their very own air-conditioned chapel, a swimming pool, an orchid garden, a uniformed staff of twenty, gallons of fresh mango ice cream in the walk-in freezer, and bodyguards. They were also famous for owning the first Porsche in the Philippines. Baby's father ordered the car all the way from

Italy as a birthday present for his only son, Baby's elder brother, Vip. It was silver and looked amphibious. Soon after his twenty-first birthday, the Porsche was crushed flat and Vip was decapitated in a collision with a truck transporting a life-size, memorial statue of Gabriela Silang on a horse. Vip was posthumously dubbed "the James Dean of Manila." The unnamed truck driver died instantly too, leaving behind a family of eight on the island of Negros, but no one gave him or the statue much thought.

I never met Vip, whose pretty face was enshrined in framed photographs strategically placed all over the Lozano mansion. On top of the unused grand piano in the living room, in the hallway leading upstairs, on the glass countertop of the vanity table in Baby's frilly bedroom. She worshiped him.

"My older brother's name begins with V," I had said.

Baby responded with a blank stare. "But he's not dead."

Baby inherited Vip's pet spider monkey, Chonggo, an unhappy creature with huge, sad eyes. Chained by one foot to his perch under a palm tree, Chonggo made anxious, grinding noises as he watched us splash around in the swimming pool. A bridge inlaid with Spanish tiles connected one end of the pool to a shell-encrusted grotto housing the Virgin Mary. A small glass-encased photo of Vip standing next to his sports car lay at the Blessed Virgin's feet. The grotto had been erected on a small, circular cement island in the middle of the water. Sometimes we would have lunch on the island, and sometimes we would pray to the plaster Madonna for the soul of Baby's dead brother. To play, to pray, or to eat depended on Baby Lozano's absurd whims. The monkey would gnash his teeth and hop from one foot to the other, singing in awful desperation.

How could I ever forget?

"Too bad," I say to my mother, years later. "I just don't remember."

"Well, Patsy remembers you."

"That's nice of her. Don't worry. I'll write Papa a letter."

"Didn't you hear me? Your father's going to die. Letters take forever. You'd better call him at the hospital. Or call your sister. She'll deliver the message."

"This is the last thing he needs to hear."

"How can he criticize you? You're such a modern girl, and he's a cheapskate bigamist."

"Jesusfuckingchrist. It's been almost twenty years. Haven't you gotten over that yet?"

"Watch your filthy mouth."

I can't resist saying it. "I'm your daughter, aren't I?"

Mother. The monkey invades my birth canal. *Chonggo. Unggoy.* Fu Lang Chang. Face of Elvis, overripe lips and wise eyes. Wiseguy. Venus. Curious George. Caimito de Guayabal. My volcanic breasts engorged with blood and milk. Milk thinned by water. By metal. By fire. By mud. Dainty black old-lady hands. Monkey paws, clasped in prayer. Diamond teardrops. Lemongrass. Mustard grass. Red dirt, oozing gaseous vapors. Umbilical cord. Venus. Won't you be my melancholy monkey? I want to go home now. Shove the baby back in. I'm not ready yet. Mother. It was like this. Equatorial heat. Bliss. Gecko tongue. Twilight.

Great Wall of China

The night Jake Montano proposed we move in together, we were snowed in at Shine's, the jukebox playing "Oooh, Baby, Baby" by Smokey Robinson. An oldie even then, but beloved by all who were stranded at the bar. The blizzard put us all in a playful mood. Sly and I attempted a backbreaker tango. He dipped me so far back that my head practically touched the floor. There was a woman my mother's age who'd been sitting by herself all night, mink coat carelessly draped on the stool next to her, chain-smoking Virginia Slims and sipping cognac. She watched us dance. "Git down, chirrun."

Elvis and Jake were buying each other drinks and singing along with the jukebox. Keiko, Shine, and Angelo were taking turns in the dark, snorting lines straight off the marble counter. Keiko had kissed and made up with them after the last deranged episode involving Arnaldo and the cops. Angelo chimed in with his impressive Philly falsetto to Smokey's bittersweet "ooh ooh ooh." Sly let go, and I dropped to the floor. Just like that. He slid down too, right next to me, and started snoring. I wasn't hurt, just startled. Jake grinned. Sobered me right up. "Want another brandy? Cold outside." He helped me off the floor.

"Let's go to breakfast," Elvis said. I looked over to where Keiko sat not too far away. "Wanna come with us?" I asked her. Shine and Angelo were cleaning up, stepping around Sly's body. Everywhere I went these days, folks were passed out.

"No thanks," Keiko said, prodding gently at Sly's rib with the tip of her flashy Fiorucci boot. "You better take him with you."

The one place open at this hour was The Pink Teacup. Elvis, Jake, and I hailed the only cab in New York and woke Sly up long enough so he could pile in with us. The snow and sleet kept falling, and the cabbie crept cautiously through the blinding white rain. "Grand and Bowery," Sly croaked, before passing out again. His body slumped heavily across my lap. "Oh shit, now what do we do?" I said.

Elvis bobbed his head to the cabbie's tape of Hector Lavoe singing "Aguanila." He said, "Ah, Lavoe. One of the greats. Whatever happened to him?"

The cabbie grunted, in sympathy or disgust, I wasn't sure.

"How's Keiko getting home?" Jake asked me.

I was back in my bad mood. "Shine'll get her there in a limo."

We were on the Bowery. Sly was as rigid as a corpse. I tried shaking him off me, but he seemed to get heavier. "Honey, you're home!" I shouted in his ear. I could swear there was a smirk on his face. He snored on. "Wake up, stupid. This isn't funny."

Jake glared at me, then opened the cab door. He and Elvis managed to pull Sly out on the curb, where his body fell on the snow with a soft thud. The cabbie stared straight ahead, as if this were all perfectly normal. Except for us, it seemed Sly and the world were asleep. Hector Lavoe's wailing was the only sound anyone could hear on the glistening streets. "What do we do with him now? He won't wake up," Elvis said.

"We can't just leave him here," Jake said. "Which one's Sly's building?"

"He's doing it on purpose," I said, leaning out of the cab to get a closer look. I was furious. Shine, Keiko, the whole drunken evening. It was too cold, too late, and I was hungry. "Leave him," I said. "This is some kinda game he's playing." Elvis and Jake stood around for a second, calling Sly's name. When they got no response, they climbed back in the cab. "See? He's just acting crazy," I said, trying to reassure them. Sly remained sprawled on the sidewalk. I was mindful of the meter running and the fact that we were all low on cash.

"Go," I ordered the cabbie, who lurched forward into the night without once looking back.

At The Pink Teacup, Elvis ate his way through two orders of salmon croquettes with eggs over easy and grits with lots of Tabasco. I picked off his plate. Jake ordered a side of grits with melted Velveeta cheese. We lingered over watery coffee, too wired to go home and sleep. The lone waitress was exhausted by the unexpected, demanding crowd of night crawlers and drag queens seeking shelter from the blizzard. We were trying hard to pull ourselves together before the sun came up and we all turned into dust. I loved it, of course, the fitting end to my backbreaker tango, the fitting end to another hard drink-and-snort-fueled night. *Bonjour*, Stevie Wonder. New York, just how I pictured it.

Without warning, Jake said, "So it's settled? We'll move in together."

I glared at him. "No, it's not settled. I don't want to talk about it here."

"Surprise, surprise," Elvis murmured to himself, attacking his peach cobbler.

"Damn," I said to him, impressed. "Where do you put all that shit?" Elvis ignored me.

"Tapeworm," Jake said. "That's why he's so skinny."

I stared at Elvis, hoping for some acknowledgment. Elvis kept eating.

I finally worked up the courage to see him alone a few days later. "I'm pregnant again."

"Figured." Elvis's eyes were flat and accusing.

I blathered defensively, afraid that if I stopped Elvis would vanish.

"I know Jake would make a great father. Jake isn't afraid of children. What the hell am I waiting for? Some kinda black prince or something? Or Prince himself? Yeah, that's it. Prince. Too short and fey for my taste, but sexy, yes, sexy, weird smart funky sexy. Definitely my ideal man, perversely androgynous with pretty eyes. Prettier eyes and skinnier torso than you, Elvis. Are you listening? I still believe I'll cut a record deal and make so much money I can go ahead and fuck myself, yeah, make my own baby. Who needs you, anyway? Who needs Jake? I'll hire one of the LaStrange sisters to baby-sit. Or a blond nanny from Sweden. An au pair. Isn't that what they're called? Better yet, I'll send for Emy, my *yaya*. She'll spoil my child rotten and cook for me. Cook and cook, just like my mother. Men aren't the only fuckers who need wives. I need a wife! Then when she grows up, I'll send my fabulous *infanta* to you for guitar lessons. Then straight to Harvard or Brown or the Sorbonne or UCLA film school. And not on some goddam minority scholarship! She. She. She wants, I want. Gonna be a girl, that's for sure. Girls are the best. Right, Elvis? She can be a cultural theoretician, or get her cosmetology license from the Wilfred Beauty Academy. The world's her oyster. I swear, I'm not a snob. Hairdressers are *artists*. Remember what Jake said? We're a generation of hairdos." I took in a big lungful of oxygen. "I already told Keiko about keeping the baby. She agreed it was right, the right thing to do."

I was angry, but Elvis was even angrier. "Lemme put it to you this way. You in love with Jake? Jake's such a *nice* guy. Why didn't you tell me you were pregnant again? Fuck what that madwoman Keiko thinks. Fuck. Is it mine? Goddammit, is it mine? Rocky, you fuckin' dreamer. There goes the band. And for what? You don't even care about kids. You don't know about kids. *Kids bore you.* Jesus fuckin' Christ, bitch dreamer."

He called Sandy in New York to tell her he was sick. "What?" She murmured drowsily, still half asleep. "What?" More a gasp of sympathy than a question, really.

He had mastered sounding detached and almost cheerful. "I was diagnosed four years ago. After Stephen. But I've been actually putting on weight and feeling fine —"

"Oh, Marlon," she groaned in sympathy.

"Until last month," he finished. There was silence, which he dreaded. He spoke in a rush, not wanting her to interrupt. "I heard about these experimental treatments, wondered if you knew about them, using bitter melon, of all things." He laughed a little, embarrassed.

"That guy at UCLA, you mean?"

Marlon exhaled. "Yes, yes. *Him.*" His tone became eager, anxious. "Do you know him? He's Filipino, I think. Some kind of activist or doctor. Claims these enemas have kept him healthy —"

"I don't know him, Marlon. I'm not sure he's a bona fide doctor, but I've read the articles, and . . ." She hesitated.

Marlon abruptly changed the subject. "How's my niece doing?"

"Great. Kinda lost and tormented at the moment, but keeps it to herself." *Like you*, she wanted to say, but instead she said, "I'm very fond of her, Marlon." Sandy Oppenheim, wide-awake now, sat up in her bed. "Marlon, I'm coming out to see you. Okay? I'll come for the weekend. We'll look into all the options, see what's what." *Options*. Another one of Sandy's kind euphemisms, Marlon thought. Another one of her safe, businesslike, colorless words.

"Marlon?" She waited while he tried not to cough. When

she finally spoke, her voice cracked. "Do you want me to tell Rocky?"

"Not yet," he said.

"Those fucking coyotes got my Balthus." Isabel struggles up the path toward Marlon's front door. She shivers in spite of the afternoon sun, wrapping the frayed silk robe tighter around her body. Beaded velvet slippers Marlon once brought her as a gift from Manila cover the gnarled, arthritic toes of her feet.

"Did you find his body?" Marlon was startled by the wispy apparition in his garden.

"Of course not. Coyotes drag their prey off before eating them." She paused. "Do you own a gun?"

"Absolutely not."

"Goddammit. Every man should own a gun. Fritz owned several, even taught me how to shoot." Isabel dabbed at her runny nose with a sleeve.

"I'm sure he did." Marlon was alert to the faraway look in her eyes. Like she was seeing past him to a graveyard. It was one of the signs. She had been getting more unpredictable lately, switching from sweet old-lady befuddlement to dreamy paranoia and constant obsessing about her cats.

"It was hindsight. Didn't do us much good after the fact, did it? After the robbery, I mean."

Marlon steered her to a chair in his living room. "Did you just get up? Why don't you join me for coffee?"

Isabel refused to sit down. "I don't have time. I must find a gun. Do you think our aerobic neighbors own one?"

Marlon chuckled. "Absolutely. That husband of hers is your typical mass murderer. Placid. Nonverbal. Seventeen dismembered teenage boys buried underneath the floorboards in his rec room. His wife's too busy exercising to give a fuck." Marlon poured coffee for Isabel and wasn't surprised when she accepted the cup.

"She's probably stashed one of those coy little pearl-handled revolvers in her purse. What do you call them? A lady's gun. Fritz gave me one, but I lost it after he died."

Marlon took the cup from the old woman, whose eyelids suddenly fluttered shut. "Isabel? Are you all right?"

"Dammit! I can't remember where I put it. Marlon, darling, hurry! I can't do this alone. Places to go, people to see." Isabel's eyes flew open, and she staggered to the door. "Cats and coyotes, cats and coyotes. It didn't used to be this way."

They hobbled slowly toward a pastel structure resembling a Taco Bell marooned at the bottom of the hill. Swirling bronze letters spelled out THE OLIVOS on top of the mailbox, a miniature replica of the ostentatious house. A ROB & DIANE WELCOME U mat lay before the front door, and chimes played the opening bars of "You Are the Sunshine of My Life" when Isabel pressed the doorbell. Marlon sensed someone staring at them through the peephole.

The door was finally opened by a bronzed and gelled amazon of a woman wearing Lycra shorts and matching Lycra halter. Her expensive high-top sneakers were intimidating, more like weapons than shoes. A colossal Rottweiler suddenly emerged from the shadows. The woman grabbed the dog by the heavy chain collar looped twice around its massive neck. She gave the collar a tug. The dog reluctantly sat, never taking its wary eyes off the two unwelcome visitors. Stevie Wonder's "Superstition" played in the background.

"We apologize profusely for interrupting your workout, Diane." Isabel's tone was sweet and sincere.

"I never knew you were such a Stevie Wonder fan," Marlon added.

"Uh-huh." Diane Olivo hung on to the dog's collar.

"But it's an emergency." Isabel hesitated, giving Marlon a frantic look.

"We need a gun," Marlon explained.

The dog growled softly. "Don't," Diane Olivo ordered the animal, jerking the chain roughly to make her point. Then she glanced back at Marlon and smiled. Her tone was mocking. "Mar-lon Ree-ve-rah, did I hear you and Mrs. L'Ange correctly? You sure don't look like violent types."

"When do you expect Rob back?" Isabel interrupted. "Maybe he can help us."

Diane Olivo shrugged. "He's in San Diego for a convention."

"The coyotes got my Balthus," Isabel said. "My second kitty this year. Murder and mayhem, Diane, in some form or other. I can't bear it."

Diane addressed Marlon. "What's wrong with her?"

"She's brokenhearted," Marlon replied.

Isabel focused on Diane as she babbled in desperation. "Ask your husband. Rob knows exactly what I'm talking about. We've discussed it. The world is devolving, and coyotes are the first to act out. Have you noticed? The sun is a toxic red ball. Crystal clear in Guadalajara. Your husband's seen it. He's been to Guadalajara and he knows. If the smog weren't so bad out here, we'd see it too."

"Rob'll be back in a coupla days." Diane started to back away from the door.

Isabel was determined and forceful. "There's a draught in the canyon. The jackals and hyenas have nothing left to eat but my kitties. Don't you see?"

"Jesus, Isabel," Diane Olivo said.

"Don't pity me, goddammit," Isabel shrieked. "Just help me do something about it!"

Marlon took the old woman gently but firmly by the arm. There was almost nothing left to touch but bone. "Let's go, Isabel."

Diane Olivo tugged at the dog and slammed the door in their faces. As if to blast them away, she turned Stevie Wonder way, way up. For a moment, Marlon and Isabel were left standing on the doorstep, unsure of what to do next.

"My gun." Isabel sighed.

Marlon guided her carefully across the intersection. There were no cars coming, and he was glad to take his time with the frail old woman. The humiliation he'd felt in Diane Olivo's presence immediately vanished. "Fuck that tacky broad," Marlon said to Isabel. "We'll find what you need. We'll find Balthus." Preoccupied with her ghosts, Isabel didn't respond. Marlon didn't mind. He sang exuberantly at the top of his lungs: "You are the sunshine / of my life. / That's why / I'll always . . ."

"Silly man." Isabel pulled away from Marlon's grasp. "My gun," she kept muttering as she dragged herself to the porch where her cats sprawled and waited. Marlon noticed the one-eyed Balthus, very much alive, among them. He said nothing. "Hello, babies. Hello, darlings," Isabel called out gaily. Stretching and arching, the tough-looking tomcats ambushed the old woman, caressing her ankles with their battered tails, an alarming chorus of purrs and impatient meowing. Isabel stared fondly but helplessly at the hungry animals.

Marlon took the keys from her and unlocked the front door. An overwhelming ammonia stench emanated from the dusty interior. He held his breath and walked in. The cats had definitely taken over. The Persian rug was soiled and ripped, and the once plush sofa was coated with hair. Scattered on the kitchen floor were open tin cans rimmed with crusty remnants of rotting fish, and a bowl of swampy water. Marlon found one can of sardines left in Isabel's bare cupboard and a carton empty except for two eggs in the refrigerator. He rinsed out three bowls, filled one with fresh water, the second with raw eggs, and the third with oily sardines. Then he brought the bowls out to the porch, and let the cats fight over them. "How nice. How very nice." Isabel sighed with satisfaction, transfixed by her pets. The skimpy rations disappeared in seconds, and the cats began making anxious noises again.

"Shall we have tea?" Isabel looked up at Marlon as if noticing him for the first time. Marlon was sure she was performing genteel white lady now, one of his favorites, a cross between Deborah Kerr and Helen Hayes. She led him back inside the foul-smelling house.

"You wait here," Isabel said, giggling girlishly. "I'll go find us something."

Marlon played along. She would return with a bottle of rum as she always did, have a few drinks with him until she passed out on the sofa. He'd cover her with a blanket before stumbling back to his own house. He promised himself that today, after she fell asleep, he would clean up for her. Even if she didn't notice. Even if it didn't matter. Then he'd drive to the supermarket and pick up some food. For her. For her damn cats.

On the living room wall hung a framed photograph of Isabel taken in her Hollywood heyday. The photographer was famous for his portraits of doomed jazz musicians, decadent surrealist poets, and pampered society debutantes. Isabel had outlived them all, including the photographer.

In the picture, Isabel drapes herself languidly on a teakwood love seat carved with dragons. A halo of smoke around her, cigarette holder poised in one hand. The photographer has used a filtered lens, attempting to envelop his subject in a soft-core aura of exotic mystery. But in spite of the gimmicky props and setup, Isabel's face emerges from the smoky mist, brazen and pantherine. She is elegantly costumed in a man's tuxedo, her almond eyes and Cupid's bow lips heavily outlined and painted like the toughest of whores. Her thick, unruly hair has been tamed, slicked back, and obscured by a gleaming top hat.

With contempt, Isabel described to Marlon how aroused the photographer had been by her androgynous costume. "He thought I was one of his slave boys." Then she said, "I wouldn't fuck him, of course. You understand."

Black soot. Dried blood. Sepia. Smoke. Isabel confronts the camera. Her gaze is direct, unflinching, defiant. Marlon loved her. Isabellina, the ruined mother. Isabella, queen of the jungle. Isabel, the perfume of his nostalgia for lost islands that could exist only in searing flashes of memory. He loved her without the selfishness that had been at the core of his passion for Stephen, the long-gone lover, also a photographer. Marlon kept lying to everyone who still bothered to ask. Stephen was in Mexico on assignment.

Marlon decided, then and there, to sell his house. Small as it was, his charmingly rustic cottage should be worth something. It was located in a fashionably seedy neighborhood, he kept it immaculate, and the garden was a miniature jewel. He'd give away or sell his prized orchids of course, send Raquel and Voltaire money, and return to the Philippines. He'd persuade Isabel to return with him. She could visit Samar, dig up whatever family she might have left. He'd stay in Manila, make amends with his brother, Francisco, maybe get to know his standoffish niece Luz. God knows how many grandnieces and nephews he had by now. There were relatives all over the islands he'd never met, even a great-aunt and her twin brother, close to a hundred and ten years old, still living in Paete, Laguna. After he and Isabel finished meeting them all, they could finally collapse in the exquisite heat and be buried next to each other.

Isabel repeated, a little louder and with a trace of impatience, "Marlon. That man was a depraved little troll. He offered me money. Can you imagine? I was tempted, out of sheer hatred. Marlon, for God's sake, are you listening?"

What had changed? Everything and nothing. Elvis and Jake remained friends. Rocky made a compromise with Jake. He'd keep his apartment, and so would she, but they would spend all their time together until the baby was born. "Then what?" Jake was losing his patience.

"Then we'll see," Rocky said.

Keiko was again unavailable, busy setting up a traveling exhibit of her work. "I'm beginning to think you're not interested," Rocky said, during one of their late-night phone marathons.

"How can you say that? I'm her godmother —"

"Keiko, please. We don't know if it's a girl."

"Well, I know. I have a gut feeling." Keiko's tone softened. "I wanted a baby girl."

"So have one."

"Easy for you to say."

"I'm not kidding. If you want a girl so much, you're certainly in a position to adopt."

"My, my. Aren't we crabby," Keiko said, coldly.

They didn't talk much after that, except when Keiko unexpectedly sent over a Shaker-style, handcrafted pinewood cradle as a gift. Rocky and Jake both called to thank her, though Rocky was a bit wary of Keiko's lavish gesture. "There's something hostile about it, don't you think?" she said to Jake.

"You mean cradle as art object," Jake said.

"Yeah," Rocky said. "Elegant and impractical." Keiko and Rocky drifted further apart.

Rocky was surprised at how easy it became to live without, as Jake called it, Keiko's constant "noise." Her demanding, exuberant presence had, for some time now, no longer been a welcome intrusion, but a chore. The nine months of Rocky's pregnancy progressed unremarkably. She gained the expected forty pounds, never threw up, peed every five minutes, and craved avocados. Rocky kept working at the Center and performing with the band until her seventh month, when Graciela Delgado ordered her to stay off her feet. Her legion of mostly female fans stared in awe at her growing belly, murmuring things like, "God, you are *so* brave."

"Guess they think you've got it all," B. Goode observed wryly. Elvis, who finally got bored with keeping his distance, teased Rocky by calling her "Superwoman" to her face. "How are you today, Superwoman?" If he was still angry, he didn't show it. It got to be a joke with the musicians, Rocky in all her strange, clumsy bigness, pouting from her corner of the dressing room, forced to abstain from everything everyone else was doing. She stopped smoking, though occasionally she'd steal a guilty puff or quick toke from someone's cigarette or joint. "Just one," they'd all say, laughing. Even Sly fussed over her. For nine months, Rocky alternated between ginger ale or Perrier with a twist. It bored her silly, but she did it.

"We should call my mother," Rocky groans, lumbering toward the bathroom for another violent round of vomiting and diarrhea. She doesn't quite make it, soiling herself. Jake helps her undress and climb into the shower. "I'm a mess." She weeps as the warm water sprays over her. "Never mind calling my mother. She's too far away. Call Graciela instead."

"What should I say?"

"Tell her it's time. Tell her the fucking contractions are driving me crazy."

Graciela Delgado sounds wide awake and chipper at four in the morning: "See you at the hospital in twenty minutes."

Graciela greets them dressed in jeans and a sweatshirt. "My work clothes," she jokes. The maternity ward is brightly lit but empty and silent. A lone nurse checks them in. "Where is everybody?" Jake asks. "They're around," Graciela answers. She examines a squeamish, irritable Rocky and pronounces her not quite dilated enough. "Walk her up and down the corridors, slowly, and do the breathing with her," Graciela advises Jake.

"But I feel too sick to walk," Rocky protests.

"Precisely," Graciela says. "Perfectly normal."

Rocky leans against Jake for support, overcome by intense waves of nausea and the undulating, tumultuous movements in her belly. "Oh God. I can't take it anymore!"

"Just do your breathing," Graciela repeats, unmoved. "Don't push. You're not ready yet." She starts to walk away.

Rocky panics. "Where you going?"

Graciela looks slightly annoyed. "To check on my other patient."

Rocky is stunned. "You've got someone else delivering the same time as me?"

Graciela's amused. "Do you think you're the only one? Stop worrying, Rocky. I'm right down the hall if you need me."

For a moment, Rocky looks lost. Then she shuts her eyes and starts panting furiously, like Graciela taught her to do in Lamaze class. Jake guides her down the corridor. They pass another couple. The young woman is in the same hospital gown as Rocky, but she's obviously in a lot less discomfort. The young man smiles helplessly at Jake. When they are out of earshot, Rocky mutters under her breath, "What's *he* smiling about? Fuck this pregnancy shit. I wanna go home right now."

As the hours creep by, Rocky becomes animal-like, clawing Jake as her contractions accelerate. "I've got to push this thing out," she wails. Graciela examines her again, Rocky howling in pain at her touch. "Take your goddam hand out of me."

"It's time," Graciela says.

Bathed in icy sweat, Rocky sits up in the birthing bed, pushing and grunting, her burning vagina about to explode. Tears mingle with sweat. *She is so tired.* "You're not doing it right," Graciela barks at her. Jake holds her right hand, and a nurse who's appeared out of nowhere holds her left.

Rocky digs her nails into both of them, moaning in exhaustion, "I just want to sleep."

"*Push*," Graciela commands. Graciela sits on a low stool between Rocky's open legs, waiting for the baby to pop out. Rocky heaves and hollers, grimacing demonically. "*Push*," Graciela commands again. "You're almost there."

Jake brings his sympathetic face close to Rocky's. "Go away," Rocky snarls, "I hate you."

"Why didn't you call me sooner?" Milagros chastised Jake on the phone. "I've been ready. My bags have been packed for weeks."

"Rocky and Venus are doing fine. The baby came a little early. We didn't want to bother anybody."

Milagros sighed with disappointment. "I'm not anybody. I'm her mother. I should've been there." She didn't miss a beat, sounding hopeful. "Are the two of you getting married? Maybe when we get there?"

"Rocky and I haven't decided."

"What do you mean?"

"We've discussed it."

"Discussed it? *Dios ko,* how unromantic."

"Well. It's been difficult."

"What about the baby?"

"She carries both our names."

"Uhm."

"I'll pick you up at the airport."

There was a stony silence. "It's not necessary. Bas and Fely are renting a car."

"We'll meet you anyway. You're staying with us, of course?"

Milagros didn't answer.

"Mrs. Rivera?"

"I wouldn't want to impose."

"It's really okay."

"Don't think I approve."

"I'm sure you don't."

"This is all too casual, if you ask me."

"It's not. We're deadly serious."

"I believe in ritual. Ritual's good for the soul. It's a Filipino thing, it's a Catholic thing, whatever. It suits me fine. Ask my daughter. She's got theories about it, I'm sure. What's the point of life without ritual? I got married in a cathedral, right when the Japs invaded Manila. No one came to the wedding. They were all too scared. But we went ahead with it anyway. It was important."

"I know."

"Do you? I'm not asking Raquel to do what I did. I don't have money for a wedding, and that father of hers won't send a dime. Raquel doesn't have to wear a white dress and a veil. She doesn't even have to go to church."

"That's not her primary objection."

"She can go to City Hall. Have a judge instead of a priest. *Be modern*. What's so bad about that?"

"Trappings aren't the point."

"Trappings! Listen to how you talk —"

"We're simply trying to assess the situation. We take the concept of marriage much too seriously to rush —"

"You rushed into bed."

"No, you're absolutely wrong. We didn't."

"Bullshit." Milagros's laugh was grim. "You're perfect for each other. So rational. Both cold-blooded, just like my former husband."

"Mrs. Rivera."

Milagros was silent.

"Venus is *gorgeous*. She weighs eight pounds. Lots of hair." Jake waited for a response and then continued when Milagros said nothing. "Black hair. Fine and long, like her fingers. Piano-playing fingers. Mrs. Rivera?"

Still nothing.

"It's really okay."

She finally spoke. "My name is Milagros, Jake. Don't ever call me Mrs. Rivera again, okay?"

Venus Sleeps, Undisturbed

At the baggage claim area, a robotic female voice makes announcements. Flight changes, white courtesy phone calls, warnings. "Do not leave bags unattended." Rocky and Jake wend their way through a maze of shell-shocked passengers and their wired, rambunctious children. Furtive young men skulk about, offering all manner of bogus transportation. Impassive men in dark suits hold up placards and signs by the exit doors. TEL-AVIV CAR #3. SABRA #116. SINAI BIG APPLE LUXURY LIMO. WHEELS ON FIRE.

"Ride to Manhattan?" someone casually asks Rocky.

"No way," Rocky mutters, hurrying past him. She revels in the music and chaos of airports, finding herself at home in the deadening glare of fluorescent light and low hum of conveyor belts.

A little girl of about seven catches Rocky's attention. There's something about her outrageous mop of hair and pug nose. "Sit down, don't move, Molly! I'm going to get our bags and look for Grandpa," a harried woman barks. Rocky realizes with some amusement that the child resembles Pedro Almodovar, down to his black curls, stocky body, and boxer's face. "Sit down or else!" the woman threatens. The child slowly backs into a chair and sits. She is aware of Rocky's presence but stares past her with a look of defiant boredom. SHE SELLS SUSHI BY THE SEASHORE and the cartoon image of a dinosaur in a grass skirt are silk-screened across the front of her T-shirt. The harried woman joins the mass of people waiting by the carousel. Suddenly overwhelmed by anxiety, Rocky scans the crowd of arriving passengers for her mother.

Venus dreams undisturbed in the Snugli pouch that Rocky wears. Where is Milagros? Where are Auntie Fely and Uncle Bas? They are traveling together, and plan to attend Imelda Marcos's trial at the federal courthouse. "Everyone will be there," Uncle Bas had said on the phone earlier that week.

"How do you know you'll get in?" Rocky asked him.

Basilio Cruz chuckled. "Don't worry, *hija*. Your uncle has *mucho* connections."

Rocky wonders if her mother decided not to come at the last minute. Milagros was perfectly capable of not showing up, just to prove a point. And hadn't Rocky offended her mother deeply by not calling her on the way to the hospital?

"Is that your mom?" Jake points to a tiny woman sitting by herself in a corner.

Rocky is startled by how her mother seems to have shrunk. Milagros looks her age, though she is impeccable in her rayon dress, jacket, stockings, and four-inch pumps. Her face has been freshened by the arsenal of cosmetics she carries with her wherever she goes. "Even to the grocery store," Rocky said, trying to explain to Jake the extent of her mother's vanity. Black vamp eyeliner and mascara, mocha blush, translucent powder, redder-than-red dragon lady lipstick — these were the basics, what Milagros would take if she were forced at gunpoint to travel light. The complete stockpile included not-yet-approved-by-the-FDA wrinkle-remover creams and jars of turtle oil purchased in Tijuana, and a bottle of Shalimar, her signature perfume. "That make-up bag's the first thing my mother will grab in an earthquake," Rocky said to Jake.

Two large, bulky suitcases are propped next to Milagros, more than she needs for her two-week stay. They're the unsightly, vinyl kind with wheels and straps that you buy from street vendors at bargain prices.

Rocky's tone is apprehensive. "Ma. What's all this?"

"Presents for the baby. What else?" Milagros retorts. "Also, I wasn't sure about the weather, so I brought extra stuff, in case."

"You look very stylish," Rocky remembers to say.

Milagros winces as she displays a swollen stockinged foot. "I could hardly get them in my shoe."

"You should stop wearing those damn high heels," Rocky says.

As if she were shaking a fan at her, Milagros dismisses Rocky with an imperious, fluttering gesture of her manicured hand.

Fely and Basilio emerge from the crowd, loaded down with carry-on bags and cameras. They cry out when they see Rocky, and the barrage of comments and questions begins. "Ay! Ay! Where's the baby? Ay! Ay! Is this your husband? *Dios ko*, it's been such a long time." The flight, they inform her, was interminable. The food, inedible.

Basilio Cruz winks at Rocky. "Good thing your mama packed some lumpia."

"You're kidding," Rocky says, then laughs. She turns to Jake, as if translating for him. "They brought their own food on the plane."

"Of course we did. And I've got some frozen lumpia for you," Milagros says.

"Hug your auntie," Fely demands, reaching out with her arms.

"Kiss, kiss." Bas leans toward Rocky and plants noisy kisses on both her cheeks.

Fely tugs at her husband's sleeve. "Look! Rocky's baby!"

Rocky collapses on the chair beside her mother so they can all peer at the infant. Flashbulbs pop. Bas takes picture after picture with his Instamatic camera, until Rocky holds up a hand, and roars, "Enough!"

"You need to lose weight," Milagros murmurs to her daughter, loud enough for Fely to hear. Rocky blushes. She thinks of a million snappy comebacks. "You don't look so hot yourself." Or, "Who do you think you're fooling with all that make-up?" but stops herself.

Fely rushes to her defense. "What do you expect? She just had a baby."

Milagros glares at her sister. "There you go again."

Fely says in a resigned tone, "There *you* go."

Basilio Cruz, with an insincere grin pasted on his face, raises his eyebrows at Jake in commiseration. "Women."

"Ma, Auntie Fely, Uncle Bas. This is Jake Montano," Rocky says.

"I thought my daughter was going to let you just stand there all night."

Milagros gives Jake her hand, almost as if she expects him to bow and kiss her topaz ring.

"It's good to finally meet you," Jake says.

"I invited your mama to stay with us at Howard Johnson's," Bas says to Rocky.

"That isn't necessary," Rocky says. "We've got room."

Milagros looks pleased. "See, Bas? What did I tell you?"

Bas throws his hands up in mock surrender. "Okay, okay. You're de boss."

The Snugli pouch intrigues Rocky's mother. "What'll they think of next," Milagros clucks. "Very unattractive."

"It's practical," Fely argues, ever the nurse. "No strain on the back. Keeps the mother's arms free." The bickering starts up again.

"My daughter isn't a kangaroo!" Milagros declares.

"Ay, *hija*," Fely says to Rocky, ignoring her sister. "I just can't believe you're a mother now. The baby is so beautiful!"

Milagros is determined not to be outdone. "You can't even see my grandchild in that damn kangaroo contraption."

Rocky unzips the Snugli for her mother. "Look all you want," she says wearily.

Bas pats Jake on the shoulder. "Congratulations, Jacob. By golly, we need to get you a cigar. Don't believe the Cubans. We make the best cigars in the Philippines."

"Call me Jake, Mr. Cruz."

"He's part Cuban," Rocky murmurs.

"Excuse me, *Jake*." Bas widens his grin. "I didn't mean to offend. And, please, don't call me Mr. Cruz. I'm Uncle Bas, your uncle-in-law."

Rocky rolls her eyes. "We're not married, Uncle Bas."

Fely and Milagros lapse into an uncomfortable silence, while Bas does an exaggerated double take. "Well, well . . . Excuse me *lang*."

"I'll find a skycap," Jake says, hurrying away.

"He seems nice," Milagros offers grudgingly. Then after a significant pause, "And mature."

"*Guwapo*," Fely says with enthusiasm.

"Mestizo," Basilio Cruz adds.

Milagros fusses over the baby, unzipping the pouch again so she can get another look. "You've got to be careful with this thing you're wearing," Milagros says. "She could suffocate." She asks Fely, "What's that thing?"

"What thing?"

Milagros's tone is impatient. "That thing! Fely, *naman*. You're so forgetful! You're the expert who told me about it. That thing that happens when babies die from sleeping face first."

"You mean face *down*," Fely corrects her.

Basilio and Fely Cruz insist on giving Milagros, Jake, and Rocky a ride into Manhattan in their rented Cadillac. Milagros stares out the window. "I can't see a thing."

"Of course not. It's nighttime," Fely says.

"I know that," Milagros snaps, then addresses Bas in the driver's seat. "Are you sure you know where you're going?"

"I love New York," Bas says to Jake, ignoring Milagros. What a devil of a woman. Basilio Cruz is relieved she won't be staying with them. "This is my kind of town."

"You've been here before?" Jake asks him.

"Of course," Bas brags. "Navy man."

"He means he was the ship's cook," Milagros informs Jake sweetly.

Bas turns up the volume on the radio. "Ooh, I like that song. *Sino ba iyan?*" he asks Rocky, who's slumped in the back with her mother and aunt.

"Gloria Estefan," Rocky replies.

"Yeah, man, *siempre*. Hmmm, Gloria, sexing-sexy!" Once again, Bas moves his eyebrows up and down at Jake for emphasis. "Cuban women are my favorite."

"Bas, *puwede ba*," Fely warns him from the back seat.

"Joking *lang*," Basilio Cruz assures her.

Basilio Cruz screeches up in front of the run-down building on Eleventh Street and sits there for a moment, gazing at it in disbelief. Garbage from slashed bags spills onto the pavement. An old man walking a pair of matted, miniature poodles pauses by the garbage. He glances at the boat-sized Cadillac, recognizes Rocky inside, and waves. "Who's that?" Milagros inquires.

"He's an actor," Rocky says.

"He doesn't look like one," Milagros sniffs, disappointed.

Bas makes a show of helping Jake unload Milagros's luggage onto the curb. "Are you sure there's an elevator?" he asks Jake, who nods. Relieved, Bas shakes Jake's hand vigorously, pats him on the back once again, then climbs back into the driver's seat. Rocky helps her mother out of the car. "Are you coming with us to Imelda's trial?" Fely asks her. Rocky is amused by the cozy tone of her aunt's question. You'd think Imelda Marcos was a personal friend of the family.

"I don't think so," Rocky says. "The baby."

Disappointed, Fely Cruz makes clicking noises with her tongue. "*Sayang*. You're missing the trial of the century."

"*Sayang*," Bas repeats, before driving off.

Milagros can't believe her daughter lives the way she does. They'd be better off in a shack in Manila. Well, not exactly, but she could've sworn she'd seen a mouse, maybe a rat, scurrying in the dimly lit hallway. Plus, the elevator stank. In fact, the whole city seemed to stink. That's what she'd thought on the long drive into Manhattan from JFK. Thank God that show-off Bas turned up the air conditioning and made her roll up the car window. Her own flat back in San Francisco was nothing to brag about either, but at least there were two bedrooms, and a bathroom and kitchen you could turn around in. Plus, Zeke's building was a certified gingerbread Victorian.

And this man, Jake, father of the baby, father of her grandchild Venus — who is he? He was so *quiet*. Quiet like that other one, the Chinese. Too quiet, really. Very nice and considerate, she could see that. But something's lacking. Milagros could see that, too. *Feel* it, actually, in her bones. Milagros had uncanny instincts. When her mother, Raquel the First, was alive, she had claimed that if Milagros hadn't wasted her time marrying Francisco Rivera, she could've been a . . . what do you call it in English? (Milagros's command of English was starting to slip these days.) A *psychic*, that was it. Not a word Milagros found appropriate or expressive, but it would have to do. Milagros found English a frustrating language. She could accept being "psychic" in English but not in the silly sense, like Dionne Warwick. Dionne should've stuck to singing. What the hell did she mean by a "psychic friends' network" anyway? It sounded so trivial. Milagros understood, just as her mother, Raquel the First, did before her, that there was nothing innocuous about this power. A *manghuhula* exists on another plane, is pestered constantly by spirits, and, depending on one's point of view, is blessed or doomed to explore the past and foretell the future. Back in Manila, her fortune-teller, the fabulous La Sultana, had observed that while Milagros was born with the gift, the gift needed to be nurtured and utilized. Otherwise it would fade away. "It's like anything else," La Sultana explained. "Muscles atrophy. Teeth rot. Bones crumble." La Sultana was no phony, predicting the breakup of Milagros Rivera's marriage and "the long journey to a known and unknown place" exactly one month before Milagros booked passage on the ship bound for America. La Sultana lived a beggar's life in a rusting Mercedes-Benz permanently parked near Paco Cemetery. The wrecked car was the only clue to her former status as the widow of one of the most feared and despised politicians in the Philippines. Thanks to her extreme faith in the Blessed Virgin Mary, La Sultana had been a devoted, complacent wife to her philandering husband and had borne eight children by him. But at the age of fifty, she was suddenly brought to her senses by a torrent of electrifying dreams and ominous visions. Two-faced, jackal-headed angels wouldn't let her sleep and engrossed her in exhilarating philosophical debates conducted in a jumble of arbitrary languages: Tagalog, French, Kapangpangan, and occasionally Spanish or Latin. All this occurred, of course, while her husband snored beside her. Invisible *engkantos* cornered her under the *balete* tree in the garden and drove her mad with their soft, childish giggles and playful caresses. A colony of termites attached itself under her bedroom window, and blacks ants swarmed across her bed. When La Sultana dared to predict the date and time of her own husband's death, he attempted to have her exorcised and committed to a private sanatorium. La Sultana's story was leaked to the sympathetic press, who dubbed her "Our Own Living Martyr." The Archbishop of Manila paid her a visit and gave her his blessing. Rumors spread that La Sultana was a healer and medium for the Virgin Mary. When her unpopular husband died at the exact time and day she had foretold, the country went wild. La Sultana left her family, changed her name, freed her servants, and renounced all worldly possessions — except for the Mercedes-Benz sedan, which she drove herself to an alley of mud near Paco Cemetery. Milagros visited her once a week, standing in line with all the other faithful, rich and poor, who recited the rosary out loud as they waited for hours, without complaining, in the burning sun.

To Milagros, the spare, joyless environment reflects how much her daughter has changed. Rocky has obviously learned to scale down everything, even dressing austerely. There is no privacy, only one boxy room where sleeping, eating, working, whatever, occurs. Books are piled on top of one another, used as end tables. Cassette tapes and recording equipment are scattered about. A mess. Milagros is forced to step over an electric keyboard lying in the middle of the floor, next to an old-fashioned, rather plain cradle. A hollow plywood door opens into a perfunctory shower stall and toilet. "Excuse me," Jake says, shutting the door behind him. The sound of running water can clearly be heard through the thin walls. Rocky refers to an alcove with prefab cabinets as a "kitchenette." The total effect is utilitarian and charmless.

"How can you stand it?" Milagros asks.

"The landlord's decent," Rocky explains. "And it's rent-stabilized."

Milagros is unrelenting. "Where's the baby's room? How can you cook in a closet? Where am I sleeping?" She frowns when Rocky shows her the loft bed she shares with Jake, and the convertible sofa underneath. "Maybe I should go over to Bas and Fely's motel —"

Rocky starts to protest. "If it really bothers you, Jake can stay at his apartment."

"I beg your pardon?" Milagros is puzzled.

"He has his own apartment, within walking distance."

"I thought you were living together," Milagros says.

"We are. Sort of."

Milagros holds the baby in her arms, rocking it gently back and forth. "She's got your frown," Milagros observes. "Your father's pout. That hair, well, Voltaire had a lot of hair. So did Luz. Fair skin — but that nose! It's your *lolo*'s nose. Ay, too flat."

"Ma. The baby's only a few days old. Maybe she'll grow up and look like no one in the family," Rocky says.

"Ha. I can see it with my own eyes. She's definitely a Rivera."

His hair still wet, Jake emerges from the bathroom, in a fresh shirt and jeans. Milagros can't imagine how he managed to change clothes in such a narrow space. He kisses the top of the baby's head and nods at Rocky. "I'm off."

Milagros is incredulous. "It's almost midnight. Where are you going?"

"To work," Jake answers. "Good night."

Rocky takes the awake and fidgeting baby from her mother. "He's a recording engineer," she says after Jake leaves. She'd explained this to her mother a million times, but Milagros hears only what she wants to hear.

"It's so late," Milagros insists.

"Jake prefers night sessions. Sometimes they go until ten in the morning. He makes good overtime."

"Why doesn't he buy you a house? This is a ridiculous way

to live," Milagros complains, plopping herself down on the couch. Rocky doesn't respond, and nurses the fussing baby. Venus refuses her nipple at first, then starts making furious bleeting sounds. "She's wet," Milagros says.

"I just changed her."

"Maybe she went again."

"Ma, trust me. She's dry."

"Then she's colicky. Voltaire was colicky. He cried morning, noon, and night for six months. I thought I was going insane. You were colicky too. Never wanted to be put down. Luz was the only one who never gave me trouble."

"I thought you said Luz was always sick."

"I never said that."

"You said it was because of the war. You were sick and hungry, so Luz was sick and hungry."

"You're dreaming."

The baby finally settles down, sucking contentedly. Two weeks of butting heads with Milagros lie ahead of Rocky. She leans back and shuts her eyes, listening to her restless mother rummaging through the kitchen cupboards.

"Gotta go to Chinatown tomorrow," Milagros mutters, "get some supplies."

"There's a grocery store two blocks away."

"Not the same. You're breast-feeding and need to eat real food. These cupboards are filthy. Ayyy, Raquel. Roach eggs all over the top of your fridge — and what's this? Mouse droppings! *Qué horror.* I'll clean up first thing in the morning. Then we'll go to Chinatown. Bas told me the Chinatown here is even bigger than San Francisco!"

"It's not necessary. The grocery store has everything —"

"No, they don't. I'll cook virgin chicken, Chinese-style. Best thing for nursing mothers. Remember Harry Fong? His wife gave me that recipe."

"Maybe Jake can take you —"

"I can go by myself, thank you."

"Jake loves going to Chinatown. He does all the cooking and knows exactly where to go."

Milagros can't make up her mind if she is revolted or amused.

"I'd go, but — it's just that Chinatown's so crowded. And I'm too tired to face it," Rocky says.

"Poor Jake."

"Why do you pity him? Jake is perfectly happy," Rocky says, indignant.

"Is that why you won't marry?" Milagros doesn't wait for Rocky's response. "Thank you for helping out with the plane ticket."

"I'm glad we could," Rocky says, relieved at the change of topic. "Is business really bad?"

"It's me. I just don't have the energy." Milagros is gazing intently at Venus. "The baby's fallen asleep again. Look, Raquel. Her little mouth's still moving." She struggles up from the sofa and paces around the tiny apartment, examining everything. There is a wedding photograph of Milagros and Francisco Rivera which Rocky has framed and hung on the wall. Milagros stares at the image, then turns to face her daughter. "You should've called me first. I'm your mother. I could've helped. Instead, I had to hear about it from someone else."

"For God's sake, Ma. Jesusfucking —"

"Raquel!" Milagros glowers at her daughter.

Milagros loved to go on about each of her children's traumatic births. Luz was premature, Voltaire was a breech, Rocky caused her to hemorrhage. Japanese war planes hovered on the horizon, air-raid sirens wailed, and snipers menaced the streets. Rocky's father, of course, was never by her side when it was time for Milagros to go to the hospital. Francisco Rivera always managed to arrive when the worst part was over. *Before the war, after the war.* Rocky could recite back every gory detail from memory, even as a child. That's how often her mother told the same brutal stories. Milagros couldn't stand the sight of blood, or anything to do with "female suffering." Rocky had long ago decided that her mother was the last person she needed during labor.

Milagros, in another snit, starts pulling gift-wrapped packages out of her suitcase and handing them to her daughter without looking at her. "From Voltaire," she mutters. Before Rocky has even begun to unwrap it, Milagros shoves another present at her. "From Zeke." Voltaire had sent a book, *The First Five Years of Your Baby's Life*. His inscription read, "I guess you really need this, ha-ha! Love, V." Rocky is overwhelmed at the sight of his elegant scrawl. "I miss him," she says to her mother quietly.

Zeke sent a perfectly uninspired but useful travel set from Macy's, flannel blanket, bib, snap-on suits, two plastic baby bottles, and a fascinating selection of oddly shaped rubber nipples. "For juice. For water. For milk. What'll they think of next!" Milagros exclaims. Harry Fong and his wife sent a red silk bunting embroidered in gold thread. The Changs sent ornate silk shoes with a whimsical frog face embroidered on each toe. "The Changs?" Rocky looks puzzled.

"That's right. *Those* Changs," Milagros says. "Elvis's mother dropped the present off the day before I left."

Rocky piles the gifts neatly on one corner of the sofa, smiling to herself. She must try to call her brother tonight, or first thing tomorrow. He'd moved back to their mother's flat, but on a very temporary arrangement.

"When are you and Jake getting married?" Milagros asks.

"Would you stop asking that question?"

Milagros pulls out her Marlboros, looks at Venus in her cradle, then puts the pack away. "Are you still in love with Elvis?" When Rocky doesn't answer, she goes on. "I almost didn't recognize that mother of his. Her hair's white from worry. She complained Elvis never calls or writes. Then she started weeping. Ha. 'Sounds just like my son,' I told her."

The baby makes tentative crying sounds. Rocky rearranges

her blankets, then gently pats the baby's lower back like Graciela has taught her. Soothed and reassured, Venus quiets down.

"Ma, what do you think? *Venus Rivera Montano.*" Rocky utters her daughter's name shyly, but with pride.

Milagros surprises her by responding in Tagalog. "*Ang haba naman.*" Too long and complicated, she complains. Unnecessary. Why do you have to make things so damn complicated? What are you and Jake trying to prove? Are you still in love with Elvis?

"I am not trying to prove anything, Ma. I'm just tired and over-whelmed. Trying to make sense of . . ."

My mother curls up on the sofa. "Don't you want me to open it up for you?" I ask.

She shakes her head, resting it on her clasped hands and closing her eyes. I drape a blanket over her, but she shakes it off. "Too hot." Then she murmurs as she drifts off, "We'll go to Chinatown first thing. Call your brother."

Venus and my mother are fast asleep. I dial my mother's number in San Francisco. The phone rings at least fifteen times before Voltaire picks up. "Who's this?"

"Me, calling from New York."

"Who?"

"Me." When he doesn't respond, I relent and identify myself. "It's Rocky." I refrain from adding, *you remember, your sister.* Instead: "Thanks for the book you sent."

Voltaire's voice is groggy. I wonder if he's stoned. "What book?"

"The baby book. Jesus, Voltaire, it's Rocky, I had a baby, and Ma's here in New York with me. You sent me a book. Are you okay?"

"The Carabao Kid sends his love," Voltaire answers.

"The Carabao Kid's dead," I remind him.

He ignores my comment. "I bought your single."

"What?"

"Found it in a bin at Tower. Hey, what time is it there?"

"Shit." That's what I'd always been afraid of, ending up in one of those bargain record bins, a has-been at thirty-three. Things are certainly happening a lot quicker than I'd anticipated. I've fixated on thirty-three, the age Jesus was when he was crucified, as the age when I'll probably die, too. Of course, in my usual half-assed way, I've conveniently forgotten all about Jesus rising from the dead. The fact that he also didn't give birth to a baby named Venus and *I did* hasn't occurred to me either.

"Your lyrics are fierce," Voltaire says, as if to remind me: "'Bed / Head / Fuck me till I'm dead.' Right?"

I giggle.

"Elvis's music is nice and edgy," he continues, sounding just like one of those pompous rock critics. "I love the song, but I pity you."

"Thanks a lot."

"No, no." Voltaire chuckles. "Don't misunderstand me, *ate*. I've been thinkin' about us, you know. I've been thinkin' for years, about what the Carabao Kid taught us."

Ah, the Carabao Kid and what he taught us. *How to be a F(P)ilipino*. Voltaire's idealized father figure. And mine too, I suppose. He was this Pinoy poet from Watsonville with the sleepy, wise face of a water buffalo, a man totally obsessed with the Philippines who'd never been there. In hushed tones, he'd describe the fiery sunsets, swaying coconut trees, and white sand beaches, sounding like some romantic tourist brochure. Kinda ironic and laughable, except the Kid thought it was funny too. "Oh yeah, sister. I forgot — I've never been *there*." America was here: vast, inhospitable, and harsh. The Philippines was there: distant, lush, soulful, and sexy. He made constant jokes out of what he called his "carabao dreaming" and wrote a series of self-deprecating haikus called "Existential Pinoy Paralysis," questioning his fears about returning to the homeland. "Maybe I just don't want to be disappointed," went one of the more quotable lines in his poem "Maybe." Another ditty was called "EXpat vs. EXile." The fact that Voltaire and I had actually been born in the Philippines had earned us his lasting admiration.

It was 1973. "*Hoy*, sister." He calls out when I stroll past Manong Joey's Kayumanggi Barbershop on Kearny Street. I'm on my way to see what I can shoplift at City Lights Books, but I can't ignore that loud and insistent "pssst, pssst." Filipino greeting. "What the fuck?" I mutter, annoyed. I stick my head into the dark, tiny storefront. Old Filipino men glare back at me from their pomade-scented gloom. Even in their humble circumstance and advanced age, they exude gangster flash and style, chewing on fat cigars while they wait for their haircuts. Acting like millionaires and preening like peacocks, they wear pimpy suits with rakish fedoras or slouchy Panama hats of the softest weave and two-tone wing tips or white patent leather loafers on their feet.

Manong Joey is in the midst of putting the finishing touches on some aging used-to-be gigolo's modified pompadour. The beat-up radio's tuned to KJAZ. In this bastion of macho vanity and sartorial glamour, the Carabao Kid stands out in his chinos and muddy work boots, his graying hair pulled back in a loose ponytail, his goatee wispy. He's right at home, claiming one of Manong Joey's unused barber chairs and swapping tales with the *manongs*. They are obviously very fond of him. Kid and the old guys could blah-blah all day and all night. "Talk story," the Kid used to call it. A brown teenage madonna in bell-bottom jeans, a Santana Abraxas T-shirt, and scuffed cowboy boots sweeps hair off the floor into a dustpan. The Kid proudly introduces her as "My daughter, Ligaya. Same age as you, sister, looks like." She's Manong Joey's goddaughter, all-around assistant, and shampoo girl.

Kid had once been an up-and-coming welterweight boxer, but he gave it up after a brutal match. The Kid's opponent beat him so bad, he went into a three-day coma. "Like Jesus," I said.

The Kid smiles. "Maybe so, sister. But that's when I decided my brain was too valuable."

He and Ligaya wander the planet, sleeping bags and everything they own on their backs, claiming no place and every place as their home.

"Where's your mother?" I ask Ligaya.

"She got fed up and went home."

"To Watsonville?"

Ligaya shakes her head. "No. To Pangasinan. In the Philippines," she adds, looking at me like I'm an idiot.

"Don't you miss her?"

"Of course."

"Don't you wanna visit her there?"

"When Papa's ready," she says, "I'll go."

The Kid's paid his dues and done his grueling summer stints at the canneries up in Alaska. With Ligaya and her mother before she left him, he's picked asparagus, strawberries, grapes, and peaches in the fields of California. "You name it, we've picked it," he'd say.

I keep thinking of Ligaya's mother, fed up. "How awful was it?" I ask.

"Sister, you don't wanna know." He laughs that knowing laugh. Manong Joey and the old guys join in. Makes me feel kinda foolish. Then the Kid switches to his favorite topic: the essence of a true F(P)ilipino. "You got your big gatherings, your big pig, lots of *tuyo*. Bitter melon. Plain hot rice. Plain and hot, to absorb all that salt. Jars of *patis* and *bagoong*, to stink up and get happy. Then you got your music and your dancing. *Voilà!* This is heaven, sister. Stop worrying about small things." I realize he sounds just like my mother and Uncle Marlon, only more irresistible because I'm not tied to him by blood.

Voltaire and I start coming by the barbershop at least once a week. The Kid calls Voltaire "little brother." The old guys tease us with "Why don't you quit fooling around and let Manong Joey give you both haircuts?"

Kid and Ligaya disappear for weeks at a time, working menial, backbreaking jobs as far away as Texas and Louisiana. Then they'd suddenly appear, browner and just as mysterious as ever. "You do what you gotta do."

"Who coined the term *Pinoy*?" I ask.

"Search me," Carabao Kid replies. "Pinoy just is."

"Part of the cosmos," Ligaya adds.

"That's an old term," Manong Joey says, "from home."

"What's home?" I ask coyly. Again, Kid and the old men laugh knowingly.

"Why do we keep coming here if we aren't wanted?" Voltaire asks.

"Who says we're not wanted?" An indignant old man in a white suit shoots back at him.

"We can't help it. We got big dreams. We know how to suffer," Kid says.

The old man in the white suit explodes. He's been sitting there fuming, pretending to read a newspaper. "Bullshit! You young people don't know what you're talking about. I'm a loyal Pilipino, a veteran, and a U.S. citizen, and I'm proud of it!"

Frankie Matuban makes a dismissive gesture. "Shut up, Nemesio."

I'm afraid the old guy might pull out a gun or wave Bronze Medals and Purple Hearts in our faces, but the Kid eventually calms him down.

Amador Reyes is the name on his birth certificate, but he's known simply as Kid, a.k.a. the Carabao Kid. Some consider him the unofficial spiritual leader of a fast-growing, chaotic, and exuberant Pinoy arts movement in San Francisco. The movement's emblem is the water buffalo, or carabao. Art and politics are, of course, inexorably intertwined. The Carabao Kid is asked to read his haikus at street fairs, beauty contests, cultural fund-raisers, civil rights demonstrations, and rallies against the Vietnam War. "You do what you gotta do."

He gently chides me for once describing myself as Filipino. "Don't say Fili, sister. Say Pili. In Tagalog, *pili* means 'to choose.' *Pino* means 'fine.' Pilipino equals 'fine choice.'"

I am impressed by his logic at first. Then I say, "But Filipino and Pilipino's not so different. Part of it's still a Spanish word."

The Carabao Kid's heavy eyelids flutter, and he seems taken aback. "Ha?" He even grunts Pilipino. *Ha* instead of *huh*.

"*Pino*," I repeat. "Isn't that simply a twist on the Spanish word *fino*?"

The Carabao Kid is annoyed and amused. "So what you saying, sister? The Spaniards actually meant to call us Fili-finos?"

Now I'm confused. It's like all the other collisions with language that occur and reoccur in my life. Amusing and occasionally illuminating but oftentimes going nowhere. But maybe nowhere's okay too. We start giggling, Ligaya covering her mouth shyly, everyone else cracking up at the absurdity of our conversation. Voltaire, Manong Joey, his clients Frankie Matuban and Dr. Arsenio "I'm sure we're related" Rivera. These young Pinoys sometimes float in to pay their respects and ogle Ligaya. They're Voltaire's age, and do volunteer work at the hotel for *manongs* across the street. The Carabao Kid calls them "my zany disciples." The volunteers transform Manong Joey's humble barbershop into a major cultural hangout on Saturday afternoons, bringing food, beer, and rum. Manong Joey turns up the radio. The Kid tells jokes. The atmosphere tingles with pent-up energy and nervous laughter. The Kid and his disciples believed that in the long run, everything could be reduced to a joke. Maybe that was the point all along, and Filipinos knew it. Jokes were in our blood, and very Zen of·us. Four hundred years of colonization and Catholicism couldn't erase it from our consciousness: *Bahala na, ha-ha-ha.* The Carabao Kid was right. Even back then, he could see I was ambitious, trapped in my media-saturated, wayward American skin.

"Your band will happen if it happens," Kid says. "You think because you're female, you have to outfox all of us. Everything in its own time. Don't force it, or it will outforce you."

Another time he says, "Why rush? Recite your poems. There's music in that, too."

Then, "Consider the yo-yo. How can you forget your roots so easily?"

I start cutting school, following him and Ligaya around. The Kid lectures me about bad karma and shoplifting books. He marches me into City Lights and introduces me to this long-haired Japanese guy who glowers from behind the cash register. "Now that you know his name, you can no longer steal from him," the Kid says.

We take the Muni everywhere. The Kid especially loves riding streetcars. Or we walk all over the city. Eat greasy noodles at Wooey Looey Gooey's, greasier French fries and hot dogs at Clown Alley and Doggie Diner. "One day I'll tell you about our historical connection to the hot dog," he says. For a spiritual man, the Kid's remarkably nonjudgmental about eating meat or processed food. "You eat what you gotta eat."

But he's no fool. "Hey, sister, I hear your mama's a damn good cook. How about it?"

I invite him and Ligaya to my cousin Peachy's wedding reception, which is held at one of the smaller ballrooms in the Hilton Hotel. Uncle Bas got a package deal because of his first wife having worked there when she was alive. My mother's catering the buffet for two hundred noisy and hungry Pinoys, her biggest job ever. Everyone's dressed to kill: Mrs. Bambang and other sour-faced matrons in their beaded *ternos*, solemn men in their shimmery *barong tagalogs*, doll-like children in organza ruffles, sensual beauties in their flouncy taffetas. Absolutely no beiges or muted pastels; only tropical colors abound, hot pinks, burnt oranges, canary yellows. Kid and Ligaya make their late entrance to a chorus of stares and murmurs. Voltaire and I rush to welcome them. "At last, ha, I meet your family," Kid says, his eyes twinkling mischievously as he scopes out the crowd. "Where's that famous *nanay* of yours?" For the occasion, he's put on dark corduroys and borrowed a long-sleeved white shirt that looks too small on him. Ligaya's got on a sacklike granny dress with her cowboy boots. "Aha." The Kid spots my mother commandeering the buffet table. "She's *maganda*," he observes. *So pretty.* Zeke Akamine hovers protectively around her, cigarette and drink in hand. The Kid swoops right in, shaking hands with Zeke and my mother, introducing Ligaya to both of them. It's as if Voltaire and I don't exist.

"Aha," my mother says. "I've been waiting to meet you."

"You from Hawaii?" Zeke asks.

"Why? Do I look like one a dem Buddhaheads?" the Kid retorts. Both men slap each other on the back, laughing. The Kid twinkles at my mother, who twinkles back.

The Kid visits the buffet several times, devouring enough *lumpia* and *lechon* to feed an army. He and Ligaya maneuver their way to Uncle Bas and Auntie Fely's table. By then the mood is genuinely festive. The Pinoy band, Rudy and the Romantics, starts playing "Plantation Boogie." Old and young men vie with each other to dance with the teary-eyed Peachy. Gifts of money are pinned to her wedding gown. Children squeal with delight, running through the throng of dancing couples. Voltaire convinces me to join him on the dance floor. We snap our fingers, doing flamboyant Latin hustle moves à la John Travolta. My mother cha-cha's expertly with the Carabao Kid, who's a smooth, surprising dancer. They dance all night, much to Zeke's chagrin. Rudy and the Romantics are absolutely amazing, segueing expertly from one musical genre to another. Everyone's a little drunk, full of food, and much more tolerant of strange, bearded Pinoys and their sack-clothed daughters. Kid gets the usual cultural cross-examination. *Where are your people from? Are you related to . . . ?*

Uncle Bas grosses me out, as usual, with his dumb remarks. "*Alam mo*, I'm an advocate of free love and the Black Panthers."

But Kid's his usual, nonjudgmental self. "Good for you, brother. Always keep an open mind."

"Tell that to my wife," Uncle Bas says.

"*Puwede ba*, Bas." Auntie Fely lets out a loud sigh of exasperation.

The Kid and Ligaya disappear again, this time for months. I go by the barbershop. "So where are they?" I ask Manong Joey, who shrugs.

"Who knows? They'll just show up, like they always do. One of these days . . ."

But they don't. Manong Joey gets a collect call from Ligaya from some godforsaken town in Louisiana. The Kid and Ligaya had gone there to look for work shrimping, but the day after they arrive, Kid collapsed and died instantly. According to Ligaya, a blood vessel burst in his brain. "Aneurysm," she said. Manong Joey and I take up a collection to help Ligaya bring her father's body back to San Francisco. *Shrimping. Aneurysm.* What the fuck is that? I ask Manong Joey, who looks permanently grief-stricken. I am stricken with grief, too, and want answers to my futile questions. "Was the aneurysm from his boxing days?" The old men in the shop are silent.

Voltaire and those volunteer guys from the hotel organize a memorial reading for the Kid at Our Lady of Guadalupe Church, in the Mission. Father Bayani, the Pinoy minister, raps from the pulpit like a poet. He was a friend of the Kid and pays flowery tribute to his wisdom, humility, and humor. Father Bayani invokes the Kid's name as if it were powerful enough to drive evil spirits away: *Amador, Amador Reyes.* Father Bayani's a born showman. He knows not to talk too long and exactly when to back off. "And nowww," he says melodramatically to all of us packed in the church, "it is your turn to remember." A red banner with the carabao emblem is unfurled. There are poets, community activists, families with children, the guy from City Lights. My mother shows up, her face grim. She and Voltaire, who escorts her, don't stay long. Ligaya sits in a state of shock, between Manong Joey and his wife, Manang Alma. I didn't know then that I would never see Ligaya again.

Poets take turns at the podium, reciting their favorite haikus by the Kid, or their own poems composed in his honor. I've never been surrounded by so many real-life Pinoy poets, colorful, inspiring, and intimidating. They strut and swagger when they walk up to perform. *Chickaboom, chickaboom.* A deadpan Pinay with outlandish eye make-up and sequined jeans chants to a conga drum. I'm paralyzed by fear. She leans toward me, whispering encouragement: "Go, sister, go."

I recite, "When I die, / eat your sorrow, / devour a mango, / then dance / a juicy tango for me." Not one of the Kid's deepest, but one of my favorites.

A *manong* is helped up to the podium. He's trembling uncontrollably, like maybe he's got one of those old folks' diseases. I recognize him as Nemesio, the vet who'd exploded in a rage back at the barbershop. He's got on the same white suit and he pulls himself together long enough to stop trembling and play a *kundiman* called "Hating Gabi" on the violin. In the front row of the church sit the other old men, listening intently to the bittersweet music, proud and erect in their sharp summer suits.

Voltaire's tone is playful. "Remember when he gave you that book by Carlos Bulosan? You got in a huge argument —"

"The Kid acted like I was being sacrilegious," I say.

"He was right. You never even bothered reading it."

"That's not true. I read the first fifty pages, then jumped to the end."

It wasn't just an argument. It was a shouting match. We were having one of our late-night noodle fest debates in Chinatown. I was in one of my dark *sumpung* moods and felt like lashing out at the Kid and the world. There was a devil comin' from inside me that wouldn't shut up. The Kid made the mistake of asking me if I'd enjoyed reading *America Is in the Heart*. "Bulosan's a bore," I said. "A noble martyr. An overrated, sentimental writer. A mediocre poet."

The Kid seemed stunned by my attitude. Ligaya and Voltaire just sat there, listening. "Sister, sister, how can you say such arrogant, cruel things?"

"There are no surprises in that book." I'm enjoying acting like a bully. "The outcome's too goddam predictable. Suffering, heartache, yearning. Pain with a capital *P* — and more pain! I'm sick of humility. I'm sick of being grateful. America in the heart? Bullshit. You say Pinoys love to party? I say we love to suffer."

"I don't disagree with you on that, sister," the Kid said calmly, fixing a steady, unsettling gaze on me.

"I'm just sick sick sick of reading about it," I whined. I felt ashamed of myself. How could I tell him I didn't need him anymore?

Voltaire's voice shatters my reverie. "Did you hear me? I've finally got enough money and I'm going back to Manila, for good."

"I had the strangest dream," Milagros says, grimacing as she sits up on the sofa. "It felt very real. I could've sworn I got up this morning, tiptoed into your kitchen, and made rice for your father. Everything was normal. I knew I was in New York in your apartment. I knew I was visiting the baby. Your father was sleeping somewhere in the shadows of this room. I never actually saw him, but I knew he was there. I heard him moaning from his bed, 'I'm hungry, hurry.' I was cooking as fast as I could, in total darkness." She gathers her thoughts. "The dream was a sign. He's going to die, very soon."

It's early in the morning but already stifling in the apartment. Rocky sits by the open window, nursing Venus. "I always hated nursing," Milagros says. "No milk with any of my babies, except you. We never quite recovered from the war, you know. Never seemed to have enough to eat. I had to give Luz and Voltaire soybean as a supplement." She looks down at herself. "How could you let me sleep in this dress? *Qué horror.*" Rocky smiles. "It's new. Got it on sale at Macy's. What time is it? Already? Ay, that's right. I'm three hours behind, right? *Dios,* I need my coffee and my cigarette." From the kitchen, a note of surprise. "You got me instant? *Salamat.* You know your mother can't drink anything else." She puts the kettle on the stove. "Whatever happened to that friend of yours?"

Rocky moves the baby up to her shoulder and attempts to burp her. "You mean Keiko?"

Milagros seems unsure. "Maybe. The one who kept taking your picture."

"Keiko," Rocky says, nodding. "Keiko's in Venice right now. She might show up while you're here."

"Voltaire bought a magazine," Milagros says. "She was on the cover."

"Yeah," Rocky says. "Keiko's in a lot of magazines. She's famous."

"That girl always knew what she wanted," Milagros says, transfixed by the baby.

Rocky is unnerved by the sight of Milagros splashing water on her face at the kitchen sink. Nonchalantly, Milagros pats herself dry with paper towels. What the hell's happening to her vain, fastidious mother? A woman who reigns from her run-down San Francisco apartment as if she were still the privileged wife of Francisco Rivera, as if her children were still children, safely ensconced in Gothic institutions run by sweating Jesuit priests and scowling nuns. Milagros Rivera is a woman just as capable of grand delusions as practical realities, a woman brave enough to abandon her marriage, but foolish enough to pine for the same man who betrayed her. Her contradictions infuriate Rocky. Her mother looms large in her life, but her father remains a jumble of fragmented images and shadowy memories, a man with a soft face and an apologetic, haunted expression. Rocky remembers a childhood of her mother's friends flirting with him quite openly, her envious cousins calling him *guwapo*. She's inherited her father's full, petulant mouth. Wasn't he fond of dressing in white? The last photo that Luz sent showed a potbellied man with a jowly face, dressed like a bum.

As the years in America fly by, Rocky prefers to think of him as dead. "I don't have a father," she'd respond when asked. The Kid used to chastise her about it. "You got to make peace with him, sister."

"I don't know him," Rocky said. "Don't remember much. Did he cry when we left? Did I? Never even knew what he did for a living."

She's obsessed with finding out why her mother gave him so much power. Her father wasn't, isn't, even really handsome. Not like his brother, Uncle Marlon, is handsome. Movie-star handsome. No one ever said anything about how smart her father was, or how clever. "Charming," was all Rocky remembered the women in her family saying. "He's so charming." Rocky resolved never to hand over that kind of power to any man or woman, never to wait around like her mother waited around. For her father to come back, for her life to change. *He'll be back.* It had happened so long ago that Rocky wasn't even sure if her parents had actually broken up over a woman. *Just another woman. He'll be back.* It was a source of painful and juicy *tsismis* back in Manila. Rocky's uncles, her grandfathers, her older cousins, her father, all the married men on both sides of her family, in fact, had strayed. Great-grandfather Rivera had actually been killed in bed with his best friend's wife. Lolo Flores was known to have an "outside" family, and more than twenty illegitimate children. But he was discreet about his intrigues, so Lola Flores kept her humiliation to herself, and the marriage stayed intact. Rocky's mother was different, confronting her husband in public, making demands, issuing ultimatums.

"It's not really about your father, you know. Your mother simply wants to go home," the Carabao Kid observed. "She's had enough of this country, but she'll never admit it."

"So why doesn't she?" Rocky asked, exasperated with all of them. Voltaire, too. Why didn't he just get on a goddam plane and go back?

The Carabao Kid said that Rocky's mother was just like the stubborn old men back at Manong Joey's barbershop. Fiercely determined to keep up appearances at any cost, strutting proudly to their graves. But why? Rocky would ask, bewildered. What for? All that bragging and pretending, all that posturing and face-saving, got them absolutely nowhere. What was so bad about admitting failure or defeat?

"I'm fiercely determined, too," Rocky said, "but in the opposite direction."

The Kid laughed. "Yes, sister, I know. Flaunt it, shake it, fuck 'em if they can't take it."

"Sounds like a song," Rocky said, laughing with him.

"What are you hiding and who are you, sister?" the Carabao Kid asked.

Rocky rolled her eyes in disgust.

The Kid teased her, "Ay, *malakas ka talaga.* I even hear your mind's eye rolling."

"You got a way with words," Rocky said.

"I got away, all right," the Kid responded.

"How come you never ask Voltaire who he is and what he's hiding?"

"He already knows. He hides nothing."

"Oh, yeah? Who is he, then? A Fili- or Pilipino?"

"Stop beating yourself up, Rocky," the Kid said. "Your mother's not Imelda Marcos, your father's not that greedy tyrant. What went wrong isn't your fault." He paused. "And it isn't your brother's fault, either. "

The kettle whistles. Milagros brings her coffee to the table by the window. "So are we shopping today? I'll cook a big dinner tonight. Bas and Fely can join us."

"Jake thought we'd take you all to a restaurant."

Milagros is indignant. "Why spend all that money for a mediocre meal? It's settled, then. You call Bas and Fely while I take my shower. Then we'll go shopping. Where's that husband of yours, *ba?*"

Rocky bristles at the word *husband.* "He probably went to *his* apartment so he could sleep."

"Well then, we'll just take the baby with us."

"Ma, I told you. I don't know if I feel like going all the way to Chinatown," Rocky says. "It's too hot and I'm exhausted."

"Today's my only free day," Milagros insists stubbornly. "I'm off to the trial with Bas and Fely tomorrow."

Rocky groans in defeat. Nestled in her grandmother's arms, Venus yawns contentedly. Her dot of a mouth opens wide into a huge black O. Her fingers curl into puny fists. "Look at you,"

Milagros croons with delight, "just look at you." The infant gazes with cloudy eyes at the unkempt old woman before her.

"I finished cooking the rice in my dream," Milagros says. Rocky gets up from her chair to stretch her aching body. "I keep filling bowls and feeding the rice to your father," Milagros continues. "The room stays dark. 'More,' he begs, 'more.' I tell him, 'I'm going as fast as I can.'"

Milagros, Fely, and Bas walk up the steps of the federal court-house at nine in the morning. Reporters and photographers are already there, smoking cigarettes and drinking coffee. Fely happily points out a few Pinoys with video cameras, notebooks, and self-important airs. There is excitement and anticipation, an odd sense of camaraderie among the waiting Filipinos. All are here for the same reason, eager spectators at Imelda's daily sideshow. Rich or poor, clad in Gucci loafers or double-knit polyester, they know it's the best drama in town, and it's free.

Fely approaches one of the men. "What time is Imelda coming?" He is friendly and answers her in Tagalog. Fely hurries back to where Milagros stands, clutching her handbag and smoking. Beside her, Bas is carefully recombing his hair. "Maybe thirty or forty minutes *pa daw.* That's what the guy said. You want to have breakfast? Should we go in? Where do we go?" she asks Bas.

Milagros is curious. "Who's the reporter working for?"

"I think the *Filipino Inquirer* or *Philippine-American Herald,* I'm not sure."

Milagros is disappointed by Fely's answer. "Look! It's that guy from NBC." She nudges Fely with her elbow and points to a beefy young man with curly blond hair and a mustache. Bas wanders off to the Filipino reporter and introduces himself. Soon the men are laughing, and other Filipino men join them. Fely is annoyed. "Bas is always making *tsismis* with everyone he meets. Next thing you know they'll come back to the motel with us for dinner," she complains. Milagros gives one of her I-told-you-so smirks. Bas leaves the reporter and goes back up the steps to the women. "Where's the camera? Hurry up, Fely. Let's take a souvenir picture!" Fely hands him the camera.

"Let's pose at the top of the steps," Bas suggests. "And maybe when Imelda gets here we can pose with her." Milagros gives him a disapproving look. "What's wrong, Mila? Don't be a kill-joy, *naman!* This is a *herstorical* event, *di ba?* Or maybe I should say *hysterical.*" Bas laughs.

Milagros is furious. "How can you even think of posing with that woman?"

"Why not? She's famous!"

The three of them huddle, Bas in the center with his arms around both women, beaming. Milagros cringes from his touch. She has taken great pains to dress elegantly but simply for the trial, a strand of valuable Mikimoto pearls around her neck. The pearls were a gift from Francisco, before Milagros found out about his mistress. He'd won them in a high-stakes poker game.

You never know who might show up from Manila. Why, Patsy Lozano had called to say that she planned to come with someone whose name Milagros can't remember, someone who made a stopover in New York from Manila on his way to Rome. Just to see Imelda! The trial has become a major tourist attraction for most Filipinos.

There are rumors that today is the day George Hamilton will be called on to testify. Wouldn't that be something? Now there's somebody Milagros wouldn't mind standing next to in a photograph.

Her friend Patsy Lozano once danced with George Hamilton at one of those parties in the old days. When she isn't in Manila visiting her grandchildren, Patsy Lozano divides her time between a town house in London and another on the Upper East Side of Manhattan. She calls Milagros whenever she's in San Francisco. They meet at Macy's or Gump's and gossip while Patsy shops. Patsy always treats her to lunch, which Milagros finds embarrassing. "I'll see you at the trial," Patsy chirped the last time. Patsy Lozano considers long-distance calls, flights on the Concorde, and intimate dinner parties with Imelda and Doris Duke "no big deal," though Patsy Lozano also considers herself a staunch Aquino supporter. She was featured prominently in a cover story that the *New York Times Sunday Magazine* did on upper-class women in the Philippines aligning themselves with the People Power movement. Rocky sent Milagros the magazine, which Milagros saved in her trunk along with press clippings of Rocky's band and other assorted Rocky memorabilia. Milagros was amazed at how demonstrations and street rallies had suddenly become chic among Manila socialites. She knew half the women mentioned in the article and couldn't believe what she read. And there was her friend Patsy, absurdly glamorous in Cory-yellow golfing shirt and Cory-yellow visor, immortalized in a photograph, shouting, "Cory! Cory!" at some pivotal rally held near the American embassy right before the Marcoses were forced to flee. Milagros almost fainted from excitement when she saw it. She was thrilled for her old friend, and also envious. History was being made, no matter how raggedy or chaotic. Yet she was so very far away from it.

"What's the difference between the Marcos regime and the Aquino government, *ba?*" Milagros had once asked Patsy. Patsy Lozano could easily get on Milagros Rivera's nerves, but she was too powerful and privy to all the latest gossip for Milagros to dismiss easily. Even more important, Patsy's ex-husband used to be Francisco Rivera's favorite golfing partner and visits him frequently now that he is sick. Because Patsy is still on good terms with her ex-husband, she pumps him for information whenever she's in Manila, then passes on to Milagros all the gossip she's gathered concerning Milagros's ailing husband. The only thing they never discuss is Francisco's son by Baby Guzman, who Milagros continues to call "that woman."

So? she would ask Patsy as casually as possible. Have you heard any new *tsismis* about that woman?

"That woman" is also what Milagros sometimes calls Corazon Aquino and Imelda Marcos. "Seems to me things haven't changed one bit. And from what people say, under that woman's rule, they've gotten worse."

"Excuse me, *lang*, but I happen to believe that Cory is progressive," Patsy Lozano argues.

"That woman doesn't run the country! The army runs it!"

"Ay, Mila! There you go again! *Puwede ba*, you've been away too long and you believe everything you read in the foreign press!" Patsy Lozano chuckles. "Put yourself in Cory's place, *naman*! She's expected to clean up an economic mess that's been going on for over twenty years."

"And why can't she? Because she's just like that other one!"

"You're being too critical. Just put yourself in her place and ask yourself what you'd do in a similar situation."

"A helluva lot more than those women!"

"Ay, Mila, *naman*! Change takes time . . ." Patsy Lozano deftly switches topics and tells her about a certain Manila matron who caught her husband in bed with the houseboy.

Fely, in sneakers and pastel sweatsuit, carries snacks wrapped in aluminum foil in plastic shopping bags into the courtroom. Milagros hopes Patsy Lozano doesn't see her enter with Bas and Fely. Bas and Fely are exactly the kind of people Milagros wouldn't have bothered with if she'd stayed married to Francisco Rivera in Manila. But being in America has changed things. As far as Milagros goes, her sister's life has been ruined by her marriage to the loudmouthed, smarmy Basilio Cruz. Milagros refers to him as a commoner. A gold-digging wife killer. But like it or not, thick-skinned, jokey Bas is someone she's forced to put up with in New York. Besides, Bas makes himself indispensable by renting a car and driving them around.

Fely is older than Milagros by four years, but people often mistake her for Milagros's mother. The image of a bewildered immigrant in perpetual culture shock, Fely shyly trails behind her sophisticated sister when they are out in public. Rocky adores her and lovingly refers to Fely as "my no-bullshit aunt." Voltaire has said she should've been canonized when she married Bas, and he calls her Santa Auntie. Milagros can't live with her, or without her.

Basilio Cruz outdoes himself today in a seersucker leisure suit, which he wears with white nylon socks and white patent-leather Florsheims. "Just for Imelda," he brags. He keeps his counterfeit Porsche Carrera sunglasses on even indoors. Basilio's open shirt displays his diamond crucifix, and the brand-new Olympus that Fely has bought him hangs from a strap around his neck.

"Poor Tiyo Bas. He can't decide whether he's a pimp or a tourist," Rocky whispered to her mother when Bas drove up in the Cadillac earlier that morning.

Milagros stares straight ahead, following Imelda and her lawyers into the courtroom. She is fascinated by how Imelda's famous lawyer towers over Imelda, who is pretty tall for a typical Filipina. The cowboy lawyer reminds Milagros of . . . is it John Wayne? Randolph Scott? Imelda, all in black, gives her fans and supporters a tentative, sad smile, the practiced smile, Milagros decides, of a martyr. Imelda glances in her direction. Perhaps she notices the genuine pearls around Milagros's neck. Milagros is sure that Imelda, at the very least, retains a good eye for authentic jewelry. Did she remember Milagros? There was a time when . . . Milagros puts the thought out of her mind as she looks around for the best place to sit.

Bas has already situated himself in the press section, next to the Filipino journalist. He pulls out a small memo pad and ballpoint pen from his pocket, ready to take his notes. What nerve! Milagros shakes her head slowly. Fely puts on her eyeglasses and pats the space next to her on the cushioned bench. Milagros is relieved. At least they are sitting in the safe, pro-Aquino section, the second to the last row on the left side facing the judge. Patsy Lozano, a veteran spectator at the Imelda trial, has warned her that one's political sympathies are determined by where one chooses to sit.

"But what if it's crowded, and I have no choice?" Milagros asked her.

"Get there early then," Patsy Lozano advised.

Patsy is one of those powerful, in-the-know Filipinos. And no matter how Milagros feels about Cory, she certainly doesn't want to be mistaken for a Marcos loyalist. It's too . . . common and vulgar. Like the way Bas and Fely dress.

Milagros glances at her preening brother-in-law. What did Fely ever see in him? "Moocher" was practically tattooed across his forehead. Milagros was sure Bas was planning to one day poison her loyal, trusting sister for insurance money, just like he did his first wife.

Milagros spots another familiar face. Isn't that ex-Congressman Diosdado "Cyanide" Abad sitting right in front of her? Definitely a Marcos loyalist, everyone knows that. Why is he sitting on the left side? Milagros panics.

The marshals usher more important-looking foreigners into the courtroom, slender women carrying Chanel handbags and balding Middle Eastern men whose various colognes perfume the stuffy atmosphere. Are these Khashoggi's people? Milagros wonders. "Who's that?" Fely whispers loudly. A bent man with white hair, a trimmed beard, and the gaunt, ascetic face of Saint Jerome is helped to his seat by a haughty woman who wears a hat. The old man is someone out of a more elegant era, with his impeccable linen suit, spats, and bamboo cane. Intrigued, Milagros forgets about Congressman Abad and Fely rustling her bags packed with Spam sandwiches and cans of Diet Coke.

Too bad Raquel couldn't come with them today, Milagros thinks. It would certainly give her something to write about. Maybe she could talk her into coming tomorrow. This was much too important for Raquel to miss. And if that companion of hers or whatever she wants to call him is too busy to take care of the baby, then what the hell, Raquel should just bring the damn baby with her. Ay, *dios ko*, Milagros sighs to herself. If things were different and they were back in Manila, she would hire a *yaya* to help Raquel take care of Venus. Then they wouldn't have to be bothered with any of this.

Three rows behind Imelda and her lawyers, a familiar woman fans herself and whispers into the ear of a short, effete young man. He is laughing softly. They are completely engrossed in each other. The woman turns, and her glittering, made-up eyes meet those of Milagros. It is Patsy Lozano. Patsy gives a little wave with her fan, then pantomimes making a phone call to Milagros later. With a faint smile, Milagros nods in agreement, noting how Patsy's surgically tightened features are frozen into a sleek mask belonging to a woman of thirty. Milagros wonders if Patsy recognizes Fely beside her.

Patsy's attention drifts back to the man next to her, and their conversation resumes. The judge enters the room. "All rise," someone orders in a loud voice. A hush falls over the courtroom.

The judge makes a motion for them to sit back down. From the press section, Basilio Cruz clears his throat so noisily that Milagros Rivera is terrified he'll forget himself and spit. Basilio adjusts the collar of his shiny shirt and brushes imaginary lint off the pointed lapels of his jacket. Milagros frowns. For a man with absolutely no taste, Basilio Cruz is incredibly fussy.

The chief prosecutor is speaking. An earnest man in a rumpled suit, he's a dead ringer for Al Pacino — but not very impressive when Bas compares him to Imelda's cowboy. Basilio Cruz tunes the prosecutor out and studies Imelda, memorizing every detail so he can go on about it later to his girlfriend. Imelda's helmet of blacker than black hair, which never moves. The subtle, black pearl button earrings. Her gray eye shadow and pale lips. A surprising woman, Bas admits to himself, one who should never be underestimated.

Over there sits Adnan Khashoggi, utterly relaxed and almost pretty. Is that rouge on his cheeks? Mascara on his curly lashes? Maybe he's *bakla*, Bas thinks. They all are, probably, including that macho cowboy lawyer of Imelda's.

A wave of pleasure washes over Basilio Cruz. He makes plans to come back to the trial for the rest of the week. After all, he is free to do as he pleases. Maybe he'll write about it for one of those local Pinoy papers, like the *Phil-Am Herald* or the *Daly City Messenger*. He could be their New York correspondent. Their *national* correspondent. Aren't they always looking for new talent? Money isn't the issue. Like he often says to Fely, "Money isn't everything." Bas understands when it comes to community and the news media. He's a community man, a proud Filipino, eager to work for a modest fee. His wife says he has a way with words. So does that *chuplada* sister of hers, Miss Big-Time Milagros Rivera. It must be true. And now that he's chummy with the reporter sitting next to him . . . what's his name? Bert. That's right. Bert Avedilla. Bert has connections.

The first witness is called. Not George Hamilton, but some FBI agent. Bert Avedilla scribbles on a yellow legal pad. Basilio steals a glance at what the reporter is writing. Today's date, the name of the FBI man, the chief prosecutor's first question. Such logic! Such detail! Basilio is inspired and copies down Avedilla's notes.

What an exciting day. This trip to New York had been worth all the expense. Bas looks back to wink at his nearsighted wife, who is nodding off into sleep. Fely falls asleep wherever they go. It's been going on since the day they were married. No matter how noisy it is or what they are doing, Fely nods off without warning. Her physician has diagnosed it as some mild, harmless form of narcolepsy and claims there is nothing one can do. There are brief periods when Fely's condition doesn't manifest itself — at her job, for example. Fely never falls asleep while she is working at the hospital.

What if Fely starts snoring?

Bas signals Milagros discreetly. In response, she nudges Fely gently with her elbow. No reaction. Milagros shrugs and turns her attention back to the FBI man on the stand. Fely's heavy body slumps against her. The agent drones on about secret Swiss bank accounts and the incomprehensible "trail of deceit" left by Imelda and her cronies. The agent gets off the stand and points to a chart. Figures are quoted, and the district attorney asks more tedious questions. Along with Fely, two members of the jury have also fallen asleep. Fely's breathing slows down as she begins to wheeze and snore, softly at first. Then the snoring becomes more audible. Basilio coughs. Milagros can feel Basilio's eyes boring holes into her, begging her to do something about Fely, but Milagros pointedly ignores him. Son of a bitch. Let him squirm. Let her sweet, tired, hardworking sister sleep.

During recess, Milagros and the now awake Fely go to the women's rest room one floor down. Fely starts to bring her shopping bags with her. "Leave them on the seat," Milagros suggests irritably, taking the bags away from Fely.

"But —"

"Fely, please, nobody's going to steal them."

Bas has disappeared with the reporter. Patsy Lozano is in the hallway outside the courtroom, waiting for an elevator with her companion. She spots Milagros and signals her to join them. Milagros points to the staircase in the opposite direction and waves goodbye to her. Patsy Lozano looks annoyed by Milagros Rivera's elusive behavior and whispers something into her companion's ear.

The women's rest room consists of one toilet stall with a broken door. Someone is inside the stall, attempting to urinate and hold the broken door shut at the same time. Two Pinay women wait by the sink for their turn. As she enters, Fely trips and bumps into the younger woman, who glares at her. The first, heavyset woman is retouching her eyebrows with a dark pencil and assessing herself in the mirror. "How boring, *naman!*" She complains to her friend, finishing with her eyebrows. After a moment, she leans forward to draw a mole on her cheek. "Too many details, *dios ko!*" She mimics the chief prosecutor's voice. "If you say you took a taxi, what was the license number? Who was the driver? What time of day was it? The exact date and location where you caught the cab? Boring *talaga!* Ay." The woman gives an exaggerated sigh. Her friend joins her in a chorus of sighs. "Boring *talaga!*" she echoes.

From the stall, an older white woman maneuvers her way to

the sink to rinse her hands. Milagros remembers her from the courtroom. Why is she at Imelda's trial? Milagros tries to work up the nerve to ask her, but the white woman leaves before she has a chance.

The heavyset woman keeps up her chatter. "Let's go home *na*! We have such a long subway ride."

"But what about George Hamilton?" her friend asks plaintively.

"*Ay, naku*! I don't think he's worth it! Too many questions about nothing!" The heavyset woman flushes the toilet.

Suddenly Fely speaks. "Excuse me *lang*, ladies, but a case like this is really complicated. We have to be patient. *Di ba*, Mila? This is history. So many ins and outs. Slowly they are building a case. They have to ask many questions because . . ." She pauses to think. "Because they are grooving in the dark!"

"You mean groping," Milagros says dryly.

"Groping, that's it," Fely says.

Milagros pays her sister a rare compliment. "That's right. You're absolutely right." Fely is delighted.

The other two women exchange astonished glances and exit hastily.

"I could've sworn you slept through the trial," Milagros says, amused.

Behind her thick glasses, Fely's magnified gaze is open and innocent. "I did."

Black

"In Spanish, *yo-yo* means 'I, I.'"
   — *Voltaire Rivera*

"Black: Nothing is black; really, *nothing*."
   — *Frida Kahlo*

Cold blue light, the ripe smell of half-eaten food and unemptied trash bins. Venus in a stroller, amps, mikes, guitar cases, a battered set of Pearl drums, the upright piano scarred with cigarette burns, our pile of jackets and bags, the piano stool underneath. Rocky's in one of her moods, bitching about last night's gig. "What are the rest of us supposed to do while you solo — dance around like the Ikettes?"

"I love the Ikettes," I say.

She reminds me, once again, that it's her band, her funky global doo-wop choir of disharmony. *My dream, Elvis.*

"It was *my* concept," I argue. "I shared it with you."

Rocky is sour and unforgiving. "Don't claim credit for everything I do."

I can't believe what I'm hearing. "I am so tired of your shit."

"Feeling's mutual." She takes a drag off my cigarette before stubbing it out.

"What the fuck are you doing?"

"The baby," she answers curtly, then turns on the charm. "So, darlin', where's our buddy?" When I don't respond, she sighs. "Sly's days are numbered."

"Why you gotta talk about him like that?"

"He's costing us money with his late shit."

"Why you gotta be so hard?"

"Hard?" She's trying not to laugh. "Gimme a break."

"No, you give *me* a break. And while you're at it, give Sly a break."

Venus starts to fuss. I go over to the stroller. Check her out. She's a wrinkled little thing — funny too, with that black hair like a Buckwheat fright wig. Venus squinches her face, crying. I pick her up, patting her back and walking her around like I used to do with my brother, Dwayne. She cries even louder. Rocky holds out her arms. "Let me," she murmurs, pulling up her T-shirt. I hand Venus over. She smells the milk, whimpering as she attacks Rocky's breast. Rocky flinches. I wonder how much it hurts her.

I wish Sly would hurry the fuck up and get here.

Rocky coos at Venus. "Hey, sweet thing."

I surprise her. "Wanna go check out Sly Stone's comeback at the Red Parrot this Saturday?"

She looks at me, suspicious. "Are you fucking with me, Elvis?" Ha, she snorts, rolling those eyes. *Sly Stone's comeback, sure.*

Rocky doesn't forgive or forget. She's the one who left, but I get the blame. If she ever got a whiff of the deal I'm cookin' up with Brian, she'd accuse me of sabotaging her. It's always personal. Shit. The Gangster of Love has gone as far as it can go. I'm forming my own powerhouse trio. Takin' Sly and E. Sharp with me. Bass, guitar, drums — that's all I need. Speed and noise. Excruciatingly simple. Low maintenance. "Powerhouse." Maybe that's what we'll call ourselves. No more confusion about who's the boss. I'm writing the music *and* the lyrics. Brian's finally woken up from his slump. Like he's ready to act like a white man and make some money. He's been hangin' out, schmoozing with A and R types, getting a buzz going. Last I heard, Warner Brothers loved my demo. The Jimi Hendrix Experience meets the Elvis Chang Powerhouse Experience. Ha.

Sly wanders in lookin' bad. Gray and sweaty and stumbling over the equipment. "Watch it, man." He's been wearing that same stinky jumpsuit all week. Rocky's doin' a slow burn. "Been to sleep yet?" I tease him, trying to ease the tension.

Sly approximates a grin, clenching his teeth at me. Mumbling something like, "Yeah, yeah, gronk it."

"Speak English," Rocky snarls.

A middle-aged white woman with flaming red hair trails sheepishly behind him, with Sly's bag of percussion instruments slung over her shoulder.

"Say hello to Rusty," Sly croaks.

Rocky's about to explode, but he doesn't notice. Sly's in La-La Land, staring at his drums, not sure of what to do first. Finally, Rusty does it for him. She sets his equipment up like a pro, then makes room for herself on the piano stool. I have a feeling she's done this before. She pulls out a silver flask from her purse. Feeling my eyes, she looks over and offers me the flask. "Wild Turkey," she says, grinning. There's lipstick on her teeth and she's old enough to be my mother, but her tits and legs are magnificent.

"I've met you somewhere," I say, taking a sip.

"Yeah. You probably have," she says. I offer the flask to Rocky, who waves it away. The baby's finished her dinner. Rocky gets up and swaggers over to the microphone, Miz Hot Shit, Miz Sheena, Queen of the Jungle. Venus does her goo-goo act in Rocky's arms, content and drooling at me. Rocky leans into the mike. "Let's open with 'Gangster Boogie.'"

Cold blue light. I'm ready, fat joint tucked in between the frets of my guitar, pick in hand. E. Sharp plugs his ancient Fender bass into the amp. Rusty leans back against the piano and closes her eyes. Beads of sweat glisten on Sly's forehead. He glances at me, then at Rocky, waiting for her signal to begin. She nods. Clutching his sticks, Sly crashes face first into his drums. Rocky can't believe it. I'm shaking him like a rag doll. "Sly, man, you okay?"

Rusty's eyes fly open, big and round. "Oh dear," she murmurs.

Disgusted, Rocky grabs her jacket and the baby's things. She pushes the stroller with Venus inside as fast as she can out of the studio. Like a fool, I keep yelling at Sly. "Don't do this to me, Sly. Not now, man. Not now."

Rusty puts a hand on my shoulder, her tone sympathetic. "It's okay, love. Really. He does this sometimes. He'll come out of it."

One love. The sun's coming up, his favorite time of day. In-between time. Sly clambers down the narrow wooden stairs. The woman with the fiery hair and exhausted face follows at a slower pace. The thumping groove of music drifts out with them into the wet, desolate streets. In the ruins known as Playland, there is no air. Sly's always been drawn to the darker shades. He thinks he's Dracula, loves being recognized and acknowledged by unpredictable men with raspy voices. Their lacquered women sip Don Q rum or Rémy Martin and rarely speak. There are mainly men in Playland, never any unescorted women. You have to identify yourself at the door, you have to know somebody. Everyone is presumed to carry a gun. The heavy bass amplified and isolated in the music pulsates in your groin, in your skull, in your veins. It is always night and there is no air, a certain kind of menace to the smoky atmosphere that Sly loves and appreciates. Back in Detroit, he was Dwight, a middle-class Catholic schoolboy. Only son of Vivian, a retired social worker, and Dwight Sr., a retired principal. His baby sister, Roxanne, is the first to dub him Sly. Roxy has graduated from college with honors, works for a bank, and single-handedly raises a son. Oh, if Roxy could see him now, playing drums, shucking and jiving, slapping palms, girls hangin' off him, heh-heh-heh, face black and gleaming, electric white smile, meticulously cultivated, bronze-tipped dreadlocks. He knows everyone there is to know, he hangs out with the heavies, he throws parties, he's the pasha of Lower Manhattan. Would Roxy pity him? Would she cry or laugh?

Are you holdin', my man?

The men pose in the shadows, hands caressing their lacquered women's thighs, hands delicately holding paper cups of rum. The weak, whorish glow of colored bulbs on black walls, black floor, the low black ceiling. Sly has long ago chosen this underbelly, this underground, this sleazy, after-hours Dracula underworld, as part and parcel of his life as a musician. He's playing the purist, the gangster, living solely for the coke, the pussy, the ultimate thrill of creating the music itself. It's a beautiful life, man. Myself chasing myself, as crazy Rocky once said. Sly loves

Rocky almost as much as he loves his mother and sister. Tough, okay women, women he reluctantly trusts and grudgingly respects.

Tonight's been a perfect New York night. He makes the rounds downtown and uptown, says hello to some people, makes new and invaluable connections. At Playland, the music is lowdown and insinuating, everyone mellow and happy. Sly and the redhead stagger out into the street, where a muscular Jamaican in a long leather coat, his dreadlocks sprouting from a jaunty leather cap, emerges from nowhere and cockily approaches. "Hey, Sly, wha's happenin'? Been a long time, man." They beam at each other. There's plenty of backslapping, hugging, and laughing.

Sly's radiant, the sun's coming up, the world's percolating. He's surprised and glad to encounter the Jamaican, who goes by the name Junior. Junior's a fixture in the East Village, attaching himself to musicians, getting wasted while picking up white girls. Sly hasn't seen him for at least a year. He's too high to care or ask where Junior's been, why he's shown up so suddenly on these wet, desolate, uptown streets. Out of nowhere. "Everything cool, brudda man, really cool." Sly slips into a flawless imitation of Junior's accent. The redhead feels uneasy around the imposing, leather-clad Jamaican, who pointedly ignores her. She wraps the Minnie Mouse–print acrylic fur tighter around her shivering body to ward off the early morning chill. It's been raining all night, and the street of abandoned buildings glistens.

Are you holdin, my man? Junior looks around furtively, then turns to Sly and pantomimes sucking on a joint. Sly hasn't slept in forty-eight hours. He pantomimes back: But of course.

Grinning amiably, Junior reaches inside his leather jacket and pulls out the biggest, shiniest, freakiest nine-millimeter gun Sly has ever seen. Jumping back, Junior aims the weapon at Sly, who stands there disoriented. His hands are held, palms up, in a bewildered, What the fuck? gesture. Pulling out his own gun doesn't even occur to him. *This is Junior, his running buddy.* "Is this some kinda tired joke?" Sly asks. The redhead gasps, scurrying behind Sly for protection. She covers her ears and squeezes her eyes shut, a childish reflex. The three of them are alone on the street. Playland, with its throbbing music, seems to have vaporized in the darkness. "One love, man. Remember, one love. This for Dirk and Kirk," Junior whispers, shooting Sly several times in the stomach. Sly collapses on the pavement, a painful smile frozen on his face. Junior bends over, calmly wiping the barrel of his gun across Sly's shirt. He saunters off, disappearing quickly around a corner. The red-haired woman gasps in wonder. It had all happened so fast. Gone, just like that.

Our Music Lesson #2, Or How We Appropriated You: An Imaginary Short Starring Elvis Chang, Rocky Rivera, and Jimi Hendrix

[*Interior of an empty nightclub. Midafternoon. A tape loop of "Voodoo Chile" plays on the soundtrack. Elvis and Rocky are kissing passionately, ensconced in a booth. Sitting across from the kissing couple is a bemused Jimi Hendrix. As he looked in 1970, the year he died. Black Western gear and a silver conch belt studded with turquoise, black sombrero and sunglasses. A bib stained with wine and vomit is tied around Jimi's neck.*]

Elvis: Listen to your own words. "Oh, the night I was born, the moon turned a fire red." You were in sync with the times, but ahead of it too. Before you, there was no one. Maybe Chuck Berry. Maybe Little Richard. I was into Chuck Berry, just like every other guitar player in the world. I memorized all his licks. And that jagged chunka-chunka thing in all them James Brown classics. Juicy horn riffs.

Jimi: Maceo.

Rocky: That groove on "Cold Sweat." You know it?

Jimi: Say, beautiful. Of course I know it.

Rocky: [*trying to appease him*] I meant "you know it." Like you know it. Not you don't know it? Know what I mean? [*pause*] Why are you wearing that bib?

Jimi: To protect my shirt, ha ha.

Rocky: Now it's my turn to be offended.

Jimi: Sorry, beautiful. I'm feeling blue. Desolate and blue. [*looks around indifferently*] Nothing's changed.

Rocky: Take off those glasses. Let me see your eyes.

[*Jimi takes off glasses slowly.*]

Listen to the wail of your feedback, so fierce against the drummer's desperate flailing and bashing. What was his name?

Jimi: Noel. [*puts glasses back on*]

Rocky: Whatever. He can't keep up. He's drowning. The song winds down, the song's about to end. Hey, it was Mitch Mitchell on drums, wasn't it?

Jimi: You mean *whomever*, don't you? God, I am so bored with that song! Keyboards like a funhouse circus, the bass thumping. Aren't you sick of it? And I'm singin' so earnestly! They never said I *couldn't* sing, but shit. I hate *earnest*. God in a roomful of mirrors. Music is strange like that. Do the old man a favor and *turn the goddam song off!* [*pause*] Nothing interests me here. It's all about money.

Elvis: Three things to remember, old man. *Uno*, we can hardly afford to rehearse. *Dos*, hindsight is easy. *Tres*, Rocky is saved.

Jimi: Put anything else on. I don't give a fuck. Funkadelic! Prince! The Art Ensemble of Chicago!

Rocky: I was fourteen years old when you died. My brother was seventeen. He wanted to play guitar like you so bad, it paralyzed him. [*pause*] If you listen carefully, the "Voodoo Chile" melody is exactly the same as "Catfish Blues."

Jimi: I loved being taken care of. All I wanted to worry about was music. Those Europeans gave me carte blanche. "What is it you want to do, Jimi?" they asked me. "Would you like to present a big work, or something intimate for forty people?" [*laughs, pleased with himself*]

Rocky: If you listen carefully, "Voodoo Chile" follows "Catfish Blues."

Jimi: Are you accusing me of plagiarizing? Do this old man a favor and *turn* that fucker off! [*looks around, agitated*] Garçon! Garçon! Goddamit, where's service when you need it, *s'il vous plaît!*

Rocky: I believe we're in the South Bronx.

Elvis: [*embarrassed*] Sorry. We'll come back later. [*gets up to leave, but Rocky pulls him back into his seat*]

Rocky: [*to Jimi*] We're in London, eternally twenty-seven years old, in honor of you. Why are you afraid? This is a beautiful song. *You wrote it.* You sang it. Before you, there was no one. Accept your role in history. Flames bursting out of your skull. Salvation funky. Redemption funky.

Jimi: Redemption? [*laughs*] I sure as hell can't relate to that, sister.

Rocky: Why are you wearing that bib?

[*Jimi chuckles. Rocky climbs up on the table and starts to dance wildly. Just as abruptly, she sits back down.*]

Jimi: "Not enough grease." "Too much grease." These kids, they're like piranhas gnawing at me. I got tired of being critiqued. Do I play like the white boys? Do I fuck too many white women? I always wanted some of that white boy money. What a dilemma. Shit. I'm just a country boy.

Elvis: I'm just a country boy, too, Oakland country. My pop taught me to love the blues. Sounds just like Chinese music, he said. He gave me my name, didn't he? And I took a lotta shit for it.

Jimi: Your father named you after a clown and a thief. You know what Elvis the Pelvis once said? "Ain't nothin' a nigger can do for me but shine my shoes." [*to Rocky*] And what about you, beautiful? Why you try so hard to be a man?

Rocky: You sound just like my mother.

Jimi: Fuck me, then. Save my soul.

Rocky: Let's get one thing straight. You can't fool me. I know all about you. I was fourteen when you died, but I'm not stupid. Did you die with that bib on?

Jimi: Have you any idea how much pussy was thrown at me?

Elvis: [*to Rocky*] Will you quit blaming him for everything? Damn. I wish Sly were here. [*to Jimi*] Sorry about her. She's volatile. [*pause*] Our friend Sly, if he coulda met you, if he coulda jammed with you, he'd've died a happy man.

Rocky: But he didn't. No stairway to heaven for that poor sonuvabitch. Sly was shot full of holes because he was stupid, and now he's burning up in hell.

Jimi: [*to Rocky*] It's a thin line between love and hate, and you sure got a filthy mouth. [*to Elvis*] Please. Feel free to call me Jimi. [*to Rocky*] Say beautiful, can you calm down enough to spare this old man one of those Indonesian cigarettes? If I have to listen to this same old tired song all night long — [*pause as he lights up and exhales gratefully*] Ahhh. Smells good, don't it? Like a man's perfume. Sweet fire. [*sheepish*] I've tried cutting down, but it just don't work.

Elvis: You get the joke, right? We did a cover of "Voodoo Chile."

Rocky: Your song.

Jimi: No kidding.

Elvis: It was Rocky's idea to do it. She absolutely loved you, man.

Jimi: [*smiling at Rocky*] Is it true? You absolutely loved me?

Rocky: Still do.

Elvis: She did. We all did. She said, "Face it. We'll never write a song as simple and as good as this one." We always gave you the proper credit. [*Hendrix laughs.*]

Rocky: How come you played dead for so long?

Jimi: I had no choice. Sorry.

Rocky: I throw a party in your honor every year, on the anniversary of your death, which is also the anniversary of our coming to America. You know that? Of course you don't. [*pause*] Has anyone ever asked you if you were Pilipino? You look like you might have some of that blood.

Jimi: What blood?

Rocky: *Pilipino blood.* Damn, aren't you listening? Haven't you heard a thing I've said? Everybody I love is dead or dying. I have outlived most of my friends. I have a baby — somewhere. [*frantically looks under the table*] Oh my God, where did I put the baby? [*to Hendrix*] Do you have any children? Lookit you, sitting there so sad and sorry and horny. A dirty bib tied around your neck, stinking of vomit. Why'd you go and die and have to be so predictable?

Jimi: Thought I was a mystic, thought I was blessed. Thought that was enough. Chewed peyote. Wrote psychedelic poetry. Believed my own press, my cocaine-induced, rainbow warrior, ghetto royalty, gypsy freedom fighter, LSD-laced, corny, cosmi-comic mythology. I wasn't as bad as you think, was I?

[*Jimi and Rocky start singing*] "'Cause I'm a voodoo chile / voodoo chile / voodoo chile / voodoo chile." I played guitar with my tongue, set it on fire, and the whole world, too. What more do you want from me? I don't owe you or anyone else an apology, beautiful. The nights were long, the dogs kept howlin'. Like Edith Piaf usedta moan, *Je ne regret rien.*

[*Rocky leans over and slips off Hendrix's sunglasses before kissing him on the lips. It is a long, meaningful kiss. Elvis picks up Hendrix's burning cigarette and smokes it. He studies their passionate clinch with detached interest. "Voodoo Chile" audio fades up as this last image fades to black.*]

Keiko sat on the sofa bed, watching me make dinner in the kitchen. "I've been traveling too damn much."

"That's great that your work's in such demand," I said, wondering if I sounded sincere.

"I suppose." She paused, studying me. "Ran into Brian on my way here. He looks . . . prosperous. Says you haven't been down to pick up your checks."

"Bet he sounded anxious."

"Of course he did." Keiko smiled. "It's funny to see you cook."

"Is it? Jake says I'm careless with food. I only cook what's tried and true. You may want to eat out tonight," I warned her. "My lack of interest limits me to roast chicken and tossed green salad, which is on the menu."

"I love roast chicken."

"Boring but dependable," I said.

Tossing salads means nothing in this world when you consider my mother's a renowned cook, and so is the man she stubbornly calls my husband. Jake's inventive. At last night's welcome-back dinner for Keiko, he grilled salmon steaks along with eggplant, zucchini, and corn. Jake's accused me of being lazy and treating the preparation of food as another annoying domestic chore. He knows I long for unhealthier times, when life didn't revolve exclusively around food and family.

Keiko nibbled on a slice of cucumber. "Brian said your royalties are still coming in —"

"Yeah, I know."

"That's good, isn't it?"

"It's great. I never thought that one little song . . . —" I glanced at Venus in her playpen. She's on her stomach, gnawing and drooling on the terry cloth alphabet block Keiko brought her. "I've been thinking of asking for my old job back at the Stress Center."

Keiko was appalled. "Good God. Why? That's beneath you. Have you been writing at all?" Then she asked that hateful question: "When are you putting another band together?"

"I can't even bear to listen to music anymore," I said.

"It's about Elvis, isn't it? I don't blame you. That fucker goin' behind your back, breaking up the band like he did. Did you see him on MTV? And Sly getting whacked. I never liked him, but he didn't deserve *that*." I didn't respond. "You don't need a receptionist job, Rocky. Jake takes good care of both of you," she said.

"We take good care of each other, and Venus," I corrected her, feeling touchy.

"Oh yes," she agreed a little too quickly.

Jake worked a grueling schedule at the recording studio, but he didn't seem to mind. It was probably easier than being around me. I've been wallowing in self-pity, spending long, idle days with Venus, renting too many movies from Kim's Video down the street, eating and sleeping too much. Voltaire has returned to the Philippines, gone and done it at last. Should Venus and I join him? My mother calls me at the oddest hours, midnight, five or six in the morning. If I let the machine answer, she leaves rambling, irate messages, then calls again and again until I pick up. "Ma, is this an emergency? I'm sleeping."

"Are you?" she asks, bewildered.

I call Auntie Fely in alarm. "Is Ma all right? She calls me three or four times a day. It's never about anything. She rants on my answering machine, sometimes in Tagalog."

"Your mother's not well," Auntie Fely snaps. I'm surprised by her accusatory tone. "What are *you* going to do about it?"

When I don't answer, she says, "You'd better do something, soon."

It's something I cannot articulate, this inertia that has settled in.

Reach for the unexpected, the jungle jingle goes. It's occurred to me there's a slim chance I may be experiencing menopause early. After all, my mother had a hysterectomy before she turned forty. Or maybe it's post-whatever depression. Like the beautiful baby's born and the party's over. Now what? Rock 'n' roll doesn't prepare you for this.

Keiko and Jake don't know it yet, but I've fantasized my next line of attack. A solo act, maybe. Duet with saxophone? Deliberately corny, like a fifties beatnik act. So corny it might work.

Once, when I was window-shopping with Venus, I was intrigued by a woman in a polka-dot dress. Something about her, the way she dressed so carefully, prim in her bearing, as if she were a TV sitcom matron, June Cleaver or Donna Reed, sexuality cinched tight and reined in by starched aprons, shirtwaist dresses, and black stilettos. She looked about my age. I followed her into a pharmacy on Sixth Avenue, the big fancy well-lighted kind that sells everything from drugs to stationery, French perfume, and toys. While Venus slept in her stroller, I eavesdropped snatches of the woman's conversation with the cashier, jotting everything down on the telephone bill that happened to be in my bag. I saw it all inside my head, another song, a poem, a possible movie, a story, a source of inspiration! I couldn't wait to get home and start typing.

Later, I went over my notes: "Her gloves. Dead brother. I coulda killed him, honey! Honey, why not! Terrorist? Bathing beauty? Her gloves match polka-dot dress. The cashier doesn't speak. She nods in agreement at everything the polka-dot woman says. Polka dots talk in a very loud voice." None of it meant anything to me.

How can I explain all this to Keiko? I am amazed at my trivial pursuits, and the non sequiturs I jot down. My cycle of depression begins. I lose myself in a frenzy of cleaning, dazed mothering, indifferent cooking, and movie watching. Uncle Marlon's classics are my favorites. *West Side Story, Blue Hawaii*, even the

Mexican Indian bit part he played in *The Wild Bunch*. Uncle Marlon is machine-gunned to bloody shreds in slow motion in a sun-baked plaza reeking of stupidity and death.

Keiko's visits two days in a row are unsettling. It's like she's trying to make up for something. I hide my notebooks, afraid she'll sneak a look. I remember that look of pity she gave me when I worked at Dr. Sandy's clinic.

At last night's dinner, Jake toasted Keiko with good champagne. "A retrospective at thirty-eight! My God, and you're not even dead yet." Keiko blushed with pleasure and laughed.

"Blue car / guitar, / pick up what else / you need. / Love's your precious / nightmare. / The rest, / baby, / is greed." My minor hit on an independent label that sometimes provides me with half the rent money. There are other tunes on a demo tape I've stashed away in a closet. Potential hits, according to my ex-manager. Brian calls from time to time to remind me that a check is waiting. He keeps pressuring me to pitch my songs to other bands. "You could make a bundle," Brian insists.

"Fuck you," I say to him. "How's Powerhouse doing?"

"We're preparing for our European tour," Brian says. "Thirty-five cities." Then he says, "You're wasting your talent, Rocky."

"Fuck you," I say again. "Fuck Elvis and Eddie. And may Sly rest in peace."

Keiko thinks I'm still her best, best friend in spite of the fact that I now treat her rudely. On purpose and with deliberate and malicious intent, I am rude. I refuse to return her phone calls or answer her letters. When the phone rings, I make faces at Jake, and whisper, "Tell her I'm not here." Keiko is relentless. She calls back and acts like everything's fine. Invites herself over. Offers me plane tickets. "Come to my opening in Houston," she pleads. When I tell her how much I hate Houston, she says, "I know the best Mexican place to eat. And this Chinese Texan photographer who'll take us there in his pink convertible." She brings toys for Venus, bottles of good wine for Jake and me. When Jake's out of earshot, she takes my hand and repeats that we are her true family. This will last, I know, until her next lover comes along.

God, Sly was dumb. Going down in a blaze of gunfire that didn't even make the back page of the newspapers. Junior shows up grinning in Sly's face, and *blam*. Sly got it in the stomach. Cold-blooded, like they wanted to make sure Sly died slowly. Junior walked away from him, picked up his paycheck, flew back to Kingston, and disappeared. Sly had trusted and emulated Junior. Junior had perfected the rap and the swagger, with his mysterioso, ex-con aura worn proudly like a cloak. "Junior's baaad," Sly would say, grunting with admiration. God, Sly could be so gullible and dumb.

Junior was way out of my league. I had known enough to remain cordial but keep my distance. I wasn't Junior's type, either. My fronting the band was something that amazed and amused him. "What you do takes a lotta heart, sister," he once said, laughing softly to himself as he chipped away at the fat white lines neatly arranged on the mirror. Chip, chip, chip, went his razor blade.

Elvis told me that Rusty flagged down one of those gypsy cabs to take Sly to a hospital. She waved money at the paranoid driver, who convinced her to dump Sly in a bus shelter right in front of the emergency entrance to Lincoln Hospital. Sly bled to death in that shelter before anyone discovered him. It was Elvis who called to tell me, Elvis who identified Sly and took his body back to be buried in Detroit.

Consider this. I've never been to a counselor, a therapist, analyst, psychiatrist, or whatever. The last time I saw a priest-confessor was twenty years ago in Manila. That's if you don't count the Carabao Kid. Keiko's been through them all. Besides Dr. Sandy, Keiko's been seeing a Reichian therapist. Keiko keeps trying to convince me to try it, but I just don't grasp the importance of orgone boxes or gurus. Before the Reichian, she saw a Jungian. Wrote her dreams down in minute detail in very expensive journals made of handmade paper. She also meditates. Claims her vision has cleared since she stopped doing dope, drinking, and smoking cigarettes. Keiko laughs and says she's almost ready for me to meet her real parents. "They're alive, and they don't live too far from Manhattan." An amazing transformation, from Keiko the wild woman to Keiko the sincere puritan. I am waiting for her to renounce fucking. Jake and I are probably two of the only adults she knows (not counting Elvis and his rock 'n' roll life) who still occasionally indulge and drink hard. Though we're absurdly cautious now. We do it when Venus is asleep, getting high with a certain amount of guilt that is new and burdensome. "Motherhood's the ultimate self-censorship," a poet I know once said.

Keiko, here's what I want to say. Right before I gave up music, I was full of myself. The happiest I'd ever been. So much pain, I had to sing. In my dream you'd always be there, slinking through the audience of a packed nightclub as if it were the Nile, or waving goodbye to us at the airport as The Gangster of Love boards the Aeroflot plane that takes us on our first and last straight-to-nowhere, straight-to-hell international tour.

We've hit the big time. The Gangster of Love opens for Sister Mercy's No-Bullshit Satin Soul Revue. They immediately expose us as fakes. Sister Mercy is a living legend and authentic survivor of the chitlin circuit, magnificent, gritty, temperamental priestess-bitch and godmother to James Brown. Hers is a twenty-piece orchestra complete with an Eldridge Cleaver lookalike emcee and sultry, topless backup singers who call themselves "The Fire-eaters." Sister Mercy marches past me as if I were invisible, speaking only to the men in my band. "I don't care for women and their whining," she growls in explanation.

Never mind. I excuse her bad manners, I eat shit, grovel like a white boy, so grateful am I to share the same bill with her. But this tour is evil. We have to pay our own way. It's 120 degrees and humid. Parasites in the drinking water and no shade. No trees left on this barren landscape, boiled English food the only thing available. I cry every day I'm here: "B. Goode! How could you be so bad!"

Brian gives us daily pep talks on the importance of working, on work as an end in itself. He reminds us, once again, of the prestige of opening for Sister Mercy, rumored to be the only female ex-lover of Little Richard and the true author of "Lucille" and "Tutti-Frutti."

"Look at the big picture. Think of what you'll learn just watching her strut onstage. Think of the riffs you can steal from that legendary horn section." Brian is dehydrated and delirious, his pale English face swollen with bug bites. Bugs so vicious they'll bite your dick off.

Once, I caught my mother in bed with the Carabao Kid. They weren't doing anything, just lying there asleep. I backed out of my mother's room as quietly as I could.

Sister Mercy, Sister Mercy. We try staying high enough so that nothing matters. Sly wanders off into the bush with Elvis. Looking for musical secrets to steal, pygmy mythology to appropriate as their own. Days later, they emerge with beatific smiles on their faces, zoned out and speaking in tongues.

Who wrote the song? Who dreamed the song? Who gets the credit? Who's paid the royalty?

Keiko, you slink down the Nile in your papyrus canoe. Walk a tightrope in your embroidered fez and gauzy veil, the lipstick slash across your mouth a phosphorescent green. My blue-faced *aswang* hovers above, hungrily flicking its threadlike tongue at me. You promise to save me, balanced and confident on your perch above the ravine. Blue-faced vampire, obliterated by your neon green kiss. Nasty nasty nasty neon green bliss.

The boa I wear is a constrictor around my neck. Sly whispers, "Does the Congo still exist?" And Elvis sneers, "I can't keep up with history."

Congo today, money tomorrow.

I am pregnant with Venus. I moonwalk and shuffle across the makeshift stage of the outdoor jungle arena. Searchlights blind my eyes. We are in Zamboanga, and I can smell the salty ocean nearby. My mother suddenly appears onstage, pushing my father in his wheelchair. His hands are clasped in prayer, his tongue hanging out, ready to receive the body and blood of Christ. We are in the Zamboanga or Zimbabwe of my imagination. Z. I'm no longer ashamed that I can't tell the difference. I've lived too long and made too many connections. Familiar foliage, familiar sun, familiar colonizers.

Sister Mercy dismisses my band as postmodern, postcolonial punks. Monkey see, monkey do. We F(P)ilipinos can imitate, but this audience prefers the real thing. She pities me. The audience clamors for Madonna and Sting. Their brand of blond exotic, without gravity. They throw rotting bananas at me. I am pregnant, stuffed into a black Maidenform corset, gasping for breath. A screeching spider monkey crouches on my left shoulder, with a face more human and poignant than mine. To appease the restless mob, B. Goode introduces me, in desperation, as "Madonna Demivida, fresh from Motor City, Detroit. You remember Motor City, don't you?" He's suffering from malaria, drunk from too much quinine.

I stumble onstage, trying to get by with a cheap blond wig. The booing gets louder. Where is Sister Mercy? She's six foot one, weighs two hundred pounds, and pities me. I spot her in the wings, fuming in the shadows. She disapproves of the covers I've chosen to deconstruct and desecrate. "Dr. Feelgood." "Heat Wave." "In Time." She covers her ears with giant fists when I recite the opening lines of James Brown's "It's a Man's Man's Man's World." The natives curse in English, threatening to throw us into the shark-infested ocean, then jeering at us, "Fuckit if you can't take a joke." A village matriarch crawls onstage to taunt me. "You are not worth killing." She cracks a brown egg on my forehead. Egg yolk drips into my eyes. Sister Mercy's had enough. She stomps out from the wings, brandishing an Uzi. I'm not sure if she wants to kill me or spray bullets into the unruly audience. She's had enough and she's berserk. Government troops are forced to intervene. We are tried without a jury, condemned to exile as second-rate, Western imperialist, so-called artists before being shoved into a Philippine Airlines jumbo jet. We are flown out of Zamboanga in the middle of the night, back to the safety of Motown memory.

I always believed that rock 'n' roll and the road would be part of my life forever. It was once easy to visualize ourselves past the age of forty, still prancing, posturing, living to dance and shriek our guts out. "The only way to live," Sly used to say, heh-heh-heh. It was our language and passion. We thought on some level the world would always owe us, at least an ear. An infantile premise, according to Jake. Forget it.

F(P)ilipinos love to party, but whatever happened to the real Sly Stone?

My arrogance about music and my immortality faded fast after Venus was born. I asked myself if I'd end up like every other burned-out musician I knew, prowling the clubs at all hours, bragging that I hadn't been to sleep in days.

*   *   *

Keiko, you're wrong. Elvis didn't break up the band. I fired them all. Fired my faithful manager B. Goode, who refuses to acknowledge he's been fired and still does business on my behalf.

So much pain, I had to sing.

I packed all our tapes in boxes, copies of the one record we made in another. Sealed the boxes, pushed it all into the back of a closet. Fifteen years or so worth of shit. Over.

Los Blah-Blahs: Three

My mother was ranting and raving, I don't know exactly about what. But her entire rant was an accusatory monologue in Tagalog. She practically used up all the tape on my machine. You did this and you did that. Why don't you return my calls? This is your nanay. Ikaw ikaw ikaw kasi! Loud and clear. Odd because her rant was forceful, but calm.

"Nothing odd," Keiko assures me. "You should call her."

I've forgotten much of the language, and it exasperates me. Big holes when I try to speak. Like, how do you say sugar? I remember aswang for vampire, asin for salt. But not sugar. I've dreamed entire dreams in Tagalog, but I don't know what I'm saying. The cadences in Tagalog are like the Latin cadences in a traditional Catholic mass.

"When was the last time you went to mass? Latin's out. You should know that. It's gotten very democratic. Sacred rituals in vernacular. How's it goin' leg o' lamb o' God? Dope. Fresh. Yo, G. There goes your liberal theology in action. Banal sightings of the Blessed Virgin in New Jersey," Keiko says, laughing.

"Middle age is turning us into fascists," I grumble.

"Bullshit. You always get fascist and Republican confused. Middle age is turning me into a neocon bitch snob. Rocky, call your mother."

"In my dream I was talking to some man, but he was out of the frame. Probably my father."

"At last."

"You know I never dream about my father. This was the first and only time."

"You never dream about men, period. Except maybe Fidel Castro."

"Not true. I had a dream about Sly. He was very much alive, grinning that famous grin. 'Rocky,' he complained, 'there are too many ghosts in your head.'"

Black: Her Story

In darkness, Milagros Rivera glides from room to room in the musty apartment, silent except for the barely audible laugh track of a "Mary Tyler Moore Show" rerun in the background. Milagros is looking for something or someone, she is not sure which. She forgets. She forgets the damndest things. The names of her children, the simplest words in the English language. Is it the gaudy pendant she is searching for? Heart-shaped, encrusted with fake diamonds and rubies. The kind old ladies with poodles fancy. A gift from her son, Victor. Victor, Viviano, Vance, Vince. A gift from her son, whose name begins with a V, she is sure of that much, at least. Milagros has forgotten that she sold the pendant to Tessie Bambang for a mere pittance, along with all those other things that Tessie had been coveting for years. Sold for *nothing*. Her platinum watch, a hand-carved, mother-of-pearl inlaid chest from Mindanao, her antique filigree earrings from Lola Flores, the Mikimoto pearls . . . No, she hasn't sold the pearls to that unctuous bitch! The pearls are still safe in their silk brocade pouch, stuffed in the back of her underwear drawer. For that elephant headache of a daughter, when she has her baby. Milagros furrows her brow. *Raquel*. Had Raquel already had the baby?

She has forgotten to turn the lights on, as she has forgotten to do so for several nights this week. She finds the darkness comforting and familiar. There are still those moments, spaced further and further apart now, when Milagros snaps out of her daze and, cursing at herself, switches on a lamp. Or the phone rings and rings, ruining her precious reveries, always Fely or Zeke snooping around, the worried concern in their voices infuriating Milagros. "Of course I didn't answer the phone," Milagros will sneer, sounding remarkably lucid. "I was in the bathroom." Zeke frequently asks her to join him for dinner at the new Thai place around the corner, but Milagros barks "Not interested!" and hangs up. She knows he is simply trying to get her to act *normal*, to *eat*. Milagros snorts in disdain. Zeke is so transparent.

Milagros no longer sleeps. She keeps the television on for company, though all she does when she can bear to sit still is channel-surf, listlessly. The ghosts pay sporadic visits: her mother, her father, her maternal Spanish Chinese grandmother, even her grandmother's lover, the half-American bastard son of some colonel and a washerwoman. Her favorite is a sorrowful beauty with a mustache, for which Milagros affectionately dubs her Bigote. "*Hoy*, Bigote. What you so long-faced about?" Milagros teases her. There are animal ghosts as well, a boisterous little monkey and a panting yellow dog, whose breasts hang from too many puppies and whose ribs show from hunger. Milagros remembers her father fondly calling such dogs rice hounds. These mongrels lazed about the yard, belonging to no one, grateful for scraps.

Milagros wears a black crepe skirt, which she has forgotten to zip all the way up, and a glittery moth-eaten sweater. On her stockinged feet are scruffy slippers, bought for $2.99 at Walgreen's. She peers into her dining room, expecting to find her guests. They're late. How she hated when anyone was late, especially for one of her dinner parties. Seagulls, Milagros suddenly thinks. Seagulls pecking at my brain. *Pensamiento*, pentimento, pimiento, *punieta*.

What to do when the English no longer makes sense? *Ay, puta. Ay naku. Buwisit. Putang ina mo. Qué asco. Qué barbaridad. Qué horror.*

Milagros trips on the curled-up edge of a rug, a woman suspended in a red void. Her daughters float in the sky above her. She reaches out, her legs spread, the palms of her hands up in a gesture of . . . supplication? beseeching? blessing? Is she screaming or laughing? Where is her son? She imagines her children into existence. She can imagine anything into existence, she is that powerful. Profane immaculate conceptions.

Luz wears a red dress, as red as the red void in which her mother is suspended. Raquel is a naked cherub with a jaguar's face. Like her sister in the scarlet dress, like her mother has taught her from the womb, Raquel keeps her eyes shut in a constant dream. Her tiny, terrifying teeth are bared in a sly grin. She is beautiful. Luz in the bloody dress is beautiful. Voltaire floats into the frame. He is his mother's twin, a gypsy moor from the Alhambra shrouded in black velvet. His glass bangles make too much noise, and Raquel the baby stirs in her sleep, letting out a fretful cry. "Look what you've done," Milagros accuses Voltaire, banishing him.

Her legs scissor the red horizon. Her back splits open: magnolia, plumeria, and calla lilies unfurl on her broken spine. Her flesh a map of scars. A map of the universe. *Manong, manong.* Walk the dog. Rock the baby.

Milagros attempts to gain her balance by reaching for a chair. Her vision blurs.

My children are afraid of me, and I love them. I'm a scammer, a thief, the queen of self-pity, the Empress of Sorrow. I paint everything gold. The stove, the refrigerator, the radio, the telephone, the bed, the plates, the silver. Midasina, Medea, Medusa. My son the poet holds up a tube of red lipstick. I pucker my lips. Find a soft spot. There. There. There are too many women in this house. A cluster of spikes, not snakes. The woman nailed to a cross grows bored with the nails embedded in her palms, embedded in her beautifully manicured feet. There is no blood. The nails are brand-new, rustproof. Dipped in hydrogen peroxide before being hammered in. I grow bored with my anguish, screech with rage, and writhe for my salvation. My children howl along with me, a chorus of thorns. "Somebody yank these nails out."

* * *

Imagine. Delicious obsessions. My children and I sailed on a ship. Magellan went looking for spices. All those mad Europeans went looking for spices. Their lives lacked chili pepper and heat, they longed for something they could not name. What was possible was not visible, so in the name of God and the Fat Pale Queen they went sailing in search of gold, pepper, saffron, and souls. And here we are, the bastards of discovery, five hundred years later! I sailed here in a rage. I sailed on a ship for an eternity of seventeen days to California and shut my eyes to save myself and dream. Little Richard, Perez Prado, Fats Domino.

How we remember. What we remember. Why. Who? What? Where? When? Who? Who else? Who with? Who said? How? How much? With what? With whom? Where else? Why? Why? Why? Why is the cross of Magellan a tourist attraction in the Philippines? Why is a scavenger fish named after Lapu Lapu in the Philippines?

O Ferdinand, O Isabella, O Cristofer, O Cortés, O Lopez de Legazpi, O Ponce, O Balboa, O Vasco de Gama, O Popes of manifest destiny. There was never enough gold to mine. My country was never Peru, and all you found was cinnamon.

The woman with a mustache is sitting in the chair, just out of Milagros's reach.

Wrong again. It is 1941, and I'm in my casita azul in Macao. I'm wearing your pants and smoking a cigarette. It's one I rolled myself. I'm terrible at rolling anything. The tobacco keeps falling out, the paper is soaked with saliva, and I keep having to relight the cigarette. But I look good, don't I? A pensive pose, with a kalachuchi flower stuck in my thick black hair, dead center, so you can't miss it in the photograph. Somber yet stunning. Just so, how I lean against the wall of my little blue house of skulls.

The woman with a mustache beckons to Milagros. "There are exactly fourteen Stations of the Cross," Bigote reminds her in a whisper. "While your children sleep, we'll reinvent geography. Recall our flight from one shifting continent to the next. Wallow in the mud of mistaken identities. Cross-dress to Calvary." Bigote's face is serene and luminous, but Milagros senses the urgency in her beckoning gesture. Milagros moans in a sudden flash of recognition. She makes one last attempt at reaching for the chair and falls.

The Fall

It was Bas who called from San Francisco at half past nine that evening. He sounded genuinely surprised when Rocky's usual clever, musical message on the machine didn't click on and she picked up the phone. "Funny you are home, ha."

"Bas. How can I help you?" Rocky affected a detached, congenial tone whenever she talked to Basilio Cruz. After her mother convinced her that Bas had another woman and was trying to poison Auntie Fely, Rocky stopped addressing him as "uncle" and let him know in little ways how much she disliked him. Bas's call tonight was unexpected. Bas never called, except that time he called collect while Milagros was visiting. He and Fely had driven to Atlantic City to gamble, leaving Milagros back in Manhattan with Rocky and the baby. There was a lot of shouting on Milagros's end, and Rocky suspected it was about money. With Bas, it was always about money.

Rocky braced herself for the worst. Bas was somber. "Ay, hija. You might maybe ask how is it I can help *you*."

Rocky knew what must have happened and did not want to discuss this with him. "Where's Tiya Fely?"

"At the hospital. Your mother —"

"Fuck!" Rocky growled into the mouthpiece. There was a moment of silence, then she sighed. This was not Bas's fault. "Is she —" Rocky found herself unable to say the word.

"Okay. She fell down. She's okay, but she's in the intensive care unit. Lucky you, it's where Fely works." Bas paused. "You better get on the next plane."

"Fuck." Rocky blinked back the first rush of tears. Hadn't she known it in her bones? Her mother had been disoriented the last few days. Whenever Rocky called, Milagros would let the phone ring and ring before fumbling to answer it. Once, she actually hung up in the middle of something Rocky was saying.

"What the fuck happened?" Rocky wished she hadn't quit smoking. With the phone cradled against her shoulder, she reached with her other hand for her old motorcycle jacket that lay across a nearby chair. She unzipped the breast pocket, pulled out her cash, and started counting. There was enough. More than enough for a pack of cigarettes.

"We were going to eat with her," Bas explained. "Now that your brother's gone, *alam mo na*, Sunday nights your mama gets so lonely. She likes to cook, but nowadays it's only me and Fely."

"What happened?" Rocky repeated impatiently.

"We ring and ring the doorbell. Fely was getting nervous because the lights weren't on. Your mama never goes anywhere except to the grocery and back, *di ba*? No answer, no answer. What is that? I say to myself. 'You wait here,' I tell Fely. 'Keep ringing the doorbell.' I call from the pay phone at the corner deli, but the phone was busy. So I call the operator to check on the line." Basilio Cruz droned on and on, switching arbitrarily from past to present tense while Rocky put on her shoes, grunting into the phone occasionally to let him know she was still there.

"And so Zeke help me pry open the bathroom window. Good thing I'm still *payat* and manage to squeeze through. I told Fely if it had been her, her fat *puwit* will still be stuck in the window and your mama would be dead." Bas chuckled, then caught himself and cleared his throat. "But she is still breathing, although completely passed out. Thanks be to God, *di ba*? Stroke again, it looks like to Fely. She called the ambulance and go with them to the hospital. We called Luz in Manila —"

"I'll get on a flight first thing in the morning."

"You know where to go? Chinese Benevolent Hospital. On Jackson Street."

"I know it." Rocky grimaced. Last time, it was St. Francis Hospital. Before that, Pacific Presbyterian. Milagros had been all over the city, wherever was convenient when she fell, whichever hospital had room. Her doctor happened to be whoever was on duty. There was no money, and certainly no insurance. Rocky wanted desperately to get off the phone. "I'll call the airlines. See you sometime tomorrow."

"Don't worry, *hija*. You can stay with us. I have my car and will drive you," Basilio Cruz assured her.

"No thanks, Bas. I have keys to Ma's apartment."

Rocky made arrangements for Jake to stay with Venus. He still had his apartment, and they continued to act as if they could shuttle back and forth forever. The morning after Basilio Cruz called, Jake found Rocky sitting in the kitchen, staring into her first cup of Bustelo. "What happened?" he asked, although he knew.

"I guess this is it," Rocky said. "I hate to leave you and Venus in the lurch."

"It's okay." Jake took a sip of Rocky's coffee. He made a stab at wit. "We're used to it." Rocky flashed a faint smile, which relieved him.

"Whatever happened to your famous sense of humor?" he asked, after one of their recent arguments. They fought a lot. Ever since Sly had been killed, Rocky acted as if all she wanted was to withdraw as far away as possible from him and the world. Even Venus's presence was no use. Rocky was inching further and further away from him. "I'm sorry," Jake would say, sick to death of apologizing constantly.

"I'm sorry too," Rocky would answer.

"Call when you get to the hospital. Let me know how she's doing," Jake said the morning she left. The doorbell made them jump. Rocky stood up and threw on her jacket. "It's the car service. I'll be gone a week."

She lightly touched the top of Venus's head while she slept. "Is this all you're taking?" Jake helped her adjust her backpack.

Rocky didn't answer, but hugged him tightly before mumbling "I'll call you" and rushing out the door.

On the claustrophobic, overbooked flight, Rocky is grateful to be traveling alone and curls herself into a tense ball in her seat. She must sleep. That much she knows. She's been up since dawn, brooding in the kitchen while Venus slept peacefully in her crib. She wonders how she is going to survive the next few days. Ghastly. She's brought along some Xanax from Keiko's stash, plus leftover Anaprox tablets from her last visit to the periodontist. The blue Anaprox are a year old. Rocky has hoarded them for emergencies. Like right now. The plane is overheated and stinks of chemical solvents and Naugahyde. Someone nearby has on too much Calvin Klein Obsession. Rocky swallows an Anaprox, plugs headphones into her Walkman, shuts her eyes, and forces herself to dream. If one counts the forty-five-minute delay on the ground "due to a mechanical difficulty," she may as well have flown to Madrid. She drools saliva from the corner of her parted lips, dozing off and on to the incessant, angry wail of a baby two rows ahead of her. Finally, the plane takes off. Rocky feels the surge in the pit of her stomach. She's timed it perfectly. Inside her head, Jimi Hendrix's orgasmic intro to "Foxy Lady" drowns out the baby's terrified wail. Lights blink off and on in the cabin. Rocky's eyelids flutter as she wakes and dreams, wakes and dreams.

Safety instructions are ignored, a movie that no one cares to watch is announced. Rocky opens her eyes, readjusts her tight, aching body in her seat. The man sitting next to her moves his elbow away from her touch. He is reading the latest issue of *Entertainment Weekly* and will never once look at her during the course of their flight. Rocky notices the miniature bottles of vodka and tonic next to the plastic cup on the tray before him. The baby is silent for now, carried up and down the narrow aisles by its drained and exhausted father. "It's not bad," a stewardess smiles brightly at another passenger across the aisle from Rocky, trying without success to rent him some headphones. "Really. Kevin Costner's great." The man has been typing something on his laptop computer. He looks annoyed by the attendant's interruption. A blue screen. How amazing, Rocky thinks. Four and a half pounds, no bigger than a purse.

Rocky arrives in San Francisco at one in the afternoon, Pacific standard time. She yawns and her ears pop. She is relieved when no one is there to meet her. She can grab a cab, get to the hospital on her own time.

The awesome cathedral-like structure of the Chinese Benevolent Hospital imposes its gothic gloom over a bustling, vibrant Chinatown. Rocky's yellow visitor's pass reads C23. She decides to walk up the two flights instead of taking the elevator. "It's locked," the security guard informs her.

Rocky forces a smile. "Can you unlock it for me?"

A teenage girl sidles up next to her. "Fuckin' thing ain't workin'," the teenager mutters, indicating the elevator with a toss of her head. Rocky starts to smile at her too, but like the guard, the teenager acts as if Rocky were invisible.

The teenager crosses her arms and grins flirtatiously at the guard. "Come on, be nice. I got family up there." She's a tough beauty, with oversize square shapes of gold-plated metal in her ears, an elaborate ponytail hairpiece oiled and gleaming down her back. The guard takes her in with his eyes. With a grunt, he produces a ring of keys, fumbling for the right one. Rocky follows the teenager as she bounces up the stairs and disappears down the dreary, pale green halls of the ICU corridor.

Fely rushes over to greet Rocky. She looks worn-out, older than ever. "Your mother's asleep," Fely says, bringing Rocky closer to the bed. Milagros is hooked up to an obscene tangle of wires and tubes. An oxygen mask covers part of her face. Her straggly, yellowish, graying hair spreads out on the pillow beneath her head. Her mouth is partially open. With her dentures removed, she looks a hundred years old. Rocky gasps at the sight of the helpless, toothless old woman. This is not her glamorous, bitchy diva of a mother, but a common hag.

Fely tightens her grip on Rocky's arm. "Lucky we found her when we did," she whispers. The lights are subdued in the crowded intensive care unit. Milagros lies on a bed directly behind the nurses' station. Flimsy curtains separate her from the other patients. On her left is a young man with gunshot wounds in his stomach and thigh; on her right, an older man, the recent victim of an auto collision. Everyone lies perfectly still in row after row of metal beds. The monitors above blink off and on. "What's that?" Rocky asks her aunt in a low voice. The young Chinese nun on duty looks up from something she is writing. She smiles, recognizing Fely, then puts a finger to her lips.

"Checking everyone's heart rate," Fely murmurs. She gives Rocky a few minutes next to her mother, then gently leads her away toward the elevators.

"There aren't any chairs," Rocky says. "How come there's no place for visitors to sit?"

Fely's smile is kind. "It's the ICU. You're not supposed to hang around too long." She presses the elevator call button. "Don't worry. She's got a good team working on her. Plus I'm here."

"I'm glad you are. Otherwise . . ." Rocky pauses, overwhelmed. She is grateful for her aunt's transformation into a take-charge, no-nonsense professional. "Tiya Fely, I'm scared."

"I know," Fely says. "I'm scared, too."

"Is she going to die?"

"If it's God's will."

Damn God, Rocky wanted to shout.

They wait a while longer, but the elevator never comes. Fely steers Rocky toward the stairway. "Come on, *hija*, Bas will be waiting outside. I have to go back to work, but he can give you a ride to your mother's. Zeke's away, visiting his family. Are you sure you want to stay there alone?" Fely asks.

"I'd prefer it," Rocky replies.

Fely gives her niece a long, hard look. "Anything can happen to your mother. You know that, don't you? You should stay."

"I can't leave Venus for too long," Rocky says.

"We have to hire someone to watch your mother when she goes home," Fely says. "*If* she goes home. Milagros can no longer fend for herself." Fely shrugs. "*Bahala na.* Whatever it costs. If I have to rob a bank myself."

"Me too," Rocky says.

Mickey Mouse Money

Rocky and her aunt are sitting at the dining table in Milagros Rivera's apartment. They have just returned from overseeing Milagros's transfer from intensive care into her own room at the hospital. Scattered on the table are the remains of their shared meal, Fely's care package of *sinigang* and rice, which she has brought over and reheated for Rocky. "Since you'll be here a few more days, we should do a little grocery shopping," Fely says.

Rocky's response is indifferent. "I'd rather eat out."

Fely worries about her niece. When she isn't at the hospital, Rocky spends too many hours alone in the morbid silence of her mother's apartment, trying to put order into the shambles Milagros left behind. As if by simply throwing out newspapers and rotting food, Rocky could right all the wrongs and keep her mother from dying. "Too many things, Tiya Fely. Mama has too many goddam things." Rocky seems astonished by all she finds in the cluttered, dusty rooms. Milagros's possessions run the gamut, a treasure trove of the beautiful, the sentimental, and the tacky. Mother-of-pearl knickknacks, capiz-shell windchimes, crumbling photo albums, sandalwood fans. Letters Milagros began writing to Rocky lie unfinished on a desk, next to a pile of unpaid utility bills and wilted plants. Her dressing table is littered with oxidized cosmetics and bottles of rancid perfume. Steamer trunks burst with more Manila mementos, bolts of piña cloth; more fans; a beaded emerald green floor-length *terno*, with one missing butterfly sleeve. A cigar box crammed with prewar photographs and a carved carabao horn yo-yo carefully wrapped in tissue. "How could she live like this?" Rocky wails. "It's become a crazy museum."

"It's the same apartment it's always been," Fely reminds her. "You just never noticed."

"My God, look." Rocky gasps at the pantry shelves stocked

with canned sardines, bars of Ivory soap, and rolls of thousand-sheet, family-pack toilet paper.

Fely sighs. "It's our war mentality. Didn't your mother ever tell you? Back then, we were desperate for basics. You'd trade precious family heirlooms for a stupid tube of toothpaste. Anything, for the chance to feel clean again. Ay, *naku*. I do it, too, buy family-size everything, even though it's just Bas and me now."

Rocky stacks yellowing newspapers and outdated magazines into bundles for recycling. She makes a futile effort, scouring twenty years' worth of grease from the kitchen walls and stove. She empties the shuddering, prehistoric refrigerator of what seems like hundreds of Tupperware containers. Unrecognizable leftovers encased in fuzzy, greenish blue mold, frozen and forgotten by Milagros God knows how long ago. Her mother's once lively kitchen has finally succumbed to despair and neglect, along with everything else in the stuffy apartment. "Why do I bother?" Rocky grumbles to herself, dragging her sorry bundles and trash bags down to the alley where rows of garbage cans await her. Back up the stairs she goes, for another round of scrubbing, scouring, mopping, and sweeping, collapsing early each night into a heavy, dreamless sleep.

Rocky calls Jake to give her daily report — "My mother recognizes me now" — and to ask about Venus.

"I took her to the studio." Jake laughs. "She's already got a great ear for music."

Rocky's attempt to reach Voltaire in Manila has been awkward. He's been staying with Luz and her family, but the young servant girl who answers the phone informs Rocky in Tagalog that everyone has gone to Kalibo. "Kalibo?" Rocky says, puzzled.

"*Oo, po*," yes, the young girl patiently and respectfully explains. Kalibo, for the Ati-Atihan festival.

"Ah." Rocky sighs. "Emergency," she wants to say in English. Her Tagalog fails her at this crucial moment. How does one say "emergency" in Tagalog without alarming the poor girl? Is there a telephone number in Kalibo? Rocky manages to ask.

"No, no. *Hindi, po.*" The young girl giggles. "No, no. *Walang teléfono.*"

Rocky comes up with an urgent-sounding "*Importante.*" Another Spanish word, it occurs to her, but it works. "*Sabihin mo,*" she says in Tagalog, "his sister called from America. Tell him to call her back in San Francisco. *Importante,*" Rocky repeats. "Please," Rocky adds in English.

Dinner with her aunt has been a welcome break from the Xanax glaze and drudgery of the past few days. "Ready for your interview?" Rocky playfully asks Fely, who laughs nervously. Rocky disappears into her mother's bedroom, then returns to the table with a microcassette recorder. She carefully positions it in front of her aunt. Felicidad Cruz gazes suspiciously at the machine. "Do I have to talk into this thing?"

"C'mon. You promised."

"I've never done anything like this," Fely says, visibly distraught.

"Tiya Fely, please, relax *lang.*" Rocky waits for her aunt to regain her composure, then says, "The year 1941. Let's start with the first day the Japanese occupied Manila."

"Yes, 1941," Fely repeats, nodding. "No, no, wait. It was 1942, I think. That's right, the Japs came in so fast they were arresting all the American citizens they could find. *Kawawa, talaga.* We had these neighbors, the McMillans —"

"Where were you living?"

"On Herran Street, near Pennsylvania. Near where your old school was located. They dragged our American neighbor straight to Santo Tomás University, where the Japs had set up a camp for all the foreigners. We never saw Mr. Mack — that's what we called McMillan — again. His Pinay wife was very" — Fely is at a temporary loss for words, then brightens — "stoic. Very stoic. Just stood there and watched the Japs take him away. Your *lola* Flores and I were peeping through the shutters. Your *lolo* had left for the mountains with the other men, so it was just me and your grandmother. And she didn't want those Japs catching sight of me, her young daughter. Ay! Those Americans were caught with their pants down, *talaga*." Fely's laugh is soft and bitter.

"Can you remember who else was in the house, what you were doing, even what you were wearing?"

"Ay, Raquel. Why do you need to know all this?" Fely sighs. "I was wearing a shapeless dress, a cotton dress. It was ugly. The ugliest dress your *lola* could find. I think it belonged to our cook, Margie. Margie was very fat. Your *lolo*'s favorite. Her real name was Maria Agustina, but he called her Margie and she loved it. She was a great cook, but very *sumpung*. When there was a full moon, she could get pretty violent. There was a story about Margie hacking her first husband to death with a *bolo*. She'd caught him flirting with another woman. *Dios ko*. We never found out if the story was just a story, although Margie was perfectly capable. She never crossed your *lolo* or *lola*, and she was very sweet to me. *Sirang ulo*, your mama called her behind her back. Your mama was very naughty."

"You wore her dress?"

"You know, Margie had a son. That's right, a son. Ay, it's all coming back to me. That son of hers, he came with us . . ."

"Wait. Go back, Auntie Fely. The dress."

Fely smiles, starting to enjoy herself. "That big, ugly dress. It hung down to the middle of my calves, no shape at all! An oversize floral-print duster, faded from the sun. The cheap kind you buy in Quiapo market or Divisoria. Lola Flores braided my hair so I would look even younger, braided tight and coiled up on my head like an old maid's crown. And shoes and socks! Can you imagine? As if I were a very young child, or an old woman. Your grandma was afraid the Japs would rape me."

"Why didn't you leave Manila and join Lolo in the mountains?" Rocky tried picturing the grandfather she'd never met as a guerrilla soldier.

Fely becomes agitated. "I told you. They promised us it was going to be a short war."

"Who promised?"

"*The Americans.*" Fely's tone is sarcastic. "A short war, you know. 'It's gonna be a short war, don't worry.' Ha! They underestimated the Japs. They were caught with their pants down."

"Where was my mother?"

"Milagros was in Hong Kong, married. She had left before it got serious. Your *tatay* saw the writing on the wall."

"They left knowing there would be a war?" Rocky feels a twinge of shame at the thought of her parents fleeing Manila, saving themselves while abandoning family.

"Yeah. Your grandpa joked with her, 'I can hear you singing 'Planting Rice' for the Japs,' and that's all your mother needed. Left on the last plane for Hong Kong with your father. *Naku*, in a way we were all relieved. Remember, your mama was a real beauty."

Rocky is silent.

"You remember that song from when you were little?" Fely asks, wistful. "You used to sing it for five *centavos*. We'd ask you to sing, but you'd always stick your little hand out first. 'Five *centavos*, please.' Very polite and serious. I used to laugh so hard. Your mother would be furious."

Rocky starts to sing. "Planting rice is never fun. / Bend some more till the set of sun. / Cannot stand and cannot sit, / cannot something something — oh shit, I forget."

Her aunt frowns, then finishes the lyric for her. "Cannot rest for a little bit." Fely pauses. "Your parents left on the last Pan American plane out of Manila. The only time I've seen your mother travel light."

"Why didn't you go with her?"

"She was married to your father."

Rocky is unable to comprehend Fely's logic. "So? You still could've gone with her. Lolo knew the Japanese meant business."

"That's why he went to fight," Fely answers.

"But he left you and Lola."

Fely speaks slowly and patiently, as if to a child. "I was not married. My duty was to be with your grandmother. Plus we'd been told the war wasn't going to last long. Nothing we couldn't handle. So we waited it out. A mistake, but that's just the way it was. Your father realized it wouldn't be as bad in Hong Kong. How, I don't know. But he was right. Plus he had business there, something to do with shipping. Don't ask me what. Your *tatay* was so mysterious."

"Why didn't Lolo Flores ever come back to America?"

"There was really nothing for him here," Fely answers, after a brief silence. "He was disappointed and fed up."

"The yo-yo business?"

Fely nods. "Exactly."

Rocky fixes them both instant coffee the way her mother likes it, with two spoons of sugar and a touch of condensed milk. She takes a sip and grimaces. "How can she stand this?"

"Like drinking candy," Fely says.

Rocky turns the tape over. "Let's go back to that day. All right, Tiya Fely. You were hiding behind closed shutters, hoping the Japanese wouldn't notice. You, Lola Raquel, Margie the cook, maybe her son."

"Her son, Henry."

"Henry? Was that another one of Lolo's American nick-names?"

Fely smiles. "You could say that. I think Henry's real name was Enrique anyway, so your grandpa wasn't too far off. Henry was about fourteen, but he looked no older than nine or ten. A small, skinny, skinny thing, which was funny, because Margie was so big and fat. She never talked about his father, but it must've been that man she supposedly killed. Your *lola* would never have hired a woman with illegitimate offspring, oh no, she never would. I'm telling you, she was tough like that. When it came to sex, she had a hard heart. Dragged us to church on Fridays for confession, on Saturdays for novenas, on Sundays for mass. Even Margie and

Henry were forced to come along. Never had any use for America either, so your grandpa had to come here alone. Some people said she wore the pants in the family."

"That day, Auntie Fely. A car pulled up?"

"They took Mr. Mack away in this black car. We found out through our houseboy, Genesis, that the Japs were taking everyone to Santo Tomás. Genesis had actually gone out into the streets, asking around."

"Wait a minute. You mean there was you, Lola Raquel, Margie the cook, Henry, and Genesis?"

"That's what I said."

"Anyone else?"

"Genesis had a wife whose name I can't remember but whose face is so clear."

"Emy," Rocky says, remembering. "When I was born, she became my *yaya*. She took care of me until I was five or six."

Fely sighs. "Ay, Emy. Margie wouldn't let her near the kitchen, but she was a good cook, too. I wonder what happened to her and Genesis?"

Rocky shrugs. "They work for Luz now, according to Ma. Ma used to talk about them all the time, talk about all the people from the war, like I'm supposed to know them. She resents it if I don't know or remember like she does."

"Of course," Fely says. "That's your mother, clinging to her past like it was yesterday." She sees the unhappy look on Rocky's face and abruptly changes the subject. "Genesis was very brave."

"How bad did it get?"

"Bad," Fely answers. "Anyone could be taken away by the soldiers. We saw things, ay, *naku*. For Genesis to go out there and risk everything, just to see what happened to our neighbor — well, it was foolish. Your grandma was angry, but she had to let him go. She had to. You know, she never cried. Not once during the war, except when she heard your grandfather survived. Your mother's just like her." Fely yawns and checks her watch. "*Dios ko*, where's that husband of mine? I have to work the early shift tomorrow."

"I'm not finished," Rocky says.

"Raquel, I'm falling asleep."

"Not much more, I promise. So?"

"So what?" Fely's eyes droop.

"So go on."

Fely takes a deep breath. "We had that old house, too many rooms *talaga*, and haunted. You could hear a little child crying sometimes, very late at night. Your *lola* had the house blessed by this vain priest, Father Guwapo we used to call him. He was staring at his reflection in the mirror, whenever he thought no one was looking. Poor Father Guwapo, he was later tortured and killed by the Japs, and the ghost-child wasn't scared away. Our landlord was a German Spanish mestizo. Did you know that? Kunstler."

"I grew up with one of them." Raquel chuckles.

"*Naku*, that's right. The one and only, high and mighty Kunstlers," Fely says with scorn. "There were four brothers, and the one we were unlucky enough to have for a landlord kept pressing your *lola* for the rent. Imagine that! Here we were in the middle of a war, with your grandpa away fighting, and this *walanghiya* keeps harassing your grandmother for the rent. Your *lola* told him, 'Trust me, there's money in the bank, but we can't withdraw it.'"

"Why not?"

Fely can barely contain her rage. "What do you expect? The Japs froze all bank accounts. But Señor Kunstler — what was his first name? Arturo, I think — he kept pressing and pressing on your poor *lola*. I got so mad and insisted we all move to a cheaper apartment. I was sick of that man and the ghosts in his house! Thank God your *lola* finally listened to me. We moved down the block to this rooming house owned by the widow Solis. She was very kind and didn't charge us anything until after the war. It was understood that if we lived through the war, we'd pay. If not, well, *bahala na.*" Fely got up from the table and peered out the window. "Where's that Bas?"

"What was it like in the widow's house?" Rocky asks.

"*Magulo.* We crammed all our stuff, including your mother's wedding presents, into three little furnished rooms. We had one floor of the widow's house, plus use of her kitchen. The servants slept on *banigs* on the floor, while your *lola* and I shared one tiny room, like a cell. We were surrounded by the widow's heavy furniture, and all our boxes of things. So many things!"

"How come you had Ma's wedding presents?"

"Like I said, she left in a hurry. Actually, they came in handy during the war," Fely says. "We were so broke, Genesis used to go out into the street and sell her gifts piece by piece, so we could have money. Mickey Mouse money that had no value, of course. But we were forced to use it. And we ate."

"What sorts of things did you sell?"

Fely laughs. "Sheets, a gas stove, a piano."

"Who would buy such things, and why?"

"You look bewildered, but you shouldn't be," Fely says. "There were rich people in the war, gangsters, farmers with cash, even the Japs. They'd buy on the black market from desperate people like us, who sold priceless things for nothing. These same clever people would hoard what they took from us for after the war. You see? They were looking ahead. While your *lola* and I used the Mickey Mouse money to buy lard, rice, sugar, whatever we could get."

Rocky turns off the tape recorder and helps Fely clear the dishes from the table. They wash dishes and clean up in a comfortable silence. It is past midnight, and Rocky wonders if her uncle is in some bar with one of his blondies.

Her aunt speaks. "You know what one of the worst things was about the war? The boredom. Rape, starvation, hunger, death, and boredom. Mickey Mouse money! Your grandmother was right. There was nothing for a young woman like me to do but hide in the house and wait for it to be over." Finished with putting everything away in the now tidy kitchen, Fely wanders into the living room and stands by the window, watching and waiting. "Had enough history?" Fely asks softly.

"You survived, Tiya Fely. You were lucky."

"I was one of the lucky few." Rocky's aunt agrees absently, fixing her gaze on the dark street outside.

Hula

Grinning and apologizing profusely, Uncle Bas shows up at one in the morning to take Auntie Fely home. She has fallen asleep sitting up in a chair by the window, and it takes me a few minutes to rouse her. "The car broke down," Bas explains. "No public phones anywhere." He reeks of cigarettes, whiskey, and breath mints. I'm too tired and disgusted to confront him, and I don't bother inviting him in. He lingers by the door, a guilty child waiting to be punished. I help Auntie Fely with her coat. "See you tomorrow," I say, kissing her on the cheek.

"Lock all the doors," she says, "and close the lights."

I put on my mother's best dress. Her amazing mermaid gown, emerald green and completely beaded with shimmering sequins. The dress comes with attachable butterfly sleeves, also beaded. When the sleeves are snapped on, the dress is transformed from siren sexy into a formal *terno* of green light. But one sleeve is missing, one shimmering sleeve. I find the fish-scale dress in my mother's huge metal trunk, the one we brought with us on the ship, the trunk packed with all her things. The dress is folded and wrapped in plastic so the sequins and beads don't snag. Next to it lies a matching sequined purse, also wrapped in plastic. I shimmy into the gown. Very Imelda. In her prime, my mother was a good half a foot shorter than I, with a tiny waist, ample hips, and high, voluptuous breasts. The gown was made especially for her. It is form-fitting and clings like a second skin. My waist is still thick from being pregnant. I hold my breath, zip slowly up. The zipper is located on the right side of the gown, a fifties style, I think. I remember the pants my sister and I wore as children. They zippered up the hip, too, and were a pain in the ass to take on and off. Our form-fitting slacks contrasted sharply with my brother's comfortable and practical trousers. I guess that was the point of our contradictory upbringing. We girls were expected to follow in our vampy mother's footsteps and show off our gawky bodies, but also make sure our vulvas were securely locked away.

I am a torch singer at the Bayside Club in Manila, I am my mother giddily dancing on a tabletop in Hong Kong, twenty-five years ago. I peel off the dress and exhale.

It is comforting to sleep on my mother's bed while I'm here. I've rearranged her room slightly, with fresh flowers and a Frida Kahlo poster that I bought impulsively from an art store near the hospital. Scattered about are my odd assortment of "things" from New York to keep me sane — my Hendrix and Funkadelic tapes, my Walkman and microcassette recorder, and a homely, framed photo of Venus taken just hours after she was born. Along with the Kahlo *Self-portrait with Small Monkey*, there's a postcard from Voltaire which I've tacked on the wall next to my mother's dressing table. The postcard is a photograph of opium smokers in Tonkin, circa 1900. *Indigène fumant l'opium* is what the French photographer has titled this portrait of a man with hooded eyes, his fingers curled around a long-stemmed pipe and what I imagine are matches. He's been caught in the act. Expectant, poised in midair. There's a vulpine beauty about this man with hooded eyes. Another man sits slightly behind him, holding a tiny teacup. His eyes are alert and cautious. An emaciated woman who doesn't seem to give a fuck about the camera's presence is in profile. She lounges on a woven *banig*, busy sucking on her pipe. Her bare, flat, slender feet are in the foreground of the picture. Nearby a boy of three or four squints fearlessly into the camera. I assume the man with hooded eyes to be the child's father, and his mother the oblivious, emaciated young woman. His mother. A turn-of-the-century junkie with eyes only for her pipe.

Voltaire sent me the postcard from Honolulu, on his way back to Manila. He'd found it at your basic depressing souvenir stand stocked with polyester aloha shirts, jars of macadamia nuts, maps of Waikiki, hokey Polynesian pinup calendars, cheap cassettes of popular hula music. What the postcard was doing among these items was puzzling. And there was only one.

Instead of my father, my mother should've married Uncle Marlon. Even though he prefers men, they would've gotten along famously and probably stayed married until the day they died. Back when my father was still courting my mother, Uncle Marlon was my father's go-between. Uncle Marlon was much younger than my father and in awe of him, so he gladly did whatever he was asked to do. As a budding teenager, the graceful and sensitive Marlon was already suspected of being *bakla* and therefore considered "safe" by my father, who ordered him to escort and chaperone my mother to dances and the movies. My father was a rare exception in Manila: a man who couldn't dance. He had a tin ear when it came to music and no sense of rhythm. Very strange, and terribly embarrassing for my father. Uncle Marlon, on the other hand, was a phenomenal, agile dancer. He loved dressing up and taking my mother out to nightclubs and parties. He loved going to the movies. They went every weekend. All these outings were financed by my father. Uncle Marlon and my mother made a stunning young couple. I know. My mother has shown us photographs from those days. The fantasy abruptly ended when ambitious Uncle Marlon took a job as the cook's assistant on a ship bound for America. Eventually, he ended up in Los Angeles. His first movie? A nonspeaking role as a waiter in a Chinese restaurant in Samuel Fuller's *Pickup on South Street*.

Uncle Marlon was strangely proud of playing Elvis Presley's happy-go-lucky sidekick in *Blue Hawaii*. That's him in the background, a heartbreaking grin pasted on his copper face. He strummed a ukulele and wore loud, customized swim trunks. A lei of ginger flowers hung around his neck, and his bare chest was oiled and gleaming.

My father once boasted that Uncle Marlon stubbornly refused

to wear the baggy swim trunks brought in by the costume designer. He insisted on customized bikini briefs that showed off his supple body. For some obscure reason, the costume designer let Uncle Marlon do what he wanted, as long as he paid for it out of his own pocket. Maybe it was his insinuating grin. When he turned it on, most people just couldn't say no. Even Elvis Presley was charmed, Elvis who was rumored to have said, "Don't let that little coconut head steal my scenes."

Since the scandalous bikini briefs were never her idea, the costume designer informed Uncle Marlon that he had to buy the fabric himself and pay someone else to do the dirty work. My uncle found and hired a Filipino seamstress to create swim trunks for five different beach scenes, all but one of which ended up on the cutting room floor.

Of course, you could never tell if my parents or Uncle Marlon were telling you the truth. A talent for enhancing the facts runs in the family. Like the thing about Elvis calling Uncle Marlon a coconut head. Or the story Uncle Marlon told me himself about Rock Hudson trying to pick him up in a bar. "Never was my type," Uncle Marlon sniffed.

Funny. As close as they were when they were young, my mother saw Uncle Marlon only twice after we came to America. He came to visit us in San Francisco on his way to the Philippines. Both times, they sat up all night, drinking Scotch and rum, giggling, smoking, and gossiping. Both times, she gave him letters and packages to take back to Manila. As dawn approached during one of those visits, I lay awake in my bed, too excited by my glamorous uncle's presence to sleep. Through the thin wall separating us, I heard Uncle Marlon's low, muffled voice and the hushed sounds of my mother weeping.

My Frida

"Her throat's constricted," I tell the nurse. This one's Irish and looks disillusioned. I dub her Nurse Irate.

"Her throat's dry 'cause she won't drink her water," Nurse Irate explains. She cranks up the bed so that my mother, who seems to be shrinking by the minute, is now in a sitting position. My mother moans. Exactly three minutes have elapsed, and we've got 180 to go before lunch.

Nurse Irate holds up a glass of water. "C'mon, honey. Have a drink a water. Open that little parched throat up."

With great effort, my mother focuses on me. "How are you, Maria?" *Maria*. Easy to remember, easy to forget. Goes well with any last name: Maria Felix, Maria Montez, Maria Shriver, Maria Schneider.

"C'mon," Nurse Irate says with mounting impatience, the rim of the glass at my mother's cracked lips. My mother's cloudy eyes don't register. Her yellow fingers fiddle nervously with her thin woolen blanket. I notice how the nails are still long and manicured, though the polish is chipped.

My mother improves enough to complain, "No one's as lovely as they used to be." She asks for lipstick and a mirror.

"A good sign," Auntie Fely murmurs, hopeful. Uncle Bas shows up with a box of See's chocolates. "She can't eat that," Auntie Fely reprimands him. "Are you insane?"

My mother stares at Bas blankly, as if he were a stranger.

I sleep better than I have in months. I dream about my daughter. She's curled up in a giant, silver egg-shaped incubator. I know she's safe inside. Keiko and I are crouching protectively on top of the incubator. Two fierce hens, hatching and guarding our chick. It is a silent dream. When I wake up, I am ravenous. I take a taxi to the airport, get on a half-empty plane, devour my pasty airline lasagna, and sleep some more. Jake and Venus meet me at JFK. Jake has a pained look on his face. "Bad news," he murmurs. "It's your mother."

"What? What about my mother?"

Other people in the terminal turn to look at me. I stifle a sob.

"Calm down," Jake says. The baby's agitated by the tone of my voice and won't let me hold her.

I go home for one night, before turning right around and flying back to San Francisco.

My mother suffers more little strokes and clots in the brain. She's wheeled into the operating room and saved by the cardiac surgeon, Dr. Chua, then moved on to a new floor to recuperate.

"Are you sure they know what they're doing?" I ask my aunt.

"Chinese Benevolent's the best," Auntie Fely says. "Your mother's lucky to be here." She reminds me that her *kumadre*, Mrs. Garcia, is the head nurse on my mother's floor. Mrs. Garcia's watching out for my mother. Don't worry, Auntie Fely says. We're all Filipina nurses at the Chinese Hospital. Well, ninety-nine percent Filipina nurses, and we're the best. What for you worry so much?

My mother's swift deterioration amazes me. She lies in a morphine haze, her cheeks sunken, her shell of a body crumbling minute by minute, second by second. On the table next to her bed, her dentures lie soaking in a glass of clear solution. My aunt stands watch, seemingly unaware of my entrance into the room. Finally, she says in a weary voice, "Welcome back, Raquel."

The bed is much too big for my mother, who is lost in all that whiteness. Since I've gone and come back, her hair has grown another foot. Unruly and long like a madwoman's hair, streaming out on her giant pillow. I bend to kiss her. A musky scent emanates from her scalp. "Ma. Would you like a shampoo?" I am repelled by her toothlessness, the brittle, crinkly parchment tex-

ture of her skin, her smell. Ashamed of myself, I fill a basin with
warm water. Someone, maybe Zeke, has been thoughtful and
left a gift set of chamomile shampoo, baby soap, and moisturizer.

Her eyes blink open. She is blissfully stoned, and I relax a
little. I cover my mother's body (she is so light, lighter than my
daughter) with towels, then begin sponging her hair with water.
She grunts. "Am I hurting you?" She doesn't answer. "Are you
cold?"

Dr. Chua pops her head in the door. She is dressed as one of
Santa's elves and passing out candy canes to visitors and patients.
My God, it hasn't even occurred to me — but it's almost Christmas. In a daze, my mother asks weakly, "What're those? Condoms?"

Another patient shares the room. Behind a white curtain lies a
woman older and sicker (is that possible?) than my mother. She
is strapped down (for her safety, I am told), as my mother is often
strapped down (for her safety, I am told). On several occasions
when neither Auntie Fely nor I was there, my mother managed
to slip out of bed without falling (the nurses were amazed). She
floated happily down the corridors of the hospital in her bare
feet, until Mrs. Garcia spotted her. "Ay! *Dios ko!* Crazy old lady.
Pitiful old nekkid bitch, lost in the wilderness." My mother's
hospital gown flaps around what was once her voluptuous body,
now a skeletal frame of rickety bird bones.

"We can't have this happen again," Dr. Chua informs me.
"Your mother could fall and suffer permanent damage."

"You must be kidding," I say. "How much more damage could
there be? It's permanent, as far as I'm concerned." I'm so exhausted, I don't mind sounding bitter. Damn age. *Damage?*
Fuck metaphor. My mother's going fast, and we're just waiting
for the maggot train.

Dr. Chua's polite. She pretends I didn't say what I said. And
so, I give in. Dr. Chua prescribes sedatives. Milagros is strapped

to her bed. (For her own good, I'm told.) The straps aren't tight, Dr. Chua says. Just enough restraint so she can't wander away or fall off the bed.

"I can't look at her like that," Zeke says. "*It's wrong.*" Zeke, whose hair is now white, looks like he wants to bolt and run as soon as he walks in. I am shocked to see him. He carries sad-looking violets in a green plastic pot wrapped with a satin bow, the kind of careless, overpriced gift you buy in a hurry from hospital shops. He balances the plant awkwardly on his lap. "How are you, Milagros?" he keeps asking. *It's me, Loverboy.*

My mother's roommate fixes her blind eyes at the ceiling, her mouth open like a black hole. Auntie Fely says no one ever visits her. I sneak a look at the name on her chart. Theresa Connors. Just like my mother, poor Theresa's got everything wrong with her. Emphysema, heart condition, diabetes, cataracts, gangrene, phlebitis, aphasia, you name it. Sometimes she caws like a mynah bird: "Help, help, they're trying to kill me." The orderlies call her the Screamer. It's their way of dealing, dreaming up nicknames for the dying and the hopeless. My mother is the Wanderer. She's our sweetheart, Mrs. Garcia says. Mrs. Garcia's taken a shine to my mother. "*Kawawa naman, ano?*" She shakes her head and commiserates in Tagalog with the other nurses on the floor. There's Miss Reyes. Miss Concepción. And the smiling mestiza, Virginia Brown.

None of the nurses enjoys Mr. Bacigalupi, the eighty-year-old man in the room across the hall from my mother. He's known as Freaky. Another one abandoned by his family. Lucky for him, he's rich. "Ay, *nakakadiri,*" Virginia Brown shudders whenever she looks in on him. Day after day, Freaky masturbates vigorously without ever experiencing orgasm, oblivious to the world. He is fed and medicated intravenously, but he jerks around so much that the tubing inevitably comes undone. Mrs. Garcia is exasperated. "Whatchu do that for, Mr. Freaky? You gonna rub yourself raw till your tingting falls off. Then what? Dirty man. Guess we gonna have to strap you down. Save your tingting for you."

The other nurses stand behind Mrs. Garcia, giggling. The bed's a mess. The old man is bewildered, but he doesn't stop. He's on automatic, feverishly playing with himself. No one wants to go any closer to him, not even fearless Mrs. Garcia. The only sound the old man makes is unh, unh, unh.

Since my mother's relapse, I've been dreaming incessantly, violent, glorious dreams. Sometimes my dreams center on Milagros in her heyday, circa 1958. Other times, the dreams are enveloped in a muted yellow fog, and my mother doesn't exist. Instead, there's Frida Kahlo. She lies doped up on Demerol in the English Hospital, what's left of her powdery spine laced into her plaster corset. A corsage of silk flowers is pinned to her hair, which her sister has brushed and plaited. Frida is vain even in her agony. Her strong hands are clasped on her belly as she regales her glamorous visitors with ribald songs and poetic non sequiturs. *Reddish purple: Aztec. Old blood of prickly pear.*

Dr. Chua appears, and Mrs. Garcia with her troop of petite Pinay nurses. Uncle Bas, leering. So many visitors hovering, so many solicitous nurses and doctors! They are all a little in love with Frida. While they watch, she paints a portrait of my father upside down on her plaster corset. Black snakes. Where am I in this dream? I am not in the room. Frida paints and paints. Time does not fly for Frida. Time makes her skin crawl, makes her spine constrict and tingle. Glass eels slither inside her skin. Except for her strong hands, she cannot move. She is strapped to this bed, she is strapped and molded into this plaster corset for safety, for her own good. The restless eels slip, slide, and slither. She cannot move.

Who will visit her tomorrow to ease her boredom and pain? Maria Felix? Ava Gardner with some lovely stupid matador in tow? Nelson Rockefeller? Anna May Wong and Leon Trotsky in disguise? La Chinita's having one of her exotic flings. She wears coolie hats with veils, blond wigs. Raybans. Men's trousers and wing tip shoes. Trotsky shaves off all his hair, wears green contacts. Borrows one of her rayon dresses. He's so trendy. Don't tell the press. No one knows the truth but you.

Zeke leaves the potted plant on the nightstand. He exits from the hospital room without saying goodbye. I don't know if he is ashamed or disappointed with me for not taking better care of my mother. I stop myself from running after him. Why do I always feel guilty? Fuck Zeke. Fuck metaphor.

I dry my mother's hair carefully, with a fresh towel. Would you like me to brush your teeth? Her smile is gruesome. Who am I to her at this moment? My father as a young man? She is flirting with me, she is flirting with ghosts, a coquette to the bitter end. "How do I brush her teeth?" I ask Mrs. Garcia. Mrs. Garcia addresses my mother. "How's my sweetheart doing today?" My mother blows her a kiss. "Lipstick," my mother suddenly says. "Where's my lipstick?" I am frantic. How do I brush, when she doesn't have any teeth? Mrs. Garcia is amused by my mounting panic. "Use gauze," she tells me. "Dip it in toothpaste and rub her gums gently. Watch out. They're pretty sore and she bleeds easy. There. *There.*"

My family is strapped to their hospital beds: my father, Francisco, Uncle Marlon, my mother Milagros, my mother Frida, Luz, Voltaire. Me, curled up next to Venus, in the egg-shaped incubator. TV a constant, soothing presence. We switch from Oprah, to Jerry, Montel, Sally, Geraldo, Ricki, Maury, Phil. Our sources of cheap entertainment, especially once the Demerol kicks in. Our favorite is Oprah. Oprah's sincere. Oprah's the one who knows the meaning of suffering. Her eyes are guarded, but she can't help herself. She's guilty too. Guiltier than all of us. But she acknowledges her guilt. That's why we love her. Compassion radiates from her every pore. The rest of them, Montel Geraldo Jerry Sally Maury Ricki Phil, are nothing but assholes. Self-righteous pornographers. Oprah Oprah what time is Oprah on? Isn't it afternoon yet?

It is exactly 8:31 A.M. and you've just finished breakfast. Mrs. Garcia was spooning cereal into your mouth when I walked in. "Look who's here," she chirps. "Your daughter. What's her name? Do you remember your daughter's name? All the way from New York, imagine. Again! Just to be with *you.*"

Your eyes are not so glazed today. You're wearing lipstick, and there is an imperiousness about you that I find promising. "You're late," you grumble. Then you make a terrible face. Mrs. Garcia urges you to eat some more, but you stick your tongue out at her. She keeps cooing at you as if you were a baby. Need to pee-pee yet? Try to pee-pee. Yesterday you were a very naughty girl.

My mother flinches when the icy bedpan is slipped under her ass. She is mumbling something we cannot distinguish. Mrs. Garcia is disappointed. No pee-pee? Okay, I'll be back later to check on you. "*Sige, ha. Milagros. Hasta la vista.*" The breakfast tray is removed by a handsome, pumped-up Pinoy with two gold hoops in one ear.

"Hey, Benny."

"Hey, look who's here. Too bad about your mama," he says like he means it. "How's New York?"

"I dunno," I joke. "I wasn't there long enough to find out."

He forces a laugh, for my sake.

Frida. The bedpan is gently slipped under your sore ass by your Filipino nurse, Bienvenido Agmata, Jr. Benny to you, me, and all who love him. You're a lucky gal. You've got bucks, you've got loyal fans, you're a Mexican diva. Filipino nurses are in demand, and here you are, with your very own Benny. You flinch from the touch of cold metal, you wince at the memory of your dead German father, your Germanness, which was actually a lifelong source of profound embarrassment. Better to be mestiza anything, mestiza China mestiza Irish mestiza Spanish, anything else but German! *Dios ko.* 8:32 A.M. When I think German, I think bad food and Nazis. I guess you could call me a racist through and through. And such gloomy, bombastic music! But why do I love you so? How much longer before lunch? before Oprah? Here come the goodies. 8:33 A.M. on the dot. Little paper cups filled with little capsules, little paper cups filled with sweet orange syrup.

"I can't swallow," my mother complains. I can't I can't I can't.

"Try," I say. "Please. Try." I hold the cup with the liquid up to her mouth. Obediently she drinks, then immediately spits every-thing back up. She stares defiantly at me.

"You're worse than your granddaughter," I say.

"You look like somebody I know," Milagros responds, before falling back on the pillow. She shuts her eyes. Her breathing is labored.

I sit. I am afraid that if I leave the room, she will die. I sit and sit. The lunch tray is brought in by another orderly, a nonde-script man I've never seen before. Where is Benny? I am hungry enough to consider eating my mother's strained turkey mash and lime Jell-O. But I don't. Another hour passes. Benny returns to take away the tray of uneaten food.

I'm relieved to see him. I am grateful, and don't mind if he knows it. My voice betrays me. "Hey, Benny."

My pumped-up, benevolent angel, Benny, smiles like he means it. "Hey, Rocky. *Kumusta?*"

Los Blah-Blahs: Four

The mortician doesn't overdo your final make-up job, Mother.

He doesn't have to. He works from a throwaway snapshot I find among your possessions. I haven't given the photo much thought, but when I return to view your body for one last time before crema-tion, the mortician returns the photo to me in an envelope.

I clutch the envelope and gaze at your corpse. You've been artfully arranged in that sleeping pose one might later describe as "peaceful." In my Xanax-induced, Catholic clarity, I know this is a ghoulish joke. You are not sleeping. You are very dead. Your soul has left your luminous cockroach shell of a body.

Kodak color print, 3 1/2" × 5". It is a sad, lovely snapshot. The lighting is bad, and your complexion has a greenish yellow cast. Your head is cocked, expectant. Listening for something, resting, waiting. Your serene, unpainted face is a revelation. Who took the final picture?

To Return

"I read somewhere that in Tagalog, *yo-yo* means 'to return.'
I've also been told that *yo-yo* comes from *yau-yau*, which
means 'to cast out.'"
    — *Rocky Rivera*

Good Friday

It's Friday, almost closing time at the Passport Services window of the Cooper Union Postal Station. Why I always choose to do important shit at the last minute, I'll never know. Runs in the family, I guess. It's another annoying Pinoy trait, something inherent within CP culture I can't shake. Colored People's Time means showing up hours late for an appointment without any excuse, and always being the last to leave at parties.

I'm trying to renew my passport and act civilized. There's a very tall black lady who's in charge, wearing a fabulous copper wig. She's taking it slow and easy with the imperious man ahead of me. She's aware of my impatient hovering, and for some reason she decides to teach me a lesson. "You had this kind of trouble before?" she asks him, her voice dripping with concern. I shift from one foot to the other. Lady, I want to scream, my father is dying and I've got to go home! The man leans an elbow on the counter and shakes his head in feigned disgust. "Day before yesterday I came without my ID. I was told I had to come back. Yesterday I came with the ID, but I forgot the photos —"

"Uhm, uhm, uhm." Her copper wig leans to one side, the ends flipped up, metallic wings. Finally, she hands him some papers. "All done. Have a good trip, darlin'."

"You bet." Mr. Imperious gives her the thumbs-up sign.

"I have an emergency trip I have to take," I blurt out, thrusting my application at her.

She immediately switches from East Village coquette to stern, Southern church lady. "Are you a citizen?" She studies my old passport with suspicion.

Out of nowhere, a short, frantic man sidles up and leans his head on her shoulder. A nametag is clipped to his jacket, but I can't read it. The old lady is bent over my application and ignores him. He's aware of my presence, but doesn't seem to care. Perhaps he is performing for me.

"Phyllis," he pleads, in a raspy voice. "You can't do this to me, Phyllis."

"Go away, Frank."

"I'm going home, Phyllis."

Phyllis fills out my Social Security number on the form. "Go right ahead, Frank. You ain't done a lick of work all day."

"Phyllis. I'm hurt. I am *so* hurt. How can my mother talk like that to me? A son needs his mother's respect."

"Whatever, Frank. But I ain't your mother, and I'm over here tryin' to do my job." She looks at my astonished face. "Forty dollars."

I hand her two twenties.

The man addresses me. "Don't you think a son needs his mother's respect? Just once, he needs to hear her say something nice? Just once?"

I shrug. I know if I respond with words I'll never get out of here.

He rolls his eyes in desperation. His shoulders twitch. I'm not sure if he's pretending to have a seizure, or if his agony is real.

Phyllis is unimpressed. She gives me back the cash. "That's okay. You can write us a check, baby."

Frank begins to cry softly. "Phyllis."

"Go home, Frank. Your parents are the best in the world. They treat you nice." She turns to me. In a matter of seconds, I've become her ally, her second banana. "His parents real nice. They give him everything."

"No they don't." He sobs. I turn to see if anyone else in the post office is witnessing this drama, but they're all too busy with their transactions.

"Go home, Frank." Phyllis practically shoves him out of her cubicle.

His rabbit eyes meet mine; there's nothing there. His smile is odd, triumphant. "Bye-bye, Phyllis dear. Love ya."

"You better stop takin' all them Valiums, Frank." Phyllis chuckles as she watches Frank go out into the street.

"Wow," I say.

"What you think. Tell me if that crazy boy got any money," she says to me, playfully. "C'mon and tell me."

"No, he doesn't."

"Ha! That boy's so rich it'd make you weep. He don't even have to work. You see that suit he got on? Frank Yablonsky," she informs me, "is a millionaire. Frank Yablonsky crazy. Frank Yablonsky a dopehead. Frank Yablonsky our union rep. The best in the bizness. Crazy as a loon, but when that boy negotiate, you better watch out. He brilliant."

"You were amazing," I say. "Both of you."

She seems skeptical, yet pleased. "Really?"

"What a routine," I gush. "I mean it. The two of you were better than vaudeville. Better than Broadway."

"Really?"

"I mean it. I know. I'm in the theater," I say, feeling a lot like Sally Field at the Academy Awards. It suddenly becomes a matter of life and death that this woman love me. I decide to embellish a little more. "And . . . I used to work at the post office."

"Is that right? Well, then you must know about the bins we got back there. Them big ones. For all them letters?"

"Of course, that's where I used to work. In the back. Sorting . . . bins."

"Well, what you think we do with ol' Frank?"

"Excuse me?"

"I said, what you think we do with crazy Frank when he git too crazy roun' here?" She pauses for dramatic effect, an absolute pro with her punch line. "We throw him in the bin, that's what. Throw him right in there and bury him with all that mail. That boy love it."

"Git outta here."

She waves me off, delighted. With herself, with me, with the image of crazy Frank in the loony bin, with the whole damn world, probably. "No, baby. *You* git the hell outta here."

Tropical Depression

A fierce typhoon occurs in the Philippines, usually around the month of August. A typhoon called, with some sense of ironic humor, a "tropical depression." This gray storm of raging, relentless force goes on for thirty days and nights, eroding the soil of the land and the spirit of those who live there. Palm trees snap in two, children and water buffalo suffocate in avalanches of mud. Entire shantytowns swept away, just like that. Novenas are offered to Saint Christopher and Our Holy Madonna of Monsoons, but to no avail. The archbishops and politicians have all fled to higher ground, but the rotting wood doors of haunted cathedrals are left wide open. Life-size plaster effigies of Santo Niño and a sorrowful, jewel-encrusted Black Virgin remain mysteriously untouched on their pedestals, safe from looters and the swirling mud waters below. On the twenty-ninth day, the rain subsides into a drizzle, but the damage has been done. Epidemics of typhoid, cholera, and dysentery are rampant. Strange scenes of violence and grieving occur without warning. Grown men weep uncontrollably. Women run amok, hacking at everyone in their path with any weapon they can find — bolo knives, scissors. Infants are born with webbed feet. The general mood of despair is alleviated by frequent sightings of the Black Virgin. She wanders the countryside, seeking to comfort those who cannot be comforted. A young woman wearing a blond wig has herself crucified in a public ceremony. Her spectacle of sacrifice draws thousands of believers, showy penitents flogging their own, mildewed flesh with dainty, custom-made whips. Blood flows, the only vibrant color in this black sea of waterlogged depression. In Manila, phosphorescent crocodiles and moray eels lurk in the aquatic ruins of a submerged mega–shopping mall on Epifanio de los Santos Avenue.

Trouble

Exactly two months before I arrived in Manila, the caretaker Teofilo was abducted by four men in a jeep from our family beach house in Banaag province. Luz writes me a long letter. Teofilo's presumed tortured and very dead by the people from his fishing village. Trouble is, Teofilo's body is nowhere to be found. On the car ride from Ninoy Aquino International Airport to Alabang, my sister, Luz, reminds me of all of this, in that curt, matter-of-fact voice she adopts whenever she's uncomfortable. "Imagine, so much trouble." Politics, she mutters. With elections coming up, the military's jumpy and the left's getting desperate. Poor Teofilo, such an innocent victim.

I shut my eyes to drown her out. I'm on automatic, nodding as if I were listening to what Luz is saying. I'm unprepared for this trip. Ordinarily, I wouldn't have chosen to stay with my sister and her family. Still, I am grateful to be rescued from the confusion of the teeming airport, too exhausted from my twenty-seven-hour journey to understand the deep-shit gravity of the situation. My sister's terse pronouncement fades in and out of the crackling radiowaves in my fatigued brain. *Teofilo. Oh, yeah. Teofilo, Genesis and Emy's son.*

The traffic and congestion are mind-boggling. We are stalled in a hopeless gridlock of trucks and buses belching black smoke. Cars and jeepneys jockey for positions at every turn. "You didn't bring Venus," Luz says.

I gaze out the window, take in the half-finished luxury hotels, the rows of cozy sari-sari stores, the lurid splash of billboards advertising the latest kung fu action movie: AK-47 MEETS JOHNNY KOMMANDO. Twenty-two years.

"Who's taking care of her?" Luz inquires.

"Her father."

"Her father?" Luz is astonished and indignant.

"We don't have *yayas* in New York," I can't help saying. She glares back at me. I've always maintained that if my sister hadn't married Charlie Fuentes, she would've made an excellent Mother Superior. "Ayyy, Raquel. How could you be so irresponsible?"

I force myself to concentrate on what's outside the car window. How many years has it been? You'd think Luz and I would be happy to see each other, but we're not. I inhale Manila and steel myself. "You look good," I say to her.

Luz sighs in frustration. "Please. I'm too fat."

We are not moving.

Eyes, eyes. I am surrounded by eyes. Probing, curious, taunting, hostile, mesmerizing eyes. Passengers in the crowded bus alongside our car stare down at us. Thank God I'm wearing jeans, although they're all wrong, too heavy and dark for this steamy, oppressive heat. A young man makes eye contact, raising his brows twice in a furtive suggestion to me. His eyebrows ask, Are you available? I avert my gaze, then sneak another look. He blows me a nervy kiss.

Genesis chauffeurs us in the air-conditioned Nissan. "*Kumusta*, Genesis?" I'd greeted him earlier at the airport. "Are you all better now? How's Manang Emy?" My sister had written me about his recent bout with tuberculosis.

"Thanks be to God, okay *naman*. All okay," Genesis assured me, in English. "*Sayang* about your mama. How is your Tiya Fely?" he asked shyly.

I'd tried helping him load my bags into the trunk, but he wouldn't allow it. "Is this all, Señora Raquel?" Genesis was both amused and disappointed by my battered duffel bag and stained backpack. He slammed the trunk shut.

"I'm sorry about Teofilo," I said, feeling awkward.

Embarrassed by my show of concern, Genesis was silent. He held the car door open for me as Luz imperiously patted the seat next to her. "Hurry up, Raquel. Get in. The sooner we get out of here . . ."

Malnourished children run up to the red Nissan to press their faces and wares against the window on my side. *Buy, buy. Help me.* It's as if all the children possess a sixth sense about who I am, an easy mark, a bleeding-heart mestiza Pinay, ridden with guilt. They don't bother with my sister. They know exactly who she is, another stony-faced Manila matron stuck in the daily snail crawl of chaos on Epifanio de los Santos Avenue.

We are not moving.

"Why did you have to take EDSA?" Luz chides Genesis.

Here's what is sold on the street: mentholated cough drops, sampaguita leis, painfully sweet peanut brittle. Rice cakes wrapped in banana leaves, still steaming. White squares of carabao cheese. Whimsical pot holders stitched from colorful rags. Local-made Marlboros and Winstons, sold by the pack or singly. Matches not included. Matches, five centavos extra. I wonder if I will start smoking again.

Elvis pointed out while we were on the road, early on, that when I travel, I feel free to smoke. I drink, smoke, and fuck with a vengeance. Death by toxins becomes another remote concept, a purely North American obsession.

Bahala na.

A wizened old man squatting under the shade of a tamarind tree shows off an eagle perched on his leathery arm. Is the eagle for sale, or some kind of living talisman? At the old man's splayed feet, stacks of mynah birds caged in miniature bamboo houses are cawing and whistling.

"Let's buy one," I say.

"Those birds are probably all sick," Luz grumbles, blind to the wonders of my old man and the incongruous eagle with unblinking eyes.

Here they are again. My teenage boys, so achingly familiar. Dancing up to the car, gaunt matadors sidestepping traffic.
Dirty towels twisted into makeshift turbans protect them from
the sun. They brandish Tagalog and English newspapers and
magazines with gory front-page photographs of decapitations,
knifings, weeping rape victims. *Extra, extra.* Glorious starlets
with fuchsia lips generate the same old headlines: *shabu* euphoria, love triangles, attempts at suicide. The articles themselves
are just as graphic and fabulous. Vampire sightings are as ubiquitous as apparitions of the Blessed Virgin in a rice field.

"How many newspapers do they publish in Manila?" I ask,
amazed.

"Too many, if you ask me." Luz shrugs. "You should ask
Charlie."

I don't buy anything. The teenage boys lose interest and wander off. "These kids have already pegged me for a *balikbayan*." I
use the term for 'those who come home,' tourists in their own
land. It makes me sad.

"Is your door locked?" Luz asks, reaching over to make sure
without waiting for me to answer.

Genesis turns on the FM radio. Mello Yello, Manila's legendary DJ, is on the air. Who knows how old he is? I remember
him from my childhood. Mello dedicates the next tune: "For
Stella by Starlight. You know who you are. You'll always be
my everything. Hugs and kisses from your willing slave, Boy
Toy Garcia." Mello pauses for a brief, thrilling moment of silence. "Wow!" he finally exclaims. "Isn't . . . love . . . faaan . . .
taaz . . . tik!"

A Whitney Houston ballad follows.

"Genesis, turn it off. That girl gives me a headache." Luz
frets, squirming in her seat. The music literally seems to pain her.
"Too big. That girl's voice is much too *big*."

"Excuse me, ma'am." Genesis's manner is apologetic. "I will
buy some cigarettes for me later, okay, ma'am?" He keeps smiling. Luz grunts her assent, then purposely says to me without

lowering her voice, "I really don't like it when the servants smoke."

Genesis acts like he doesn't hear, rolling down his window quickly. He buys a pack of Marlboros and matches, then shoos the vendor away. He rolls the window back up, hiding the cigarettes in his shirt pocket before my sister can change her mind. Luz pulls a fan out of her straw shoulder bag, fanning herself vigorously while dabbing at her neck with a tissue. The heat from the sun manages to seep in, even with the air conditioning. We are wilting in the back seat. "*Dios mio*, this is terrible. Terrible terrible." Luz sighs, fanning me.

"Is Voltaire still living with you?" I don't know why, but I ask this question.

Luz's tone is condescending. "He may as well be. You know, the last time I heard from Voltaire was exactly a week ago. He doesn't have a telephone and likes showing up unannounced. He tried to borrow money from Charlie. Money to see a lawyer, *daw*. Says he wants to renounce his U.S. citizenship. Did you know that? Crazy, *talaga*. Charlie told him, 'Voltaire, you're really backward. Everyone else in this godforsaken country is trying to leave, and you're trying to stay!'"

Rocky laughs.

Luz continues, "And Tiya Fely and Tiyo Marlon, how are they?"

"Auntie Fely's depressed. Never got over Ma's death. Uncle Marlon's trying to sell his house so he can move back here."

Luz seems pleased. "When? When is Tiyo Marlon coming? He keeps saying he's going to visit Papa." Luz fans herself a few more moments, then hands the fan to me. "Is it true what they say? That he's sick? He's got that thing they're all getting, doesn't he?" I don't answer her questions because what everyone says is true, and she already knows this.

"I want to see Voltaire," I say. "I've got things for him. Ma's things."

"Don't say I didn't warn you," Luz says. "He's been living in

Pasay. In this . . . *dump.* He takes the jeepney to visit Papa. Can you imagine?"

Another child with a delicate, dirty face appears at my window. She holds up a bunch of woven palm fans in brilliant hues of purple, red, yellow, and lime green. Dyed feathers have been glued to the edges of some of them, bits of lace and gold trim on others. "We have millions of those things back in the house. Don't bother," Luz says.

I roll down my window to address the child, letting in a blast of heat. "*Magkano?*"

"Ten pesos, *ho*," she answers. No older than five or six, she wears an oversize, soiled T-shirt as a dress and rubber-thong slippers that she has long outgrown. The sun has streaked her matted hair copper.

Luz haggles with the child. "Ten pesos! *Qué barbaridad! Puwede ba*, I can buy those same fans at Divisoria for five pesos — no, three!"

I am appalled by my sister's cheapness. "Luz. *Three pesos?*"

The child pleads with her eyes. "Eight pesos."

"Too much," Luz mutters, shaking her head.

I choose a loud purple fan shaped like an upside-down heart and hand the girl ten pesos. The child snatches my money and scampers nimbly away through the maze of stalled traffic. Luz clucks her disapproval. "Ay, Raquel. You never listen and never learn. You think that money goes to feed her? It goes straight to those crooked cops who pimp her mother."

"She must get some of it."

"Ha! Maybe a bowl of rice and a beating."

"Better than nothing."

"Ha! If she's lucky, maybe a bowl of rice and some *shabu.*"

"Are we going to fight? I just got here." I am sweating. The dye from my new fan stains the palm of my hand. Without letting Luz see, I quickly rub my skin clean on my dark jeans. I wonder if the passengers in the bus are watching.

Luz finally breaks the silence. "You understand. We couldn't come for Mama's funeral. Not with Papa sick. You took care of her, and I'm taking care of him. Voltaire was devastated, of course. Didn't know whether he was coming or going. But what could I do? Carlito's having a lot of problems."

"What kind of problems?" I know Luz and Charlie are mystified by their son.

Luz grimaces. "The usual teenage — what do you call it? Generation gap. He fights with his father all the time. He's been doing *shabu*. I have to mediate. You have no idea."

But I do, I want to tell her. Instead I say, "It's been awful —"

"It's awful *here*," Luz interrupts. "All the violence. Incessant rumors. You remember what it used to be like, lots of shooting? Now it's even worse. And the economy, *dios ko*! I can't keep up with it. Inflation, deflation. Now they're saying if the army doesn't get its way, there'll be a coup. Charlie'll tell you. And wait until you see Papa. Since the last stroke, he's like a child. He knows you're coming, and he keeps asking, 'Is she here? Is she here?' Like a two-year-old. Awful."

"What about the cancer?"

"Amazing. His doctor can't believe how strong he is. How he's lasted, even with the bad heart. The diabetes. He's got the best oncologist at Makati Medical. Doctora Katigbak," my sister says with pride. What the hell. Since my father's lost his money, she and Charlie are probably footing the bills. Let her brag. For her, even sickness and suffering could be made bearable by status symbols. One had to die with style, surrounded by Harvard-trained physicians and gleaming, state-of-the-art equipment. "Didn't you go to school with a Katigbak? They're all doctors."

"I don't remember," I lie. But I do. There were two Katigbaks, actually. Emma and her twin sister, Erlinda. Erlinda was one of my best friends. I nicknamed her Erly, which made her laugh. She loved to dance. We'd practice together. I'd always lead. Cha-

cha. Boogie. Were the twins sought-after surgeons now, cutting open the rich and famous, working side by side in some fancy hospital?

"The doctor assures me Papa's pain is manageable," Luz says. "For now, anyway."

Benigno Aquino's widow, Corazon, has been running the country and making a mess of it, according to my sister. The widow's backing General Ramos in the upcoming elections. A supreme irony in a cynical culture loaded with irony. "Wouldn't you agree?" Luz asks me. "I don't know," I say. "I've been away too long." The prevailing mood in the country is one of bitter disappointment. "Nothing's changed," Luz insists, almost gleeful. "You'll see . . ."

My father was diagnosed with bone marrow cancer in 1982. "You'd better come," Luz had said on the phone. "He won't last." A slow painful death was predicted. That year I also cowrote and recorded "Greed" with Elvis Chang. I never made it to Manila. I was still too angry. My father refused chemotherapy and surprised us all by surviving. I've finally returned to say goodbye to my father, a man who's been dying for ten years.

My first morning back, I sit at the breakfast table between Carlito, my nephew, and my sister, Luz. My three young nieces sit in a row across from us, slurping up their Tang and ogling me. Carlito slouches sullenly, picking at his food. "Why can't we go to Banaag this weekend?" Carlito whines to his parents. "I want to get out of Manila and go windsurfing." The beachfront property in Banaag province belongs to my mother's side of the family.

"Absolutely not," Charlie Fuentes says. "Are you crazy?"

Luz's tone is gentler. "Carlito, please. Tiya Raquel has just arrived, and we have to stay close to your grandfather."

"Did Luz tell you about our trouble?" Charlie Fuentes addresses me. He sips his coffee, engrossed in the latest issue of *Far East Economic Review*. My brother-in-law's a publishing magnate and information freak. He subscribes to *Time*, *Newsweek*, *Asia Week*, *National Geographic*, *The Wall Street Journal*, *Christian Science Monitor*, *U.S. News and World Report*, *Reader's Digest*, plus three Manila dailies. He reads everything, cover to cover. Newspapers and magazines are scattered all over the house. He won't let Luz or the servants throw any of it away until he has clipped every item of possible interest for his "files." He considers himself an expert on everything. I've never liked him, not even when we were children.

"Raquel, I mean, *Rocky*." Charlie's grin is evil. "I'm talking to you."

"You mean about Teofilo's disappearance?" I ask, sweetly.

"He didn't disappear," Charlie scoffs. "The NPA killed Teofilo. You know what I mean? There's a lot of NPA up in those mountains."

I know Charlie's setting a trap, but I can't help myself. "NPA? In Banaag? You don't know that for sure," I argue. "No one's found his body. No one knows the real story. He's probably alive. Maybe he ran off to another village. Maybe he's in hiding —"

"Ran off to another village!" Charlie snorts in contempt. "Did you hear that, Luz? Your sister thinks Teofilo's just another neurotic New Yorker, running away from his problems!" He laughs derisively, then goes back to his magazine.

I glare at Charlie, but he ignores me. Carlito and his sisters stop eating.

My sister's tone is conciliatory. "What Charlie means is . . . well, Teofilo's a humble fisherman, very religious, with a family. He would never abandon his family like that." She pauses. "Remember when Charlie's family's farm in Tarlac was burned by the NPA?"

I nod.

Charlie frowns at me. "Those self-proclaimed insurgents demanded twenty thousand pesos a month, for so-called taxes. Can you beat that? Nothing but a bunch of extortionists, gangsters, and goons. I refused to pay."

Nanette enters the lanai. "Señora Raquel, telephone."

Luz gives me a questioning look, then says, "I think it's your old sweetheart."

I blush. There's a phone in the room, but I pretend not to notice and excuse myself. Nanette and the other servants, Celia, Jing, and Manang Emy, are cleaning rice and chopping vegetables for a late Sunday lunch. I feel like an intruder in the kitchen. "Good morning, Raquel," Manang Emy greets me, smiling broadly. Yesterday, when she saw me walk into my sister's house, Manang Emy burst into tears. Then she went right back to whatever she was doing, just as she does now. Chopping meat with her cleaver, barking orders at the other servants in the kitchen. She is an attractive woman, wiry and small, her long gray hair coiled in a bun on top of her head. I've been studying her for signs of trouble, but like her husband, Genesis, Emy remains inscrutable. Her youthful face betrays no emotion, no signs of grieving over Teofilo. The only hint that anything's wrong is the intensity and silence with which she works. The other servants glance over at me as I pick up the receiver of the old rotary phone on the counter.

"I've been waiting for an eternity," Jose Mari groans dramatically, then switches gears. "How's your jet lag?"

I want to laugh. "Oh, hi." I force myself to sound casual, aware that everyone in the kitchen is listening.

"Eternity's too long a time without you."

"Like I said. You should've been an actor. You're perfect. *Guwapo*," I tease, unable to resist the Tagalog Spanish word for handsome. Even Manang Emy looks up from her cooking. "*Guwapo* and *gago*." I add the word for stupid. Then I ask, "Do you have any relatives in New York? There's a famous leftist lawyer named William Kunstler who lives in my neighborhood."

"You're so mean to me. All these years, why did you keep me waiting?"

"You're a born matinee idol. Never shoulda gotten married. Doesn't suit you. Or maybe it does." I am enjoying myself now, couldn't care less about my hostile brother-in-law or who's eavesdropping. "Marriage keeps you on a leash. Makes you strain. Makes you hungry."

"Feed me, then. You broke my heart. Humiliated me. Practically left me at the altar."

I catch Celia and Jing snickering. "Don't be an idiot. *We were children*. So how are you?"

"You sound so American!" Jose Mari exclaims. "I'm not fine, I'm miserable. You know that Roland Gift song, 'She Drives Me Crazy'?" Jose Mari's voice drops. "You drive me crazy."

"You don't even know what I look like," I remind him. "It's been years —"

"I've been keeping up," he says, smoothly. "I know you have a daughter. I've seen pictures."

I know better, but I'm titillated. He's so good at it, such a professional loverboy.

The flirtation feels oddly playful and innocent, something I desperately need. "I flex my biceps to that song. Flex and release. Stretch my hamstrings. My aerobics teacher plays it all the time."

His voice oozes sex. "Are you alone?"

"Of course not. What a stupid question."

"Meet me later, at my disco. I'll send the car."

"It's Sunday. *Big family day*. Remember? I'm going to visit my father." There are tiny red ants climbing on the counter toward an open bowl of sugar. I glance down at the floor. There are hundreds of them, swarming in an orderly path.

"I mean later. Come later, after dinner. You won't be sorry. My disco's the best in Makati."

"I loathe discos." I regret sounding bitchy. It would flatter him to think I was angry. Manang Emy drops what she is doing and grabs the bowl of sugar next to me. She covers it with a saucer, then places it in the center of a shallow tray filled with water. The ants will keep coming and surely drown. She goes back to the table and takes a colander of rice to rinse under the faucet, humming to herself. Nanette brings out a large fish from the freezer.

Jose Mari chuckles on the phone. "What have I ever done to you? Rocky, I'm not your father. You're the one who left." He pauses. "You still call yourself Rocky, don't you?"

"*Siempre*."

"And you weren't going to tell me you were in town, were you? If I hadn't run into Charlie yesterday —"

"Thank you for calling."

"Tonight. Around ten-thirty. Everyone will be there. You remember Baby, my wife. You were classmates, *di ba*?"

"I remember her pet monkey."

"You're such a bitch." Jose Mari chuckles. "Come on, don't be a killjoy. I'll pick you up at your father's. You want me to do that?"

"No thanks."

"Then I'll do it. How is he anyway? Sorry about your mother." Jose Mari pauses.

"Sure," I say.

He prattles on. "I saw your father about a month ago, at the Peninsula. He suffers but never complains! I was so glad to see him out and about. My father-in-law visits him all the time. They used to be good friends."

"I know."

"Golf partners."

"I know."

"Like your brother and I used to be good friends," he reminds me. "I miss him, too. I hear he's back. How is that crazy Voltaire?"

"Still crazy. Haven't you heard?"

I am watching the old woman. With one swift stroke of her

big knife, Manang Emy slits open the belly of the giant lapu-lapu. My mother used to tell me stories of boats capsizing in the sea, lapu-lapu and shark devouring drowning passengers. "There was a rich fat woman whose emerald ring and diamond-studded watch were found inside one of those monsters, along with part of her arm," she said. "Dirty fish. That's why I won't eat lapu-lapu to this day."

Jose Mari sounds annoyed. "Rocky? Are you there?"

I hang the phone up gently, so as not to hurt his ear. He will call back, I am sure of it.

I am mesmerized by Manang Emy, scraping the insides of the fish, getting ready to stuff it with onions, tomato, garlic, baby shrimp. After we visit my father, Luz has planned a late Sunday banquet to welcome me home. Voltaire's coming, plus one or two boring friends who Charlie has invited to meet "Luz's baby sister."

"You didn't need to do that," I say, trying to sound polite.

Charlie feigns innocence at the breakfast table. "It's not like you're actually married."

Luz comes to my defense. "*Dios ko*, Charlie. What are you trying to imply?"

Charlie's silent. Maybe this is his perverse way of getting back at me. Maybe he's jealous. "I appreciate your hospitality," I say to Charlie, dryly. "And your obvious concern for my social life. But can't you pick more exciting friends?"

But I agree to put up with a young hotshot army colonel named Eddie something ("Please be civil," my sister begs, "he was educated at West Point") and the owner of a fast-food franchise named Ramon Ong. Ramon Ong owns several condominiums, a yacht, and a bulletproof Mercedes. "And he's only thirty-three years old," Charlie says, smugly.

"Jesus' age when he was crucified," I remind him.

"Do you believe in God?" my brother-in-law suddenly asks.

"Of course," I reply.

My nieces, Ming Ming (for Milagros), Cookie (for Carmen),

and Pepsi (for Penelope), start giggling. They've been following me around the house since I arrived, whispering. Carlito glances at me curiously, then shifts his gaze to his father.

"Do you consider yourself a Christian?" Charlie continues his interrogation, his manner bland and congenial.

"Of course," I answer. "Who isn't?"

"Let's change the subject," Luz snaps.

"You'll like Ramon Ong," Charlie says, smiling back at me. "Smart fellow, loves music. But he may be moving to Hong Kong or Taiwan soon. Maybe San Francisco."

"Too many kidnappings. All the rich Chinese are leaving," Luz says. I can't tell if she's sad or glad.

My nephew looks up from the papaya he's eating. "Can you blame them? Tiya Raquel, do you know what they say? You can't even go to the cops. The cops are behind it all."

You know what they say, you know what they say. What am I doing back here? I've run away, and my father's illness is an excuse. It's been only forty-eight hours, but I already feel like I've been gone from New York for years. Venus surely misses me. Jake surely misses me. I miss them back, miss the brutal clarity of New York. My ears need to pop. I'm suddenly overwhelmed by fatigue. "I can't wait to meet this Ong guy," I say. Lying comes so easily to me these days.

"He's not bad." Luz shrugs. "Not bad for a Chinese."

The monstrous, pinkish gray lapu-lapu's belly, bursting with diamonds and emeralds, is sewed up tight with catgut by Manang Emy. Its razor teeth are capped by lustrous pearls. I take a deep breath. There. Manang Emy's task is finished. But what about her son, Teofilo? Has she resigned herself to the situation, envisioned him already dead, his headless, handless corpse floating down some muddy, poisoned river? How will Manang Emy ever be able to identify her son? Let us pray. She puts the fish in the gas oven to bake slowly until the guests arrive. Today it's a soldier. Today it's a fast-food millionaire, uncertain of his future. Chinese

Filipino, third generation. But no matter. Does he travel with bodyguards?

My brother-in-law teases me about becoming "Americanized," and persists with his sardonic observations. He begins each damning sentence with *You Americans:* "You Americans don't care about us anymore. We're disappearing fast from your collective imagination."

I finally confront him. "Would you prefer it if I moved to a hotel?"

"Joking *lang,*" Charlie says.

Manang Emy smiles at me. I know that smile. She is pleased I've come home. She loves me like a mother, I know that much about the old woman. My mother is dead, I want to tell her. And so is your son. As for everyone else . . .

She lifts one of the cauldron lids to check on the rice. "Don't want to overcook," Manang Emy mutters in English, turning down the flame on the stove.

The petite but sturdy sixteen-year-old servant helps the old man from his bed to the leather easy chair facing the window. She gives him a kind, encouraging smile. She pities the sick old man, his limp, ugly body wracked with disease and pain. She understands what heroic effort the simplest of his movements require. "Very good, sir," she murmurs, as he collapses, groaning, into the chair. She looks at him with downcast eyes, so that no one who suddenly enters the room would misinterpret her actions. Or his, toward her. The absentminded way the old man keeps patting her hand, for example, letting her know he is grateful for her presence.

"Thank you, Naty." The old man speaks to her mostly in English. He moans, wincing. Naty rolls a leather module under his scarred, spindly legs, propping his swollen feet on it. He needs a pedicure badly. The yellowish, calcified nails on his toes have started to curl into talons. Naty tries hard not to feel squeamish, making a mental note to talk later with the old man's wife, Señora Baby. She could send for one of those *pedicuristas* who make housecalls. Señora Baby usually takes Naty's observations seriously. "You're a smart girl," Señora Baby often says. "You should go back and finish school."

Naty is silent, her expression sullen. The old man sticks out his lower lip and gazes pensively out the screened window. Naty knows he is capable of sitting and staring like this for hours. At what, she never knows. Where the old man and his family live is a new subdivision built next to a mall on the farthest outskirts of Makati. An expensive wasteland, inconvenient, soulless, arid. The view from the top-floor window is a joke, nothing but a dull, vast expanse of white-hot sky. No lush green treetops, no wafting sea breeze, not even the music of birds or clamor of traffic. What could the demented old man possibly be looking at or dreaming about? Naty wonders, fascinated.

Naty makes sure the old man eats and doesn't choke on his food or medicine. She gives him sponge baths, brushes his teeth, and half carries, half drags him from bed to chair to toilet and back again. She has gotten used to seeing him naked and the unceasing demands of her job. When the morphine doesn't take effect fast enough, for example, and the old man spends the night thrashing and whimpering, Señora Baby sends for Naty and moves into her son's room across the hall. Uncomplaining, Naty lays out her *banig*, sleeping on the floor by the old man's bed. Señora Baby makes jokes about their somewhat perverse roles. The old man is an infant, Señora Baby says, never to be left unsupervised. Señora Baby is his mother. And Naty, his teenage *yaya*. "You are totally responsible for my husband. If he falls, if he drowns, if he chokes . . . if anything happens." Señora Baby leaves it at that, smiling at Naty.

"Nothing will happen," Naty vows.

In the sweltering afternoons, the old man succumbs to a drugged sleep. Naty dozes off on the stool next to him, resting her weary head against the window ledge. The woven fan she uses to keep flies away is clutched in her fist. When he is awake and the pain manageable, the old man hums an eerie melody, or mutters incessantly to himself. He draws shapes in the air with his forefinger. Naty recognizes the letter S, triangles, the numbers three, four, and eight. Sometimes, the old man reminds Naty of the catatonic inmates at the insane asylum in Mandaluyong, where her father works as a guard. The inmates rock back and forth for hours, singing and laughing softly to themselves. Naty isn't afraid of them, like her father and the caretakers are afraid, believing the inmates possessed by demons. Naty knows better. She pities and prays for them, like she pities and prays daily for the demented old man.

Lupo or Ramona is sent to relieve Naty, who scrambles downstairs, gobbling a meal in the kitchen or taking a quick bath in the servants' quarters. Fiercely protective of the old man, Naty trusts no one else to care for him properly. "But I don't want *you*. I don't know you. Where's little Naty?" the old man demands in a quavering, anxious voice when the other servants approach. "I want Naty."

Naty gets two days off a month. She takes the tedious bus ride to her hometown of Bocaue, in the province of Bulacan, spending precious time with her boisterous, beloved family. Naty's mother, father, her tubercular, cigar-smoking grandmother, a widower uncle, one male cousin, one older brother, four younger sisters, and a prized, pampered rooster all live under one roof.

Naty is awed by Señora Baby, a sad-eyed woman of regal beauty and many secrets. Though twenty-one years younger than her dying husband, Señora seems genuinely devoted to the doddering, helpless old man. Is it possible? Naty considers Señora Baby may even truly *love* Francisco Rivera, maybe not with the weepy, acrobatic passion that megastars like Sharon Cuneta or Robin Padilla demonstrate in those tumultuous melodramas Naty finds so bewitching, but who cares? Love is love, just the same.

In the privacy of the kitchen, Naty listens with an unhappy expression to the older servants snickering about Señora's little boy. Leila the cook, a squat, intimidating woman, dismisses all of them as idiots. "*Mga gago kayong lahat.* The boy can't possibly be a Rivera. Just look at his so-called father's features," Leila suggests slyly. "Then look at the boy's . . ." Her tone is triumphant. "*Di ba?* Don't you idiots agree? The boy's definitely mestizo! Look at his nose. He's much too fair to belong to that crocodile upstairs."

Naty speaks up. "But Señora Baby's mestiza *and* pretty. Isn't she proof enough?" Everyone laughs, except the infuriated Leila.

The servants refer to the old man as Sir, making *tsismis* about his prodigal son's return from America. "Imagine," Leila says, "he just appeared one day, like a ghost at the door." With a tinge of cruelty, Leila mimics Señora Baby's voice, speaking sweetly in English. "*My goodness, Voltaire. How did you get here?*" She approximates a gruff, male voice in response: "*Aba, excuse me, lang. What do you think? I took a jeepney from Pasay, then I walked.*"

Everyone bursts out laughing, including Naty.

There is tension in the household about Sir's mysterious daughter, who's expected to arrive at any moment. The old man hasn't seen her in more than twenty years, and Señora Baby's nervous about meeting her. Know-it-all Leila has seen a photograph. "*Naku!*" she exclaims, rolling her eyes. "Purple hair, what's left of it, anyway. She looks just as *kalug* as that brother of hers."

"Obviously, it runs in the blood." Lupo, Leila's common-law husband, chuckles. Leila purses her lips, shaking her head in dismay. She clucks and wails, stirring them all up. "*Ay, Dios ko.* What if Sir's daughter tries to kill Señora Baby and the little boy? With that hairdo of hers, she looks capable of anything. Poor Sir, with all his vain wives and wayward children. Poor Sir, suffering alone in that stifling bedroom upstairs." The servants sigh in mutual resignation. *Bahala na.* God works in mysterious ways. Finally, after all those years living blithely in sin, Francisco Rivera is being punished.

Señora Baby glides into the room. Startled from his reverie, the old man makes a feeble attempt to get up from his chair. "Is Raquel here?"

Señora Baby's tone is soothing. "No, no, not yet. Sit down, *amor.*" Seeing the disappointed look on his face, she quickly adds, "Soon. I promise. She'll be here soon. Luz called to say they're all coming."

"Voltaire? Milagros too?" The old man's watery eyes dart around the room. "Naty?"

Naty rushes to his side. "Sir?"

The old man extends his withered arm. "Help me up." Naty, unsure of what to do, turns to her mistress.

"Take it easy, *amor,*" Señora Baby says brightly. "They're all coming. All your children. But we have to take it easy. Not get too excited. We'll get you dressed. There, there. Ay! Naty, it's too hot in here. *Amor*, why won't you allow Naty to turn the air conditioner on?"

"No." The old man snarls.

"But Dr. Katigbak says the heat isn't good for your heart —"

"No." The old man glares at the woman standing before him, so costly, so sporty, so perfect in her Ralph Lauren shirt, Banana Republic Bermuda shorts, and metallic Charles Jourdan sandals. She is disturbingly familiar. A thought suddenly occurs to him. "Where's Kikoy?" He hasn't seen his son all day. Maybe he's been kidnapped.

Señora Baby is amused. "Outside playing, where else? Don't worry, *amor*. I'll bring him to you. *Sige*, Naty. Get his white pants and shirt ready." In a panic, she watches as her husband drifts away from her, tracing the five points of an invisible star. Her voice becomes shrill, and she switches to Tagalog. "Naty! Are you deaf? I said, get his pants and shirt and dress him right *now*!"

"Look, Señora." Naty points to the old man's tray of untouched food.

Señora Baby flails her braceleted arms in exasperation. "How can you get well if you don't eat, *amor*? I can't give you medicine on an empty stomach." A threat insinuates itself into her voice. "Would you rather I call Dr. Katigbak and ask her to put you back on the IV?" She pauses to consider his agitated reaction. "No? I didn't think so, *amor*."

Naty starts helping the old man on with his white shirt. Señora Baby grabs a comb from the table cluttered with bottles of medicine. "Don't we look *guwapo*! Wait till you see yourself, *amor*. Wait, wait, let me comb your hair. Look at you! Ay, Naty, bring over the mirror. Hurry."

Shrieks of excitement come from the patio outside, where a boy of four brandishes a toy sword. He duels vigorously with a swarm of mosquitoes lurking in the dark thicket of wild ferns and gardenias. Ramona, a woman in her late fifties, is paid to watch over the child like a hawk. "Uh-oh. Careful. Careful. Too much jumping! Too noisy!" The *yaya* admonishes him. Ignoring her, the boy lunges with his sword. He lets loose a bloodcurdling wail, stabbing merrily at his imaginary foes in the bushes.

The old man stares at his reflection in the mirror. Who is that? He marvels, distracted by the tiny, exquisite flowers embroidered on the pockets of his white shirt, the white monogrammed handkerchief Naty has so thoughtfully . . . white on white. So clean, so . . . Milagros in a saucy halter dress, cat's-eye sunglasses. San Sebastián, Spain, 1955. She thinks she's Ava Gardner. Ha. *Puwede ba*. The spicy scent of cologne slathered on his neck nauseates him. The little dwarf Marlonito follows her everywhere, begging her to put on his rubber shoes. Let's dance, Marlonito says. Milagros laughs, but Marlonito doesn't seem to mind. At the bullfight, she sits behind Ava Gardner and . . . *Who does she think she is? Who do you think you are?* He shivers at the mottled, wrinkled texture of his skin, the horror of his old man's face — foolish, sunken, cadaverous. "Aren't we *guwapo*?" The beautiful woman kisses him tenderly on the lips. How can she stand it? His dry, parched lips. Who are you? He wants to ask her, unable to speak. Evelyn. Baby. Milagros. *Wife*. How absurd, he thinks, wanting desperately to laugh, but afraid of how it might sound. His eyes dart frantically around the room. Where is she? His eyes, frantic and stinging with tears. *Naty, Naty, help me.*

Naty takes the mirror away from Francisco Rivera. A car pulls up in the driveway. The old man hears crunching gravel, car doors swinging open, car doors slamming shut. Hushed voices. A young child — his son? — whining. The beautiful woman takes a deep breath, forcing herself to smile at the old man. "See, *amor*? Didn't I tell you? She's here."

FOR THE BEST IN PAPERBACKS, LOOK FOR THE

In every corner of the world, on every subject under the sun, Penguin represents quality and variety—the very best in publishing today.

For complete information about books available from Penguin—including Penguin Classics, Penguin Compass, and Puffins—and how to order them, write to us at the appropriate address below. Please note that for copyright reasons the selection of books varies from country to country.

In the United States: Please write to *Penguin Group (USA), P.O. Box 12289 Dept. B, Newark, New Jersey 07101-5289* or call 1-800-788-6262.

In the United Kingdom: Please write to *Dept. EP, Penguin Books Ltd, Bath Road, Harmondsworth, West Drayton, Middlesex UB7 0DA*.

In Canada: Please write to *Penguin Books Canada Ltd, 10 Alcorn Avenue, Suite 300, Toronto, Ontario M4V 3B2*.

In Australia: Please write to *Penguin Books Australia Ltd, P.O. Box 257, Ringwood, Victoria 3134*.

In New Zealand: Please write to *Penguin Books (NZ) Ltd, Private Bag 102902, North Shore Mail Centre, Auckland 10*.

In India: Please write to *Penguin Books India Pvt Ltd, 11 Panchsheel Shopping Centre, Panchsheel Park, New Delhi 110 017*.

In the Netherlands: Please write to *Penguin Books Netherlands bv, Postbus 3507, NL-1001 AH Amsterdam*.

In Germany: Please write to *Penguin Books Deutschland GmbH, Metzlerstrasse 26, 60594 Frankfurt am Main*.

In Spain: Please write to *Penguin Books S. A., Bravo Murillo 19, 1° B, 28015 Madrid*.

In Italy: Please write to *Penguin Italia s.r.l., Via Benedetto Croce 2, 20094 Corsico, Milano*.

In France: Please write to *Penguin France, Le Carré Wilson, 62 rue Benjamin Baillaud, 31500 Toulouse*.

In Japan: Please write to *Penguin Books Japan Ltd, Kaneko Building, 2-3-25 Koraku, Bunkyo-Ku, Tokyo 112*.

In South Africa: Please write to *Penguin Books South Africa (Pty) Ltd, Private Bag X14, Parkview, 2122 Johannesburg*.

P.O. 0003631801